Sarah Murphy

Lilac *in* Leather

Sarah Murphy

Lilac *in* Leather

A Tale of Forsythia, Bedbugs, Faded Cotton & Time

PEDLAR PRESS

TORONTO

Copyright © SARAH MURPHY 1999

ALL RIGHTS RESERVED. No part of this book may be reproduced or transmitted in any form or by any means whatsoever without written permission from the publisher, except by a reviewer, who may quote brief passages in a review. For information, write Pedlar Press at P.O. Box 26, Station P, Toronto Ontario M5S 2S6 Canada.

This is a work of fiction. Any similarity to real events or to persons, living or dead, is coincidental.

ACKNOWLEDGEMENTS
The publisher wishes to thank the Canada Council for the Arts for its support of our publishing program.

CANADIAN CATALOGUING IN PUBLICATION DATA

Murphy, Sarah, 1946-
Lilac in leather: a tale of forsythia, bedbugs, faded cotton and time

ISBN 0-9681884-2-7
I.Title

PS8576.U67L54 1999   C813'.54   C98-931473-1
PR9199.3.M87L54 1999

First Edition
Printed in Canada
Designed in Toronto by Zab Design & Typography

ACKNOWLEDGEMENTS

For Jean and Marcella Jean and all the women who have walked the edge and for Leila and for Buffery and all the women who have tried to pull them back and for the ones who have given up and the ones who have kept trying and for Tom who walks with me and for Lee who leaves me alone and for The Alberta Foundation for the Arts and The Canada Council who bought me the time and for the folk at the Word Hoard in Huddersfield lifting another one for me Thursdays at the Slubber's and the Yorkshire/Humberside International Writers in Residence Scheme which got me there and for all the others who have been with me through the process and especially for my editors the late Mort Ross who first believed and Beth Follett who saw it through. THANK YOU.

Because I am not myself
I know there is no end to knowledge
—JEAN MCMILLAN, *New York 1964*

FORSYTHIA

We giggle snug

would
and
gle
down

under the covers like little girls, wiggling our feet. That's why I gave you the skirt.

Or didn't give exactly. At least that isn't what I said: I'm giving you this skirt. I just said you could keep it until I wanted it, that we'd shorten it for me later. And I didn't let my mother shorten it at the time to allow us both to wear it, either. Although I knew that would have been all right, it wouldn't have been too awkward a length, right above your ankles: a lot of women were already wearing things like that.

Which is what made it a gift. Really. And you knew it at the time. Even if you think now that it's just guilt that's stopped me from coming by to collect it. What you probably say to yourself when you put it on. What you've no doubt been saying for years: Guilt, guilt, smoothing your hand along its ribbons. Guilt. Guilt. If you still wear it at all.

You must remember sometimes, though. The way I do. Often, in fact. How we stayed at my mother's place. How wonderful that was: an extended sleepover party with the mother in the next room. Listening until we whispered. And making sure nobody smoked in bed.

You even braided my hair. I remember your fingers. And your feet too. The toes. Very far apart. And neither hot nor cold.

It went perfectly on you. That skirt. It always will. It was my mother's favourite from the summer she finally got to visit her old friend Nancy down in Arizona. From Mexico. In Mexican cotton. Though she never actually crossed the border. Only got as far as Nogales. And looked across. Staring into a whole other world while she talked to an old friend she hadn't seen in twenty years.

But I always wanted it. From the minute I saw it I longed for that contrast. The soft bright multicoloured satin ribbons sewn in squares across the harsh textured blue cotton. Patching it the way the roads patch the land she must have crossed. So bright that I never forgot what it looked like then. Even if it appeared that I had.

Nor do I think you will ever understand what that skirt could say to me when it was new. With the big sky in it and the sunsets. The green edge of treetops or the yellow and orange, even purple, of badlands and deserts: how it contained so many other places. Other times. Ancient lore: faraway dreams.

Because you're like everyone else. Everywhere outside the City that I've ever lived. And half the ones inside too. Native or recent arrival. With someone always after me to do New York. Or maybe just the Village. Who thinks you just go there and do it. Do New York do the Village do SoHo do the Artworld do the Modern do the Met do Central Park do Coney Island, even do the Bronx Zoo. But DO Something. Do some particular Something. And then you don't need anything else. Because you've had The Experience.

And maybe the Mexicans feel the same way, or the inhabitants of Venice, but then to top it all off I get stuck with the inevitable electronic umbilical cord, one you can't cut, that snakes out from the centre, only the centre, and New York these days is still the centre, with all those references in the papers and the magazines, bringing the origins, or at least the importance, the stamp of approval, on all glamour all trends all art all knowledge back to that particular place, so that it would be possible to believe my mother's languid comment that everything that counts happens first in New York, even if you did manage to smile and say, throwing out your hand, languid yourself:

–We-ell, everything that counts for New Yorkers, anyway. Then followed it up with some comment on the media and American magazines and New Yorkers writing most of them so what can you expect? Though the problem for me is more just being forced to recognize my mother's apartment on television, the building must be in some stock footage somewhere, followed always by looks up at the Statue of Liberty or the Brooklyn Bridge, so it's always a Technicolour reference that I just can't get time and memory to blur. And then there's thinking that just being there puts your life into the big time, that you can just insert yourself, like into a soap opera, talking to the characters between the commercials, quick quick, get right in there, no matter how small that life is, or how sordid. Or how short.

So that it's always:

—C'mon Alma, let's do New York. You and me, do New York. Let's do New York together.

As if I could ever do New York. Or believe it could be done. As if New York doesn't always do us. All of us. The deserters and the runaways. The inhabitants too. They're not decoration, those people on the street corners and subway platforms. Though none of you ever believe what I say about leaving, so superterrific it sounds, so Fan J. Q. Tastic: Do New York. With my fast escape just adding to the legend, the myth of the Big Apple. So that it doesn't matter if we're the ones who get chewed up and spit out.

But I'm not being fair. I know I'm not.

You did make that other New York come true: you're the only one who ever did. Even if the trip started just because I needed to go home. Still, you made it real walking around the city with me, holding me by the elbow. Giggling.

And in SoHo you looked up. Looked up laughing so pretty and so fresh that you became New York. That other New York. A *Breakfast at Tiffany*'s vision come back to haunt the dying city. The image the developers just keep on selling. Only fresh. Made so real on your face that it was obvious to everyone how becoming you were to New York. How well your smile went with the best of the buildings. Whose facades still reminisce about the white gloved elegance of my childhood, while their structures sour and ulcerate with the undigested ghosts of sweatshop labourers. With all the passersby loving your smile as much as I did: never have so many people smiled back at me as when I walked with you.

Which is another reason I gave you the skirt.

My mother was so unhappy

when it faded. When the ribbons ran. She lent it to someone for a party and they threw it in the washer. A shame she said. Though I tried to convince her it would be all right. That it was a New York summer now and not a Mexican winter. That it was loyal to us in its colours, and that its faded survival made me like it even more. Especially after that last summer, when it came to its damaged maturity: the summer that I left.

Until my mother offered it to me finally. That night with you. To make it so much more beautiful. You can't have forgotten. How it lay among the other things she took out.
– God that's gorgeous, you said. But then nothing looks faded on you.
  Your voice echoed as you said it. Even out the window. Suspending itself there in the thick air over Central Park. As opaque as the colours of the skirt or the other voices drifting up, the park still full of joggers in the light, though the supper time jogger rush hour had finished long before, the crowds going round and round the reservoir, their bright coloured suits like an extended carousel, up and down and round and round, like the skirt twirling. Though the Columbus Avenue voices of my childhood, in a Spanish that no one who has studied two years in high school could possibly understand, warm as the ribbons on the skirt and as staccato as the static from their radios, were nowhere to be found. Columbus is an upwardly mobile restaurant and boutique street now, and the side streets where everyone once hung out on their stoops and shouted has filled with silent solid middle class elegance. Until I missed them. The voices against the dense evening.
  Only you were there. Your voice instead. And still early: with the twilight colours bleeding slowly into each other. And the edge of the buildings on the other side of the park. All New York a sudden twilight ice cream candy swirl. Disappearing into dark as fast as you can eat a one scoop cone.

My mother took out a tawny skirt too. The one I thought went with your hair. Only you hardly looked at it. You just ran your fingers along the other's ribbons while your gaze wandered off through the window. So that you held a dense grey-blue in both your eyes and hands. With the purples in the sky fading as they had on the skirt while you repeated:
– Lovely, lovely, this is just lovely. And looked out into the thick enclosing distance.
  But it wasn't until you held it up against you that I said you should take it.

Right after Laura left. Because that was the night she finally came over. We had just watched her walk out from under the canopy and off down the street. And we had leaned out the window. The two of us. Giggling and waving from eleven stories up. So that she had giggled and waved back. I'm sure she must have. Or at least smiled. And I can see the wave: how the white hand stood out against the grey concrete pavement so clearly. To contain the hugging warmth of the evening we were all part of. Even my mother. Smiling across the room with her arms folded. Giving us her old pyjama party look before she said:
— Have I got some stuff.
— Girls, she said. And clapped her hands: Have I got some stuff. A perfect gesture; getting out the costumes for the dress up. Only I wish it had occurred to her before. When Laura was still there. But I guess it would have been hard to do; hard to read the moment; harder to take it all in.

It had been so long since

I'd seen her. Not that I hadn't known what happened. I'd been to the hospital often enough when her head was practically shaved, and she was so skinny you wouldn't believe it of a person who hadn't just gotten out of a detention camp.

Though she was beautiful. The way it made her look all punk and androgynous. So delicate handsome that a couple of teenagers had threatened to beat her up right there in the common room where everyone was allowed to socialize, male and female, if she didn't give them her best leather jacket, the one with the painting on it.

Then they apologized when she took it off, meekly I think she must have done it, I can see her looking down, the shoulders poised forward ready to accept a fight if it came to that, while making her slightly amused Christian gesture of charity more than of fear, almost in ceremony by the time she had the jacket in her hand, like a propitiation or sacrifice to the spirits of the City.

Until they ruined it by refusing to take it from her hand once they could see her body clearly.

– Oh, you're a girl, they said, and she had to let the laughter surface into her eyes, she was apparently wearing one of those semi-transparent Indian cotton blouses, so that she threw her shoulders back to make the heavy breasts that never went away no matter how skinny she got, more clear; rubbing the nipples against the cotton a bit with the motion of her shoulders as she laughed, as they were forced to clear their throats and look down. While she insisted on giving it to them anyway. Holding it under their noses and laughing.

Until she had to leave it on a plastic chair for them, kneeling like before an altar and arranging it carefully, the sleeves folded over each other in front. Only by then the orderlies or the nurses had noticed, and they made her put it back on, even if they disapproved of it. So that I don't know how she finally managed to give it away. Just that she did.

But all that happened later when she turned herself back in and was allowed to wear her own clothes. Which means she must have told the story to my mother, not to me. Because what I remember was the hospital robe all white and shining and so gigantic it made me want to tuck her in my pocket and take her home. Only I gagged and rushed out onto the street instead, then left town as quickly as I could.

Maybe I wouldn't have had the guts to call her again if it hadn't been for you. With your chomp the Big Apple smile. That made me think it could be done. Not just the phone call but all of New York. That we could walk in, you and me arm in arm, and do it, just do it. Do in New York. Bury all that was left over: the past like piles of garbage.

Like from that last summer, when the sanitation department was on strike and the garbage piled up on the streets, underlining the waste in my life for months, before it was taken away and dumped. By scows that would take it far out into the harbour, to make ground fill in New Jersey. For the new container ports maybe. The ones that circle the City now. That are its only claim to still being a working harbour. Port Elizabeth et al. Bunches of them. And soon to come to Brooklyn. Cement cities built on used tampons and orange rinds and the peels from the bananas the same ships still bring from Central America. While the old warehouses in the deserted old neighbourhoods have become luxury lofts. A process that hadn't started back then, you could still smell the spices when you walked a lot of those streets, even if the buildings hadn't been used in years.

  I would watch the scows go, standing on the bicycle path or out on the pier where the old 69th Street ferry had left from Brooklyn to Staten Island, as they moved out under the Narrows bridge, days the sky and the water were the same thick birthday cake icing blue and I could watch all the boats, freighters and tankers and tugs and scows and ferries sink into it, be swallowed by the icing. Or maybe it was playdough, more salt than sugar as my nostrils would expand to take in the slightly cool harbour smell, overlaid with dead fish and creosote, the only cool part of that whole summer. Waving Goodbye to Garbage a big joke that later became an important part of one of Laura's performances, or maybe it was one of Sandro's rituals, I seem to have an image of large numbers of people standing around with bright coloured handkerchiefs in some form of Rite of Passage. If only out from the mouth of the harbour, to let go of all the old and already digested. Although I no longer believe you really can let go of all of that, the way I never let go of that last summer.

That's why I clipped all the articles I could find on that garbage scow that was doing the rounds of States and third world countries, as far south as Brazil I think, trying to sell its New York garbage. Because even if you'd say the major networks do a better job of that, still it seems so appropriate, especially thinking about it now that we're moving again, just across the city to a bigger house this time, though soon we may go south instead of north. But I love that idea of hauling my New York detritus with us, it makes a wonderful illustration, I can see it in my mind on a page from one of those books I grew up with, anthropomorphized tug boats plying the harbour, with Jeanpierre, complete with moustache, the tug; and me the scow, my back piled high with old cans and old papers and old condoms and old thoughts and old friends and older dreams. While the seagulls dive in, the way they do even onto the grass of our neighbourhood park, landlocked as we are, after whatever refuse they can find, to play with a candy wrapper or anything bright, the way memory plays with me, tugging out whatever she can find, broken machinery or bedbugs or coffee grounds, astonishing textured days, or intense loud nights, cries and outcries and rotting loves. As we sail on. Jeanpierre and the kids alternating pushing and pulling me down through the harbour of our days towards the open sea. And no place to dump this load.

Only with you I thought I was immune. That no seagulls would pick at my body. There would be texture and feeling without pain. A memory without mass or inertia to be overcome. Not a garbage scow but that skirt. The past faded only a little and spinning beautifully, the way you did in it, round and round. So that in passing I would get to see Laura. To give her my best.

Again.

A good way of putting it my mother would say, since that's what Mother accused me of doing with Laura all the time.
— You're giving yourself away, dear, she would say: You're selling yourself short, you're selling yourself cheap, you're worth more than this, what are you getting back, you're giving her, or sometimes it was them, the best years of your life, you should do something with yourself, what are you getting in return?

Something that Mother started as far back as our years together in High School, telling me that I could be, could have been, so much more without Laura, without Laura's influence. That I was well on my way to being popular, to being influential to being class or school president or head of some committee that would get me into Radcliffe or Vassar or Smith or Berkeley or something as I brought together my brains and my poise and my diplomacy, the quiet maneuvering she wanted me to have inherited from her. That was spoiled when Laura came in, January of my first year.

Because she never got along. Never fit in. And she never showed defeat by caring. Although she did complain a lot, especially to me. You must remember that too.

How she started in with that:
—I remember.

While she fingered the astronomy text she had in her lap, the one she was using to calculate the proportions of the universe, the relative size of the consciousness of its inhabitants. Pressing her hands against it until I was sure her memory would consist of just that: how to do those operations. And I didn't want to listen at all, I even remember how my heart started to beat faster, trying to find some way around letting that hollow flattened voice enter our evening, some way to avoid her extrapolations, all full, if you listened, of the howling emptiness of interstitial space, leading me to want no part of the explanation of her arrival at that text, the beginning of her calculations in that one high school astronomy class we had taken together, where she would sit in the back and concentrate, attempting to put the correct value on each formula, that would lead her to correctly correlate the coordinates for the landing of the alien ship, and its E.T.A. Through use of the mental vibrations sent out by all the rest of the students as they studied, or gossiped about boys, or about her. About the way she dressed or smiled: what was wrong with it.

Only it wasn't that. She wasn't into that at the moment. How it hadn't been a joke the way she'd told me at the time: no one could talk like that who wasn't under the influence of an alien being, she might have said, looking around her, they have to be the key to the Arrival. Because by the night you met her she was convinced she had purified all the nastiness all the trivia, made it precipitate out, with her atonal universal formulae. She knew they were all that had protected her even back in school. And would say so if you asked.

Even if she was into that trivia herself now, the 'they said' and 'we said' of the classroom and the lunchroom and the washroom. Not a universal energy but a commonly constructed remembrance, the way high school always becomes an adolescent movie in the mind, with its lessons about jerks and geeks and creeps and nerds, whatever the 'in' vocabulary of the moment should happen to be, and popularity and loyalty and how you can't judge a book by its cover. In which all the very real torment we once felt becomes the basis for laughter and object lessons, as she took out and dusted off one by one, the detailed memories of a shared world that no longer fit the one she was trying to inhabit.

That I think she remembered and mentioned to tantalize me. Perhaps to tantalize us all. Performing for her supper again as she did her best, now that the text was closed, to make us feel that we were all living an episode in *Fame*, where it was simply natural that she had become the crazy artist. Making herself a caricature with those highly polished but ever so slightly unlived incidents and coincidences of our common memory, trying to fold me into them with her gestures and her giggles. Meant to signify how much fun it had been sometimes, being so 'out' and then so 'in'.

Until the memories themselves caught her. And there came the little break in the voice. Not flat but grown all small and far away as she suddenly said that thing about how she couldn't understand how they had hurt her so much. Or why either, she just didn't understand it, while she looked from me to you, all little again and shrunken.

And you smiled then. And it was so warm. And so real, as if you could pick her up and wrap her in a blanket like a baby, that tears sprang to my eyes. Because it was so good that you could do that, try to encompass without consuming her. Even if she couldn't expand into it. But settled back into the hoarse New York whine she had cultivated for years against the efforts of all her teachers. As she started to complain.

While the voice took on yet another timbre: not far away and hollow, or small and close, but drifting in the middle distance like the smell of the ginkgo tree fruit in her parents' backyard: acrid and permeating, attractive and rotten. In a diatribe against rich bitches. How they looked and what they acted like.

Maybe you thought she was implicating me. That her bitterness against me was finally coming out. Only she wasn't. It wasn't me at all. It was all the others. She and I had been the United Front Against Rich Bitches.

We were both scholarship students at that school. And the girls she was talking about had homes in the country and suites on Park Avenue, or a brownstone, at least in the Village, but to really qualify, on the

Upper East Side. The kind that had their own horses in the Central Park stable and bragged lazily of their clothing from Bergdorff's and their jewellery from Tiffany's and their vacations in the Virgin Islands or Europe or even the Far East: There is nothing to match the beaches of the Aegean one would say in her mother's voice, while another replied: But, of course, you haven't seen Bali, as they drank their parents' scotch or rye or imported vodka poured from crystal decanters when the black maid had an afternoon off to see her relatives in Harlem, where the truly adventurous had also gone. Obviously not for a vacation and just once you understand, to visit.

With all of the above accomplished while their parents weren't looking. After all, drinking the hard stuff wasn't allowed and going to Harlem was dangerous and bragging wasn't nice. Especially in front of the underprivileged.

There was even one whose house Laura visited once. Sonya with a 'y' or Sofia with an 'f', something all sibilant and sophisticated like the girl's colour coordinated silk scarves and tweed suits, in contrast to that preppy crowd still in plaid skirts and shirtwaists and circle pins; and secret minis or hip hugging bell bottoms away from the school. Which made Sonya just about as 'out' as we were, but 'out' different: Just too-oo much, they used to say imitating her accent, while with us they just used names, calling us the slobs or the brains or the beatniks. Or even the hippies, I think they used hippie uptown by then, it was no longer a Village word for weekend hip; while they oinked in our presence.

Though I'm sure it was our similarities, maybe just the bohemian edge, that made Sofia entice Laura over there that day. To the parents' New York townhouse (this family was New York, London, somewhere in Italy, Acapulco or Puerto Vallarta and I always want to say Melbourne, but I'm sure it's not true) with the bidet.

It's got to be the quintessential error. One they ought to mention in all the etiquette books for the lower to middle visiting the upper to haute upper, along with the one Sylvia Plath talks about in *The Bell Jar*, not drinking the water in the lemon or rose scented finger bowls thinking it some kind of exotic soup with its floating petals or lemon slices; with this advice for use with that class's European style component, though even Laura said she wouldn't have done it, after all she'd read about the things and even seen them in those French movies with streetwalkers or couples who stop in hotels and wash their feet, that we were always sneaking off to the Bleecker Street Cinema to see. Besides which the difference in mechanism is pretty obvious, the taps you turn for the central spray instead of the handle to flush.

Only it was dark and the bathroom was huge, huge and navy blue and she couldn't find the switch, and it was her first time with the hard stuff and she'd gotten so drunk while she tried to pretend she knew it all, almost choking on that smooth aged whisky as she knocked it back like water when she'd only ever drunk wine. And then to be immersed in that soothing darkness with its brass fixtures that barely glimmered with the little late afternoon fall light from the one high curtained window, and its white trim that was grey in the dark. It was like a cathedral, a goddamn cathedral, she said later, with its awesome spaciousness and its low light.

So that she just couldn't tell. Even that there were two of them, standing side by side. Until she tried to flush the thing and found herself staring into it confounded. Her mouth hanging open as the Great Turd she had left received, true to place, its graceful and elegant baptism.

Quite a lovely scene it must have been too, she said so herself, with the playful sprinkle just catching what little light there was, glowing silver in contrast to the brass, while she knelt down, utterly prayerful, as she studiously took stock of her situation. Weighing all the possibilities, examining the potential outcomes, until she became convinced there wasn't time to let the water melt the whole lump down. And almost anything seemed better than leaving quickly and letting them find it hours later, solid and stinking, a gift from the sewers she was supposed to inhabit. She even contemplated putting it into her purse for a while, she told me, she got as far as looking around for something more or less impermeable to wrap it in, where she could keep it safe by her side until she left, only to find as she looked that her purse wasn't in there either, so that she had to quickly find another plan before the turd became too soaked and squishy to move.

Which meant she finally just grabbed as big a handful as she thought the toilet could take of the scented and colour coordinated toilet paper, and, in the logical desperation of drunkenness, she formed from it a baptismal robe. With which to transfer her creation to the correct apparatus, taking it out of its reserved High Anglican sprinkle, to give it, plop, a more vulgar low Baptist full immersion. More fitting she felt to her class, and to her father's class consciousness. Though not a Baptist he had attended in his youth enough of those prayer meeting derived radical tent meetings, identical down to the linking of arms and singing of songs, that she was able to hum one to herself, to stop the mixture of smells from overwhelming her resolve.

Then, while she watched it sink delicately to the bottom, its robes floating up diaphanous about it, her hand reached out and she flushed. Waving, she flushed. A bright little goodbye to her newly baptized offspring before she took up what she told me she felt was her only proper role in that house, just a lace apron and she could have been the French chambermaid in one of those movies, scrubbing carefully to erase the Great Turd's traces from its former bed.

What I remember, despite all the jokes and our christening it – after all it had received the rites – The Great Turd, is how angry I was at her when she told me what had happened. Enough to challenge her about it, asking her why she had ever gone there, and what did this So-fee-a, this Soan-ya have to say anyway. Repeating this part more than once to jostle her back into our usual way of talking about the other girls, trying to get the drop on them for when they talked about us, when they giggled in the cloakroom on the second floor, and whispered. Until we would ask ourselves, if they ever talked about anything besides boys, or us, if they ever talked the way we did, and we would look away across the park or the playground, or out onto the water, profound concentrated looks before we said of course not, Julie and Mary and Sandy and Dusty and Rachel and Raquel and Holly and Ivy and Barb and Hook and Sofeeya, hardly: They don't talk the way we do, they don't figure out the world.

After all we did mention physics and mathematics and art and alienation, and read Sartre, and called him Sart, or at least she did, I've never read Sartre, I just talk about him, though by now I've delved a bit into de Beauvoir, not *The Second Sex* or the memoirs so much as the novels, but we did already know about alienation, though not about reification, and something about what was happening in the world, civil rights had given way to the war while we all stood for some abstract concept of world peace and visited the U.N., so that we nodded sagely again. Of course not of course not, they were all just so *utterly* superficial. Which is the tone I took that time.

– Was it *in*terest*ing what she had to say? I inquired. Making sure that interesting was a four syllable word, just that trifle sarcastic. What I used to like to think of as sardonic and worldly. Though this time even I could hear a whining tone sneaking in, maybe in how I said she, or the earlier Soan-ya. Because I had to move on fast as this 'you're just jealous and she's not even a boy' expression came over Laura's face, making me continue, the sarcasm dripping now.

– Did she talk about her vacations? I said.

– No, Laura answered. Careful now and possessive. Enjoying how much it bothered me as she took my arm and looked me in the eye.

– It wasn't about her vacations. Not mostly anyway. Then she broke the mood by giggling: She did talk about all the museums she went to in Europe. Just to interest me.

She contemplated that fact a moment, maybe it was the first time it had happened, that attention, so that she had to try to explain, how she had liked it, how it was different from our friendship, but she had liked it.

– Sofia wanted to make me interested in her, *me* in *her*, Laura said: So I talked about the Museum of Modern Art, and ye-es, Sonya said she goes there often, and sits in front of the Guernica. Just in front of the Guernica. To try to understand war, she said. Its meaning in the modern world.

And then it was my turn to laugh as I sucked in my cheeks and tried to imitate Sofia's look. Because it was easy to imagine, Sofia on the bench in that white white alcove especially designed for it, the giant painting in front of her, years before Picasso's agreement with the

Museum to repatriate it to Spain on Franco's death could be fulfilled, as she took in its sharp edges and its desperate yet somehow controlled grey howlings.
– Yes, I believe you, I can see her in front of the Guernica, staring wide eyed and then crossing her legs when some boy...
– Young man, for Sofia they are all young men. Or just men, Laura interrupted in Sonya's accent.
– ... comes in. Then she kind of twitches up her skirt, like in the movies.

I shoved my hip into Laura, regaining the initiative as I tugged her sleeve.
– Does she do that, did she tell you, c'mon, tell me?

We both burst out laughing. The two of us together as we separately imagined a studious Sofia in her horn-rimmed glasses smoothing her manicured hands over her tight tweed skirt, I could even hear the faint rustle of her quality nylons, and envisioned them silk, against the lining of the skirt, as we laughed so hard that Laura took a deep breath and gave me the blow by blow, the stuff I'm not sure she meant to ever tell anybody. Except that image, so very movie French, the horn rims even matched Sonya's hair, while I'm sure she did at least let her leg swing slightly, made Laura skip and clap.
– I'm sure she does that I'm sure I'm sure I am I am, she chanted as she danced: Maybe she even wears greys to match the painting.

Warm greys.

Guernica Grey. At last, a fashion accent that understands war.

With the whole afternoon with Sofia suddenly in the realm of the absurd. Allowing Laura to describe in all its decadent detail what it was to sit in that living room and have to go to the can, detail after detail until we could name the whole incident *Life and Times of the Great Turd* while we laughed and laughed, and it lost its capacity to hurt or to wound. As tears of laughter ran down our cheeks and we fell into each other's arms, and I wasn't jealous or even angry anymore as the interchange took on another tone.

My anger wasn't born of jealousy alone. I knew it even then. It arose because I could see something had hurt her. Because the point was that no matter how: Rich, rich, Laura said throwing her hands up in the air, Sofia was, you still don't make yourself vulnerable to people like that. You don't play their clown. Make yourself ridiculous and vulnerable, drinking stuff you've never had before. Just because they have money and a house: something to offer. Because you become a story to them, or not even a story, just a collectible.

Something I couldn't explain very well back then, I hadn't really thought it out. Though I tried to put it together, why she shouldn't have gone, how I wasn't just jealous, Sofia wasn't for her, she didn't want to be Sofia's pet poor person. The one from the slums, or the edge thereof, introduced to all the parents' friends in some way that would allow them to zero in on it, this product of interestingly safe slumming their friends' daughter had brought home, even if Sofia was more 'out' than us.

Only Laura just laughed at me, and said it again, softly, wonderingly, almost the way she talked about how they had hurt her that night with you, looking off into the distance and rubbing something.
– I enjoyed the attention, Alma, the attention. Not Sofia. That's what stars must develop a taste for, you know?

So that if she didn't hang out with Sofia much after that, it had nothing to do with my reasoning. And though I knew at the time she was refusing the overtures – and there were more – for my sake, I didn't mind. I was convinced that a taste for that kind of situation would only get her hurt.

Which it did, of course. Because there's no question but that she did develop that taste. And that similar situations hurt her a great deal over the years. Their echoes still do. That's what that complaining tone was. Even at her most confident, I've heard it sneak into her voice. Though I've never understood how she let it.

I don't, even now when her confidence is gone. It's just one of those contradictions that can't be resolved. Though I do feel a little bit too much like my mother when I chalk it up to genius. Even if that's what so many books say. That it's people with immense talent who can be so fiercely strong and driven and ambitious, and still do things like that. Be so absolutely insecure. Or passive the way she was in front of those who had more of what she thought she wanted, making herself, on purpose before them, often before all of us, before anyone, as defenseless as a snail without a shell. A delicately beautiful sea slug. Whose poison works only against itself.

Until she needed that whole schemata, those astronomical/physical/mathematical rules, to protect her. After I walked out on the job. Because that was the best I gave her: I gave her protection. And though no one ever thought I was as dramatic or as interesting, much less as brilliant, as she was, still I got to take care of her, and pull her back when she got herself too far out on a limb.

While the audience she was developing, even some of those same rich bitches, applauded. As she jumped out of the grasp of this one woman fire department, and meowing ran to press her starving nose (she could stay out on those limbs a long time) up against the butcher shop, or the Bergdorff, window. Making herself their victim again and again.

It was much harder for her than it was for me, hard as that might be to admit. Because no matter what she did in the art room – and it was so much more than anyone else in the class or even in the school ever did – it terrified more than it pleased. The way watching that kitten venture further and further might make you want to applaud or to close your eyes and be told when it was over, but certainly not to go along. So that even those who spent time telling her how talented she was how there were just so many things she could become spent just as much time lecturing her on being more cautious and more conscious, mostly of how she walked and how she talked and what she said. Just, please, a wee little bit less intense over all, it might let her be, well, at least a tiny speck more popular. Though I think that everyone knew, that of all the things she could become, none of them ever included acceptable.

With her thrift store blouses at a time when nobody did that, and her too fast hands, which at least one girl said made her so Eye-talian, though lord knows how she found out, that heritage was on the mother's side. And more than anything, there was Laura's overeager grin, and the words behind it, how she would talk about anything that moved her with a complexity and an enthusiasm that could drive anyone away, or make her a fast-talking ornament, like in that house. The way she would always be someone's form of slumming. Or, moments she would surface from her intensity, be made to feel that she was.

For my mother and me it was all very different. My mother at least had that part of the performance down. It was good if slightly unconventional (that made people notice you) taste in everything, and all the right names and knowing when to use them. When to call the people who counted. Like for getting me the scholarship to that school. Which put Laura and me into more or less the same category, at least for those girls.

Though maybe you couldn't tell that from looking around the apartment on Central Park West. You'd have to know how it was rent-controlled for years before it was co-oped. And how Mother finally pulled out all the stops to get the money, mortgaged to the hilt and all, to come up with the insider price when they converted the building, my inheritance she calls it, while still, compared to most New York rents, or buying in cold, she got off easy. And while she could have kept the rent-controlled apartment without actually owning it, she tells me now that the last tenant in the building who has neither sold out nor bought in keeps getting threatened with having her apartment sold to the Russian Mafia. To someone who specialized in getting people out of rent-controlled apartments in Moscow, the real estate agent who currently owns it tells the woman in a creepy voice, because he can't make any money out of it till she gives it up. There's even that story about how Mother got the call from an agent, I think she told this one in front of you, for some Hollywood star, Richard Dreyfuss it turned out to be, who would pay her eight thousand a month for six months, if she'd just move out. And then when she said yes, the agent decided the apartment, magnificent view and all, was just too little, its third bedroom too much like a closet.

Because in terms of real money, in cash flow, there's hardly been any of that since Daddy divorced Mother and went to live with the Young Wife out on the coast. A pattern I'm sure you're familiar with. Day time soaps drive in movies prime time TV art cinema features New York L.A. Toronto Vancouver Kansas City Sault St. Marie Calgary it's all the same thing. And my mother much too proud to call him on alimony, or even child support. Although I do think she finally asked, when it came to the apartment. For Alma's future, she must have said. You do remember her? She even got some money from Jeanpierre and me. So that if it is my future, I already have an investment in it.

Mother went back to work immediately after the divorce, and let me know every day how hard it was on her, getting absolute loyalty from me in lieu of child support. And while she couldn't keep up the life to which she had become accustomed as far as travel and food and that kind of thing was concerned, even you could tell from the walls, covered mostly with prints from what are now called 'emerging' artists, and the white painted baby grand over in the corner; she would never give up that pretense to high culture. To being a part of at least that very small elite. And the doors it opened. So that I did grow up used to that.

And to the role Laura seemed to want, that entrance at any cost, that being a pet in the houses of the rich. Though my mother never thought of any of that, the way poor cousins used to work for richer cousins or go to their houses and entertain them, as a form of begging, like for alimony. What the richer friends she had when Daddy was around and the contacts she got through them gave or helped out with was objective aid. Based on merit. On getting what my mother was convinced we deserved: what I in particular deserved.

The one thing my mother thought Laura and I had in common: deserving. Laura deserved more than anyone I've ever met. And got less. Even my mother thought she had Merit, and liked that part. Even if Laura's no holds barred enthusiasm, her blind dedication, scared my mother as much as it did anyone else. With our friendship scaring her more. Almost as much as Jeanpierre scares her. The way I never quite go for the right people. Or never quite keep the wrong ones, even if they're interesting, at a proper distance.

The way Mother asked if I was going to play Alice B. Toklas to Laura's Gertrude Stein. Though that was much later. When I had already done a year at University and Laura was at art school in her sophisticated phase. And I was leaving my mother's place to get our own tenement apartment. The year before that last summer when I left.

But I don't know

why I'm going over

this. When I can't even be sure if you remember her. Or if hers isn't just another vaguely drawn face jumbled up in all the other impressions from your trip to New York. So that it might be there in your archives, perhaps you recorded it into memory, that one face whose secretively beautiful outline could still be discerned as she looked down at the heavily veined hands in her lap. With the grin that breaks through, the world opening grin that the two of you have in common.

What I noticed about you that first time I saw you, when I came to the Yoga class at the 'Y' and you were there and you took the ten minutes you always did at the beginning of each session, to talk to us about theory and about what you would do, and to welcome the newcomers before we went on, and to ask if there were any questions, always you asked if there were any questions, so that I raised my hand, the piece of paper describing the class in my hand, and asked what we were to call you, all it said there was Ms. A. Thorne, and I knew you wouldn't want us to call you that. Which made you laugh.

– A good first question, you said. No, hardly. People just call me Thorne. But you can't put that on a brochure. Instructor: Call Me Thorne. And when I was a kid, it was Thorney. Hey you, so Thorney. Probably still am.

And that was when you grinned and looked directly at me. Before you looked at your hands, graceful between your cross-legged knees. And I knew, as I stared that instant into your face, that I liked you. More than I had liked anyone in a long time. So that I blushed, while you covered it with your warm laughter. I think you thought you were protecting me from a social blunder.

It was only that night that I
noticed how that smile connected you. What little Laura had left of it. And it does make it perfect for her to be your New York crazy person, you know, Thorne. I've always loved rolling that name of yours around on my tongue, I said it as often as I could from the moment you told us to use it.

A New York crazy person for Thorne. I certainly didn't think it right then. That's not what we invited her over for. But it is a phenomenon most people who do New York only get to contemplate from a distance. The bag lady in five layers of rags on the corner, the man who talks to himself in four languages, all his own, as he walks down the street in ten varieties of ethnic clothing, the young girl on the bus holding wilted flowers who cannot stop crying. All of them somehow just that little bit out of focus. With Laura a much better show, so genuine, better even than having someone come to the door collecting for Aliens Anonymous. Though she was a bit like that too. Get yer Aliens, yer red hot Aliens.

Only I don't mean that. There's no reason to be cruel. To her or to you. That shows the way I think, the cynicism I've developed over the years. Not the way you do, Thorne. It's just that I've learned how easy it is to collect people impressions when you're just passing through, your own personal animated postcards to take out back home. That make people part of the scenery.

I do it all the time, in fact. Much as I hate myself when I do. In all the moving around with Jeanpierre. Travel. Hit the hot spots. Dig the local colour. Groove on the exotic, the different. The new. What I thought I was doing when we went back. Making New York new. You might think that's what you were for me too. The liveliest scenery of a new place.

Or a new space. The new world the yoga class and then the women's group that grew out of it opened to me. When I finally bothered to enter it. To take up issues that had long affected my life, to move in again from the world's periphery. I had probably thought that admiration over distance, for Laura's works or our new female, role models, I think we're supposed to call them, or even horror at the issues women face, and fight, was much more elegant than brighter or muddier immediacy, tacky involvement, the way the skirt became more refined after it faded. Laura would probably have a formula for that too, how concern becomes more tasteful with the square of the radius as you travel from the source, or let it recede into memory.

So that maybe you think that's what we're all like. Us south of the border big city folk. Intellectuals or with intellectual pretensions. Slowly sipping exotic tastes through some fine bright straw, or a rolled up New York Times, a siphon at least long enough to reach to the street below my mother's apartment. Or down to the Lower East Side, or up to East Harlem. To suck up its denizens. Just long enough to taste them and spit them out.

Only I have no way of knowing, mutatis mutandis, that the opposite isn't true too. That Laura wasn't part of your exotic. I don't know if you've ever noticed how many friends, maybe they're more acquaintances, you have who talk like that, the ones from your other community, that dancer's world. Who urged you to do New York with luminous eyes, and always spoke to you about the wonders of SoHo or Off-Broadway, or the Staten Island Ferry or the Brooklyn Bridge or the Village or even Pier Sixteen. Or funky blacks with ghetto blasters, the way that one guy said that, when I told him I was from New York and didn't much like it. Don't you like funky blacks with ghetto blasters he said, forgetting poverty and unemployment and lack of health care and beggars on subway cars and street corners and crack and smack and crime and pain. And pain and pain. Blasting out of funky ghetto blasters.

So that there's no way for me to know she just didn't become part of that same tourism we went out of our way to be guilty of: just a pair of nervous hands on an astronomy text that passed in the night.

Maybe you never even understood that she's the reason I gave you the skirt. The reason for so much that happened between us. Or you think she didn't mean much to me because I did give it to you instead of saving it for her. Or saying I would. For when she came back from wherever she had gone. To try to convince us all that I thought she still could. Maybe you think I should have said: I'm saving that for Laura, instead of giving it to you the minute you let it go and let me hold it up to you. Even if I had just said how much I had always wanted it. And how Laura had admired it too.

The truth is I don't know what you thought. We never talked about it. Not until now. When I stand here addressing you, packing and thinking about that skirt and addressing you, cloth passing over and through my hands as I think about that material and how you felt it with your hands and how I wanted to tell you the whole story even then. And about all the things I have done to try to make myself tell the story since, to the world perhaps, but at least to you. At least to you.

And I think sometimes of how I must phone you. I say that often to myself: I must phone Thorne. We must get together. I even say it to you when we meet, and you say it too, but it never happens. And it's not the space for the call that's missing it's the space for making it all come together again once we've made the call, I think we both know that. Maybe you even say it too: I must phone Alma. Maybe you even think: I must phone Alma to return the skirt. The way you wrote in that note you sent. Asking what I wanted you to do with it. Or something. An excuse like giving me something or getting something back, to talk to me about what you're doing now, the way I tell this story to myself over and over. And even when I toy with writing it, it's still for you.

She was important you see, Thorne. Just the way I told you. And that was her name: Laura.
Laura.

Even if she did call herself Lilac that night. And wore purple. Even a purple headband plunked down in the middle of that spunky kinky hair. With a matching purple skirt. Not beautiful or even long, or satin smooth and cotton rough and faded to twilight sky, glowing and opaque at once, a fog to walk through, like the one I gave you. But thick polyester knit and short. And even if minis were coming back in, well just a little bit, at least in the crowd she once ran with, still they would never be like that, unless you walked the streets. Or maybe if she'd had the black leather jacket still, with its purples painted onto the back, she could have brought that juicy material off, with its texture like a fruit waiting to be peeled, or a trampoline ready to bounce off of. That could be crushed too perhaps, and the liquid expressed between the fingers like the lilacs she wore. Except that cloth wouldn't have given off any perfume. Except patchouli oil and coal dust, and polyvinyl resin maybe: the bag lady modification of the look she's had since art school.

Art school and the commune and Sandro. With the few changes in hairstyle and the overall loss in weight making it seem older by then, and far more worn, just as she seemed more strange. As if she had walked onto the set for the wrong movie. And she couldn't even make any of it comment on itself the way she once would have, as she looked around confused out of the burning depths of her eyes, and touched the flower pinned to her dress like a corsage. With a diaper pin. A big yellow duck shaped one that she said was just for the occasion. Because it was a special night. And only my mother had trouble calling her Lilac.

Though it is hard to figure out how she got the flowers. I don't remember lilac summer well enough in New York to even know whether it happens at the same time as anywhere else, Calgary or Quebec City or Montreal or Toronto or Vancouver or Thunder Bay, or whether it's different, four to six weeks earlier than Toronto or Calgary, later than Vancouver, like a lot of spring flowers. Hyacinths or crocuses or daffodils. Or the forsythia.

She would have had to buy them anyway. Or steal them or find them in the garbage. Lilacs just aren't common enough in New York City, at least in our part of New York City, to have been picked. Even in season.

It goes without saying that my mother thought she was wearing them for me. Only in that case she would have been better off calling herself Forsythia and wearing yellow. With a purple diaper pin. Hippopotamus shaped maybe. I've seen those. Because unromantic as it must sound forsythia is still the flower we really have in common.

They grow all over the city. Even along Riverside Drive. They're that low growing bush with the long smooth branches and smooth leaves. You don't see them in Calgary. Except maybe in the supermarket around Easter, for a couple of bucks a bunch they mark a spring that's only come in another part of the world. But in New York they substitute for caragana, or that other funny low growing stuff with the yellow roselike flowers and a strange Latin name.

We would always make the four block walk from the apartment down through the *cuchifritos* and the hum of voices to the Drive to see them. In March. They bloom in March. During the first month the truly poor down there below would come sit out on their stoops, or stand by wide open windows, watching a more intimate complexity bloom in each other, the way we would watch Central Park. The way the Yuppies down there now probably watch the Dow Jones.

When that same spring longing made Lilac and me sneak out toward the polluted waters of the Hudson we would find the bushes there along the edge of the highway. Where access is restricted by spiked steel fences, grey or green or Rustoleum red or all three layered together by turns. Which we would climb over to hide under the plants while we gossiped and giggled and held each other's hands and felt the early spring sweetness of the ground and the air, mixed with old debris, car exhaust and flotsam and jetsam and shit and traffic passing and radios and creosote, while we would look up through the long whiplike branches with their heavy load of yellow flowers bending them so close. To the grey of river fog that seemed to push against them, or the higher cloud, or sometimes to the final blue of sky beyond. On the best days far beyond. And bright instead of pale. Like the colour of the skirt when it was new. As close as New York ever gets to that: deep translucent blue crisscrossed by yellow orange tan green ribbons of closer colour.

With the best times of all those when we would come and there would still be flowers on the branches but the green leaves would be starting too so that there would be flowers, thousands of flowers, already on the ground: freshly on the ground to let us lie in their blanket. With a feeling so special and so vivid that we couldn't help ourselves, that going back to childhood and to playing, after all we met in the first year of high school and we'd both been streamlined through New York's best public elementary schools skipping two grades to make us barely thirteen, and at that age almost all social contact is still fantasy anyway, more a form of realistic role play, imitating books or television or our parents, than reality itself, the squeals of 'does he like me', another form of playing house, aided by the increasing pressure of sexual awakening between the legs, that inevitably propelled toward a far more real future. In a longing outward, toward something more, beyond the house or even books, the same prickling sensation in the back of the mind that came between the legs to let you know that something could be made the future could be created out of the melding of mind and action, just like the body could act to meld to create a child.

And it would often as not be too heavy to bear, perhaps that feeling that knowledge always is at its most raw, so you fit it into patterns that are less than real, that are partial fantasies, just as her life and mine always would be, even as she pursued that need to get closer and closer to the centre, the essence of things, still it would be too difficult to say, except in passing: The future is yet unmade and we can make it. It's always easier to fantasize, conversations or adventures, and let it grow, the way a mother's face dreams out a window while she feels her pregnant belly, just letting it grow, eyes still closed to any possibility but unconscious nurturance, sensation used to fill in fantasy's gaps, the way we would use what we saw on the ground and in the air and in the distance and in ourselves to feed those games we played until they could become more real than anything else we knew. Were perhaps more real for years than anything else we had between us, those wonderful days when we would be witches and mages and time travellers; with amazing powers and contacts with other forms of terribly intelligent life, extra or unknown terrestrials, and we would have spaceships that were clear bubbles and special houses in the woods that were the woods themselves, with branches that grew specially to house us while blanketing us with multicoloured flowers soft and liquid just like the yellow ones that surrounded us.

While animal friends would come and stand guard over us, picked out of the picture books we still secretly adored or the biology texts on animal life we rigorously examined, tigers and pumas and ocelots and small deer, howler monkeys that transmitted secret messages, zebras or giraffes who bore us on their backs, whales that bore us away through clear water, noble golden eagles crossbred with king vultures or iridescent peacocks to help us fly. Animals that might in reality only be dull grey pigeons, their iridescence confined to neck or eye, or mean-voiced grey squirrels chattering at us about our closeness to nest or stash, or just the one eyed soot black neighbourhood alley cat, come to hunt mice, or rats. That looked out for our sacred places, and the magic they produced.

And best of all we were

Amazon warriors, she the Queen and I her lieutenant. In a fantasy for all spaces and times and ways of life, a permanent secret society of women warriors, fighting for a better future, a permanent peace with lions lying with lambs, or at least alley cats with squirrels. Though we would avoid Wonder Woman, she was a travesty of the true myths we said, especially in that ridiculously reconstituted American flag, we had both inherited other myths from our parents than truth, god and the American way, while we invented our own, allowing ourselves to be anywhere and anywhen we wanted, and believe in our powers, especially those times we knew that evil invaders were coming to take our haven.

When we would sneak through the branches, to come up behind them or to escape, depending on the game, and they would be couples with babies in strollers or prams, space capsules we called those, or older women walking dogs, or boys playing tag, until one day we found a lone man at the very edge of our domain. A presence horrifying more than evil, we never talked about it, not specifically, but it shouldn't have surprised us, how we had finally managed to incarnate, wormlike or sluglike he seemed somehow as he stood there, that other side of first awakening, as the longing to move outward creates the knowledge of the edge of the world, the one that can be fallen over.

Because the world we share is not our fantasy, not even our fantasy of making the future: there is never complete control. And sometimes no control at all, the way it feels at twelve, at thirteen, especially for girls, it still does, I know, I can see it growing in my daughter, that's their delight in horror, not gaining control but celebrating helplessness, though we didn't do that. Our Amazons, our animal friends, our secret codes, were to give us control, to allow us to practice it, the way boys play sheriff and football. While tales grow of the near fatal accident or fight that would have only scraped a knee or broken a nose, talking and playing it over and over to gain some power, even if only magic, over that world that is always there, the one in which the other guy has the knife, the motorcycle skids on the oil slick and the front wheel locks at a hundred and twenty, there are twelve of them and one of you, the rapist has a gun and twenty-five feet of telephone cord, your father's gone crazy he's killed your mother they're both dead in an airplane crash you've just survived you are failing to survive ecological catastrophe a nuclear war, you're completely in the power of aliens or terrorists or satanists or the State, an unfriendly force you don't yet know how to overpower or manipulate, that maybe you never will. Because there's a crack a void always something to fall into on a lonely night in a shared disaster through the whistling wind at the tunnel opening between the bedroom window and the door by the edge of the subway platform, always a place to fall over, onto the tracks or into the water or just down and down and down, to sink into the wide expanse of air or ocean toward rocks or trees or sharks unable to move or even to breathe, just to disintegrate body and soul beyond the whine of the civil defense siren that hurries you into the air raid shelter: an end to everything, to everything, to everything, growing up with the nightmare of the edge in which no one quite dares to believe.

Aliens save us we would cry. Save us.

Though our own edge was dreamed was fantasized by then so much more readily and easily and often in men, the nuclear holocaust was for the nine to twelve age bracket, though we still spoke of those old dreams. While these were men, all kinds of men, though not in white coats, not the ones that would finally take her away, it would have been impossible to dream them, though not the slobbering grey faces that pursued us around corners, breathing hard and ugly and hot, grabbing at us as we only barely managed to escape the hand, its touch still on us as we convinced ourselves we could fly, out into space or into our favourite trees, the ginkgoes in her backyard offered protection from those dreams that would be spoken in shortness of breath and giggles, when we woke up from our sleepovers in the middle of the night, saying:

– Do you ever dream that, do you ever?

Our eyes sudden hot centres that passed us on to the other side of the pit or left us on shore or at the edge of the wrecked city. The way his presence did that day. The fact that we could incarnate him could sneak up behind him could whisper about him made him not an object of fear but our talisman as we reached out toward the shore of exploration, the one she always loved the most, that tempted and seduced and tamed the edge of horror as well as possibility, that did not fear, but told stories constructed images made totems to celebrate the edge, the constant falling, the way she would say much later: A finite consciousness in an infinite universe is a constant falling. So that as long as we were both there together we knew we would be allowed to cross at least momentarily, in private rites of passage, to the other side. Which meant it was in that spirit, in the knowledge of our own invincible connection, that we watched him there, with his own worm in his hands. Massaging it gently, outlined against the sky.

Although what I remember of him still, far more distinctly than the shape of what he held between his fingers, are the scaly chapped lips. Or what might better be called a chapped face, a reddish raw area extending down almost to the chin and up to the nose, that he just kept on licking.

And for all that later we would laugh at how we acted, at the childishness of it, and never mention how we reached out to each other, afraid of that, or taking it for granted: then. Then when that incident happened it echoed with a depth of truth that made the monster with the red face take on the symbolic beauty of a Greek sentinel, of Achilles looking onto Troy as Penthisilea arrived with her band to defend the city. Only spying on that man then coming up behind him would allow us to change the outcome of that ancient battle. Speaking of that change in literal terms as if we were writing our own adventure, our own comic, or forcing ourselves to become impossibly literate and terribly profound, talking instead about the meaning of that battle in the overthrow of the matriarchy.

—Oh! if only it could be changed, we might say, swearing not on our mothers' but our Robert Graves, that such an event had taken place, that was what we were reading then, Graves' *The White Goddess* and Fraser's *Golden Bough*, the old patriarchal texts on matriarchy, there is no other way to describe them, that would make even us agree with Mary Renault — we were reading her too, her novels were the fun side, a background for fantasy — that maybe such an overthrow was necessary, after all you know how women are with power, though we didn't much like what her Theseus did to his Hippolyta.

We wanted to win, to win, to WIN the great battles, whether it was right or not, or even if the men just had to take over, if that was historical necessity, all the books did seem to say that. So that we would let Penthisilea take Achilles to an earlier grave, even if he was fleet footed and so handsome without his beard and just the right age for us. Instead of raping her the way he did, fallen on the field of battle, something we could still see as an act of romantic love, of tribute to a beautiful enemy. Though it would have been far more fun we thought to be taken alive or better to make him get captured and switch sides, after all he'd almost done that, because we wanted him too much. Only there was no way that final battle scene would be worked out, not to our satisfaction, and anything else, well it would take place in our tent anyway, where we could work out better scenarios, there under the forsythia, or with her parents in the country, laughing and laughing about those fanciful scenes until we could leave them and go on, a bit sadly, to acknowledge the accuracy of the *Iliad*. And then, even more removed, to speak of the meaning of the Great Goddess and all the smaller ones.

We did know a lot of the Greek and some Celtic or Hindu names, though not much from anywhere else, and we did prefer Jung to Freud, in myth and in literature and in history. Archetypes will always seem more interesting to the adolescent mind than Oedipal Stages, even if they get to ham it up on them, and the penises we had seen offered little enough to envy, like that man's, just enough to giggle over before we would go on to analyze myth and legend in our tired intellectual voices to avoid our overidentification with it.

As we plotted how I would be a great anthropologist when I grew up and she would be a great artist, the one to illustrate and make real the tribal rituals that I would unearth. Which was not altogether a joke, I think I did intend that once, I always did love anthropology, and archaeology too, I still do, that's why I collect so many little artefacts.

We would laugh and laugh then, to make ourselves so cool, and sometimes when we threw the flowers in the air, that year or other years, living our own cyclic time, we would look at each other and say:
– That man, you remember that man.

Which would make us get absolutely giddy, the way you can laugh until you're ready to throw up, as we would say:
– He was the first tribal ritual, New York second half of the twentieth century.

Though when we caught each other's eye, and the sky was blue, the surge of joy was for that day: and each other.

Even perhaps for his gift to the earth, because I would swear that it was a gift, just like I would swear it was a gift for the man who shocked you so much on the Crescent Heights Hill, when you couldn't believe what men will do, you even said that.
– I don't believe what some men will do, shaking your head.

While I said: You haven't ever wanted to?
– What, jerk off in front of little boys? you replied.

So that I turned away a little before I could go on.
– No, c'mon, it's not for little girls, there are no little girls here. He just isn't afraid, Thorne. He thinks he's got a weapon in his hand, and that if we look it will impress us. I'd be terrified. But I've wanted to. Not so much in the open as in the woods, in the spring sometimes, with the smell of the earth, the way he's doing it for the sun, for the earth turning and growing ripe, for nature for the world, haven't you ever wanted to do that? Just snuggle down into the earth and come and come?

Or maybe I didn't say it out loud, maybe I wasn't brave enough, maybe I just heard her voice speaking in my mind, the way we would have spoken together, and I remembered when I had been with her and the smell of the forsythia, and maybe I just wanted to speak but

the power of that image overcame me so that I shrugged instead and what I said was:
– Uuuhhh. Yeah.

While I just kept watching him, and pushed the stroller, noticing how he commanded all that wide view, with its brilliant yellows to purples its tumbling afternoon descent into summer cloud, as the sky reflected back from the buildings in the downtown and the lights came on to almost sink him into the sunset, inlay him in it really, the glowing red orange almost eating his edges, clear like the ribbons once were on the skirt.

And he was the sentinel again, our enduring immortal archetype, going on and on, year after year and place after place, a strange compelling image whether or not he could have felt it, the way Laura and I had, as he made his unconscious living gift to earth and sky.

I would

like to think it was that. The truth of a need that in the end must make a gift. The way it must have been on that day in the park when Laura and I were so close to him that I still remember the smell of his sweat, the hollow echo of his breathing. The earth and sky through the forsythia, the eggshell delicacy of the firmament, the other side of that terrible testimony to loneliness, its longing for attachment, echoing the way the sky did on the buildings its longing for union.

That it had to bring on our own gift. To ourselves or to spring. Because we had to affirm awakening, we had to, as we would have to again and again. Making our prayer to keep away Tinker and Pooka and Blackhearted Stranger so that the world would expand to wonder rather than shrink to terror, reweaving between us as the branches did above us all possible growth. Growing the earth the city the woods our fantasies our futures right there between us as we turned ourselves over and rubbed ourselves into the earth. Wiggling into the flowers until they covered us, grabbing last year's humus cover with our hands and smelling its rancid richness as we wormed ourselves in more and more, massaging the pubic bone and the clitoris.

As we looked into each other's eyes and we created our own love ceremony to the spring, the blooming children of the sun and the earth as we squirmed and rubbed in propitiation of them, in identity with them. Until I saw her catch her breath. And the world expanded. And throwing flowers into the air with our arms, we turned back to face the sky.

And the look that passed between us was as it was that night at my mother's in that one enduring moment when time stilled. And the sounds and smells the same: dampness and echoing distance. Except that first time we did not break apart. Or look past each other to find infinity, or something to hold onto. We reached our hands up from under the flowers and held on and held on while we looked into our eyes until we thought we were each other. Taking in the world from the other side of terror. Or of time.

Which is maybe what that man was trying to do too; both those men.

And that was the first time we knew we were just one person in two bodies. And that too is the place where we became blood sisters. And that is why the forsythia really were our flowers.

Not those overwhelmingly country-scented lilacs.

There was just no

vay I could tell my

mother that. Or anything about the forsythia. I couldn't chance reminding her of that era. With the questions or emotions it could bring. Not when she thought Lilac had named herself for me. It was easier to repeat what she already knew. To speak of Laura's love of country freshness. How her loss of that part of herself must be where that name Lilac came from.

– Lilacs just don't grow in New York, I mused: Not unless she went down to the Brooklyn Botanic Garden, she did hang out there enough, called it her country estate the summer she studied at the Brooklyn Museum.

Or maybe she went out to nether Brooklyn, Far Rockaway or the Bronx, on a major quest to rob the garden of the frame house of some Archie Bunker Goetz type, without getting shot. A trial by fire, more or less, of her new name.

A sophisticated and cool enough statement, a New York in-joke, while in my mind I laughingly told myself how it would be a difficult task for the knight to take on for love of his lady, much less the Amazon Queen for her lady-in-waiting. Because there were certainly never lilacs in the inner city, not in any of our neighbourhoods, not where we hung out, I did say that part, with exclamation points even, almost waving my hands.

Which is when Mother laughed. You must remember that. And arched those plucked eyebrows.

—Well, you're not exactly growing in New York anymore either, dear, she said: Maybe that's what it's about.

And then she puckered her mouth. Without the eyebrows lowering. Very precise. Her I-see-right-through-you expression. So perfect for a teacher. To intimidate you into telling the secret whose nature she really has no inkling of. Though with my mother that expression is sophisticated enough to have made her a commentator or a courtesan.

The way she was always the most interesting teacher in her school. At least that's what the students always said. Part of the assessment no doubt on course content and name dropping. The rest on dress. And that expression behind its desk a category in itself. The one that always made me want to choke it off her face. That made my voice change and go up. Squeaky, before I could answer.

Except that one time. When you sat opposite me and smiled and I felt mature. And responsible. With something in me feeling a bit of power. That maybe made me show off: sophisticated for you. A New Yorker. So I just arched my eyebrows back. Dueling eyebrows, I thought. The way Mother used to do with Sandro. And call him Young Man. The winning touch that no matter how high he raised his brows always drove him crackers, I guess it reminded him of all the things he hadn't done, and made me want to be like her for every time he ever called a woman a bitch or a cunt or a cow, the artworld tags of the time, because I would remember him cowed before my mother, and think how perfect it was cowed before the cow – and giggle inside.

Only with me it isn't nearly as effective as with either of them. I neither pluck my brows nor pencil them. Nor are they dark and beautifully defined. Jack Nicholson brows like the ones Sandro has. So they just disappear. Become fat pale caterpillars in the middle of my forehead. Trying to escape to safety in the bush of my hair.

This time the voice did the work my eyebrows couldn't. I pitched it low and cleared space around it, like you taught me to do in our yoga class. While I told her just what she wanted to hear. That if Laura's new name touched on me at all, it was only for the country good times we had shared, she must remember those few times I had spent out in the country with Lilac's family. As I went on about how innocent and open and beautiful they were, how lilacs must remind Lilac of the few times she was ever able to get out of the heat of New York's summer when she was a kid, memories of trees and bugs and open ocean and scallops with their blue eyes hanging out, and a greater purity.

The one Laura never found. That she had given up on when she took on the urban decadence of her artworld persona. That she tucked away somewhere for future reference. That maybe she was trying to recapture with her talk of high school, with her thumbing of the absolute rules contained in her astronomy text. Something my mother might know more about than I did.

The brows finally went down after my explanation. I'm sure it made her feel good to know I would think of that, as if Laura and I had been living the right story, if only in the right location the few times that one summer we got out to the Island together, in the days of malteds and lilacs if not wine and roses. I just thought it should have been egg creams and forsythia, that Laura should have given up on those purple flowers, the way she gave up on leaving New York. Settled for what was really hers. That by now this Lilac business was just a greater alienation. Even if Mother thought it might mean Laura still thought about trying to follow me.

Only I wasn't going to bring all that up. Urban alienation and class identity. So I pouted instead. To ruin the whole effect.

It's true
Laura's family didn't get out much. Any more than we did. Especially once Dad was gone. Though I did get the one trip to California by myself the summer before I met Lilac. The summer I was about to turn thirteen. But even then the countryside was all from a distance looking down from the plane. Plus a few picnics. And the large garden with its high walls like a huge salad bowl accidentally left by alien giants, to be groomed by illegal alien gardeners, in the smog and movement of Los Angeles, thrown in for good measure.

Because the country was something Mother just didn't care about. It took me a long time to figure that out but it's true. Not even enough to get me placed in summer camp. The *mens sana* didn't need the *corpore sana* as far as she was concerned. Whatever extra money we had went into the theatre, into music lessons, into culture. Not into making it more convenient for the mosquitoes to eat us alive. Enough of them got into the city without us leaving to look for them.

The *Better House and Garden* side of the country was all that ever counted for Mother, she had endless questions, disguised often enough but endless, about Dad's; the house the garden the cars the pool and who came over and why. If I'd ever heard of any of them, if he and the new wife went out much. Even if she did know I was still too young to answer the way she wanted, to give her the lowdown. Though I don't think she ever wanted the down to sink so low as the descriptions she would get later of East Village/Lower East Side/Brooklyn bohemia, when what she desired was house parties in the Hamptons with all the right people. Though the nether bohemia at least amused her, the counterculture subculture was still culture, not like the descriptions of tent camping and wildlife and the best new hiking gear, which leave her eyes glazed, that she gets now from me instead.

I did make one Hampton house party. I repaid her work to get me a scholarship to that school at least that much. Though even then it wasn't in one of the mansions. Just a small but adequate house owned by a psychiatrist whose daughter was friendly to me for half a year because our parents had decided she should be.

But if Mother had wanted to she could have gotten me a scholarship to camp too, or even done the country thing as well or better than Lilac's parents. With their rented trailer.

That psychiatrist and his daughter certainly would never have lived there. Or even stayed for a weekend in anything so vulgar. Such eyesores were forbidden in that area of Long Island even on private property, even hidden from view. Lilac told me that. They'd tried one summer. Some friend of her family with a little bit of property had come up with the idea, they had connections too, though they liked to deny it, from living on the edge of Brooklyn Heights, I think, and her father, injured and unemployed, telling stories in the bars. Which got them onto this property near Hampton Bays, very isolated and undeveloped, with a lot of trees still on it, and no buildings, away from the ocean where all the huge houses are, near one of the interior Bays. Shinnecock maybe. The one where the clamming is supposed to be so good.

The owner just said try it and gave them a map to follow, I think he wanted to live on it in a trailer himself while he built, only the cops ended the little experiment by ordering Laura's family to move. Even if no one could see them. Hidden away inside their disgraceful aluminum can they still might have served as an example to the other less than well-to-do. Articles have been written on that. Many of them. Even you were aware of the cachet of the Hamptons. Not only its wealth, but its history of wealth. Not its beauty, but its Who's Who. Knew the Eggs in *Gatsby* were really the Hamptons. Asked me, too, why there was no North Hampton since the other three directions were represented. And even if you were just curious then, it was certainly tongue-in-cheek by the time you got to that other question you asked.

Where was the short island, you asked me, giggling, after I explained, in a rather pompous and school teacher fashion how the boroughs of Brooklyn and Queens were at one end of Long Island and Montauk Point at the other, the Hamptons just before, with all the good addresses, the elegant towns, always on the ocean side of the Island, never facing Long Island Sound and Connecticut across the water. Maybe it was Manhattan you added, nudging me out of my tour guide mode, until we both laughed.

Maybe it was. But no Manhattanite would ever admit it. While suddenly I found us acting the way Laura and I always had with our sophisticated Sophia voices. There we were, you and me, Thorne, looking at a well-dressed woman in some SoHo cappuccino bar, while you held out your hand toward her as if to shake hers in introduction, and said:

– Perhaps I should ask her if she is from the long island or the short?

Though I don't think that with all your reading of Big Apple nuances in all of your perusing of big art magazines you were aware of the enormous effort, intellectual and otherwise, that had gone in over the years to keep the Hamptons pure. And not by race, but by class. Though they do get mixed up. Since to act African or Hispanic or Asian or Irish or Italian or Jewish or most anything else that isn't the historic imitation of Britain's aristocracy that defines the eastern seaboard's upper class – you can even note it in the accent of actresses of the forties, though not always the actors, the way you would make fun of me sometimes with my stress induced dyuties and styudents and to whoms most deeyootifully learned at that school – is already to be vulgar, you can only cross the true Hampton barrier, or whichever other one it is, by giving up some part of the identity that defines you. And though changing your skin or hair colour or having your nose bobbed is not a strict requirement for the ordeal of purification the way changing your voice or your preference in music is, still it might be preferred.

With article after article dedicated to the horror of the lower middle class hordes advancing across the Island year by year. Their approach to the Hamptons dutifully chronicled bubble gum wrapper by bubble gum wrapper. Each loud radio or louder shirt duly noted and marvelled at. Another domino theory giving rise to questions like: Where do we draw the line? If Sag Harbour falls is Hampton Bays far behind?

All of which meant that by the time Mother allowed me to take Lilac up on her invitation to join her family for a few days they were further up the Island toward Montauk in an overcrowded trailer park, nesting among the transistor radios. Where Laura had an old Army tent to herself to give everyone else a bit more room. She'd pitched it off to one side, they'd been lucky enough to get a spot right at the edge of the park since no one else wanted such a long walk to the laundry room and the showers, there among the lilacs.

When I arrived in late summer they weren't in bloom anymore and there was none of that spreading night perfume. Just green heart shaped leaves and old brown dusty spikes and a certain shelter. Though I think she fell in love with them then. During the period that she was alone in that tent. Looking through the screen window at the waning and waxing of the moon, and imagining the loud transistors a gentler music, to which she could dance in flowing skirts under Japanese lanterns. The real old-fashioned printed paper kind. While a slight cold would touch her shoulder and laughter absorb easily into fog. The way it would in the gardens of those huge forbidden mansions her family would pass on their way to the beach. Complete with topiary teddy bears, or, I would swear I saw it once, the white rabbit from *Alice in Wonderland* complete with pocket watch.

Though when I was there she just kept apologizing that it couldn't be like the forsythia. And once even tied a goldenrod to a branch. Just for me.

Her love of *The Great Gatsby* must have been born out of that summer too – and it was a love, Thorne, not just an acquaintanceship like yours – since that was the only summer she spent on the Island, the next few summers another contact lent the family a whole house for a month in the Delaware Water Gap. Where there was honeysuckle but no lilac. Though she wouldn't discover the novel until the summer I left, when she was already into black leather and William Burroughs, the things that would finally gain her entrance into those *Gatsby* places, though it seemed a total contradiction, how she held forth on the novel for at least one entire evening, telling me and anyone else willing to listen – she was holding court by then – why Fitzgerald was America's only true great twentieth century novelist, adjective after erudite adjective, like the Island tide inexorably rolling in, or maybe more the ocean fog she so desired, slowly obfuscating everything, the way the fog would the Japanese lanterns, while she tried to look literary and brilliant.

Because she had some method for resolving all the contradictions inherent in Fitzgerald's work, things about class and vision and women and America looking at itself, with much longer words that I can't remember thrown in, all concepts that she was learning at school not so much to be radical as to be safe, which amounted to the same thing on that edge of the art community during those years, to finally let her feel some comfort in coming from where she came from, especially with her father's socialist aphorisms. So that the poverty of her origins finally became a weapon the way the rich girls' riches had always been, which meant she was really arguing her right to that longing to be like them she just couldn't get rid of no matter how much she tried.

Which was why it all seemed such a work of prestidigitation as I sat there listening. Because what that new déclassé young intellectual crowd of hers truly wanted, even demanded, was for the few representatives of the working class among them to hate the bourgeoisie more than they with their bourgeois origins hated themselves; you had to be their scourge, you couldn't go around demonstrating the envy that was, in the end, more integral to Lilac's class origins than the Brooklyn bray she couldn't altogether shake either.

So to protect herself she made her argument transcend into some realm of the absolute where it became terribly important that she be right, because she had convinced herself and now tried to convince us all, that her rightness would have some resounding impact on the future of America, of the world perhaps, because the knowledge in her ideas could somehow become concrete and save us all. We would see who we are, even Gatsby could see who he was, the way she always wanted people to see who they were, the refrain grew louder over the years, and peace would reign, the lion would lie down with the lamb the squirrel with the alley cat the characters of her mind with each other the secret agents of interplanetary harmony with the sound of the universe.

In the same need for complete resolution of all conflict that would increasingly drive her crazy as she became more and more willing to invent new and nonexistent schema to make everything she ever thought fit together. A gift of inclusion that led to great visual beauty; and intellectual chaos.

I did read Fitzgerald once. Just like she told me to. That very night in fact. Within the white walls of my room. Her annotated *Gatsby* given into my hands so that I could contemplate its already incomprehensible marginalia. That I tried my best to decipher, I was still part of her world then and as convinced as she that there must be some transcendent significance in whatever passed from her mind to her hand. And if these large multicoloured phrases were dictated by aliens, well then invasion was near, I would have been the first to admit that, though now I am sure all those words would look more alienated than alien dictated. Just like the Beatrix Potter book she gave me that night with you, Thorne, I don't remember if it was for both of us or just for me, or even which it was, except that it wasn't *Peter Rabbit*. Only that I kept it, and keep it still, I haven't dared throw it away, for all that it terrifies me sitting there among Amber's old children's books – I'm sure I will see it again as I pack – it still connects us, and me to that night. Because there is part of me that still believes in such an accumulation of concrete connections, that passes its fingers over that book like Aladdin rubbing his lamp, thinking it just might bring her back to earth. Or at least some part of me to her.

You must remember the book, or at least the incident, it was important she said. It would bring luck to my children, the notes together with the text would combine to multiply good thoughts, perhaps even to broadcast them with the help of the illustrations, I don't remember. Besides which the observations contained seminal ideas for the future of the West. No one had yet comprehended how truly misunderstood Beatrix Potter was. How much she had known. The way no one had yet truly understood Fitzgerald.

Only when I did finally give up on the Gatsby marginalia, or just took to noticing the bold roundness of the hand, and tried to decipher that, to see if it could give the text meaning, I started to cry. And berated myself with thoughts about how the aliens must have had a very good reason for picking her and not me for their messenger, because she obviously had the better mind for these things.

I felt terribly inadequate because I could no longer understand. I was still sure there must be something absolutely necessary there in her text, something in the combinations made between her text and the text of the book, that would have very important ramifications. So that I turned back to the book, and was suddenly caught, and it was more like I swallowed Gatsby whole, like a suburban commuter might an oyster at the oyster bar in Grand Central Station; and I understood even less. Especially of her preoccupation.

Maybe the situation the book spoke of was just too familiar by the time the book reached me, I don't know, but I didn't believe a word she had said about it, or understand how she could put such energy into explaining that work, I thought it was stupid, just stupid. Only because it was Laura speaking I turned it around and concluded that I was stupid instead. That there must have been something solid in that oyster, some pearl in that huge formless creature, that three hour swallow of a long meal that I never noticed chewing. Because everything, including that long ride back to town had that same texture, that oyster slipperiness like slightly salty whipping cream. Or that old saw about Chinese food that was still around when I was a kid: how it's very filling, you might even feel bloated, but you're hungry again an hour later.

So I might be completely mixed up. All I can bring into focus is a scene in an apartment. I don't know if the beautiful woman was with her lover or her husband or if Gatsby was there as well. Or if her face was really bruised or just her soul. And I always see two women when I'm sure it should be two men. So that the texture is of those summers with Lilac. The summer of the lilacs or the ones to come. After we left the Hamptons just the way Gatsby did. To take our own long year's journey into the city, with its hot winds through fire escapes and blowjobs.

Maybe I yawned and put the book down and went to sleep.

Maybe I never read *Gatsby* at all.

I'm the one who loved that trailer park. Without need of any fantasy to flavour it, or even any flowers to give it scent. That place, for all its pure and terribly salty water, was far closer to Coney with its crowds than to any Island you might have wanted to do spinning around in the skirt and saying you wanted a hat: A hat and I'm ready for the Island, you said your voice gone all breathy and small like Mia Farrow simpering at you, so that I was sure it wasn't the book but the *Gatsby* movie you'd got it from, that you were conjuring its blonde on white on grey on ice blue images, with even the skirt suddenly genteel beneath your pretending hand: The Island the Island, you said, spinning, the Hamptons the Hamptons or was it the Eggs, the Eggs, North or West, East or South, I don't remember, but talking like the upper crust again: The Island the Island, the way those who go out to the Island for the summer always do, the ones who just wouldn't be caught dead saying Lon/guy/Ind, the way the inhabitants of its closer suburbs and of Brooklyn and Queens often do. The way Laura did long before she was Lilac or ever crossed the Brooklyn Bridge into Manhattan to our exclusive school to learn better.

Or to say it as a joke on a previous self. Before it turned into an act of class war. In which she won enough battles to triumphantly enter enemy territory, at least briefly, to drink champagne in crystal, though never to wear white lace. When she would wear that jacket and introduce herself with a tough handshake and purposely vulgar laugh.

– Oh, I love Lon/*guy*/Ind, almost as much as Coney.

In fact

Coney Island was always mine. I might call it the Island myself if I could get away with it. Mine. Even without a black leather jacket.

By the day

I got you there it was pretty devastated, with the rides gone. Though it had partially recovered from its worst days. And you can still get good clams and oysters on the half shell even if you wouldn't dare swim. And even if it would never have been the Island to do in that skirt, it was one of the small indulgences that Lilac always made for me: she would always go to Coney Island when I asked.

It didn't matter that its atmosphere was something she always wanted to get away from, like going down to the bars to get her father – or to ask him for money, he was always more generous when her mother wasn't around – with the guys always leering at you. All those young black leather jacketed punks, the jackets have been *de rigueur* a long time, though they haven't always worn earrings or attached the word rock after their name, punk was just another name for young and stupid back then. Or the common garden variety drunken dirty old men. The latter still white, the former already mostly black and Puerto Rican by the summer I left the city, although there were a few young Italians left. While the colour in her father's favourite bars varied more according to location than to age, there was even an Indian bar a few blocks from where she lived, native that is, called the Wigwam, where the Mohawks in from the Canadian reserves to do high steel construction, or to string the cable on the Narrows Bridge, would hang out, another element in New York's working class exotic, at least they seemed so to the inhabitants of the middle class Heights, where when Mack crossed over, he was an exotic himself. With Laura starting to see Coney Island a little that way too the last few nights we went, the New York exotic and testing herself against it, testing her roots, seeing if she could incarnate that too as she made Coney Island into a source, until she was the one to ask me to go.

– To do research, she said laughing. And added, a kind of needling: Tribal customs.

It was more physical anthropology she was actually into, an archaeology of the present, she may even have used those words, it was the kind of thing she said by then. As she talked about the secrets in forms or in images, secret messages for her art as well as from her aliens, with the former far more productive.

She would walk around and look carefully at how the piers were starting to rot, picking up old pieces of board with algae and barnacles growing on them, and mussels as well. The same ones she admired as they clung to barely submerged pieces of pylon, waving and turning on their seaweed mattresses, fluorescent like the neon signs along the boardwalk, flashes of green and pink and blue against New York nightsky maroon to black.

They reminded her of little leather jackets she said, of the punks on the boardwalk in their leather jackets. And she laughed the throaty laugh she was already cultivating, though even then she would not have dared to say out loud, what she would say in a later interview. Still, the image must have been there. Or growing. Out of eating mussels as a kid, something not many people did back then. But which her mother fixed in a particularly succulent sauce.

I only got to read about how she sat in that fancy restaurant with its menu in French making it impossible for her to even know what she was getting, after all she'd been true to her working class roots and Mack's desires in high school and studied Spanish, New York's most recent immigrant language, though she'd had to lisp out a Madrid accent instead of a staccato Caribbean beat. So that I'm sure she felt, if only for a moment, just the way she had in Sofia's house, awkward and unworldly opposite the interviewer who knew exactly what was what, making her wait in trepidation to see what she would get, surely not a giant turd in a bidet, surely it wasn't the *Return of the Great Turd*, surely not that, as the waiter, his arm behind him: *Voila, Madame* removed the cover from a steaming pot of mussels, the sweet cheap orange purple seafood of her childhood, rich in a way that pallid clams or oysters could never be, so that she could smile in recognition and kiss her fingertips to the waiter, and grin perversely as she told the woman opposite her, after all it was the kind of outrageousness the interviewer had come for, and she was intimately acquainted with the anatomy by then, she used it in everything, how they looked like sweet little cunts in their tough leather jackets, pointing out the vermilion swollen clitoris at one end, with the ochre flesh of the labia swelling out around it, their purple black ciliated edges, so much like the partially shaved pubic hair of porn models, just leaning in to almost but not quite cover the vaginal orifice there below.

– Lovely, she is reported to have said: Absolutely scrumptious, picking one up in its shell while she let the juice run down her hand, as she slurped it up by sticking in her tongue, twisting it sharply around instead of using a fork to loosen the mussel's grip.

– Oh Mother, that's good, she said, staring at the interviewer all the while. Until she chose to wipe her lips most genteelly on her linen napkin, and lean back, and then, to make sure readers not get her wrong, and think her a lesbian, especially with the way she appeared in all her pictures with her short hair and that beautiful jacket she gave away to the punk in the hospital, painted with its ill concealed vaginal symbology in day-glo colours, she told the interviewer, her jacket swinging open as she leaned even further back in her chair, arms out to show how she wished to embrace the world while revealing a filmy spaghetti strap blouse and soft cushiony breasts, their brown nipples hard and searching like eyes for all the world to see, how Sandro had steamed her open out of her own hard shell, to allow her to look upon the world, and make it anew in woman's image, while he slurped her up, a constant challenge, to make her what she was today.

Only that

today wasn't the today we saw her, the today some might accuse Sandro of making her. That today was the day of the interviews in top arts magazines when she was 'up and coming' and 'emerging' and 'someone to watch'. 'A new kind of woman artist' who was one of 'the hot new city lights' herself. Where they didn't even spell out her perversity but just printed little 'c's or 'c – ts', I don't remember. Although I know for sure they spelled out 'clitoral' and 'vaginal' as you would any other good solid polite clinical Latin word.

That brief golden today when she knew exactly which unprintable word was expected of her to make her printable. When she was part of that dark side the beautiful people have always needed, and she played it beautifully, young and shining and dark and wild. Only I remember giggling. Imitating her throaty laugh for just one moment, then giggling. Over that clipping my mother sent. Then fixing the mussels that had become *de rigueur* trendy by then, just as I suppose we had become yuppies, though the term wasn't yet there, while I drank too much wine at my dinner alone.

Jeanpierre was off in the bush and the kids, however many there were of them, were far too young to join me at table, to watch me raise my glass to my reflection in the window over and over as I drank to her and her triumph, how beautiful it was that she had gotten it all, while staring at those mussels, so beautiful on our best black porcelain plates, I don't know why I'd used them, but they made it all a picture for a design magazine, the mother of pearl glints off the grey insides of the shells, the neon glints off the black outsides, my reflection arising out of the black of the night between the drapes, transparent fork and knife held over the real lilac cloth, as I thought about how she'd got it backward, that she had always had it backward: she had been warm and open, the ocean currents running over and through her, an Amazon with weapons enough but no shield. And that what Sandro had lent her, or taught her, was the leather jacket shell: the hard image. The one that they wanted. That could say Lon/guy/Ind and bray and use it to open doors. While I was convinced she still dreamed of lace. Like the porcelain figurines in her mother's living room: the fairy tale.

– Congratulations: I muttered. To all you cunts out there.

And I raised my glass again and again in toast to my reflection and that new light of the artworld, with each gesture more lonely. Myself the designer photograph: young Canadian homemaker salutes the work of avant-garde artist Laura Mack, more and more soft focus. Until even my reflection disappeared before my tears.

Although that last time in Coney Island with me she still didn't say things like that.

– Such cool jackets, was all she said. Mussels must be the punks of seafood. And she laughed. Still her open braying déclassé laugh.

– In more ways than one. They're what poor people eat. If you tried to eat this bunch though, and she poked with a stick at one of the clusters of mussels clinging to the breakwater just below the tide line: You'd probably die. Croak. Instantly. Right here.

And it was me who had to add that the same thing would probably happen if you tried to eat one of those punks.

Those punks had always been just water off a duck's back, or maybe I should say in the context, the dark glimmering shell of a mussel, to me. Literally, they kind of oozed over me as I walked down to Broadway to take the IRT to school, mostly the Puerto Rican variety, it went with the neighbourhood, all the *qué linda linda* anybody could ever want to hear, followed by suggestions as to what they wanted to do with you. Usually in English for your benefit, though sometimes in Spanish for each other's. A dose of the streets on the way to my private school or the exclusive public junior high I'd previously tested into. An old coat my protective coloration for the neighbourhood, what was under it, protective coloration for school. My wardrobe as often as not selected by Daddy's new wife, it was his one gesture toward child support, something he knew my mother couldn't spend because it wouldn't fit her.

Though I'm sure right now Ms. Youngwife's selections would fit the neighbourhood better, with its restaurants and classy boutiques (you must remember the guy who swore he didn't dare take his clothes to the drycleaners anymore because he was afraid that when he came back for them, the old drycleaners might have turned into a Benetton), than they did back then when in the late spring my wardrobe would just get me called what I was pretending to be: Central Park Rich Bitch. Even if the last word was really the only one that ever fit.

Though in those days the punks didn't attack. At least not often. They just slunk about the neighbourhood. Their own neighbourhood. They weren't marauders disturbing its peace.

I've never missed them. One way or the other. It wasn't nostalgia for running that gauntlet that made me return to Coney Island once I'd abandoned the lonely height of my mother's apartment. And I had never loved knishes so much, or the other stuff you could stuff yourself with after you did the rides, the little neck clams or the fried oysters or the four kinds of soft ice cream you could get piled into one cone, pistachio vanilla banana and chocolate. And of course I hate hot dogs, even the world famous Nathan's frank.

And as for the rides themselves, they were never that great. Except maybe for Steeplechase Park, so different from anything else, with its moving slides and spinning hills like a wooden topographical map, a playground in non-Euclidean geometry – Laura said that, how those rides were the new math made concrete – that you paid for once and climbed into again and again. Or maybe the Wonderwheel and the Parachute Jump, that was closed shortly after I got old enough to ride on it, where you combined all the amusement park colours, and the sudden thrilling drops, with the view out to sea.

It was just that when you put those things all together, painted metal and wood and loud voices and hurry hurry hurry see the tattooed lady and recorded laughter and shrieks from the fun houses and the colours of ice cream rolling down your arm and then the summer with the thousands of people huddled on the beach, or bobbing up and down in the water holding on to ropes stretched out into the ocean, something you know almost nothing of, something almost unknown on the Prairies in fact, on any given summer day the entire population of Saskatoon was probably on the beaches, though the feel is there in fairs and stampedes and exhibition midways and maybe a little bit by now at the waterslides at Sylvan Lake or south on MacLeod Trail or in the artificial oceans of wavepools and West Edmonton Mall, but back there and then you would consider yourself lucky just to find a spot where you could spread out your beach towel anywhere between the current tide line and the boardwalk, and you would make it your own, a strange but acknowledged personal space, even as you stepped over the bodies lying in your way, still you would avoid eye contact, and never never even so much as touch a toe to the corner of a towel. At least I wouldn't, being a polite young lady. Though on really hot days it was a great temptation. Which bolder souls would not resist.

With such bright colours such infinity of movement, that I loved it, especially against the infinity of calm repetition that was the ocean. Nature nurture culture rubbing against each other at their most vulgar and glorious, like Lake Louise or Sunshine Village in winter more than anything else you know that I could compare it to. Because it's the contrast that matters, even if I did enjoy West Ed when I went there with the kids, except for the buzzing, the gradual dizziness I experience

in the repeated controlled spaces of all shopping malls. And I laughed when I saw the Beach, the beach and Fantasyland together, coetaneous so to speak, like four dimensional icons of Coney Island sent out into hyper-space, making me giggle a moment and wonder if I had entered her world, the world of her astronomy text, and the aliens had us in some kind of zoo and were observing from the roof.
– Look dear, the mothers would say to the children: There's late twentieth century humankind consuming. And I thought of you, and the skirt, and how I could use West Ed to explain myself to you, we could tour it the way we did New York and I could try again to make everything clear, from inside its museum-like spaces.

Only it's really more the lift lines that compare, we could ski together and I would explain as we would stop at the edge of a new slope to catch our breath, pointing with a pole at the metal structures of the lifts and the bright colours of the people moving along suspended in the air, so like the Parachute Jump, but looking over a different, a white infinity, that is where the oceans start. Scenes that make me laugh, and love skiing, downhill skiing, although you would probably tremble and rebel, call it a traffic jam on the Crowchild at rush hour, that skiing with the groups of crazy men drinking beer and shouting and too far out of control. Though as a dancer you love the beauty in how the body feels itself into the snow, you skied a lot once, you told me that. While for me it's the people that make me glory in downhill, more than in the absolute quiet of moving cross country, just the schuss of your skis and the occasional plop of snow dropping off a tree. And silence. And space. Natural perfection.

And still I don't know why.

Except that it's never been a love of slumming or of dirt. Maybe just for the reality of human space. The space we make between us. With all the joy we can find. A tolerable margin of joy. To keep us going. So that even when I travel I love places like that. And when some of our friends look at me and say: Well I hope I will be considered a traveller and not a tourist, I kind of giggle inside myself. I'll tour anything. And feel good. As long as it's not people that I'm called upon to gawk at.

If I can just gawk with them, instead. The way I did with you, Thorne. Or at Niagara Falls. Gawking with the best of all those gawking people, the millions of metric tonnes of water just flowing and flowing, halfway between Sunshine Village and Coney Island, ocean river and source, something nothing could trivialize. And everyone staring. And knowing it. And the little tentacles of understanding between them: a cat's cradle of human contact, loosely woven the way you sometimes weave the audience when you dance.

It's my love of tourism that made me a prime candidate for uncomplaining habitation in that trailer park on the Island too. A guilty invader even, like all those of my ilk, who exemplify the qualities pop psychologists assign to the lower middle – really the upper working – class, though how my mother could have engendered that I certainly don't know, with all her desire to inculcate good taste. Maybe that's even what did it, crossing the heights with the depths, aristocracy and poverty. So that she just wound up with the vulgar middle she always tried to avoid: me. With my love of the disconnected intensity of neon flashing on and off, or of Laura's mother's knickknack shelves, warming myself in the busyness dictated by the constant *horror vacui*, in sound or sight or smell or taste, or touch.

I even enjoyed how Alicia fussed around the trailer, all the cooking and the little touches she had added, even if it was rented. Or for that matter Laura's father, the constant games of cards, the attempts to show me how to deal. And the stories that accompanied the beer. For all of us. The whole trailer park. Though after a while all that activity in such a small corner would make me restless too, make me want to move, to do something, to swim or walk or play, and I never liked the way he looked at me, not ever.

I do love the empty too, and the elegant. I just don't prefer them. The way we all pretend we do, calling our row houses down by Fish Creek townhomes, and thinking of ourselves as living in privacy even as the neighbour's bassline enters through the wall. Pretending we are on our estates as we listen with intent pleasure for the sound of the neighbour's beer can opening, the smell of his steak sizzling, just as we once loved the clean look of the now prohibited laundry flapping on the lines.

And all of us, the articles would say, moving out like interchangeable ants onto Long Island with our neon and our transistors and our ghetto blasters and our beach umbrellas and our gum wrappers and our coke bottles and our beer cans and our flavoured condoms and our plastic flowers and our aluminum siding and our whoopee cushions and our carpet look linoleum and our plastic flamingoes and our macramé plant hangers and our black velvet paintings and our overcrowding and our braying loud voices, destroying the peace of nature: the peace of the rich.

Because the rich, they love to be alone. They love silence. And safaris and deserted beaches and lonely climbs and big elegant houses. Solitude. From where they can look the future we are all afraid of straight in the eye. I read that somewhere. It might even have been in that article on the lower middles' invasion of the Island. Stopped by zoning laws against trailers right as they reached the gates of the Hamptons, the last refuge.

And I even bought it. For at least half an hour, probably more, propped in my bed with the article in a moment of intense loneliness with the man away, maybe I had woken up in the middle of the night on the evening I'd almost drunk myself into a stupor drinking to Laura, maybe it was even the same issue of the same magazine that exalted her working class edge. But a late night in any case, with that feeling of vulnerability to possible attack curled into the back of the neck even as I pushed mine into the pillows, feeling alone and afraid for some reason even with the kids. And the paper thin walls I probably could have punched through with my fist to get into the place next door. So that I got up to turn on the radio, and admired the bravery of those solitary members of the Sierra Club, they'd never drive a trailer to Yosemite, and park it on concrete and turn on the TV. Until I suddenly felt a longing for a cup of tea.

And shortly thereafter, I didn't feel like removing myself from the bed again, an even greater longing for someone to fix it. And bring it to me on a silver tray. Or even on a cheap stainless steel imitation with sharp edges. Which made me start to fantasize. Imagining those possible parties I had always run from, what I had missed that had been within my grasp: the gentle beauty, the soft night. The silence only broken by the ocean's far away pounding, and the quiet voices in the fog. And no one to interrupt one's pleasure in it.

Until I realized suddenly that no matter how fog bound, those voices would always be heard, whether they screamed for help, or just whispered: Tea please, the sound purring out along the texture of the sofa. Because there would always be at least one person paid to listen, to make the tea, or give the CPR, arriving without your ever noticing who placed the tray on the table, who pounded your chest for the better part of an hour.

Which is what I thought about as I got myself out of bed to move around my house, my down booties slapping against the floor, and I went into the kitchen to pick out my tea, and reached up into the cupboard for it, and thought of Sir Edmund Hillary on his way up Everest. Step. Step. Step. Alone. Alone. Alone. Just like I was, except there had been that man, probably men, with a name just like the tea I had picked out: Lapsang Soochong, or some such. Only who would want to share the credit with someone with a name like that. Not when you can reduce to nonexistence anyone whose silence you can command.

– **Tea please Alma**, I then said to myself, and it appeared.
– The lights, dear, I continued, and out they went.
– Sleep, now, I said and even sleep obeyed.

Hurried along without doubt by a bit too much brandy in the tea. You never know what these modern servants will do, good help is damn hard to come by these days.

Maybe
you can understand now why I loved that army tent Laura had pitched in the bushes. It was just far away enough from the noise to please me. Though she spent the whole first evening apologizing for it. She had never had the advantage of the distance my mother's apartment, my mother's professionalism (she wasn't working class even if she worked, she was a professional, she

always said) had given me. Laura had never floated eleven stories above the park. She was right down on street level, with the clotheslines stretched out from her mother's window, or walking from bar to bar, feeling that street life suffocating her, pulling her down, until she would just turn to me and say:
– I want a life-line, a life-line, something to pull me up. Up and out.
Until I became one.

– **Wow, what a treat**. We'll be alone, was all I said about the tent that night. It was the first tent with a floor I had ever been in. Although I have had a lot of experience since, I had always thought of tents as blankets lifted up on poles. So that I was surprised to find it so solid and so sealed. With its screens over the doors and its translucent heavy canvas sides and its smell of the heat of the sun and some kind of waterproofing. And a self-contained population that got inside somehow.

With a crawling element: daddy longlegs, a variety of ants, the occasional real spider, that stuck to the floor most of the time but would do the walls too; and a flying one: moths and mayflies and the mosquitoes we tried our hardest to keep out. With the largest population, and the one that fascinated me most, forming the link between them: a reddish round beetle that mostly crawled but sometimes flew, and that always buzzed on and on and on, even more than the kerosene lamps. Which they never hit, even if the lamps formed the funeral pyre of all the lighter winged creatures. The beetles' weight was too solid and too crunchy, with their hard shells and uselessly diaphanous inner wings keeping them from ever getting much more than two feet above the ground: the level of our faces asleep on the cots.

Laura just didn't think it was proper to be inside a tent with such things. They were far worse than the tent itself.
– Well really, the bugs, you could tell she was imitating Sofia: And oh, the *noise* let me tell you, de-ah, we're never staying at *this* hotel again, she would sigh. The allusion brought on by the interior echo of all the outside activity, gargles and throat clearings in the morning, the howls of laughter and TV voices late into the night.

After all we probably would have been able to get through the horseflies and the mosquitoes, and still imagine it the Hamptons, or for that matter the Eggs. But it would have been hard to make up a movie for yourself, at least a genteel one, with that heavy presence. Which is probably why our thoughts turned, not to ancient Amazons, there could obviously be no mythic greatness in this tent, though it would probably do for sulking, but to secret agents.

They related quite easily and quickly to the beetles, and to all the other buzzings. Until we finally decided that the whole scene was part of the attempts being made by some definitely alien hardshelled creatures to take off for outer space, to escape earth orbit or to teleport themselves elsewhere, only to fall to earth again. With a few more bruises and a little laughter all they had to show for it.

So that in the end it was just something else to bring us together, as we laughed at ourselves and everyone else while the beetles buzzed and landed on us like little planes: so concrete. And definitely unromantic.

Since it was still our own world, sealed away like that, we knew we could still pretend. Which meant we integrated our days into that extraterrestrial buzzing, the beetles and the gargles, deciding on the little myths, what we sometimes call myths instead of lies, which might be, at any rate, the archetypes of our culture. So that as secret agents among the insect/aliens, come to root out some dreadful secret, make some clandestine contact with the denizens of the place, we moved among the trailers discovering them to be, like the people's minds, giant radio antennae, quasars, she called them, she had read that word somewhere, attuned to different sources in the stars.

And because we were undercover, we did our best to meld into that alien world: chewing gum and pretending to be just like the other teenagers hanging out. As we watched them and took notes, saw how they picked up boys and where they went to make out, intergalactic anthropologists assigned to observe and assure the next agent's disguise. Until we decided that if we really wanted to understand the aliens' habits we would have to try it at least once ourselves.

Which giggling we did, parading around the beach in our respectable two piece suits, throwing our weight, or at least our hips, around until, beach ball in hand, we captured ourselves two natives at once, down by the main road in a little white MG. Two richies from the Hamptons we decided later, as we tried to insert them into their proper slot, they seemed part of an overall pattern, seventeenth year locusts we decided to call them, following the lines of our insect logic, descending as they did, with their new drivers' licenses, to slum by the trailer park and pick up the poorer more easily consumable, what they think of as loose, women. The ones you definitely don't take home to the house party.

We rode about on the back of that car, sitting out over the trunk, our feet pushed down into the space behind the seat, and we held each other's hands as they drove. While they didn't notice or thought we were scared, the way we clung to each other, and they tried to make conversation while we saw a scene from James Bond unfolding before our eyes, the car going at a hundred and twenty or forty miles per hour that was in reality probably a quite respectable sixty to sixty-five, considering the road and how the car belonged to Daddy, while we pretended to blow up every VW or other small slow car we passed.

And she got the cute one and I got the one who was tall and gangly, with their techniques much the same, I'll never know if from porno flicks or locker room advice or the parents' purloined sex manuals or from practicing on each other. Because they were a dead loss out there on the sandy beach with no noise and no beetles. Though it wasn't unpleasant, somehow at just the right distance, to let your mind drift away, to the sound of the surf and the continuation of our fantasies.

Which we pooled later on, weaving them together with our accounts of the experience itself, calling it our debriefing I believe, I don't know which one of us had found that one, or in what spy novel, I know it wasn't in common use then, the way it is now, when everyone debriefs everything. Just as we did our encounter as we lay in our sleeping bags in our nightgowns after having a shower. And we talked about how disgusting it was for them to think they could just finger you two hours after they met you, which we hadn't let them do, of course, our legs tighter together than a beached mermaid's tail, more offended with their thought processes than their fingers, knowing their deployment signified what was thought of us, though the sand on them was pretty bad too. And their breath worse, I said hooting hysterically, with the taste of that young man's saliva something I have in fact never forgotten, I could conjure it right now if I wanted to, your basic bubble gum yuck, which I tasted again as our laughter lent strength to the late evening gargles' attempts at interstellar communication, telling her how my guy's breath had smelled exactly like the beetles and the sun on the tent.

After which we started to work them in more seriously, like we did the man in the park, making them the enemy, our opponents, nothing like Achilles in the field, but enemies to go with the territory, the ones we had sought out on the beach and finally encountered on the road, those fiendishly clever agents of some terrible power out to enslave us all. Without conscience or scruples.

Or for that matter culture or taste. Or appreciation for the finer things this planet had to offer. Such as ourselves.

We passed the remaining days between the tent and the dunes and the trailers and the salt sea, laughing and deciding upon, from our hideaway, what became each day more complicated plots, all of them prohibiting any closer contact with the local population than a game of softball, but with the next moves dictated, just as they always were, to coincide with simple things like a picnic with her family or going to the bathhouse by ourselves or taking a swim at the beach or just pulling out the antenna of her parents' portable to see what stations we could get and where they would be broadcasting from, sure when it was rhythmic static that it was something we must decode. And in the most secret grassy places in the dunes or enclosed among the beetles at night we would look at each other and kiss each other and try out the boys' techniques, the pressures of the hands without the encroaching fingers, then kiss again our eyes wide open, the way we always would when we were pretending not to be ourselves.

Those wide open

eyes would always

catch us. Because we were always ourselves in our eyes, no matter what we would pretend. So that it was that gaze that would make us gasp or giggle, or rise to our full heights, standing tall like true Amazons. Or fall to our knees and hug each other harder, with tears of pain or laughter in our eyes.

The same eyes that caught and held me that night at Mother's. When we moved together again Lilac and I, in a catastrophe of gazes crossing while she sat on the chair, her astronomy text in hand. Making me wish for a moment to read it, to talk to her about it, to find out where she'd been and how we could go there, the two of us, as I forgot suddenly the dull hammering voice expostulating on something, or waiting to. Like an obedient schoolgirl on line to be a teacher, Lilac ramrod straight in her chair, the text full of the lessons to be taught us all.

Because she had looked from the text to me, and in that moment she was there. Laura was there. Laura. And all the time came rushing back. Of living inside that vibrant magic world with her, as her eyes made me solid inside that moment, as only she and the moment of giving birth have ever been able to make me, as she called me once more, down off the couch. And she too sank down onto her knees, as I fell into the warm pulsating circle of her thought and of her arms.

Into a place that I had not been in so long that I had forgotten it was there. Forgotten her inside it. Forgotten she could be there still. So that I thought for one brief instant what I had not thought in years: that she could be my Laura, and be with me. All of her, as brilliant as ever. And certainly better informed, after stepping out a time to navigate among the stars, elsewhere if not elsewhen, a space academy graduate on assignment, organizing her own mission to seek out new lifeforms, with that book as her guide, her system of coordinates, her own astrolabe.

While in that instant when I looked at her, she took a brief leave from her important duties to drop an instant back into her body, into our time frame, to say: Hello. To remember her first aliens and our Amazons and her art and our laughter. As I hugged her and hugged her. Feeling with the fullness of myself her breasts large and warm against my own, the hard breastbone behind them, the heart inside beating, the expansion of her ribcage as she breathed.

Until I was there with her. Really there for just that one moment: perfect and spontaneous.

And it was just Laura. Laura and Alma. The way it had always been Laura and Alma. Laura and Alma hugging each other. Laura and Alma smiling at each other and bumping shoulders and giggling at sleepovers in high school – and whatever it is you talk about then that has more meaning and importance than you would ever imagine or dare to remember. While I felt it all again. All of it again until that evening started spinning. And gave off sparks. Because it was that moment that made my mother take out the skirt. That made me give it to you.

That makes me stand here, moving from window to closet to bed to door, to listen for the kids to measure the day to feel the cloth between my hands as I lay out the clothes, packing and thinking of you, packing and thinking of her, packing and thinking of that night, trying to find a way to tell it, to tell her story. To make it real to give her at least the weight in this world her body has long ceased to have; the weight in my life she deserves. While I find myself close to tears, packing yet again, sure that I will never have that concentration or that energy, to allow me alone, without her astronomy text, without her marginalia, her Thomian discontinuities, without her voice and her guidance, her infinite laughter, to ever find that place we were again.

Any more

than Wendy could make never-never land without Peter Pan. Or was it Tinkerbell who took them both? I can't remember. Just that there is a sensible good girl part of me much like an observant social worker, a Wendy all grown up, that weighs me too heavy to the ground, that by now finds it hard even to believe that such a place could have existed. Who would never again let me become a moth to Laura's flame. Or even the beetle in her tent I had once been.

Because I don't think I ever was in any danger of burning up, even back then I was too hard for that, but just of falling onto my round back, buzzing and struggling, my legs flailing around, the way we would spend hours watching the beetles do, like the oars on punts rowing slightly out of time, one two three four five six, rocking from side to side like a canoe about to capsize, or one of those children's toys that always bounce back, spending all their energy going nowhere, repeating and repeating their actions, until finally one or another of the animals currently on the floor would tip just far enough to get a leg under and flip itself upright to try to fly again, while yet another fell, whump, to earth to take its place, flailing and flailing, just the way I would, flailing, to get up again and reach out, to protect her to find her centre to listen to her ideas to share her projects, terribly and constantly exhausted by it all.

Until finally I couldn't do it anymore. Which is when the good girl self must have taken over, the one that had originally grown to protect her, that had fed on all my mother's advice on proper etiquette for put downs and dinner parties that got Laura through bad scenes and hard times until it turned to rescue me instead and took that beetle up and tethered it by the leg to a gold chain, the way they do with beetles in the Yucatan, larger and prettier ones for sure than the ones in Lilac's tent, beige and black and about three inches long, elegant really, I saw one once, mounted with jewellery, red and green and yellow diamond cut glass, or plastic pearls, mounted in gold plate or just gold painted metal, and the chain glued on too, a pin at the other end so that the insect can slowly do its convict's walk over a small circle of dress, or guayabera, the way my beetle was pinned to a stronger more stolid being, such a walking jewel would be so perfect for a sober and pompous social worker going to a conference to speak of her equally captive clients in a grey flannel skirted suit, where it would be weighed down against ever again having to try its Evel Knievel Beetle daredevil leap into the sky.

But just go from suit or blouse to tabletop or its small cage to eat wood chips the way all those beetles do, thinking in silence to itself. Or very occasionally be let go, in places where there is no temptation, no flame of great new ideas, just open skies and campfires with children and the same old stories to make up to tell them, the ones we have all heard again and again, nothing new at all, just the same old tomorrow over and over, of diapers to be changed or dishes to be done or courses to be passed or reports to be finished.

Small finite jobs to be done, like all the work in the Peruvian blanket behind Lilac on the couch which still held the shape of her body its fine raw wool threads moving in and out to form the traditional patterns, again and again, deep natural reds and greens that I watched until my fingers went numb and my consciousness moved once more back from my body. While the social worker politely removed herself to the couch with you, brushing herself off and turning her wine glass, her legs crossed and her caterpillar brows raised: How did that ever happen? that social worker self must have said looking at us entwined there in the middle of the floor while she pushed away the feelings rushing through my body, and watched them as if they were part of a movie, evaluating the emotion, the acting, as she thought:

– Here I am hugging Laura. Isn't it dramatic being here in New York again hugging Laura.

I watched myself doing it, then. Removing all but the most delicate feelers, like the creepers on ivy or a hothouse passion vine, or the sensor mechanisms of an alien bio-technology, back from her body, allowing those to continue monitoring the rough texture of the polyester she wore, to note how below the patchouli and the dirt she smelled the same as she always had, as they sent the message back to me that this gesture was right, right, absolutely perfect. And so sad, so very poignant, that tears came into my eyes right on cue. While the social worker continued explaining to me how this Lilac was a very problematical case, that she was in fact quite deluded, that I would no longer find even the narrowest comprehension in anything she said.

With the scene itself just as it should be: It's perfect dear, she said, patting my hand, so that I let her do it, all terribly stiff and syrupy sweet as she continued her orchestration, the way she had so often, from that moment when I let her lift my feet one in front of the other, to walk slowly since I could not fly, to turn those feet away from Laura, those many years before. While she now smiled like a nurse in a commercial, measuring out our contact like cough medicine: Take one spoonful it's good for you, as the one perfect moment ended. And I knew that nothing had been accomplished. Or repaired.

Except a bit of my pride. As I felt you and my mother sitting there watching me. Hug the shell of my best friend.

And a voice in my mind said: See how Alma has it together, see how good she is. Watch Alma watch. Watch Alma watch Laura. See how good Alma is with Laura. Watch Alma be spontaneous and open. Alma has what Lilac doesn't. Watch wonderful Alma be good. Smile Alma smile.

The worst of my children's textbooks come to life to match that brighter than bright whiter than white unfaded TV advertising science fiction fantasy world of plastic permanence in which the clothes and the apartments and the spaceships and even the minds are always clean and nothing and nobody ever gets accidentally put through the wrong wash cycle.

As I felt how my right hand wanted to reach out and wave to you. The way people do for tourist photographs. To say: Watch me watch me. And it was: Do it do New York. And the tears. Like crying in your own home movie. That could be played again and again. With each gesture so well acted; so felt so right. While the mind behind counted the seconds, one one thousand, two one thousand, three one thousand. Repeating: soon. Soon. Waiting out the end of the scene. For the director to yell: Cut. To say: That's a take.

To say: Cut and that's a wrap.

It's over.

As my eyes closed again. Only this time squeezed shut in waiting for the end to be accomplished. So that I could no longer feel her body but just my own pulse counting, through the blood in my veins the saliva in my mouth, crooning a lullaby beat by beat, myself unmoving except for the place where a slight pulse moves into the fingertips to feel the texture of her blouse, to sing along, the words from the old song repeating in my mind: All my trials, lord (this one at least) soon be over.

Soon be over.

The way it has been since I left.
Although I have never been sure that I was whole, or even that I did not steal the best parts of me from her, the ones that impressed you so much, Thorne. What you called my quirky, or maybe quarky, sense of reality. All those things I say, the way I put things together, my frames of reference, that twenty-odd years later still keep me up to date. Things she already knew back then. At least I think she did. I'm pretty sure of it. That knowing was her genius. Though I haven't been sure of very much, you see, Thorne. Not ever. Since then.

Even when I search memory over and over trying to find the fairy dust, or the will or wish or desire that for that time kept my own fairy, the fairy inside her, or inside us (what I should, perhaps, in greater sophistication, the way she once did, call 'duende' or 'daemon' or at the very least spell 'faerie') from dying, I mostly find nothing. Except that same empty shell you saw that night, that says she was never more than my own illusion. Or delusion. The way they tell her she has delusions.

That I once shared.

BEDBUGS

We did apart Laura

get an
ment,
and I'.

That first year in University when she got the scholarship to the Art Department of NYU, and various other places besides. Only she wouldn't leave the city, that's what she always insisted on calling New York: I will not leave the CITY, she would say: This is where EVERYTHING happens. Which, as we both know, whether everything does or not, made enough sense in her case since it is the New York artworld these days that decides the fate of artists everywhere.

And I don't think she did either, except for those trips to Long Island or the Catskills or the Delaware Water Gap, not even for a brief tour of European Museums, or to hitchhike to California, maybe once as far as Yale, but never more, not ever. Not even to go to her own openings.

While I got offers from Oberlin and Vassar with a scholarship rolled in, and though I wasn't at all convinced that EVERYTHING happened in New York, especially when it came to the right University, still what was important in my case did. Which meant I stayed in town to go to City College, just to be with her.

I told my mother it was the money, with the City University still completely free then.
—Even with the scholarship you know we can't afford it, I said, then added after a pause: And I don't want to owe money for the rest of my life.

But she knew that it was just for Laura that I stayed. So that she arched her eyebrows at me and spoke in her bitterest voice.
—I'd never stop you from doing what you want, dear. Please, don't let my thoughts on the matter get in your way.

And I had said: But City is as good as either of those two schools, and you know it as well as I do. Looking at it objectively, of course.

Which made her smile broaden, because she had to acknowledge that she had taught me how to argue if nothing else, and she must have recognized her favourite words on my tongue. Though she sighed too.
—That's hardly the point, dear, you know we're talking the advantage of an Ivy League degree. Or even one from a school like Oberlin. City College is what you can't afford in the long run.

Then she gave me one of her hardest hard-nosed guidance counsellor looks and turned away. Musing, her hand on one of her little art objects, in a soft voice, as if it were an afterthought only the soapstone statue should know about:

—I guess you're just not as strong as we thought.

After which she walked to the window to look at the sky, never mentioning who 'we' happened to be, her and the statue her and some mysterious spirit or just the royal we. Nor did I stay to ask. But just said, with the cards on the table:

—I'm strong enough for two.

Then charged out the door to take a long walk in the park she was pretending to be busy looking at. Though maybe she even saw me head out on the path toward the reservoir.

Then after my first year as an

Anthro major I quit school completely and got a job as a waitress. Where the tribal life around me wouldn't be so complex. Because it was just too hard to do it all. To clean the apartment while Laura studied and sketched and painted and designed and sighed and complained and wrote down her impressions. Then sighed and complained again because there was always something just so important coming up, and she was sure, just sure, this time she wouldn't be able to get it together, not on time:

—You know how rotten I was at this in high school.

Managing our Lab time they had called it, the free periods we had during the day to do ongoing work were called Laboratories, and it was true she was rotten at it, that she always got lectures: You're not making good use of your Lab time, Laura, teachers would say looking down their noses, because she was always in the art room, if it wasn't one of the times she had fallen asleep on the subway she took all the way from Brooklyn. So her University papers too were always late.

Sometimes it would be a paper for art history she would be moaning and groaning about while I listened to her ideas for hours and went over the books until I knew the material as well as she did and could help her put the thing together, just the way I had in high school, only then I'd had to learn the material too.

Which made that year too much like taking two majors at once, writing my own papers first, then, because I did it so much more easily than she could, I would as often as not end up doing her writing for her, too. But from her ideas, or the ideas we had had together.

Brainstorming I guess it would be called today, those wonderful ideas that came from those wonderful conversations that were what had built our relationship in the first place, where you wind up so far from where you started that you can hardly believe you got there, what you once said in the group you invited me to after I finished with your yoga class, is what *really* teaches us we can change the world, because we've changed each other. What I used to feel with her, and hadn't felt again until the group, so that the group, you and the group really, taught me how at least that much of our relationship had been real, that there was something true in my enthusiastic worship of her.

Though back then what I told myself as I sat down to write from the notes that I'd made while we'd talked was just that it didn't matter if I did that for her, it wasn't cheating, after all we were one person. So that I shared in what I was sure was her budding genius too, because how could it be otherwise. I could accompany her on all her journeys, because we were one. Apart we were fragments but if you put us together you would get all the aspects of one personality.

Only it would be a megapersonality. A metapersonality. Which, if we just worked on it, her travelling further and further into experience, into the uncharted depths of the universe, me building frames and boxes and carrying cases for her discoveries, arguments to bolster her position, to make sure that others could understand them, would carry us into a future, a very different future from the war scarred streets of the early seventies, as yet unmade. That we would have the opportunity of making.

Because I did feel connected to tomorrow with her, in a way that I never have. Except by instants. As I walked out of my house to greet the green grass of my yard Jeanpierre at my elbow the contractions every five minutes, the moment hours later defined in white cloth and blood when son or daughter slipped into the world, the line of orange against the trees as your eyes met mine in my mother's window. But never like that, never every day like that, each moment so clear precisely because it could, at any second, turn and be utterly different, reveal what was hidden, hide what was obvious.

I usually wrote her papers because she had a design assignment coming due at the same time.
—You have no idea what a *bastard* this one is, she would say, meaning the teacher not the assignment: If he doesn't like what you do he'll tear it off the wall, and he's so insulting, she would add as she worked and worked with paints and inks and rulers and drafting pens and designers' gouache and all the other materials of the trade she was learning. Until when she got to the mechanical stuff, the stuff that didn't take any inspiration she would ask me to help her.
—Help, help, Alma I'm drowning she would say raising her hands as if above the water, or, with a sigh: This Amazon just can't fight no more battles today.

Either way I would wade right in, to the water or to battle it didn't matter, but always to her rescue, and when it wasn't to write the paper for the other course while she did the design assignment, it was to work on the assignment itself, the minimal stuff anyway, matting and cutting paper, making frames and preparing surfaces, things like that, things I still do for myself, as she explained endlessly why she was doing this and not that, what the ideas behind each work were. Although I do remember that every once in a while an idea would be mine, like the infinity on the telephone box, one of her first successful projects, that let her know she could do it, she had the edge. Something I suggested just because those boxes did always seem so infinitely lonely to me, especially at night when we would walk by them.
—Yes, she said: The infinity of language, words repeating out into the wires, arranging and rearranging themselves, through the satellites. I think telephone satellites were the most talked about of the new technologies right then, so it was something she would know a lot about, of

course, it was the kind of thing she always did know. She would tell you how at certain electromagnetic frequencies as of sometime in this century between radio and television and radar and all the other microwaves the earth started to glow brighter than the sun, a signal to the aliens she always said: They've seen us and they're coming. And I couldn't help agreeing with her, on some level I still think I do, though I'm no longer convinced that they're here, or that she's their contact.

Then while we were talking about that, infinity and telephones, I asked her if she'd noticed how 'time' and 'emit' are mirror image words, except for the 'e' of course, which is directional, an idea that made her laugh, she hadn't thought about it. But she did incorporate it into a design, the two words expanding out from a sun, EMIT TIME in a hexagon, the capital 'E' reversing with each word like a traditional border design, so that the words were clear in exactly two places, to the left and right of the sun. And I remember looking at it, how proud I was that I had started it, the way she said she was proud of my papers, how much sense they made, even when her name went on them, how well thought out they were. Mentioning only in passing how her ideas were the kernel, the seed: which we both believed. That she was at the centre and that I wove an explanation around her like a cocoon, that I let her grow. Which would make us hug each other or kiss each other lightly on the lips each time such a special collaborative mission was accomplished.

And then, when she wasn't talking about her ideas she would continue on about that one particular teacher, and about the A's she got from him and how, at least, it was never her work that got torn off the walls. And when he wasn't an absolute bastard he was the best teacher in the school, he knew more than the rest put together and besides he was the one who sent them to all the galleries, and talked about what was happening *now* and was closest to her surrealist bent, he was the one who loved not only her designs but my papers or more: he let her know they were lovable. He was the one she let tell her who was okay and who wasn't.

While the other thing she kept saying, was:
—You have no idea who he knows.

And she was right: I didn't. Not at all. Because even when she told me their names I had no idea who they were, or why they mattered. Though it never stopped me from wading right in to help her, or from feeling so very good when I did it. So good in fact that it never even occurred to me that I should be keeping up, or for that matter, that I had an alternative. That I could or should be doing anything else.

So that
I'm sure you can see why I quit. What with how hard it was to do my own course work and to work with her so much, and to rescue her when she needed rescuing, and to work part time to support myself, to support the whole apartment in fact. And though neither one of us ever said it, we both knew that my work was nowhere near as important as hers, I never even thought I learned as much in school as I did talking to her, and besides: her work was really both of ours.

So when I told everyone I was just taking a year off school, to find myself I might even have said, using that oldest of excuses, though I was convinced that I was quite well found, I guess I really was acting the typical role of artwife: cleaning the house as well as bringing home the bacon. While she told me I was her source, her ground, her inspiration, her twin, her other half, her blood her soul sister.

As I ended up just the way my mother said I would, with her pointed remark about Alice B. Toklas and Gertrude Stein. Though I had nothing to complain about: it seemed at first to be working out beautifully. Was, in fact, almost idyllic. With the apartment in better order than it had ever been, me less tired and more cheerful, and the job waitressing really sort of fun. At the place I had already been working part-time since the year before, mechanical and chatty at once, with always enough time to relax except during the lunch or the evening rush, if you were good at keeping track. Which I was.

So that I've thought about it a lot since, that role and all the feelings around my betrayal. Like when that woman Maureen brought it up with the group, you must remember, the one who was married to the writer, not famous but well enough known I guess, to have a reputation but not much money, and her talking about how she didn't get to stay home and be told she wasn't working, even when she produced a gourmet meal, or have her avocations, or maybe even her vocation, even you said you went through that with your ex, Thorne, called a hobby because it didn't produce revenue, she got to do both: the job and the house.

And no one would dare call what he did a hobby, or talk about his lack of income, that would be ball-breaking. Only even if you didn't, when that kind were finally successful, or just when they gave up, they would have come to think you were doing it anyway, the criticism of their role, with the artist's marginality in our culture echoing in the air until they would put all the necessary words into your mouth and come to hate you. So that you were damned anyway. Probably from the start, because you would be the controlling mother whether you tried to control them or not, the bourgeoise who broke their bohemian wings even if they lived off you, and she started to cry and everyone clucked and said: Then why don't you leave him? The way women always say to each other: Then why don't you leave him? As if they don't already know and she sobbed even louder.
—Because, because because because between hiccups as we all awaited the final hiccupping out of: Because I love him.

Only it wasn't. It was:
—Because I believe in him. I. Believe. In. Him. Repeated. The fists clenched around the wad of tissue you had given her, the voice fierce. A mother, controlling or not, defending her child until it echoed in me, the way it may have done for all of us.

Only suddenly everyone started to attack: him and her. How women have to stop doing that for men expanded finally into no one should do that for someone else. Until I said, without even thinking about it:
—Wait wait, maybe it's worth it. Maybe that person could have a vision that doesn't allow him to live a normal life. Maybe he needs that other person's protection. Maybe he needs protection for life. Maybe his hatred is worth enduring if the vision works. While all of you, at least three of you, anyway, snorted.
—No man's worth that. One of you said.
—And most considerably less, another one added.

And I could feel it coming. The discussion of what it meant to be a man-identified woman, how we build them up and make them what they are, just like Virginia Woolf says in *A Room of One's Own*.

So that I said: Wait, again.
—I'm not talking about men. I'm talking about people.
Drawing even more snorts until I desperately went on.
—Look the point is that I have a friend in New York, and SHE. And SHE and SHE, repeating the word SHE until you all understood and stopped, thinking I would talk about another woman in Maureen's position which might have been my position too, only I wasn't about to admit to that.
—And she, I repeated again, not really wanting to talk about it, but saying it anyway, for the first time, looking down at the Birkenstocks that had accompanied my tired feet since my first pregnancy, when I got them without even knowing how totally politically correct they were, while talking very fast.
—And she, anshe, shedoesntgetawife. No wife. Maybeifshehadawife. Maybe if she had a wife. Shewuntofwounduponthestreet. She wouldn't have wound up on the street. In New York. Pushing a shopping cart. Fulla-evrything. Everything she owned. Maybe she wouldn't have? You know?
And I don't think you did. Any of you. And I wasn't exactly telling the truth either. But my voice must have had an authenticity in it, to make you all look down, and think about it, to ask yourselves if that was an answerable question, if women should do that for each other, or make men do it for them, be wives like that, artwives, if that was one of the new role possibilities for the enlightened male, or of being a woman-identified woman. After all, another woman's vision could surely be more worthy, maybe the problem was just that we only ever got men's visions out of this, thus tipping the cultural balance, terribly, in their favour. Or maybe, truly, it shouldn't happen at all, that kind of self-sacrifice, because it might be the sacrifice of the other that irrevocably faulted the vision, no matter whose vision it was.
But whatever you were thinking, when I looked up you were all looking down. So I played with my sandal strap and pretty soon the subject changed.

And only later at my mother's in New York when Lilac had just left and we no longer leaned out the window would you look at me and say: That's her isn't it? Has she ever really lived out of a shopping cart? And I would have to say: No.

I had exaggerated. I hadn't wanted to explain all of it to the group, and I still didn't want to tell you about how I too had played that role. Though maybe you could tell, looking into my eyes and rubbing the skirt, so that instead I told you, and that was the truth, how the week of that meeting, it made me terribly upset, my mother had called to tell me about Mandy, Lilac's beanbag frog. The one stuffed animal Lilac had kept on her bed throughout her childhood. And even when she moved in with me. Until Sandro, and then she put it in a drawer.

I don't even know why my mother bothered, I would have thought she'd be through with such object lessons by then, or at least with making special long distance phone calls in order to give them, though maybe it was because she was upset, her voice was cold as usual for such things, her you-see-what-happens-in-this-world-if-you-don't-take-care-of-yourself tone, the one that automatically causes her to lean back in her chair, so that I imagined her doing that, leaning back and sipping at something, coffee or wine, even as she spoke. But the voice was angry too, maybe at Sandro still or at some general nastiness most aptly expressed in that old song about how nobody loves you when you're down and out, how easy it was for all those people who had exalted Laura and lionized her and said they loved her, to just let her go, to drop her, to let her sink really, like a pebble into the polluted water of the East River.

And maybe my mother was trying to imply that I'd done that too, that it was one of my other firsts, discovering her first and dropping her first, but I don't think so, I just don't think either of us expected what had happened to happen, maybe that she'd never be able to get off the back wards of the hospital, but never that, being so alone. Just the way she was the night you met her; alone and unprotected and far too hungry as she alternated between horribly skinny and terribly skinny on her tranquilized roller coaster ride, not even enough energy to scream as she started down, but just staring wide-eyed once more, calm enough as her car was hauled to the top for the people at whatever department it is in the States that covers disability pension to tell her she was too healthy to keep getting hers:
— You'll have to go out to work now, dear.

And she would nod, not even aware that she'd just been pushed over the edge, that it was down down down now, although later at some in-between point, coming around a low banked curve maybe, or hanging upside down from a loop, her hair and arms flying, she would be able to tell my mother, or someone else who still stayed in touch enough to ask, that it was a brilliant catch-22 this getting you well enough just to make you crazy; but right then she would say nothing. She would just go home, to the apartment where she was living alone because she refused to live with her parents or even with Sandro, besides which her shrink didn't recommend it, one of the foci of sickness the Laingians were calling the family then, but there are advantages to eating, and she would stare at the walls, and the next morning, she was tranquillized enough to be obedient, she would start looking for a job.

Which she would do for a couple of days or maybe even a couple of weeks and sometimes maybe she would even find one which would save her for a while until she began seeing the filing system as the enemy, or forgot a couple of tranks and thought that the aliens were telling her to rearrange it into some magic order that would change the world. Which I really think it did sometimes, on a small scale perhaps, when everyone the company invoiced would receive someone else's bill, or other tiny interventions in the great order of things, social workers losing their clients at the welfare office, case histories splitting and recombining while she worked there, with some rumours she even snuck in and tried to rearrange the library where her mother worked, the aliens knew better than the Dewey decimal system, than the union catalogue; though the world such actions most often changed was her own. Losing her the job and putting her back at the start of the roller coaster. While most times she would get no job at all, even after a couple of weeks of looking, and there would be no more disability cheques and she wouldn't qualify for unemployment, and the wait was far too long to get on welfare. So that occasionally she would beg and sometimes she would steal but mostly she would just wait until she ran out of food.

Whereupon she would do something fairly dramatic, and it would be back to the little men in white coats. So that she really was heading for the streets, even if she never quite got there, it was close enough, in that little hole in the wall basement on the Lower East Side with its smell of mildew and garbage where her parents did their best to pay the rent, to do something for her they said. Because they knew too, even if they wouldn't say it, that the streets came next.

Only this particular time, the one my mother called about, before she hit rock bottom, or maybe exactly when she did, Lilac took poor Mandy, truly a magnificent creature, large and bright and calico, with Italian glass bead eyes. And she gutted her, that last remaining part of her childhood, and, since Mandy was a real beanbag frog, she took the beans, or maybe lentils, inside her, and she cooked them into soup and she ate them. And then, laughing (my mother said she was laughing), on a full stomach she took what was left of the poor carcass and pinned it, like they do with bear skins in luxury retreats here out west, to the wall.

Only with coloured push pins in one last artistic effort toward the kind of documentation she had so fallen in love with, that she spent so much time working on, so that the push pins, maybe some of them were even map pins, with little round heads, made up a last map of her world. All arranged in some symbolic order, coloured threads running between them to correspond to some visiting alien cosmology, a magical New York frog map with different elements in different colours, some representing the places she'd applied for a job, some the jobs where she'd received the aliens' messages, some the places she'd been hospitalized, and maybe even some the aliens' landings, as she pushed them in very carefully with an eye to colour and to form. Even if there weren't any more friends or artworld hangers-on to invite over to witness what she did, any photographers to take pictures, onlookers to ooh and ahh, gallery contacts to take the developed photos or videotape to, in what could have been her First Disability Performance Piece, to help her get off the Mental Health roller coaster and back on the artworld carousel, for another chance at the brass ring, right where she'd gotten off. Only she didn't know who to call anymore, except my mother. —Tell Alma I killed Mandy, she apparently said. Skinned her and ate her. I never knew frog beans could be such a delicacy. Better than frog legs.

And she giggled. Giggled and giggled. Then told my mother all about her new Mandy-skin wall hanging. Explaining in the thrilled tones that had explicated all her work the exact ramifications of the piece's cosmic meaning before she made her second call, this time herself, to the little men in white coats. They try to get them to do that. Regulate their own craziness. But like everything else, it's always too little, too late.

Only maybe you can understand now why I was upset that night at the meeting. Why I thought it could have been better if she'd had a wife. How I even thought without thinking it that it might have been better if I'd stayed. If I'd just recognized that she still needed me. Even if they do all say, the old artwives, that it will only destroy you in the end, maybe I still believe somewhere that I should have had the strength for two, like I told my mother, or that it's only the worn out ones who say that. That there have to be success stories. In all of this. Somewhere. The way I thought Laura's and mine would be. The two-in-one personality against the world.

What I still think about a lot. Right now in this room or to the sound of the vacuum. Whistling to myself, content with the sun shining into the living room, the children out with friends, or in school. I think about how happy I was then, especially at the beginning of that year. And the tune my mind hums is not *All My Trials*. And I certainly don't count the seconds, one one thousand, two one thousand, the way I did as I hugged her in my mother's apartment. Or say: Soon be over.

I ask myself what I could have done to make it last.

I would always buy a small treat with my paycheque, we could afford it by then, mostly special food, lobster or shrimp or soft shelled crabs, the occasional steak, and she too would bring things, though they were mostly found objects, from parks or alleyways or her haunting of the piers. With us both bringing home the occasional man, only to dinner of course, when we would both behave quite seductively, trying to imitate the eating scene from *Tom Jones*, but looking more at each other than at him, over our spaghetti or chili, or if luck would have it, the mussels that she would pick but I would buy, at the little Italian seafood place fairly close to us on Union Street, that we would walk to, where she would dig deep into the barrel and pull them out with her hands, laughing.

With such joy in that ceremony of looking and touching and even tasting that she would sometimes order clams on the half shell to eat right in the store with lemon juice, and she would pick out the prettiest shells that had come in with the catch asking the proprietor if she could keep them, and he would say: Sure, Laurie and: You're lookin' good, Laurie and: How's the family? How's Mom and Pop and the little ones? While she would just laugh and reply: Good, good and: Thank you, thank you, while her hands continued to root around in the barrels her eyes to take in the colours, so that anyone could tell this wasn't a part of her roots she objected to. That being here didn't make her feel freaky at all, like she was someone in one of Diane Arbus's photographs the way she sometimes said. Not in her mother's old neighbourhood, where even her grandfather was known. It gave her a sense of place, of security. Which is why really, it wasn't the money, the Lower East Side was cheaper, we'd rented on her side of the bridge.

And besides the shells there would be the beautiful designer egg cases, sharks or skates, skates mostly I think though the shape is the same, but black and shiny, that she actually included in some of her first constructions, tucking them into old type boxes before that was the 'in' thing for your walls, or printing letters on them to make miniature wall hangings. They do look like those leather bags you see all over, with the straps a continuation of the case, I've thought of suggesting one to my daughter for a doll, I'd just have to attach the two longer hooks to make the straps and let the two shorter ones hang down, they're even stiff and shiny and hold their shape like some of the newer plastics you see in the stores.

You might remember them, we went to that store too, I don't know why, even why we were in Brooklyn, maybe it was to do Brooklyn Heights, the Promenade, so famous now from so many movies with its view of lower Manhattan, and the house down by the end from that movie of the nun guarding the gates of Hell, or just the Bridge, maybe we'd just decided to do the Bridge and walked over eating an ice cream after sitting out on those crazy bolted down deck chairs at Pier 16. Where we'd stared and stared at the traffic moving, the wonderful dull almost summer colours of it, but all melded and urban, ochres and oranges and pollution yellow/pink out toward the horizon, and the bright turquoise of the Brooklyn piers, until you'd said: We can walk over there can't we? And I'd confessed that we could and besides there were wonderful views on the other side, especially of the Statue, I'd lived kind of around there for more than a year.

And you'd raised your brows from where you were leaning back taking in the sun and I suddenly realized it was the first time I'd told you I'd lived anywhere but at my mother's. So we got up and brushed our imaginary crumbs off and went back in to where the seafood and the beer kiosks and the boutiques are, Cotton Ginny's and Au Coton and all the other ones you can just as easily find in the Scotia Centre back in Calgary, so that you'd suggested: Look let's duck in here and get out in the Toronto Dominion Square and take the C-Train home. Only I'd reminded you we were doing New York, and that in New York you walk, which was what you wanted to do anyway. And, by the time we got to that seafood place, which miraculously was still in existence, considering how trendy everything else was around there, it's another gentrification centre, though some of the old families have managed to stick it out, Laura's parents among them, we had walked for miles.

Strangely enough, after all the years and all the changes the man remembered me, too.
– You're Laurie's friend? he said. How's she doing?
   While I stared at him, filleting sole while he talked, it still amazes me how quickly an expert can do that, biting my lip, until I finally spoke.
– Seems to be getting better, I said. Just to say something.
   Then I turned away and picked up some of those egg cases along with the soft shelled crabs that were in season then, maybe that was why I'd dragged you so far into Brooklyn after so long a walk, it was the best place I knew of to get soft shelled crabs. And I tried to explain the egg cases to you only you wouldn't understand at all. How something that sort of looked like the manta rays you had once seen from an airplane as you went on your one tropical holiday, much less *Jaws*, could have eggs like that, with the hooks attaching them to the seaweed until the wee ones inside were ready to take on the world.

Though you did think they were brilliantly designed, so elegant and sleek and lumpy at once that we even tried to bring them back with us, only to have them confiscated in Customs. Where the officials located them by the smell.

And then when we turned to leave I went through the ceremony, asking his permission to take them with me, and he sort of smiled and said: Sure sure.
And then he added:
– Laurie always did that.
And I almost wanted to tell him they were for her, only I couldn't, knowing they were for you, and he just went on, musing:
– Such a shame. So talented.
And turning back to his work: A bad egg that husband of hers. But you're all right. If you see her say hello. Tell her to come in for some clams.
Which is how I found out the whole neighbourhood knew, and I had to explain her to you. At least a bit.
– An old friend, I said: Who went crazy.
And you said: Was she important?
I almost told you what an important artist she was, but you went on.
– In your life I mean.
So that I answered.
– Yes. In high school, yes. Very important.
I didn't tell you about the rest. About what had happened. But you somehow knew there was more to it than I'd said.
– You should call her up, you said. You know that.

– **Call her up**. Have her over. Buy some clams. From here. We'll come back here. And you clapped me on the shoulder. And winked: You can tell him they're for Laurie.
– Laura, please, Laura, I said. He's the only one I ever heard call her Laurie.

And that's exactly what we did. To make it all happen. So that even if the moment that I hugged her gave that skirt to you, made that skirt moment happen, you made happen the moment of the hug, so you gave that hug to me. Which makes it like you gave them – skirt and hug – to each other. Or something like that.

She gave me to you and you gave her back to me. At least for a moment. So that it's a circle, Thorne, a circle. Like you're always talking about the circle of the dance. Or maybe it's a spiral. She would have had it a spiral. Changing levels. In the four dimensions of space-time.

Laura would also

se those egg

cases as a centrepiece for what she referred to as our formal dinners, meaning dinners with a man in them. Together with the seaweed and the shells she would find in the barrels. Arranged in a small fish net she had found down near Sheepshead Bay with a fat candle planted in its middle that she would allow to melt onto the old wood table. With the man, usually it was a man not men, we liked to have them outnumbered, looking at it all, and eating quite tentatively. Except sometimes, if it was oysters or clams on the half shell that still wiggled when you squeezed lemon on them, or the steamed mussels nobody ate in those days, when he wouldn't eat at all.

And we got to imitate *Tom Jones* to our hearts' content.

Until the first night Sandro came over.

And it suddenly felt like Laura and I were no longer a megapersonality but 'roomies'. As if we'd been 'roomies' all along, the way all those women I worked with had 'roomies'. To drink with and cry with and plot their next move with, whether with the boss or the day's man, the typical plot line for the movie or TV serial or bestselling paperback of the girls in the big city waiting for the big man to come along. As I watched her look at him through the wine he had brought, and drink him up with her eyes. While he ate and ate, everything we served, and looked around, from me to her to the apartment, with his eyes coming back, always back, back to her, with a sigh of sated contentment.

And then by the third time over he was coming into the kitchen to tell me how to cook.

And by the fourth time they were both in the kitchen. With him there to teach her. While by the fifth I was out. Asked by Laura with a wink, if I could get a dinner date and take in a movie. There was a good one at the Thalia she said, though for all she cared it could have been *The Monster that Ate the Bronx*, since what seemed to count was that the theatre should be way uptown. And with the Thalia at 96th and Broadway, right near my mother's in fact, or at least it was, I never even made a note to see if it was still there – it used to be the best repertory theatre outside the Village – it would be one helluva ride back to Brooklyn.

Then by the sixth time it was the words: Alma, please make sure you stay out till after eleven. A phrase that became more and more sure with each repeated utterance, her voice less and less apt to end in the rising inflection of an unconscious question, until along about the tenth time when the tentative note in her request returned. Which was when she said, accompanying her words with just the tiniest smile as she looked away:
– Your Mother's?

Then pretty soon after that I found myself one weekend working with a chisel and a rubber mallet, humming to myself, maybe it was even, *You can't always get what you want*, as I unsealed the door that had been painted shut for decades, between my room and the common hallway.

We had chosen an old railroad flat, not the kind Laura's parents had, where there was an interior hallway with rooms opening off, but the kind that appeared often enough in an art

project she kept doing over and over, the reason she said she wanted to rent the place, in fact.

— Oh, Alma, Alma, she said, her hands clasped in front of her the way most girls clasp their hands for something wonderful, a present or information that a certain boy likes them: It's perfect, perfect. It's the one I dream of.

And I guess I thought she'd said: It's the one I've always dreamed of, or that she meant something along those lines, because all I replied was: — Yes, I do suppose it's nice enough, compared to some we've seen anyway, as I went over its proportions trying to figure out how it could be organized to accommodate us both, thinking it would make an interesting adventure.

With its lack of a true bathroom, just what is euphemistically called a water closet, the wooden closet with the water tank high above the toilet bowl, and a pull cord to release the suspended water to make the machine flush, with just a slight leak, more a sweating through perhaps, so that water would sometimes drip onto your back as you sat on the hardwood seat, separated by a door from the rest of the place, the way they are in so many old Canadian houses, utterly genteel, with two separate rooms, one for bathtub and one for toilet. Only in this case gentility had gone by the boards, or under them perhaps, the water closet was tiny and the bathtub under a cutting board in the kitchen next to the only sink. Which must have been convenient enough in the days it really was a cold water flat, when you would have heated the water for the bath on the small gas stove, I even remember checking to make sure there were two taps and that the water ran hot, thinking to myself what a remarkable anachronism we had run into. It could have been from *A Tree Grows in Brooklyn*, we even had a fire escape in front and out the back windows I could see the gnarled branches that in the spring would produce the smelly palm-like fronds of ailanthus trees that gave that book its name. Along with a pole at the end of the yard you could crank the laundry out to no matter what storey you lived on, the pulley squeaking the laundry dancing with each pull, and the fig trees shrouded in the winter protection of burlap with buckets over their tops, that are always cultivated, with great care, by the Italian community. There was sure nothing elegant, even leftover ginkgoes, here.

The rest was typical enough of buildings in that area really, at least of the ones that were wide enough to divide up into flats at all, the ones like her parents' apartment were even wider and definitely built to contain apartments, with ours I could never be sure what it was meant for, elegant family dwelling or tenement, it was three windows wide, while there are those narrow two window ones that could never be divided under any circumstances, beyond basement apartment and upper storeys, because you couldn't take the stairwell out of the living space without eliminating too much room, the houses whose unchanged insides in the end promoted the gentrification of the area, when suddenly all the more well-to-do in the burbs wanted urbanity or at least the city again, a proper townhouse.

I even found myself wondering again about the whole gentrification process as I wandered with you through the neighbourhood that day, and other days too in other places, looking at SoHo or the warehouses or listening to everyone talk about the price of real estate. I don't remember anything under six figures even for a co-op loft in an industrial building in a remote neighbourhood, the kind that when Laura got her SoHo studio was still two figures per month and illegal for living. So I wanted to know if the next generation of young artists might not have to break down walls in suburban split-levels to find cheap living spaces.

Those kinds of railroad flats were incredibly cheap back then too, if you knew to wait for a rent controlled one to open up. The landlord could only raise them five percent or something, unless he renovated. So that if you had no friends about to move, or friends who knew someone who just might, who were leaving a controlled apartment, you would run out to buy *The Village Voice* at six or seven in the morning when it had just hit the newsstands on Thursday, I think that's the day it comes out, standing around in the close to dawn light waiting.

I can still feel those days, the leaves were already off the trees by the time we got it together to make our move, so that I can see my breath and feel the cold in my feet as I waited. Although in the end that wasn't what did it for us, it was hard for single girls under twenty-one to rent back then, the landlords could turn you down just because they felt like it, and the few places we saw in Manhattan, East West or South

Village, much like the one she lived in by the time you met her, terrified us more than they gave us any sense of bohemian romance, even if St. Mark's Place was right there, or perhaps because it was. Neither one of us was quite ready for that particular stoned psychedelic counterculture bellbottom bigtime. And it didn't matter how close it was to NYU, we were both subway old-timers.

Which is what drove us to Brooklyn, or ostensibly did, a lot more people were starting to live in that area then, it was even taking on its present name, Cobble Hill, instead of just being a zone of Red Hook, and even if it was mostly young couples just a few years older than us with babies, besides the old Italian families, still there were enough poky little shops and ethnic restaurants for us to feel trendy as well as safe. To maybe even think we were starting something.

We wound up renting from an agent too, just like any of those families would, there were three strollers in the hole in the wall storefront when we went in. And though I still think we could have held out for a better cheaper place, or even a slightly cheaper rent on that one, there wasn't much I could do once Laura exclaimed:
—This is the one, Alma, the one.

Because she wouldn't budge an inch. Even when I kept mentioning the lack of a separate room for the bathtub combined with the price. Or reminded her that only one of us could have a separate bedroom.
—It's the one I dreamed Alma, was all that she would say: But it's the one I dreamed, exactly the one I dreamed, over and over. Even as she climbed out onto the fire escape that ran down the front of the building.
—This is exactly the brick the sun shines on, she said. And it was then I remembered.

—**I thought you** made that up, was all I could think to reply. Telling her I thought it an invention for some class or other, from living somewhere around there, because she knew the buildings. It was her Moon Shines in Brooklyn Magritte, she'd even said so.

And I laughed tentatively, while she just stared at me. Offended.
—Gawd, youse guys from across da bridge, she said, putting on a Brooklyn accent heavier than anything she'd ever had, the dentilated 't's and 'd's exploding out of her mouth like missiles, You tink Brooklyn

109

is all one little turret bowl. Down by Toity-Toid Street. Then, back to her So-fee-a voice, My parents live *miiiles* from here.

Which I suppose was true. One and a half to three miles anyway; a long walking distance. Enough to keep them out of our hair and gossip about us out of their immediate vicinity, yet still the reason I think she wanted to live there, and still a part of Brooklyn in which all the houses are basically the same. So that I sighed. She didn't try to pull class rank often, but she did do it. While she looked around. Hurt again.

–You know I dreamed it, Alma, you know that. We talked about it. I thought that maybe you would have had the same dream. That you would recognize it too. That you too would know. This is our place Alma, ours. Something important will happen here. For us, Alma, I can feel it, she said.

And I shivered.

Even as I said: Yes, Laura yes. And followed her around, plotting what we would have where, with the place in the shape of a 'c', the way all those apartments are, the ones three windows wide anyway, just five rooms, or six if you count the w.c., with three of the rooms lined up, which is where the name railroad flat comes from I guess, front room, middle room, back room, engine, coal car, caboose, more or less. The front room in this case the biggest, with a gas burning fireplace, only the gas was turned off, linoleum in the back room and soft wood in the rest, no hardwood because the top floors were once where the servants or children stayed, or just the poorest of those who rented, if the place was built as what were once called 'rooms', and with lower ceilings too.

There is a whole mutating sociology to houses, even New York row houses, that would be wonderful to do a thesis on, Laura and I would talk about it as 'urban archaeology' again, mentioning those houses in Park Slope that had two staircases, one for family and one for servants, or the ones in the Heights (and even where we were renting) that had separate servants' entrances, with kitchens on one floor and dining rooms on another, a dumb waiter running between them, definitely meant for having a lady of the house and at least one servant, not just a housewife to hold down the fort here, running up and down the stairs panting – herself the dumb waitress – to get the food off the dumb waiter then take her place at the table for dinner. But no matter what the design the top floor was always the plainest, even the arches between the rooms less ornate than on the lower floors, square instead of curved, the windows higher and smaller, and in the case of this one, no doors to be pulled out, of glass or wood, but just the arches to mark one room off from the other.

So that we made the front one the living room and she got to sleep in it, with the middle and smallest room, the windowless coal car on this train, outfitted with a desk, my study space, while the rear room next to the kitchen with its sink and tub was Laura's studio. And I am still not certain whether she picked the front room to be her bedroom — I'd have thought we would have had to fight over the one side room no one would have to walk through — because she would have easier access to her studio at night, as she said, or if it was to continue to design the place to match her dream. Or her design of her dream. But in any case, I got the one independent room, in the front opposite the kitchen across the stairwell in the back, those are the two rooms that account for the third window in that style of building. And though it never would have occurred to us as we looked around in those first enthusiastic moments that there might be anyone around ever who could make my access to the rest of the house difficult, with my room giving onto the stairwell it did have a second door, just the way the toilet did. And it was that door I was busy opening.

Opening and still shivering because she'd been right and she had definitely dreamed it. Or at least invented it before we ever moved in. And now it wasn't just the fireplace that was chillingly identical to all those sketches she had been doing since the beginning of the year, she had even placed the drafting table in the position she insisted was correct, so that it would be barely visible through the front window. Because she had done the sketches from front and from back, taking in either bed and fireplace, or drafting table and easel.

111

Mostly in the manner of René Magritte, that least painterly of the surrealists, with his dependence on plain flat pigment – more like old stage sets than Dali's or Tanguy's hyperrealism – and juxtaposition of contemporary common images for his effect; so that he had slipped through into the sensibility of the recently deceased pop art, and influenced design as well, still does as far as that goes, from the CBS eye through all those floating men with their umbrellas.

Though the ones that really grab are somewhat more sinister and therefore useless to try translating into ads. Like his precisely fragmented female torso – each piece smaller than the one below – with cubed sky behind reminding me for some reason of her parents' backyard or the backyard of our tenement apartment on days when the harbour is fogged in and the light is pastel and refractive, days that seem to want to absorb light and time and not let it go, when the foghorns sound as if they come from inside the air. Or his stone birds halted in flight over the ocean or his fish women thrown against the shore, the ones I would think of later again and again. With all of them adding up to quite an incredible body of work, Laura and I did get to see a retrospective, though the painting that really took her consciousness by storm, and I think it did start the dream even if it was a dream and not a construct, was kept in a small dark side room housing part of the permanent surrealist collection of the Modern.

Empire of Light it was called, and combined day and night to make an expression of utter calm come over her features, the same one that interrupted her diatribe just once that night with you, when she looked out the window for what seemed the longest time, again into twilight. With that painting not so much the between time as a remark made on it by juxtaposing night and day, letting the eye mix them together, so that it was almost like one of those games you can play in the Saturday comics, What is wrong with this picture? Because it does take the longest time to realize what in that picture is out of whack, and even then it's just a slow exhaustion. A tiredness coming over you, like hypothermia or sedation, a prickling at the back of the skull and a winding down, a sense of time stopping. Then when time has completely stopped and you catch yourself like a dolphin waking itself up, noticing that you have failed to breathe, you realize what it is, and it's strangely scary: the bottom half is the simple black silhouette of houses and trees against the sky, one yellow street light off to one side, while in the top half the sky shines midday midseason all day blue, cerulean straight from the tube, with the little white cumulus clouds, so like Alberta or Texas, drifting in it evenly spaced like herds of cattle. Those clouds the worldwide Magritte trademark that always seems to be present, even in the imitation of his paintings.

Lilac would stand in front of that painting again and again, slowing her breathing, until she told me she had started to dream it. Or maybe she did say it the other way.
—This painting calls me, Alma, because I've dreamed it, she might have said, adopting a dramatic art school style, I think all art students say things like that as they try to find something in their depths that separates them from the competition, that makes them as special as she so obviously was. So that I would just say:
—Yes yes, Laura, and wait for her to go on. To tell me more about it.

While her teachers would say: Wyeth right? Wyeth and Dali and Tchelichew, the one with all those veins and the babies, that's the stuff you all like, *especially you girls*, because it's so obvious. So obvious so illustrative so literary, those same words repeated again before the teachers would go on: Well, look again. Or just learn to look. Painting is about form. *Form.*

Words that had managed to devastate more than one, and especially more than one girl, though, still Laura did not do as badly as some. Her self-confidence boosted by the fact that she had managed, besides the Guernica, to pick up on Arp and Miró on her own, if not on Motherwell, so that she could pretend to at least a little autodidactic sophistication.

Then when she discovered that first year that Magritte was still safe, with his illustrative style so bent on shaking one's belief in the firm steadfastness of the everyday, she loved him even more than she already had. And clung so tight to him perhaps because she had to give up all the other so-called 'literary' painters she had liked in high school. Burying Tchelichew as deep as she could.
—Oh that, she would say, as she passed his work — the painting with the blood and the babies really had been our favourite when she first heard that speech — while she treasured him secretly, and probably

unconsciously, till she could dictate her own maximalist terms. And revindicate him through her Thomian catastrophes and her mother's knickknacks, when art in New York briefly took on a lot more currents than the mainstream, and 'good' galleries came down to SoHo.

So that she started trying to make that dream real for one of her classes, painting or drawing or more likely design with the 'bastard', I'm sure that's where Magritte would fit, like those forks she painted on plates of sky, or emit/time, although at some point I think she was doing different versions for all her teachers, she might even have managed to fit it into colour theory by using it to explore vibrating colours, as she tried various flat Magritte style renderings of it, as well as posterizations, or thick palette knife impastos, never totally successfully, I'll agree with her teachers on that.

Because the central problem in the dream never appeared in the images she chose to transmit. And although the drawings and gouaches that she did contained a little of the horror she must have felt, they never contained the full of it. What it must have been like to dream this night after night, day after day, it didn't matter. At night or evenings she would come home exhausted, times she would fall asleep in the middle of working on an assignment, or later on the couch as Sandro talked on, when the dream would enter her and jerk her awake, startled, as if ready to scream or howl, her hands shaking. Or it would come after one of those times she was terribly frustrated and alone at her parents' place, or sitting in the apartment, but by herself in the middle of the afternoon she would come home and hammer her hand against the wall, the mattress, the pillows, and howl for it to change: for the world to be anew so that we could live in it.

And mostly I believed her, how she described it, what she said she howled then, at her personal moon hanging on her window shade or at the sun: All I want, all I want, and when she first mentioned it, it was still high school, so that she said: Is to understand it all, just for one moment to understand it, though by midway through the first year of art school, when she was well into sketching the room it was: For it to mean something. Or later when she was politicized and we went to demonstrations and Sandro had taught us all the terminology and we discussed Brechtian theatre, and dedicated time to talking about reaching inside people to let them know they were capable of change, she would say instead: All I want is a revolution, now NOW, imitating *Marat-Sade* which was very popular at that time as she lay on her bed, crying herself to sleep. Only to dream again of her bed, or of her drafting table, in the exact apartment we had rented.

And her bed empty. Her drafting stool unoccupied. The sheets all warm and wrinkled, moving even, as if a body were there, the drafting table abandoned midstroke or the line of the drawing flowing from the drafting pen. But empty, empty.

And the room night, and the sky day.

Always. Always.

Until it started to happen when she was awake. She would lie there and her soul would leave her body, she was sure it was her soul leaving, her soul or her astral body, it depended on the phase she was in which one she said, or whether it pleased or horrified her, although it seemed to please more and more back then, especially in the apartment when she got to look around at all those faces so recently attentive to Sandro and say, God, goddess, I was gone again. Because it marked her somehow, made her special, that must be why she insisted in turn on getting the apartment marked by such a dream. For all I would tell myself it did not have to be this one, it could have been any one of hundreds, even if the fireplace with its mottled green oblong tiles was the same, she could have seen one like it a million times in the houses of her parents' friends, the ones from her childhood. After all it did go with the neighbourhood.

Because I would not have chosen the place. I would have gone to a different architecture, any different architecture, even back to the Lower East Side, just to get away from such a dream, I wouldn't have courted it. While she seemed so sure that if she could be in such a place, it would give her shelter at the same time as she searched her universe, the world where time had stopped, that she could wander its interdimensional interstices, unharmed.

—**Especially with you**, Alma, she said squeezing my hand as we stared out onto the fire escape.

While all I would answer, at the same time as I shivered, finally remembering her dream, was:
—But I'll have to get window shades, you know I hate window shades.
—But I love them, she said. They work for me. Especially with those little moons hanging on them. And she made a round gesture with her hand, she had obviously thought of those circular handles at the end of those pull cords as moons for a long time, probably since childhood. It was how she would place the moon in her compositions of that dream, dangling from the pull cord of a window shade.

And she giggled.

And that was all.

Then later out on the fire escape, she turned around toward that front room again and looked in, and said, Look Alma, how perfect it is. My fate will be decided here, I know it. I know it. And I was unable to reply at all, not even to state my preference for blinds.

Nor was I ever able to explain to her my sense of foreboding. Or even put it into words for myself. Not even at the Kienholz exhibition when she wanted to do the dream the way he had done his figures.

This was one of those times when her design teacher had sent her out to the galleries, something he was always doing, telling the students they would never be artists if they didn't take it upon themselves to find out what was going on, while he underlined that she of all the students *must* get to this particular show, he knew well enough about her socially concerned love of surrealism, since she was handing him mini-Magrittes every other day, maybe he even thought this installation would move her beyond them. It was certainly the first of its kind we had ever been to.

Though the scene in the gallery was the same as ever, the way we would try not to tiptoe in, but step boldly to look as if we belonged, glancing down and at each other as if in deep and profound conversation. Because the galleries did still scare the pants off of her, she would even

say it, especially the uptown galleries, the 'good' ones. It was a world so imposingly of, by and for the rich, that it was worse than Bergdorff's. Expensive to start and then there was learning the code, far harder than dress, about which style was taking over and why, with little signals in the canvasses or the paper or the found objects or the description, that you had to learn to read. Though she had already promised herself that she would learn it, learn it until she could break it – in more ways than one – that this would be one world of the rich she could enter, even if only by the back door when the movers brought her stuff in. She would even whisper to me as if we were in church, maybe she did that day, as if she were telling me a special sacrilegious secret.
–You'll see my stuff on walls like these, Alma. You'll drink champagne at my openings.
–Yes, yes, I would answer squeezing her hand. And although I never did, the openings were still plentiful enough. While we would just stand there leaning into each other, looking I'm sure like every other scared set of students who ever came into those places that as often as not seemed a cross – just as this one did – between a cathedral and a bank vault, as we hung onto each other. With the sophisticated employees, usually female, giving us the once over and doubtless thinking we were whispering things like: My three year old sister could do better.

While the one thing I don't think they would have believed from looking at her, certainly not that first year, was her plans. Or that she could so quickly hit the artworld like a shooting star to make them come true.

While this show demonstrated to us both that some art makes a statement so strong that all its surroundings can disappear. Tearing apart the elegant complacency of the place as surely as it ripped away our facades of pretend sophistication, to bring hands to open mouths that wanted to howl, the tears standing out in both our eyes, our posture suddenly vulnerable our voices squeaks, as we stared at something we never would have expected, especially with all that stuff about form, form, form, that she was going through and doing her best to explain to me, however unsuccessfully.

And now there was this: the brilliantly obvious. The real, the surreal, the literary, the concrete, the narrative, the specific, the universal, the tragic: pain beyond all possible eloquence in three dimensions.

Epoxy resin and wood and god knows what else, to make a box like a jail cell so that you could only peek in, making me think it was a jail at first, a jail with bunks. While on each bed, so perfectly made, cast I think really, except for the heads, were two perfect and identical old and naked men, I cannot be sure now if they had one hand between their legs or not, because I do remember the genitals, how they hung there all wrinkled and so terribly tragically helpless, so vulnerable, that my hand reached out. A kind of epiphany of the sense of grief that the man in the park that day had awakened in us, a sense of the helplessness located finally there, the senile old man gone back to touch his, just as the boy baby, the flasher does, a final desire to ensure his reality just there, in that place of ourselves that is still most profoundly ours, there, the tragic helplessness not only in the human, but in the male, condition. So that her hand too, moved, we must have looked so odd, as if we were ordering something, one of those please, and a bit like the two men too, twins, with our identical gestures, one hand to mouth, one hand out to man, one after the other.

Only as we reached, our gestures must have changed and become different, because it was then I started once more to shiver. These men were not two men, but one. And the other his reflection, or not his reflection: his thought, his dream. Because the man on the top bunk, though just as three dimensional as the man below, had a two dimensional plastic cartoonist's balloon circling him from head to foot, outlined in neon I think, a thought, not a speech, balloon, since it was not unbroken lines but small discontinuous plastic bubbles that led back to the head of the man below.

So that I turned abruptly away to find relief in the artist's statement, a cooler explanation pinned to the wall behind glass, of how this box or cell in which the two men were contained represented a home for the senile insane. While this man, suffering senile dementia, had just been beaten by an orderly. So that it was not just himself, but his pain the man dreamed.

—Oh God, we said then to each other, on identical breaths again, before we rushed on, our words coming too fast, to cover, or perhaps to give shape, to our emotion, to speak of how our society had betrayed the old and the infirm, the senile and the disabled, and above all the mad.

While we looked back again and acknowledged what more we had seen, allowing it to surface to consciousness after our shock. That we had known of the man's pain and hurt and his need to escape, not just from the helpless pose of the bodies, but because both the man dreamed, the man thought, and the man dreaming, the man thinking, had goldfish bowls inside their swollen hydrocephalic heads. Goldfish bowls. Each one with one goldfish. Swimming, swimming.

– **That's too real**, Laura gasped, still staring at the men. Too real. Her voice almost a sob. Her breath ragged. So that she breathed a moment before she could go on. Then pointed at the piece as if accusing.
–That's not right, she said. It's not. It's good but it's not right. There must be some place that man is. There must. Some place he is inside, that's better than that. Where he can travel. Like I do in my dream.

And I was sure that she was talking about her own body. How it was never there when she dreamed. How she believed herself to be in a better somewhere else. So that I looked at her, and started to do it, to imagine what she must be doing, painting with her eyes those Magritte clouds and sky onto the white walls of this construction, darkening the room with her mind to give the old man just such a moment of transfer, so that I almost sighed in relief, wanting to give her that power. As looking around the gallery she repeated it. Only now she said: Better than this. Better than this.

And I thought that maybe she was right. There would always be somewhere else to go. The way I still like to imagine her doing sometimes. That the thing with her astronomy text is real. That it takes her somewhere better.

And then, because it was impossible to sustain the pain of that vision – even if we might be trying to fill it with puffy sweet Magritte clouds – to be open to the horror of it, with a strange hysterical ebullience rising up in us, we started to joke.
–Well, there should be fancy guppies at least in that place, I said, looking directly into the goldfish bowl. Doing their mating dances with their long multicoloured tails.
–No, it should be a seaquarium with those wonderful bright striped fish with their pouty mouths, she countered.

—No, anemones and starfish and sea horses and long-legged shrimp and scallops with their bright eyes.
—No, no, no; mussels, sharks, mermaids, squid.
—Manta rays sting rays sea slugs sole.
—Horseshoe crabs king crabs hermit crabs moray eels.
—Sea cucumbers sea slugs sea urchins sand dollars.
—Crustaceans cetaceans cephalopods old tin cans.
—Bivalves monovalves annelid worms.
—Tetrapods hammerheads nuclear waste.

We started to chant. Going back and forth from one to the other in four four time, as we leaned into each other and whispered and giggled, and grabbed hands and swayed until the woman who ran the gallery must have thought us pretty warped: Such inappropriate affect and so young, we could almost hear her clucking her tongue behind us as we moved toward the door, her finger itching to dial the phone to call a friend to tell all about it, how little young people understand these days, how little empathy they have, as we staggered down the stairs instead of taking the elevator, knocking our shoulders into the walls, still laughing and trying to go each other one better.

Then on the street it became a little dance: step step step skip, step step step. Until we were able to settle on the chambered nautilus, what should be inside those two round fish bowls was a chambered nautilus: perfect for its neutral buoyancy and its golden mean and its long long history and its tentacled head and its striped face and its wide-seeing almost human eyes.

We told each other that such a silent and perfectly balanced creature just might be able to transport that old man off his bed, his wrinkled pissed on sheets, through the interstices of time to a dimension he just might wish to inhabit. To that place that was better than this. Certainly more quickly, or at least more elegantly, than a goldfish could. While we walked along in the vague wintry light toward Central Park, calmer now as we passed F.A.O. Schwarz to walk by the Plaza and admire the hansom cabs, and maybe stopped by the lake to watch more mobile old people feed the ducks.

And we put our arms around each other once more, so that this time she could feel me tremble as she said:

—Such power, Alma. Such power. I'd like to pack a wallop like that.

While I thought only of our apartment and her empty bed and the goose pimples passing all the way up my arms as she went on. She had obviously thought of it, too.

—Maybe that's what I should do with my dream, the sun the moon and a bed, with a clear plastic woman full of glowing night sea creatures lying on it in pieces. Fragmented, like Magritte. Like the Magritte torsos only with fish swimming inside the aquarium fragments of my body, inside a darkened room.

And we walked on.

—**Just don't try** to go there Laura, I finally said, realizing what it was that was really making me shiver. To that better place. Not even to take him there. You could get caught you know, where he is.

And I won't let you dream me if you try that. Or put me in a thought bubble, either, Laura. I won't. I won't. And my voice whined like a child's. I even stamped my foot, so that it stung against the cold ground. Wanting to tell her I would not even be her shieldbearer then.

As she laughed again and squeezed my hand harder.

—You're not my dream, Alma, she said. You're my lifeline. My umbilical cord. No matter where I go, where I travel, or who I search for, you'll be able to pull me back. No matter what.

And then she shrugged.

—But don't worry, she said. It probably wouldn't work anyway.

And I never knew if she meant an attempt at that man's rescue, or that last plastic version of her dream. Because she never did try it. Maybe it was just too difficult, beyond her current technical means.

But I do remember

working with her on another version, Thorne, the last one she actually finished. And though it was in three dimensions, it was hardly sculpture in the round, and hardly frightened me so much as thinking about her fragmented body, at least I didn't think so at the time.

She would always work by placing the furniture just as it had appeared in the preliminary sketches she'd shown me before we moved in together, so that those first months seemed as if our whole apartment was a studio set for that dream, which maybe it was. With this particular version a small relief, more collage than sculpture, that the design teacher had demanded contain some kind of three dimensional structure and plastic transparencies. Which forced her to use a sheet of plastic for the window of the converted tenement building and to construct a foreshortened fire escape out of balsa wood, I actually did that part, painting it with model airplane lacquer to simulate the black-painted iron, while the dull red bricks behind it were scumbled into brightness with yellow acrylic that made them appear brightened by the direct sunshine, just as they had that day when we stood out on the fire escape and she told me her fate would be decided there. Only in this case the window was closed and the sun was picked up and reflected back like a star from the window that took up almost the whole piece.

You could only just manage to see in, that was true in all the versions, whether the room was hidden by reflection from the glass or partially pulled window shades, or sometimes there was a lot of brick, even the cornices showing a little, so that the angle was high and there was just the first room with its window-sized sunlit patch of floor, and various pieces of furniture, her messed up bed or her equally disorderly drafting table, though sometimes you could see through to another window like you always could in our railroad flat, with a clothesline suspended outside if it was front to back, or the fire escape if it was back to front. But always, either out the opposite window or reflected on the floor there hung not the sun but the moon. As often as not from the small pullcord at the bottom of the window shade.

She would sometimes even manage to get in all the phases of the moon, one after another passing across floor or sky, with only one suspended from the shade, another way of stopping time as well as commenting on femininity, she already seemed to be doing that, through comments on traditionally feminine symbols, though usually influenced still by male painters, this one another in the surrealist room at the Modern who always painted women and moon phases, not so well regarded as Magritte, at least by her or her teachers, or the more superficial art histories that I've read, not enough that I remember the name, except that it was French.

But in this case the window and the bright brick was cut like a mat and placed over the black and white interior, the way we always see night in black and white, black and white pen and ink and just a little navy and a little crimson gouache, and then between that sketch and the cut out window frame there was the window's transparent plastic sheet on which the sunlight was painted, and the moon out the back window, cut through onto yet one more layer of a differently textured paper, so that it was very clear indeed what the juxtaposition was, and how the empty bed nonetheless contained a female form, she had managed to make it feel almost warm, so that you wanted to reach through the plastic to feel the sheets. And then there was finally the black fire escape placed upon the mat of the window.

And because I had always cut her mats, I cut out that window too, with the plastic sheet to one side and the sketch to the other, and me sitting in the middle of the floor leaning onto the utility knife, though not as hard as I often had to do, at least in this case I didn't have to bevel the mat, something you can accomplish by hand only by bending the blade of the knife. But still I was trying to score the first layer of the board only once, and then to make one clean cut through to finish, clenching my jaws and humming in my mind already on the third side of the bottom half of the window, there would be eight cuts this time, and so far I had managed to accomplish each one in the two required motions, with all my weight going onto the knife for the cut through, so that the window would not have an edge that looked lumpy and shredded, though perhaps that would have captured more verisimilitude considering the shape our windowsill was in, exactly what I was thinking, Why am I being so careful this time, it hardly matters anyway, the edge is straight and will be painted, almost laughing about that when the knife jumped the groove, always the other danger, and embedded itself deep in my thumb.

And the blood started to spurt all over, even onto the design project, onto plastic and window and room, before I stuck my thumb into my mouth and started to clean up, and she came over to help, and we both wiped desperately at the project until we'd done as much as we could, the plastic was perfectly clean but there was blood soaked into both the window and the interior, and I took some toilet paper from the heap we had used and held it against my thumb to try to put on enough pressure to stop the bleeding. Which went on and on, pulsing out, taking what seemed like forever before it slowed down.

And though we did make jokes about the sacrifices you have to make to art, blood sacrifices we said laughing – Whaddaya want, blood? – we giggled – Look here's mine – and she made me take the toilet paper off my thumb long enough to print it onto the bottom left hand corner of the window like a signature, still I knew that as she calmed down and looked, her eyes wandering over each inch of her design, she was angry because of what had happened. At my blood pouring out over her version of our apartment. Though blood would later enter so much of her work that sometimes she would even credit it to that moment. Only she would say it was hers:
– I got the idea of using blood from when I cut my thumb doing a design project, she would say winking over at me.

And I could hardly object. Besides being part of our metapersonality, it was the cover we'd decided on. When she'd looked at me panicked, and said:
– But what will I say, what will I say, what will I tell the teacher, I had removed the bloody toilet paper bandage from my hand, loosening the blue designers' tape that by then attached it at the bottom. And I put it over her thumb, replete with my blood.
– You cut your hand, I said, while making the mat.

She laughed then, and kissed me quickly on the lips.
– We are blood sisters, flesh of one flesh, she said very solemnly the way she always did when she was an Amazon warrior, my Amazon Queen, the way we both had when we vowed to each other, stabbing our fingers under the forsythia and mixing the blood those many years before.

Then she went off to school like that, wearing my old bandages, while I held my hand up, the thumb all swollen and white like a maggot, the red blue gash across its top like a mouth, squeezing it to keep the bleeding from starting again, before I put on a tight new bandage.
– I will bear proudly the wound given me in your cause, I said while we both laughed.

The way we would each time I changed the bandage and gave the old one to her. Which went on. At least for a couple of weeks. Complete realism until I didn't have to wear a bandage anymore.

I guess no one ever asked her why she has no scar. Because I do. A big one. It's still quite visible. I probably should have had the cut stitched. Because it hurts sometimes, sometimes still. And when it does I put my thumb in my mouth and I suck on it, and still I taste my blood. And that too, is the only nail I ever bite. Even you commented on that, Thorne, holding my thumb in your hand, Why this one? you said, but I never did explain, anymore than I ever went to see a doctor about it. Out of penance, I guess. Or pride. Or maybe just so I could remember who it had really happened to.

While she never did let me cut a mat for her again.

And as for that design assignment, it was lost in a shopping bag on the subway, bringing it back from school, when the door caught on her wrist and she couldn't shout loud enough. Or wasn't able to shout at all.

—It felt like a nightmare, she said. I couldn't keep running with the train as it started, and I couldn't say anything to get the conductor to stop the train. So finally before the train could sweep me off my feet, or twist my arm so I couldn't get it out, I let go of the bag, and pulled my hand out. And for once there was no melodrama in her voice.

Then after that the piece disappeared completely. Or maybe she never looked for it. Never phoned the lost and found. But whichever way it was, although she didn't talk about it so much, and the art work with that image stopped, still, the loss of that piece didn't stop the dream. Or my foreboding. The way I think about it still. The dream, and that version of it. As if it could still be travelling the subways, replete with her fears and my blood, dictating how she comes and goes, when she is present and when she is not, whether I could see her if I looked into her eyes.

Though, as I worked on the door, humming and pounding and shivering, it was my resentment that was foremost. And what I repeated as I looked from the white door to the white walls of my tiny cell-like room, was: There must be some place I am that is better than this. Better than this.

I must be somewhere better than this.

Giggling and humming bitterly to myself, fully aware that it was merely black humour, I had forgotten in my jealousy the look on Laura's face that afternoon, and I knew that my jail was nothing like that old man's, even as I thought of the Coney Island Aquarium. Only it wasn't the chambered nautili that entered my mind, the ones I had gone there just days before, by myself, to see, to contemplate in their sealed silence while I thought of Laura off somewhere with Sandro, it was the whales. Beluga whales I think they are, white and smooth, the silence of their unheard song overwhelming, as their eyes moved, roved, questioned. Especially that day, as they swam about each other, uttering calls I could not hear until the male extruded his penis and they came together front to front. A cosmic joke I thought it, and heard their silence echoing against the flapping screaming quacking of the ducks in the pond the last time I had gone to Central Park, quacking as the male mounted the female, so different from their calm winter floating when Laura and I had been there together.

Because now I seemed caught there all the time, between those two places, the white echoes of my white walled room reverberating with the moaning quacking screaming whalesong from next door, so that I couldn't get away from it. Wherever I turned there was sex and there were couples: and there was them. Until I did want my own room to be the chamber of the nautilus to transport me to some other place, it did not even have to be better, but any place at all that was just easier than this, easier than this.

Even the Coney Island Aquarium.

As I worked my way down through I don't know how many layers of paint, how many layers of relationship, the still white of now through the pink and blue and yellow and green of yesterday. My thumb, long healed, but throbbing at each hit of the hammer, each tug on the knob. Until I could free the hinges and the doorknob, turn it so that it worked its bolt in and out, while the door opened and closed. Then a few days later I went to an antique dealer's and bought a pile of skeleton keys, trying them out one after another until one fit and I could actually deadbolt the door.

Though I often didn't. We weren't afraid in that part of New York back then, no one would come in with the landlady right downstairs, and besides, what would they steal? So it didn't bother me at all that the lock would be easy to open, I just liked knowing I had my own key. I still have it in fact. It's the strange big brass one on my key ring everyone always comments on, they did at the group if you remember, you were the one who laughed and said:

—Maybe it's the key to her closet. Don't you think?

I guess it was in a way, in a lot of ways probably. That room was certainly enough like a closet, and there was certainly enough I was hiding from. Even after I got it free the door to the outside hall could never open completely, it banged against my mattress on the floor and I had to kind of squeeze out around it, so that the room did seem almost a cell, you could take your pick whether convent or jail, especially after Sandro had managed to make his home on the other side of the wall.

When all the space became hers, or maybe hers and his. Because he wound up with the desk we had put from arch to arch in the middle room for me to do my work, we all agreed he needed it more right then to organize his theatre courses.

—You're not doing too much studying these days, Alma, one of them said.

So that just that one small white ascetic room, with the desk I actually used, a plank on bricks right there under the window was mine. Only that mine.

It was a Saturday afternoon and they had gone somewhere, maybe even to buy mussels, because Sandro had made Saturday night official seafood night. Or maybe it was somewhere more formal, she was doing New York with him then, helping him take in all the tourist places, she even did the Statue with him once. Of Liberty of course, he was an immigrant, and even dug that Give me your tired your hungry your poor, and wanted to do theatre on the grass in the star at the bottom, which I think he has even done, though I'm not sure, just that someone has. Much later of course, long after that afternoon when I cried and cried, even as I carved my small exit into the outside world.

Even if she had hugged me, hugged me close and put her head on my chest when she told me he was moving in.

– He's our soul twin. *Ours*, she said, underlining the Ours with her voice.

But I knew better. I knew it would never be the same again. He had come for her. And even in my most generous moments, I was afraid of where he would take her. If only because it would be away from me. And it was then I would see, not her dream but her hand holding her image of the dream, her hand holding the dream of her absent body as if holding her body here in this plane, and then after that it wouldn't be her anymore, it would be me holding on, holding on, trying to hold her here, and sometimes I wouldn't know if it was her outside the train car or me, which one of us it was who would be smashed against the concrete wall when the train left the station, and that no matter how many times she said I was her lifeline, I could neither let go nor hold her here with me. And that whatever it was that had happened in that apartment, it had already happened irrevocably.

Just like she had said:

– My fate will be decided here, Alma. It will.

Though even that image, that image and that throbbing in my thumb and the blood red foreboding behind it, none of it stopped me from trying to convince myself that it was for the best, that he was what she had always wanted, that truly he was the best thing for her: what she had always needed. After all we'd both talked about our princes coming.

So that in my blows with the mallet, my scrapes with the chisel, my feelings would shift back and forth like a giant tide. Between trying to feel all right about it: He's good for her, Alma, I would say to myself, scrape scrape scrape, scraping away at my insides: He can do well by her, Alma, scrape scrape scrape. Until I would dissolve into self-pity: You're hardly doing anything to make her proud, just a waitress that's all you are, just a waitress, scrape scrape and a blow with the mallet through two to three more layers of paint: You can't even bring home interesting stories, you're not even learning anything anymore, pound pound pound with the mallet even if it damaged the wood a bit. Until it all became anger: Who does he think he is, and: Why am I so stupid, and: Why doesn't this door open?

Anger at him, anger at myself, anger at the door, until I would even give up my slow deliberate logical efforts and just push and pull on the doorknob for a while, bracing my body as the tears ran down, while I shook the door and shook it, a bull terrier that won't let go, while I repeated: That phony, that phony, she'll be over him soon, almost howling as I shook the door. Until I would calm down again, and pick up the chisel, and scrape gently, soothing myself: It's all right, Alma, It's all right, scrape scrape scrape: He's very good for her, he's giving her a new confidence she's never had before. Look at how she's blossoming. Pound pound pound.

Though
I never could stand it when she talked about him with worship in her voice. In a tone I had never heard. —Alma, you have no idea how big he is in scene design, in *theatre*, in Europe, she would say all breathless: And a brilliant director besides.

All information I already had, of course, as it was only the tenth or twentieth time she had told me. While for his part he kept telling her she was the most talented. The most talented what I don't know, or wouldn't acknowledge or can't remember: designer or draftsman or painter or artist or thinker. But something we both wanted to believe, that we both wanted to have confirmed so much that it was easy to congratulate her, however I felt inside, the soft queasiness or hard red nausea in my stomach, congratulations repeated over and over in fact, times we were alone.

—He's wonderful, he's perfect for you, I would say and kiss her and laugh. And almost believe it. Even if I should have known better. Really known better. The way she should have. He didn't bring just dreams and forebodings of Kienholz horror.

He brought the bedbugs.

Not so big after all,

repeated to

myself. When he moved in and they crawled out of his luggage: Not so very famous.

Or maybe just in Europe. Some obscure part of Europe. With the one little course he got to teach at NYU hardly helping out with fame over here. He was obviously having trouble. With the States. Or with himself or with his design; or with his concept of theatre.

So that he'd taken a little apartment, over in Manhattan, not so very far from Laura's and mine, we walked at least that far the day we bought the crabs, Thorne, but you would have turned north once you'd crossed the bridge. On the Lower East Side, close to NYU and dirt cheap, like the one she had when you met her. Only bigger.

He had furnished it with old castoffs from just anywhere, crates and cable spools and other very trendy things among the artistic poor, except that he had made the mistake of adding at least one old sofa he'd found outside his place on the street. That's why he got infested. And not just with your run-of-the-mill cockroaches that everyone gets, Laura's parents, my mother, Sofia, her black maid, it's always a constant battle with the cockroaches, though it seems there was a time Lilac did declare a truce with them.

She would even let them crawl on her, a prelude to what happened later my mother thinks, Laura apparently told a reporter who saw myriad antennae peeking up from behind some object in her studio that you couldn't kill what was probably the only intelligent life left in New York, while she laughed then added something about stimulating dinner conversation. Done for shock value of course, though I'm pretty sure she must have held the conversations, or maybe they were more talks, at least that's what I said to my mother: At a high diplomatic level I added, laughing myself, what else was there to say to news like that, Laura probably did think their antennae communicated them directly with the alien space ships.

But then again I would suppose it easy enough to tolerate crawling cockroaches that only make holes in overripe potatoes once you've had bedbugs. Bedbugs. I didn't even know that people still got bedbugs.

Though Laura knew. Immediately in fact. It was the first thing she said.

—Good god, bedbugs.

As the infestation spread over the days that became weeks and months after he made his quick move, Sandro was still no less her one true love. She just kept on repeating: No one here understands him, he never even made enough to afford that hole he lived in, as he became as much her Holy Grail as her Prince Charming.

With finding him, the true him, of course, a quest she didn't even have to leave the apartment to go on, as she just followed the interior road of her mutating self-image, as if each recommended costume change brought her closer to his essence. Or the far more twisted pathways of the lines of argument used at the Thursday night meetings that he soon organized to show off the step he'd made up in the world, with the fresh clean apartment that came fresh with the cleaner, as well as the bright-eyed young thing to pay attention to him.

To which he brought other bright young things. Male and female. Who alternately preened and showed off their knowledge or hung on every word he said, while they smoked joints and drank wine and left the place a shambles. And you could see how good it made him feel, how his smile would grow brighter and his gestures wider all evening. Until they took on a particular quality after the meetings that would make him pat me possessively on the ass as I bent to pick up cigarette butts from the rug or to crush the bugs between my fingers. With Laura not minding at all, she even thought it cute and would kind of giggle when it happened, as far as she was concerned it was wonderful he thought her best friend's ass worth patting.

She would just get up to help me, or to fix him coffee, while she would wiggle her own ass around a bit, something she had never done, or even known how to do, while she looked at him with those same eyes, goo-goo eyes I've never seen her make at anyone else, the way the rest of the students both male and female looked at him. Only she got to add a special body language, even in the meetings, though more pronounced later, an exclusive hand patting and shoulder stroking, with a dedication that let everyone know where he spent the night.

I never did figure out if it was natural, an unconscious by-product of a new kind of relationship, a new mode of gesture of the kind we always add to our vocabularies as we mature, taking little motions from here and there, just as we do tones of voice, movies or friends or someone watched across a room, without really knowing we're doing it. Or if there was a great deal more intention. If she had, in fact, watched the others carefully, watched the romantic European movies they went to more carefully still, cataloguing the details of each and noticing Sandro's reactions so that she could have the right gestures ready, imitating exactly the ones discovered to please him.

Because during that first period, she gave it up later, she really would stand among the pots in the kitchen and pretend to let him teach her to cook, though she knew well enough already from her mother, whose dedicated and specialized and time-consuming Italian cooking was more a symbol for Laura of isolation than oppression. That would make her impatient even with the walls of the apartment, and more so with the heat of the kitchen, so that she always hated cooking, and let me do it. Even when she supplied the recipes. Like for the mussels.

Then much later when they'd both given up on her and he'd fulfilled his role as Pygmalion, when she was famous, he took it over completely, fixing gourmet meals for the theatre group or artworld hangers-on or curators or agents or dealers, art or dope, while alternately talking her up, or himself, as he moved over the pans. Until it became just 'the' thing to do. And one of the key questions among certain New Yorkers in the invitation game was whether you had been to one of Sandro Yurasic's dinners at Laura Mack's studio.

While later still she would just eat out of cans, and the only thing she would heat would be water, with an old-fashioned heating coil. Of a kind probably banned now for poisoning the water, which fulminate within a minute of plugging in if you don't have them submerged.

I would grind my teeth to listen to her giggle and to watch her be clumsy as she kissed him lightly and asked again what something was for, which she knew about already. She would even practice this or that dish with me sometimes, telling me how Sandro liked his food just so: *Al dente, al dente, il spaghettini al dente*, even briefly taking on her mother's accent until I would get angry.

And also conclude, watching the way he licked and whispered in her ear, the evenings I was superfluous watching the two of them standing there over the steaming pots, that the new gestures might very well represent specific instructions, like the two tablespoons of olive oil in the water for a perfect spaghetti. Started perhaps with a distracted: I love it when a woman... that later became: I love it when you... take my hand or look at me like that or lean over our pot to smell our next meal: It's so primitive, so ancient, woman at the hearth, at the centre of man's world, or lord knows what all else. But definitely ended:
– It inspires me.

To new heights of love. And insight too, I suppose.

Her dress style started to change
then, too. It had always been pleated collegiate. Secondhand pleated collegiate. Carefully ironed. Like a European school girl, down to the never quite hidden sensuality present in all those movies we would go to, one who had lost her uniform, but knew of no other style. What her mother

must have considered necessary from the moment the acceptance with scholarship to the uptown all girls high school came in the mail.

Or jeans. She would wear jeans on the weekend, and still call them dungarees. Men's Levi's or Lee's without the ever so popular bellbottoms. Until she came to wear them every day at University. With just a little bit of paint on them to show that she was serious. Sort of left over fifties on the cusp of the seventies: a polyester preppie or a dungaree doll.

With the new look fitting her perfectly, even I had to admit that, and to admire her, while I resented it, I'd never been able to get her to so much as put on a mini: My legs are too heavy she always said. Though their heaviness only added to the way Sandro had her put the look together, especially then, when she wasn't all skinny punk the way she was when you saw her. It was essentially the way she had always looked, only skewed. Now the student at the lycée had snuck to the Left Bank over the weekend, the way we would to the Village, with that hard-edged European look giving her an air of disciplined freedom, of absolute adulthood despite her baby fat cheeks. So that she achieved an easy edge over the totally loose Indian cotton hippy clothes and free grown beards and hair of the other students who came over. Or even my disappear-into-the-woodwork uptown waitress mid-thigh minis.

While Sandro still tried to imitate James Dean, the essence of America he must have thought, and she tried to imitate him, putting that slightly dykey style into her now short hair years before it became popular, making the two of them look almost like twins from certain angles. On dungaree days, the only difference her shorter stature and more wiry hair.

Then when she turned the mask of her face toward you, you would discover that Sandro had managed to include Dietrich and Garbo in the portfolio too, with the one lock of hair, never exactly floppy, trained down over one eyebrow, and the precise make up that said not so much 'I vant to be alone' as: follow at a distance. Which made the whole well calculated package, heavy legs and breasts and ass and all, sort of like wrapping raw meat in plastic, the substance and odour always leaking out.

Especially of those wonderful straight micro-minis in leather and even plastic which barely covered her ass, or evaporating off her acrobat's legs wrapped in sheer coloured pantyhose, or even net, with a special aura given off by the transparent red-blonde hair sticking through. She didn't shave her legs anymore. Not for any feminist reasons, though the women's movement had started and we were both vaguely aware of it. We would even assert certain slogans, though we laughed at others, just as we did other slogans from other political arenas, with one or another of them always coming up in the Thursday night conversations that we had named, or maybe Sandro had, The At the Edge Theatre and Art Study Group.

His remark on hairiness and women in Europe must have come up in a more intimate context. With the way she told me about it later, practicing the beginnings of that straightforward vulgarity that became her trademark, with her voice containing enough theatre for me to tell she was still playing a part, one of her Thursday night specials in fact. The one that would eventually make a lot of people in the artworld think what some of those guests already thought, that she was a street kid from the nether reaches of Brooklyn, her pain rescued from despair and expressed through culture. She's so real they would say, as if a million mile gulf separated their alienation from her authenticity, although, in fact, the two worlds overlapped.

We would even take the occasional detour into one of her father's bars, at least we had in the first year, where it turned out not to be slumming at all, even if that first time she was afraid to take me in, afraid still of what I would think. Though the way they treated her was the way relatives who don't quite understand what you do but who like you might, most of the kids from around there still hardly ever made university, which made those bars occasional places to go to be unusual and get stroked for her accomplishments, family bars complete with a family life, as well as the rare brawl, the owners celebrated our eighteenths with us in one, or really with her, making everyone in the bar toast her while they gave away free drinks. Which is what she'd learned to expect, as the overprotected pride of a deprived and resentful family that was going to show the world. And not her hairy legs.

I didn't know whether to be shocked or to find it funny when she made her voice all breathy, and told me how, she was still not ready to say cunt out loud:
—The short reddish hairs, here, on my thighs, they make him think, aahh, of what I have ...

And maybe she said: Further up, or maybe it was even: At my centre. With a little aside for something about the forest, the small trees leading into the thickest of the bush, and the fresh spring in its centre, the cave at the break in the trees.

Although I might be making that up, I knew back then you could use bush for pubic hair, but to use it to designate a forest seems so Canadian, sure as I am that the conversation took place. And that there was something in it like that, and something about the fresh smell too, the natural: 'Parrrffumme', she even imitated his voice amid dabs of patchouli, he was getting her into that as well, the animal musks, she called them, applying them to all the pulses.
—Especially there, she said, the way it does in all those sophisticated sex manuals that I've seen since.

Though she did go into the bathroom to take care of that one. While I imagined her with her leg up on the toilet like a French whore at a bidet, and thought how far we had come since the Great Turd, which made me want to laugh when she offered the small vial to me, and to make some remark about relics and holy water and baptisms, only I yawned instead.
—Ooooooh, I said, and put my hand in front of my mouth, kind of shrinking into myself, inside the limits of my body. Because I suddenly didn't want to share that thought, or to reach out to touch her, even with my emotions.

I just said: That's interesting, in my flattest voice, while my own mind switched, I don't know if I wanted it to, to the bedbugs. To thinking: It goes with the smell of the bedbugs. We could use it to baptize the bedbugs.

It would be very hard to explain how dreadful they were. To even begin to express how dreadful the apartment became as even I gave up on trying to clean it. Or at least to clean it well. As the summer approached with the warmth of its days like the tent with its beetles all over again, except that there was no ocean to escape to, only the city.

New York with its polluted water: its summer panting. And inside no buzzing, just an airless silence, as the new bugs never even attempted to take wing. Or fell panicked onto their backs on the floor. They just walked slow and deliberate from place to place like Sandro, picking up our things and putting them down, always finding what they wanted: the blood they needed.

I don't know if you've ever actually seen a bedbug, Thorne, most people haven't these days, they're few and far between and easily avoidable, I almost don't believe Sandro could have done what he did. Maybe he was fooled by their scarcity too, or thought America too newly civilized to have them, though my mother had warned me against his mistake all my childhood: You never pick up upholstered furniture from off the street, she would say. Never even sat on it no matter how tired you got.

All those couches left on the street between Central Park West and Broadway where I caught the subway represented a real and present overstuffed and fuzzy danger, as far as she was concerned. Like carnivorous plants or crocodiles, mysterious spoor from outer space, that would leave you never knowing what you had brought home. Or where it would start to grow.

That's what makes it so ironic that I, who most obediently never sat in one, got bedbugs anyway. In what I suppose could be felt to be, if the *qué linda linda* boys were to find out and talk about it, a marvellous reversal. It could be made into a very good joke, a kind of shaggy couch story: Hey, did you hear the one about the Central Park West rich bitch who got bedbugs?

A strange but definite comeuppance for my elitist ways.

That's what I would think days I could manage the irony, when I would overcome my squeamishness enough to examine the small brown things I would kill, with their bodies like miniature hot water bottles, only segmented. And just about no visible head despite what must be the efficiency of their proboscises. Amazing little machines really, apparently ancient among insects, and almost immortal too.

I even managed to bring one across the border into Canada with me. That for all the care I took to hang my clothes out in the sun, the way folk wisdom instructs, still must have climbed into the suitcase. It was certainly no independent epidemic, not after just a few weeks in Canada, plus finding it the way we did, moving slowly around the married students' residence, to become the centre of attention for the whole building. Which meant, since we were surrounded by scientists, that it was made into an exhibit and placed under glass, an upside down shot glass to be exact, where it lived for months, without anyone offering it a finger or a toe or a leg, an armpit or a pubic area, to sink its proboscis into. I believe it survived, with less difficulty than I did, my first Canadian winter.

But the funniest thing about them, if you try to keep that edge of humour, is how they pop when you crush them. A sound remarked on, I'm sure, in prisons and slums around the world, probably the original 'pop'. Though they do say 'blop' or 'bup' sometimes too, almost a tongue articulated sound, a click from another language or universe, made only when they're full. Empty they say nothing at all, and you can't burst them either, they're like walking pieces of polyvinyl, you have to slice them in half very carefully with a fingernail or a knife, and even then sometimes the legs keep walking, though not for too long. Not like fleas that you can split in half and have both sides leap, so you can't find them again.

You really can get into the sound of it: The Sound and the Bathos. Which no doubt would have made a better name for the Thursday night meetings with their ostentatious poverty and their endless talk and their expensive drugs, acid and mescaline and psilocybin on the weekends by the time I left. With Sandro's portion of the rent money that he never paid probably going into the more costly varieties, the guaranteed natural capsules of one or another perfect peyote button that would make everyone but him sick, or a magic mushroom to be chopped up and eaten, or the pure uncut powder from someone just back from South America with tales of Andean magic and alpaca ponchos and cocaine.

We had all somehow come to know it was the superdrug, the one hundred percent natural stimulant that didn't do to you what speed did, or even Benzedrine or Dexedrine to get through exams. Though it didn't yet have the cachet, certainly not the horror, attached to it that it does now, there was no crack then, and no one I ever heard about freebased it, there was just heroin which was already organized crime, and Methedrine and heroic hippies with their speed kills campaigns, but except for that all drugs were thought friendly if you knew how to handle them, and freelance too, there was always someone selling off a couple of ounces of something, to pay for the trip south or east. And even if I'm sure most of those kids went home and fumigated, and changed their clothes, maybe even their style, they still got to take a perfect image away, of difficult but noble, beat or bohemian, almost revolutionary, poverty.

Then there would be, to add to the sound, the blood the miserable creatures are full of, which gets all over whatever you pop them against. 'Plup' they go and there's a bloodstain: each one a mini-bomb in a mini-war that would lead to a mini-joke. Because we were all going on the anti-war demos, it was just something you did, once every three months or so. Though some of the guests were more serious than others, talking about street or guerrilla theatre, and getting into doing a bit of it, even in the tourist areas, Wall Street or the Statue of Liberty or the bridges. That may have been where Laura's idea to do performances started, though I think that was more eclectic, coming out of more intellectual influences, and the happenings and be-ins and all that stuff, because she was harping on immediacy even then.

With Sandro the one to advise them, he had done that kind of thing before he said, and talked of knowing Julian Beck and Judith Messina, though I can't remember from where. Only when they would ask him to participate he would say: No, no. He couldn't, he wasn't a citizen, he was barely a resident.

—No, no, not yet, I can't. And then he would laugh and imitate that part about 'I can't travel without a passport', making it: I can't stay without a residence permit, in an overly solemn actor's voice, from The Living Theatre's *Paradise Now*.

Which is when it would start.

—The war, the war, that's how we look on those people, small and brown and sneaky and close to the ground and EEEEIRRROW bombs away 'plup'. And a dead bedbug. Followed by the blood spreading.

With people mostly polite enough to aim for the floor. Though there were stains all over the wall too, and besides that a smell. A strange sickly sweet scent that truly was like the hot enclosed smell of her army tent during the day. With its brown sun-glowing walls.

This smell didn't sting the inside of your nose. It went directly for the vital organs, the central abdomen, just like musk or blood always does. Not quite your period on a baby powder perfumed maxi-pad or slaughterhouse on the wind, but a variation on the same theme, Bedbug Blood-Musk I would think of naming it, leaving out the patchouli. Though I fully believe the blood would make it hold its special cachet a long time the way ambergris does perfume, to make a scent I would recognize now anywhere if I ever had to sniff it again.

—Why that's bedbug digested blood on cheap apartment enamel, I might say. Oh, how it reminds me of days gone by.

While doubtless it would make me itch all over the way I did that summer. Especially in the Coney Island sand, with bites all over my body. I didn't need any sand fleas, as I would lie on the beach amid the umbrellas and close my eyes and see my own red blood through a paisley pattern while the salt of the ocean spray became spiked with a sweetness that was hot dogs and Coca Cola and sugar and the seaweed rotting in the sun and the dead mussels opening. As well as creosote on flotsam and jetsam and the pylons of piers and the semen from condoms, white eels they called them in Lilac's neighbourhood when they saw them coming out of the conduits into the river. White eels like lampreys I would see them then amid the red of the small capillaries of my eyes, as if the whole world had turned cannibal: the street the night the air the voices the laughter the Japanese beetles.

Even the transistor radios. There on the beach or back in the apartment those forebears of today's ghetto blasters that had delighted me from their distance far below my mother's windows as they made that then Hispanic neighbourhood dance, had taken on an insistent repetitive beat that rose toward hallucination as I leaned out my small front window or actually crawled through it onto the fire escape to lean into the twilight to await full night and their silence. When they would be replaced by the quiet buzzing of the blue lights of the still black and white televisions from the windows across the way, that seemed to suck in all our new neighbourhood's energy. While my arms rested against the heat of the metal and I could feel myself making up my own pattern, breathe and breathe and breathe and think, full of dizzy thoughts as if I were floating in the belly, the stomach or the huge twisted intestines, of some transparent monster that had eaten us all. The only sound its digestive gurglings and slurpings, the rising tide of its vital fluids full of slaps and rushes and moans and groans, that was the TVs and the streetlights and the tomcats and the occasional fight and the slamming of a door and the squeal of brakes and above it all, rising and rising, rising and rising, Laura and Sandro consuming each other, the lapping and slapping of their tides, rising out of the living room. Through the two windows directly next to mine.

Sandro would laugh about the bug-popping
and the bloodstains. To the point of telling someone once, someone stupid enough to ask why the stains were there on the wall behind their bed, that he would throw Laura, her legs flung wide in ecstasy, up against the wall during her period. While he grinned that avid grin of his, and fixed the person with his acid green eyes.

He repeated the story often after, and laughed again, the way he said he had the first time, when that woman, that girl or bitch or cunt or cow, or other permissible art community slur, had either melted or withered or let her mouth, or maybe it was her legs, drop open, depending on his mood when he retold it, or the company. As he inevitably brushed his moustache or slapped his thigh.

  Because it was his idea of a very very good joke.

Though the really

unny part, I think,

in that sense of historic irony or poetic justice, or just enduring comic gesture, was how it all ended up because Laura took such remarks seriously. She thought them symbolic of some form of meaningful freedom, sexual or otherwise. She even went around telling me, telling all of us, how he loved all her juices, so that she actually did try to make some menstrual prints for him that summer.

Lovetotems she called them, she wasn't up to cuntprints yet, while she giggled in just that dizzy way that made her the free spirit he always loved, and the others admired. The typical bohemian earth goddess, wearing her Village sandals while she tried to print herself onto various kinds of both cheap and expensive paper, from pastel rag to the brown paper fish comes wrapped in (with an extra giggle for that one, as she sang, *Keep on Truckin' Mama*), rather than the wall.

Only they didn't work. At least not the way she wanted. Which shouldn't have come as any surprise. The brown stains on the wall, or just her own sanitary napkins, should have told her how their colour would turn. The darkening of bright blood to brown seems a fact of time passing no woman would be unaware of. Just the way they all became hairy sepia Rorschachs when she had wanted something so much brighter.

That experiment must have awakened something in her. I don't think so much the feminist, or even the feminine, side – though it did call forth into the public light for the first time her sense of herself as mythmaker – as her need to prove that it could be done. That the problem before her could be solved. Whichever one it was.

Because the problem she set herself did seem to change, to mutate, with whatever new language she was currently using. There was probably one for each class, so that the surrealism of our early visits to the Modern was gone, there were no more dreams and connections and meanings, those were reserved for her talk about her life now, but a million combinations of modern or postmodern (I think that term was already in use, though I can't be sure) or formalist or conceptual or minimal or informational views of the problem, her allegiances changing from day to day, as she found in each, a new way to come back to:
–The conflict, the tension, the confrontation... her hand gestures always seeming to hold a brush or knife, to work from the ball and socket joint of the shoulder. As she attempted to carve concepts if not words out of air.
–The the the, she would repeat like a motor revving, hands now raised in a desperate Thursday night attempt to articulate, what it was that was inherent in the ephemeral nature of the event and the permanence or semi-permanence in its record. Or at least the difference between the event itself and its record's duration, how they spoke to each other those two, how they resonated, resonating frequencies she called them, to create a dialogue around the meaning of the moment, or perhaps of moment, and its relationship to momentum.
–Does the record of the event change the event's nature? You do know about the Heisenberg uncertainty principle, don't you? she would say. Before speculating that perhaps this particular record of this particular event in this particular dimension which was after all art, perhaps changed something else through its attempt to represent the moment, not so much frequency as trajectory perhaps, or angle of attack, the moment's outcomes as it moved or its wavefront moved, or something about its having existed moved, through a space time continuum. If in fact there was a continuum, if in fact it. it. it. we.

everything. anything. something. were not in fact. discontinuous. Discontinuous.
—Discontinuous. A word she seemed to savour or get stuck on, a record repeating: discontinuous. As if the word itself actually went around. Speeding up and slowing down. Diss.cn.TIN.youus. So that she made that part of it too. You. Us. You-us. We are discontin. You-us. And leaned back and laughed. And savoured it some more. So that you knew that she would have to keep it. That this one was important. That she would keep and use it. Even as she went on.

To talk about barriers. How important it was, event or continuity, I couldn't quite catch it, but especially there, at the barrier, at that barrier, where her prints took place, at the limits of inside and outside.
—Has it occurred to you, she asked, that the female body is a finite space that contains an infinite one?

And she compared us to some curve in mathematics, even art students had to take Math, not that she wouldn't have anyway, she loved it, but whose name I'll never remember: It is a body whose finity gives birth to infinity, continuity to discontinuity. Just there, right there, at that barrier, and her hand cut down across her belly. The place of sex and birth, birth and sex. Sex and birth and luck and choice, choice was very important, but luck was more so.
—Semen is luck, she said and she giggled, she still couldn't quite say even words like that without giggling: Probability, accident, the essence of the male, luck and probability, there just there, the temporal visitor, the visitor from time, and out of time, making time or cancelling time, while my mind raced to keep up: to stay on time.

Is this the male(mail) from outer space? she asked as she placed death there too, square at the border, the barrier, a place she still couldn't quite name. As she kept going round and round again, with life and death and birth and death and life and moment and duration, in all the implications of The Menstrual Moment, its symbolic bloody spread. And the barrier.

Like the sound barrier, or the light barrier that leads to elsewhen, there was the barrier nature of the orifice she wished to portray, caught in ecstasy (a giggle and crossing of the legs here) between time and time again, elsewhere and elsewhen, she even defined elsewhen relativistically, drew its presence on a map, showed how it could not be reached in our time. That it was another dimension, that sexual/ menstrual natal/prenatal choice, an intromission/penetration intrusion/ extrusion, reaching an unreachable to distort and make different to puff out or contract or bend over backwards the shape of time or of space, change its nature along that barrier/wavefront. With The Menstrual Moment, speaking to all those probabilities, those possible acts. Or to their energy gathering, their possibilities of or for change, calling to time to make itself new, commanding it to reshape, again and again and again with the tides. Exhorting it to change; there was always some it she wanted to change.

–Since it takes place somewhere beyond our perceptual plane, it must be above an elementary catastrophe, I think she said.

That was when she pulled out the diagrams, she must have been thinking about the problem for days, spoken to her math teacher or gone to the library, because she had them with her, she had come to this Thursday night prepared, it was prepared oral report time, advanced show and tell – however ad-libbed – as she showed us the shapes, and made me come over next to her to look at them closely, what in particular the catastrophes, the diagrams of discontinuous events, what they disclosed.

And god knows how she had come up with it, maybe it was because of all her curiosity about topology, about points moving across surfaces and Mobius strips in three dimensions, but she had managed to dig out of somewhere, maybe her math teacher enjoyed her curiosity and knew all this stuff, and got it for her, it would be hard to tell. But she had discovered the Catastrophe Theory of René Thom, to be her other favourite René, right next to René Magritte, looping and doubling back and juxtaposing a different kind of image, of event, sundering them and putting them back together, each type of catastrophe named by Thom for the beauty of its topographical shape, cusps and butterflies and hyperbolics and parabolics and butterflies and swallowtails and folds and elliptics and parabolics and butterflies and hyperbolics and swallowtails, seven of them in infinite combination, as many as it will take to define our perceptual dimensions, three plus one for time, but if you included more, oh yes, the number of catastrophes would permute out to infinity very quickly but in the meanwhile seven, seven is the number of the godhead, don't you see, the magic number to describe all discontinuous events, to show what happens when an event leaps, the point falls off the surface and lands on the other, continuing but discontinuous, you-us, you see, don't you?

And then she went on to describing it all more closely, and truly they were beautiful those shapes she had found, beautiful convoluted curves, telling us how the zone of overlap where the discontinuity formed, and here she giggled almost hysterically, it was called a hysteresis, can't you see, a womb-space, and she giggled louder: It's a womb-space, the place where the discontinuity forms is a womb-space, a hysteresis, that's what he called them, and she laughed again, just like I said, the womb-space, the hysteresis, the barrier.

And then she turned to me.

– Can't you see, Alma? The greatest discontinuity is the discontinuity of god. While I just nodded, and let it go, as she went on to talk of heavenly bodies and the strong force and the weak force and the gravitational force and all the other forces that can't be accounted for, while I gave up, I was doing that more and more, to let her too be discontinuous, as I watched her hands, and felt her presence, and loved her more.

As she got up and walked deliberately across the room, a catastrophe bent back on itself, to the desk in the little middle room, that should have been my writing desk, to get her prints from where they were piled, next to some scene designs Sandro was doing, a desperation in her voice as she said:

–But doing it, doing it, it's probably not possible to do it.

Which she repeated.

–Not possible. Not possible. As she moved back toward us. Her arms waving. Each movement a minor catastrophe. A cusp or an elliptic or even a swallowtail I could feel rumbling through to my feet, as she ripped the prints up slowly in front of all of us, and let them drop down on the floor amid the bedbug stains, her face full of desolation and disgust, tears welling in her eyes.

And all of us mesmerized.

I realized that when I shook my head, as if shaking off a spell, to bring myself back into the room and look around. Where I saw everyone doing the same thing. Shaking their heads or stretching their arms or their legs, shifting positions or reaching for cigarettes, rustling the way the audience does after the play or at intermission, not yet looking at one another, until my examination reached Sandro, where he sat his arms down between his legs, still staring intently at her.

He must have noticed me looking, somehow felt my eyes on him. Because he shifted his gaze to me, and leaned back and spread out his arms, and grinned. A wider more avid grin, yet more relaxed, than the one he usually wore. And then he winked.

He winked. To tell me that Thursday evenings had a new star. And he was proud. The way I should have been. Only I couldn't stand it. I didn't know where she was going and my body felt all hollow and I couldn't stand it. So that tears came to my own eyes, as I bit my lip and quickly looked away.

Toward one of the other students, or even out the window, I can't remember. And although I have always told myself that it was because of her, and her terrible pain at tearing up her own work, at not being able to do it, that I cried, I think I knew even then that it was because Sandro wore the same expression on his face as I am sure I'd had on mine only moments before. And that the pride I saw beaming from him was the same one I had felt for years. At how I protected her. Or created her. I don't know.

Even if what he offered me with that wink was conspiracy in our triumph. Because the fact is, I didn't want to know. Not even that it had happened. That whether or not she could ever solve the problems she set herself, she could hold an audience riveted as she tried. I just turned away from him and got up and went to her, and put my arm around her.

—Don't worry, you'll solve it, I said, and whether or not I believed it — after all she'd never solved the puzzle of rendering the dream — I added: You always do.

And then only days later, this time, she did. On a morning when we were alone together in the apartment she picked up all the pieces again, from where they had been left on the floor all crumpled and stepped on, and placed them together again in a new order. Or played at placing them, moving them about, saying that she knew now, knew from all the things she had said, that she would have to do more than she had done, much more than just make those momentary prints, to make such a thing into a totem.

A thing would have to carry more thought, contain more mental energy to be a totem, she said. Not that it mattered much how that energy got there, but it did have to be there, she was sure of it, like with those little totems my mother had brought back from the Southwest that Laura had seen in the apartment, you saw them too, in my mother's study, Mother loves them, they were the small clay animal sculptures that look like any other small clay animal sculptures. Except that Laura was right, I can still always feel the energy. That I am sure is there because they are made with fur and feathers and blood and prayer: the blood of the animal the prayer for the animal mixed with the clay.

Laura thanked me for the idea. It was terribly condescending really, she'd never thanked me for anything before, just talked about how we were one, our ideas one. And now I was being thanked for my mother having totems from some Southwestern native group in her apartment, while Laura went on, talking as if I had spoken to her that other night, when I'm sure she knew I hadn't. That my role had been the same as everyone else's, even Sandro's, just to give her energy, the energy of our concentration, a kind of soul blood like the prayer blood that glued the totems together. That was what she had grabbed and spun into shape, it wasn't our ideas, that brought her to understand how you had to work with the event image.

–**You have to** put hands thoughts teeth on them, she said and ripped one with her teeth and chewed its edges, to make them work, to feel right about them, mold them right. Because making a special effort to see from all angles, to comprehend, apprehend, would give an energy that could make up for the loss of freshness. Until she would be able

to make it a moment folded in on itself. Like the catastrophe, discontinuous. But possible to see from all angles, to make re-continue in the act of seeing, the act of seeing suddenly becoming like the act of sex or birth, an act of making, of giving life. Making love or babies or the world through seeing, all of it the same. So that seeing would make, or perhaps it was re-make, the way we are always re-making, re-marking, and her hand tore a page, the world in our seeing of it. Which is what would make the 'totem' become a 'work'. With autonomy in space and time, yet continuous with the seeing 'I'.
–You get it, she said: The seeing 'I'.
–Dog, I added, and she started to laugh, suddenly convinced she had the hook, that it would now be possible to do them that way.

Because they would be looser, more concrete but less specific, they would be able to relate to what was around them as we did, at least when we were standing still, or better perhaps, she said, as any syllable we spoke did, dynamically linked always to what was there at the time it was spoken. To before and to after and to the weight of its vibrations in the air. So that it would change with each speaking as well as carry something, traces anyway, not only of our individual memories of what it was the last or first time we uttered it, what you could call its flavour perhaps, or maybe charm, like for a quark, but what it meant the first time it was ever spoken, and all the speaking acquired since, which might be more akin to mass, with all the tracings of what had been around it that first time it was said, the time of its making always with it, its spin perhaps. And the totems could share in some of that, carry their trajectories or be their trajectories, I'm not sure, like the little ionized water droplets in a cloud chamber, or the particle traces of a point blank bullet wound.
–Aren't they always referring to that part of us as a wound anyway? she laughed as she titled them all: *Particle Traces of the Menstrual Moment*, though in the end only one would bear that title.
–They will all carry the moment of happening itself, she said to me right then with absolute determination, the moment of change, of mutation. They will shut down to death or to life, they will. Be just that moment, the wound the flow the entry the exit the choice, when the particle is stopped and becomes other in stating itself, stating its presence.

Heisenberg and uncertainty at the centre of our lives from the moment we had talked about his principle on swings in Central Park, wondering where we were, if we could be found, stopped or changed.
—Only these, she said: These will never fade and rot when they change, not when they are, and she giggled suddenly: Put together, composed, you know, compost, and we both laughed.
—They're menstrual compost, we said at the same time: Fertilizing our gardens.

Which made her call one that too, *Composed/Compost,* probably thinking up other titles as she stirred the torn parts with her now bare feet. Still planning them into totems with her eyes.

She would look over at me every once in a while for my approval, it was the kind of thing we had always talked of a lot, with all its ins and outs, that vocabulary of observer and observed: Who am I when I look at you? and is it me looking? as we tried to figure out why we were not each other. Only I couldn't do it any more. Even if I could still giggle with her I couldn't do it any more. Because I knew that we weren't. Even if I still didn't know why.

I wasn't willing to sophisticate it anymore, making up those questions whose answers seemed already foregone conclusions. And rather sad ones really, at least to me, their moments plunging ahead discontinuous and catastrophic and already enough for me just to bear, without ever trying to explain them. So that I would just look back at her, and maybe I would say, spreading my hands and looking at the bloodstains behind her head:
—Sounds great Laura, just great, before my eyes would wander back to those torn up brown on pink or blue or white or brown or graph paper concretions of a part of her body I had never contemplated. Lost in the impact of my own moments, the way I would choke in the summer heat of the fire escape, asking myself what the precise trajectory was of those sounds that seemed to enter my lungs.

And if I wondered anything at all, it was about Sandro. Why I wasn't Sandro.

Although I did watch her, as we talked a bit more from time to time, a morning or an afternoon or an evening here or there, the best times we had, sometimes even approaching the way we had always been, that could still make me want to breathe that bedbug ridden air and stay and stay, making me late for work more than once.

While she spent the summer collaging those prints back together in acrylic; adding lines and photos and found objects, even letters to go with her syllable theory, compacting them into far more intense, far denser spaces, in her newfound sense of the concreteness of form.
—Art is concrete, concrete, concrete, she would say as she mixed and marked the work; as it all intertwined perfectly with her old surrealistic imagery to form those white dwarves she often called them, already astronomical, or even black holes. Some days she was sure those menstrual catastrophes with their graph paper and their torn lace and their blood and their seaweed and their seagull and pigeon feathers, their tiny black mussels we had found together on the piers, their egg cases from the Union Street market, that they covered and disguised entrances into other dimensions. Laughing, while she talked about space travel, how those totems might show the changes in the nature of space.
—Around the vortex, my vortex, she said: All our vortices, is that right? or is it vortexes? and she giggled: Each person's vortex, in any case, or each woman's, do you think men have them? Vortexes I mean, or vortices, maybe they only have vertices or vertexes, and we both giggled.

While I told her that I was sure that one at least was vertices, the great prick leaning forward into life.
—Creating its own wavefront in the space time continuum, she added, then went back to black holes: My black hole, while she laughed again. And told me how we too were discontinuous.

We were definitely shapes like those catastrophes if viewed from a fourth or fifth dimension, though without doubt far more complex, with that vortex central to the discontinuity, the jumping of levels or lives or surfaces or selves, the command to the embryo to become other.
—We are not ourselves, she would suddenly pronounce, more than once she said that: That's why you can't find yourself, none of us can,

even if you told them that's what you quit school to do, Alma, we never find ourselves, just trail our particles our lives behind us like a comet's tail, that's why there is no end to knowledge, Alma.

She even wrote that into her journal, a sketchbook full of drawings and written asides, and strange little poems. And marginalia. On her own margins.

Then she wrote that remark into mine, too, taking up a whole page with flowers and stars all about, while she added something about how what you had to do, the one thing you had to be sure of, was that we, me you, whoever. Or whatever. It might be whatever, but that thing we carry around that is different from everybody else, it must not be blown apart by the discontinuities. Somehow that mind, that soul, that guide, that something, that body maybe, had to hold all of us together.

And she would stop when she said things like that, the pen or the knife or the brush, whichever tool was in her hand or no tool at all as she manipulated paper or plastic, suddenly still. Until she would kind of shake herself, in a don't-mind-me gesture.

—But you never have to worry about your mind do you, Alma? About losing it? Really losing it? You know, like leaving it somewhere? On the subway maybe. Like I did my dream?

She would never give me time to answer. To tell her of my vision of us, there on the subway unable to let go, the train rushing on, or just to say: Yes, yes, I did worry about it, I held my head between my hands listening to them some nights thinking it might explode, wondering about what I really was going to do with my life, if I would have a life at all. Only she would change the subject quickly, instead.

—And what about you? she would say. But not about my mind. About my men. Had I found any men, met any interesting men, did I want any of the Thursday night men, did any of them appeal to me? She was sure I could have any one of them for the asking.

I would turn away, then, and look at the laundry hung out across the back yards, beautiful cloth sculptures flapping in the thick air, discontinuous, just to avoid her eyes. While she would go on, she would never await an answer, but go back to work, her eyes once more on what she was doing, on pressing or ripping or manipulating, the sensuality apparent in the movements of her hands and her voice.

—It's so good, she would say. So-oo good. I just can't wait.

And she didn't mean for that night, but for me to catch up, to find one of my own. While I would say nothing. Nothing at all.

I would just enter the kitchen to fix us a cup of tea or stare out the window or back at her hands, moving, moving, while she went on. With the work, or with talking about her plans for the work, or with doing both at once, sewing her rough edged meteors to the backs or frames with an awl in purposely awkward stitching, or suspending them between the four stretchers which would in turn be suspended from the ceiling, to be changed from side to side with the phases of the moon as she looked at them and changed their name from love to Moon Totems: For the Great Goddess she said.

—And for you, Alma, for you. Who walk in and out of the apartment (maybe she even said: My life) with the tides.

And we would suddenly be Amazons again, our fantasies real again. Amazons and Goddesses, with Laura Artemis to my Athena, the changing moon to my rock, we would say, her tides lapping at me. Because it was her tides that dictated my movement in and out, and she knew it as well as I did, discontinuous emotion to my steady logic.

—But we are one in the goddess she would say suddenly: One person.

And I would put my hand on hers, palm to palm, and we would stare into each other's eyes and there would be that quickening again, there, deep in the belly.

—They will be Moon Totems for you, Alma, she said.

The last things she was to name for me. Until she named herself.

Moon *Totems for Alma*, months after Alma had gone, became the title of her first solo show at a small gallery in SoHo, to really launch her, still a student. They were beginning to look for people by then, at least in that area, the way the whole artworld would be shortly, who they felt could express the new women's consciousness, who could become examples of that, a new woman's art, which is what they said she did.

People even asked who Alma was, looking for her lady love, while others thought it meant just what it said, that it was the Spanish, or Italian for those who had researched her roots, for soul. *Love Tokens for the Soul* one article on the show called it, making her suddenly part of real artworld New York, and far more than Sandro's girl in the eyes of many.

Nor could she let it go. So that she said she didn't feel that totems could be enough, this thing needed monumentality, Athena, Artemis, called for that, she wrote me in a letter, it was one of the big themes, history had no right to deny her a big theme. To deny us a big theme, she would say by then, and she didn't mean her and me, but all of us, all women, because she had taken on the position that had been given her, to represent us, and what she knew she least wanted to see denied was her place at the centre, at her vortex. With that world whirling around her, something that would continue for the longest time before it forced her to become her own black hole, with none of her energy able to escape, even to communicate her position, long after her first truly important show.

Her first *Resolved Events*, Catastrophes numbers one through twenty-eight, seven elementary catastrophes for each quarter of the moon, to come up with the menstrual number in a way she thought perfect. And she could say it by then, subtitle it *Dis.Cunt.In.You.Us, The Discontinuity Continued*, convinced now that she had finally done it, articulated the moment the *Moon Struck* (that was the name of one of them), with prints of the *Space Between* (*Her Legs*) (another title), made with god, or maybe Athena and Artemis and all the Amazons know what, kind of paint or epoxy resin or other material, in order not to wind that part of her anatomy up permanently coated in plastic. Because they were in their final and most brilliant form reliefs, hailed as a new threshold in art and the honest – no, truthful – rendition of female experience.

Praise she deserved. Even all that stuff about how she had dived into that emptiness, or that fullness (whether it was empty or full, the void or the primordial soup, seemed to depend a good deal on the gender of the critic) to become daughter womb and mother at once, the forming body the transforming mind, that so few dared be. Which is when Sandro passed definitively to being Laura's man, or Mack's man, she went by her last name often then, she liked the androgyny of it, especially that: Hey, Mack, you still hear so often in New York, I think an article in a women's magazine got called that, complete with exclamation point: "Hey, Mack!", emphasizing how out of the ordinary her so ordinary name was. And I guess I was Mack's woman, too, because she had taken to telling those who still asked, making tragic eyes, that Alma was:
–The One Who Left. Making it sound like yet another title.

So that I've always thought it ironic how it all started. Because no matter how often she said, in interviews she would say it sometimes, how she had been inspired by her closest friend, and years later, would still name me, Alma, The One Who Went Away, as her Muse, what had really started it all was that crazy stuff among the bedbugs, that Bloody Cunt Up Against the Wall joke of Sandro's. Which made the first totems something akin to wearing a slave bracelet, because she had started doing them to please him. To give herself to him. All of her. Including her black hole. So that she could become his inspiration. Not he, her Pygmalion.

And for all that I could laugh about it, still it frightened me, made me mildly nauseous. Even when I would see the articles in the paper I would shiver, and see that vision of the dream or of the train. Though I don't think I ever brought myself to look at it directly. To remember that first time after Sofia's when in a small breathless voice she told me how much she'd enjoyed the attention. To think how dangerous it could be, how dangerous it was to her even then, or perhaps more than ever: that need to be pure and different, to go where no one has gone before, combined with a puppy's need to bring back the toy, the cat to bring in the dead bird; that terrible outsize need to please. And not just her public, but him.

To please Sandro.

Which is when I thought: it's Sandro. Sandro is the onrushing train. And whether or not I still held her hand, or tried to bring her back, she could never stop running.

But that was all long after she had stopped looking over toward me for my approval, in the days when I read the articles about her over wine or coffee, when I had truly Gone Away. Although she would still write me letters in which she traced how she would do it all, sending me sketches and diagrams, models of the catastrophes of her most recent universe, and telling me how they all related to the event enclosed. Each letter still with the desperate tone of a best friend or a lover finally keeping a long awaited promise. And beautiful some of them, there was a time I probably could have sold them for a fair bit of money, maybe still could, I have no idea how much that early work is going for now: if that world still remembers her, or even her work.

Though how they could forget, I don't know. With all those articles in *Art Forum* and *Art in America* and all those other magazines, with those lovely diagrams that were sometimes related to math and sometimes to astronomy and always to catastrophe. Or all that documentation of her performing, in which they called her the 'spirit of a new era'. Besides which that world never wants to lose money on its investments. And there was certainly enough invested in her. So they probably keep her work going. Selling and re-selling. And she is probably a tragic, if not an Amazon, queen there, where many will weep over her but hardly any will ask what she is doing now. Or mention they saw her on a street corner. Or how different her performance was.

I never answered. I meant to, but I never did. I talked to her every once in a while over the phone at my mother's or she would call from her new studio, and we would talk forever, ending always with something about how we could feel each other, even when we didn't speak, and I would promise to write after she would say something about how she needed me, something of me, even if only ink from my hand, something physical, not just this electronic connection, to keep her going.

But the letters didn't seem to require answers, not really. They were more reports than anything else, the way she had always needed me to figure out her ideas, even if it was just telling them to me, and then saying: This is wonderful Alma, whether or not I'd said nothing at all, and it was hard to say: Uh-huh, Uh-huh, Uh-hah, Mmmmmmm, Mmmmmmmm, That's great, on paper. Which meant that I didn't even know how to begin, even if some of the letters did in fact impress the hell out of me. You can hardly send an audiocassette of one hand clapping. Though I'm quite sure she did keep copies, just to know what she'd said, or seen or done or felt.

It wasn't too long either before I'd had my own much more common rendition of the truth and honesty of female experience, when I gave birth to Jason in a riptide of blood and amniotic fluid and sweat.

Ocean and river and chemicals and just the tiniest bit of excrement brown on the white of the hospital sheets making up yet another sweet sticky summer day perfume. An event so profoundly resolved, so specific and powerful, so just itself, that all I can remember doing in my hospital room, isn't unwrapping him and looking at his tiny perfect fingers and toes the way all new mothers are supposed to do, but sniffing him, sniffing him again and again, and remembering how, against all the antiseptic hospital smells, I had recognized him. That his smell was the same as mine, as the slightly sweet smell of my sweat, the way it had changed in the last months of pregnancy, until I wondered, is this the way we are supposed to recognize them, as I rubbed my nose into his body as he sucked at the breast.

I remember too how I specifically wanted to tell her about that, the strange specificity of discontinuous connection, especially as I would hold the curve of him into my breast as his small hands reached out to grab and my knees would raise him against me, and I would think we were a Mobius strip, or the three dimensional equivalent she always talked about, or I would remember the hysteresis, the womb-space in a Thomian catastrophe, and I would think that she was right, that was what we really were, with all our complex curves in and out, we were her final perfect catastrophe of the menstrual moment, sitting there in the insipid pink comfort our society extends to the blood and guts of motherhood. With its heightened sense of smell that I really wanted to tell her about, to speculate on how there might be a smell that connected the two of us too, an essential odour that linked us, that between blood relatives or blood sisters there might be a particle movement of smell, both the simplest and most complex of our senses, which could carry some sort of mental essence that might improve our telepathy, not just our reminiscence the way we all know smell does. If we could just sniff it at the same time, we would fall into mental harmony, mental linkage. Only the one smell I could ever connect it to, that I could even think of trying, wasn't the freshness of forsythia or lilacs or even the summer heat of her army tent, or the saliva of those boys, but just the bedbugs, the bedbugs.

There was something in the blood essence of birth and of the bedbugs, and in those first totems of hers, that made those terrible walking bloodbags the only smell I could think about to connect us. Yet I could not bring myself to speak of that, not even in our most intimate phone conversations. So that I just let it go. And never really shared with her the terror and beauty and absorption of it all, nor spoke to those documents that were events resolving so differently from the ones in my life, after all I had no diagrams to send back to her.

Jeanpierre did that, it was his contribution to the birthing classes we went to, with his trying to diagram the descent of the head, the turning of the body depending on presentation, flexion or extension, complete with pressure arrows in colours, because I never could diagram or draw. But I knew she wouldn't appreciate having it sent to her, not if I said it was his, even if she might have had a use for them.

And everything felt strange anyway, my whole life just slightly out of phase, so that I wanted to tell her of my new dimension and resisted telling her all at once. With my tits aching to nurse and the bath waiting, I kept looking at all those little numbers and letters and graphs and saying: What do these have to do with me, What do they mean in the context of the three A.M. feeding? Joking with myself like that, so that I still don't know if it was jealousy of her experience, where she was, or jealousy of my own, wanting to keep it to myself, to have something she didn't have, or just plain exhaustion, that I could never get it all down on paper anyway, that provoked, at least in part, my resistance to writing her. At least in the same exalted tone of voice she always used. So that I would always end by putting away my pen and paper, playing some soft music, and going to sleep to the rhythms of Jason's or even Amber's soft suckings.

And letting my mother keep her up to date. Because writing the kids are fine Jason just cut a tooth Amber is walking now Jeanpierre has received another promotion aspen and pine dominate the horizon there are raccoons living under the eaves and squirrels in the bird houses seemed worse than trying to imitate her wild documentations. Than trying to join her again in her world.

My mother would keep me up to date too. On the more specific side of things. Shows and dates and articles and envy. Laura was seen here and Laura was talked about there and Laura was written up again. And again and again. The magic road had opened to her and she was Cinderella. The menstrual pains the sanitary napkins the used tampons of her experience had magically changed to her coach, six little bedbug carcasses their broken legs splayed out had become her six white horses, and she was finally off to the Hamptons, and later even, to Studio 54.

With the great green monster appearing to me on cue, even the miracle of birth or the naturally tranquilizing effect of oxytocin weren't able to overcome the twist of anxiety in the gut, that would make me get up out of my lawn or easy chair, and walk around, the garden or the kitchen or the living room, reciting over and over to myself: But I love my husband I love it here I love my children the outdoor life the flowers in the garden the barbecue on the deck the colours in the fall having a driver's license having a car to drive, learning a new language the trips to the North the occasional vacation south or east, while knowing all the time that she had what my mother had always wanted for me.

So that I would experience that moment of anxiety again and again like the sharp clenching of Jason or Amber's mouth over my sore and chapped nipples, the wince of the moment before the letdown reflex would cut in and complaisant calm would take over from pain. As she did New York, really did New York, was present every day on the carousel of doing New York: the New York I could only see on late night television. That matched the Hollywood of all those bodice-rippers I would watch the other women pick up at the laundromat. Because those were the facts of the case: I was in the laundromat with *Chatelaine* while she was in Max's Kansas City with Andy Warhol.

And then somewhere in there, in the years of our abbreviated telephone relationship, interrupted only by the one brief trip Jeanpierre and I took to New York, when he and Sandro faced off like two hockey players, leaning in toward each other, and I didn't know if it was her or me or some other part of what they considered to be their male property, or perhaps propriety, they wished to bash about on the ice, but sometime after that, when the steady stream of objects in the mail had abated somewhat, one arrived. Larger than usual, and with instructions, a reproduction, but personalized just for me, through collaged-in elements. In an envelope and wrapped in tissue paper, because some of the parts did protrude, accompanied by a long letter full of instructions, that said I should use it as a focal point during my next labour, since I was pregnant again.

I guess she'd been talking with some friends who'd had babies, or maybe it was just reading, a kind of research without firsthand knowledge into her preoccupation with female experience, and birth was certainly one you had to cover if you wanted the whole thing, Mary Kelly might even have started her postpartum document by then, I don't know, but I certainly never expected Laura to know anything about contractions and exercises and the Lamaze recommended focal points for the moments when the contractions are the worst. How concentrating on one point is a way up and through your pain and your nausea, up onto another level and a bit of peace. Or maybe I'd even mentioned it to her myself once, and then just forgotten, talked about how it's almost a transcendence, how you can almost see through whatever it is that you pick to use, because this thing was very specific and very thought out, even the postcard was of a painting I'd never expected her to use for anything again. Not after she'd abandoned it like a hot potato, the gauchest of the gauche, that first year in art school.

Because it was the terrible Tchelichew all those teachers accused the female students of liking. The one with the veins and the arteries and the fetuses growing on the tree of life; that might even be what it's called: *Tree of Life*.

It's no surprise it would be the painting to most incense the New York art establishment of her art school days, far beyond any crimes committed by a Wyeth or a Dali or a Tanguy, who, for all they were illustrative in their depictions of loneliness or horror, maintained a straightforwardness of form that might be boring and unpainterly but which was at least acceptable, the way a student's first renderings for fashion illustration might be. So that Tchelichew's rococo exuberance, his lack of decorum, would offend even the young up-and-comers, which she hadn't become yet, but wanted to be. Which meant she had reversed herself utterly the first year in art school and said she too hated that painting.

Even if we had sat in front of it for ages our last year in high school and even more the summer between high school and university, when that Tchelichew had come to symbolize our symbiosis, we might even have formulated our megapersonality for the first time in front of it, I'm not quite sure. It had just taken on the role of our emblem, the one that told us we would make it through, interconnected and organic like all those blue and red and yellow and pink creatures on that tree, all of them different sizes and stages of development, perfect for us really, the way we saw ourselves as growing and intertwined, and besides that, it was as maximal as she was.

As exaggerated. Nothing I don't think could be as totally even sickeningly maximal in an age of minimalism, than that tree of life, almost enough to make you puke, really like transition in labour, I don't know how she could have sensed that, though maybe she didn't, maybe she just sent it for its obvious symbolism, so that I would look once again on those mouths open as if about to scream, those curving circular movements of the veins the branches the trunk, so somehow reminiscent of childhood femininity, lace and china animals and all the other protective girlish frills the ones that still inhabited the knickknack shelves in the *horror vacui* of her mother's living room, the constant confusing movement of line and form and colour, that expressed Alicia's Italian working class origins, and her fright at losing her community upon marrying Lilac's father, so that it must have been the sweetness, like the suckers you stick in your mouth for sugar during labour to get through, combined with blood and guts, that moved her. Maybe even that formed the beginning of an idea in her. The one that would only emerge much later in her *Resolved Events*, but which she might owe to Tchelichew. From those days when all of us, even the girls at school, looked for experience almost like grubs, looking for a place to pupate.

Because in the end, in what they call her mature work, I guess they measure it now not against her age but against the length of her career, the stuff that must still sell though she would get no benefit from it, with its wild busyness, it's obvious that painting influenced her more than the minimalists she picked up on at university. And I guess I always did like it better than all that Zen koan minimal stuff, although I couldn't have said it any time after her first month in art school without feeling that I'd just contracted the disease of literal mindedness, so that it was wonderful to get this large reproduction, to feel vindicated, because it was obvious that she had finally admitted her love of this painting and its influence on her, if only privately and to me, just in the way she had appropriated it, making it over like one of those huge Christmas cards,

Advent calendars I think they're called, Jeanpierre's mom always sends one, it was just about the right size and the right season, which have little doors that you open day by day until the twenty-fifth, with little messages behind them, or sometimes little chocolates.

  The way there were doors, usually cut behind a fetal head, or maybe a uterine bubble or root, or even a bunch of smaller heads, each one coded to an instruction on her sheet, open when contractions are five minutes apart, or open when they are two, or open when they are irregular, or open when you first get the urge to push, so that I followed them exactly, even if Jeanpierre thought I was out of my mind. Because it was the strangest of my births, I had gone overdue and was taking on water like a sinking ship which meant I finally allowed for induction and monitoring, and was so strung out by the drugs that I didn't know for the entire last part if I wanted to shit piss or go blind looking at that thing, quite literally, I was peeing and puking and shitting water and my waters broke and I didn't know what was what barely which end was up, with liquid streaming out of both and the monitor over my belly or its wires in my hand as I made a desperate dash to the john while I kept on doing it, opening the little doors like her instructions for a calmer moment said to open the little doors, even if I didn't know if I had the urge to push or just further diarrhea, until I opened the last one just before I was taken into delivery and it was one small pressed forsythia flower on its branch and: For us, it said: For us.

  While all I remember is a small cry as I moved onto the gurney. And the one nurse who picked it up for a moment, then holding it away at arm's length while she looked at me just the way Jeanpierre had, said:
–You don't want to take this with you?

Then after

that came the time of everything happening at once when you can smell your own blood in your nostrils, see your own veins, the veins of the baby, the veins of the placenta with the umbilicus pulsating in its last moment as the uterus pushes and pushes. A moment so perfect and present as Jeanpierre rubbed my back that I even remembered, or not so much

remembered as felt how her hand covered mine and I heard, a voice whispering, the way she had said it in the museum, so that I even said it out loud, the nurse and Jeanpierre thinking I referred to the baby.
—That's us, I said: That's us.

Before I stopped, out of breath. So that he did not hear the exact words. How I had gone on, repeating what she had said that day as she pointed with her free hand to all the smaller and smaller babies with their smaller and smaller heads.
—Us, giving birth to each other, growing each other, she said: But we'll always be attached. Always.

And maybe too I didn't say it because somehow there in that birth of my third and last child, in the birth of my second son as I had watched that reproduction she had sent, I knew that I had also finally birthed her, birthed her somehow free of me.

While I saw her face in the face of my son when he was put on my belly and I breathed:
—She's beautiful Jeanpierre she's so beautiful, and Jeanpierre smiled into my eyes that alternately saw him and saw veins, his veins the veins on my retina the placenta's veins, there is no way of knowing as the nurse said:
—She's starting to go. It's the Demerol. While she shrugged at Jeanpierre: She'll find out which it is when she comes around.

Then she said something about how she hated induction with pills, if things started happening too fast you couldn't control them the way you might with a drip, while I tried to smile at her and make some intelligent comment only I saw Laura instead. And I would still swear it was just the way she must have been, sitting in her New York studio awaiting news of the birth, concentrating on my labour just as I was, leaning over her own Tchelichew reproduction, but one cut and pasted back together like all her catastrophes, so finally separate from me, that I could not help crying.

Crying and crying as I felt my son's wet little head, in what seemed an excess of exhaustion, of exhaustion and pride.

Which it was. For me for him for her for us. Because I was sure that I had birthed Laura into a brilliant future, even more brilliant than the days she was experiencing, the way you can think anything is possible at the moment of giving birth. So that I was sure all that hard parting like all that hard labour, was also for something positive, so that she could make the journey she had to make. And that it could never be toward that place. Where there were only goldfish, or chambered nautili, swimming.

I hadn't fled just to save me, but so that she could have it all, everything she had ever wanted. And it was good, so good, as good as my son, as my son and daughter before him, sucking at my breast; so good all that time of nurturance that had helped to birth her. To birth Laura Mack. And her new world.

And it was only later that I realized I had never been her mother, that mother my mother through Anaïs Nin has always referred to as the mother of the artist, or even her co-mother, the way we had said, giving birth to each other, but just the womb. Which has come in my mind to resemble over the years more and more the dried placenta, its veins standing out as brilliantly as the ones in that painting, except that there is no tree rooted in the earth, and no small and large bright coloured babies waiting to burst out into our new world. Because the truth is I never had become Alice B. Toklas to her Gertrude Stein the way my mother suggested, all that time I had only been Avila, to her Santa Teresa. All I had become was her convent. Her bloody, her oozing, her amniotic convent. Inside whose placental walls she could discover the mysteries.

But by the time I figured that out Mother would have given just about anything to have me still with Laura, to have me call myself Alice B. Anything (Alma Be Anything): except the suburban housewife that I was.

Yet for all I tried to convince myself that she had made it, free and clear with no encumbrances, that she was happy and wonderful and brilliant and exactly where she wanted, even congratulating myself for my part in birthing her as I changed that last round of diapers or ground up baby food, still I can't say that the phone call surprised me.

With my mother's voice echoing through the long distance echo, an echo within an echo, hollow and disembodied, as she spoke her four words. Each one as if it were a sentence. Or a chapter from a book we were both reading. Or a blow, each word a different blunt instrument. A sentence of a different kind. That had travelled all the way into orbit and back just to adjust its aim. So straight and so sure, deep into my brain.
—They. Hospitalized. Laura. Tonight.

She said. And I knew, just as I had always feared, that the only thing I had birthed Laura clear of was her last remaining attachment to the earth.

And though I held the phone away from my body, as if it were a container filled with poison gas, about to open or explode, still I didn't scream or even sob, but just stood numb, as if the terrible contents being gathered from space into that container had already deadened my nerves, exploding me out of myself toward the edges of the room. From where I looked back stupefied on that black hole that was the black receiver that I was still trying to hold away from the centre of myself, as if the slivered words like the sharp metal of an anti-personnel bomb had not already penetrated as deep as they could to sever some interior emotional artery inside my brain, red and swollen leaking out feeling in pulsating bursts as I tried to make unhappen what I already knew had happened, what I already felt I had known forever had happened, my mother didn't have to say another word for me to know it wasn't a broken leg or a broken neck or anything broken at all except herself, that had hospitalized Laura.

As my mother went on to say, trying to be terribly clinical, not nervous breakdown, 'n.b.', as everybody says these days, something that just anyone could have, they even have them at Jeanpierre's office and blame them on stress, with a certain degree of pride. She said instead:
—Psychotic episode.

What the doctors must have told her. Which she passed on to me. Not so much to make Laura sicker, I don't think, as just to continue to make her different, to have her contract the kind of thing only geniuses have. Or that maybe only geniuses have any hope of recovering from.

While my sense of *déjà vu* continued to grow, I don't know if this has ever happened to you, Thorne, it's like a pregnancy of the mind, things grow and grow inside you until they are born in pain and contractions and nausea and occasional triumph, a flooding wonder that is then pushed out, where with a last: Ohhhh, it is obvious that you knew all along what they were going to be, like with you and me, I knew who you would be from the first time our eyes met and you put your hand on me to adjust the position I was in, and we smiled. And something bloomed.

Only that time it was more like a bomb blooming, the way pilots say bombs bloom, the sudden red flower like a rupture. Except that it wasn't below where you could see it but inside, rising red into the eyes, boom boom boom out into the extremities again and again, stiffening my body and then letting it go, mobilizing it to action then stopping it dead, mid-gesture or mid-sentence, with the deep knowledge that I had travelled this road before: that I had been travelling it a long time.

I would travel it again.

On the train that had brought Jeanpierre and me north when I left, that moves from underground into the old neighbourhoods out across a bridge into the Bronx, moving alongside Manhattan until it ends in Inglewood Park, a view of the city you never otherwise see, complex bridges and overpasses and concrete pylons, that always reminds me of the first postnuclear holocaust story I ever experienced, read aloud to me in Junior High, a strange and terrible vision of a primitive man rediscovering this concrete and asphalt place. That even holding Jeanpierre's hand caused a moment of terror before the city was through and the train was moving peacefully along the river, the intense suburban development somewhere up a hill or behind trees on the train's right, while out the left window we stared from, high I think on someone's dope, the world seemed suddenly idyllic, palisades and swans and wide blue river vistas with only the slightest bit of mist, an occasional turn-of-the-century factory building all complex stone and wrought iron, and the weirdest thing, on one island a facsimile castle, that we giggled at as we kissed. Fucking our way north together in that small roomette.

Only it was back into New York this time. And alone. More time than I had had alone in years, since Jason's birth, in fact. Days across flat prairie and bush and the startling outcroppings of the shield; then on to smaller farms and thinner bush and a greater variety of trees and bungalows and suburban houses; with all that time, all that landscape, dedicated to thinking about a New York I had visited only the once. When Jeanpierre and I were still in Quebec and we finally consented to come down for Christmas, my mother begging on the phone, and even bringing Laura over to her place to beg too: It will be wonderful Alma, you can see my new work, our new studio, I'm having an opening she would say, while my mother would just mention the City at Christmas while I would reply that Montreal was just as nice, though it did sound like fun, I'd always loved New York during the holidays, and besides I would see the ocean and I was mature and I was sure I could take it and it would be great, the one time I ever came into the city by thruway, surprised and almost terrified by how far out the city starts, as if the slow loss of the green edges of streets was my own entrance into some sort of futuristic technological nightmare, I was pregnant and it was the only time the city had that effect on me, the shimmering glass buildings pushing down so that I was afraid all the time, even if the first thing we'd done was to pass through them on the way out to Coney Island so that I could feel the ocean salt sting my face.

I was almost waiting for the same thing to happen with you when we came in, only it is so different when you fly, you get a distance that makes it almost exemplary, a lesson in the demographic patterns of late twentieth century North America, first the big suburban, almost country, houses with their huge dark green treed estates around them, the houses slowly taking on more of the area of the land they occupy, and looking larger because the plane is closer to the ground, the house/land ratio moving toward one and then less than one as you get into the smaller outlying bungalows, then disappearing to have the empty lots near the bay occupied by old cars, in the same proportion to their land as the houses, and kind of glowing with that light typical of ocean mist, kind of beautiful really, all thick blue to orange, because it was early, we'd been on the cheapest emptiest all night flight, leaving Calgary at one and Toronto shortly after sunrise, so that we'd giggled at it, all those changes in proportion as we went out

over the water to come in for our landing, with everything so fresh that I wasn't terrified at all. Which meant I squeezed your hand in thanks, just as I had Jeanpierre's to relieve the tension. Looking up at a building and whispering:
—Let's get out of here.
  While he replied:
—But we haven't arrived.

We went out to Coney Island right after that and I tried to gulp in the ocean air, only I couldn't get rid of my nausea, and didn't, not the whole trip. I was just sick sick sick, the way I hadn't been with Jason, and wasn't again with René, and I never got to Laura's opening, just to the gallery long enough to find the bathroom and puke and puke, and to watch them move the works in through the back door and to puke some more, while Sandro looked sardonic and Jeanpierre awkward, as Laura and I tried to convince ourselves we were still blood sisters and that we communicated telepathically, even going over dates to be sure.

  Only when the first early arrival arrived and Laura took me up to her, and did her: This is Aaalma number, the first syllable of my name all stretched out, and I knew that she'd do it again. Do it again and again, all evening in fact, more than puke I just had to run: Oh, I'm sorry I said, just as the woman started to look me over and offer her hand, and I ran to the john, and came out to demand that Jeanpierre take me back to Mother's right away. Even if he was doing his working class hero number on Sandro, and bringing it off beautifully, something that surprised me immensely considering how resolutely upwardly mobile he is. I suppose it was the only way around Sandro's pretended sophistication and cutting curiosity, that speaking the Montreal *joual* he'd learned the summer he came down to New York and met me, refusing the more correct French he'd learned in school or the lingo of his own working class Sudbury family. It was just a rabbit I'd never seen him pull out of the hat before. So that I was quite proud of his resourcefulness, I almost thought I should get him a black leather jacket to match Laura's, amazed that he could tough it out like that. The way he did with my mother too. Since he got no protection from me, with my infinite though discontinuous trips to the can.

While that trip back alone I was hardly present in the moment at all, the way I was with you, or even with Jeanpierre and the child in my body, although I did feel pregnant again, and sick too, with a future I did not want to birth as the train started to pass through industrial neighbourhoods and emptied tenements until finally even the green weeds at the edges of the railway ties were lost as the train crossed into Manhattan to elevate and run along Park Avenue.

In that section where it doesn't have a park, only a name and the metal scaffolding that allows the train to look into the windows of East or Spanish (read Puerto Rican) Harlem. Running by buildings always the same and the same and the same, clackety clack, the same and the same, only the figures by the windows different each time, looking out or looking down, seated or standing, women in housecoats men in tee-shirts with cans of beer in their hands, like Marlon Brando in *A Streetcar Named Desire*, passing by and passing by, until they were cut-outs like the ones Laura had pasted onto canvas in her student days, cardboard backed photographs each one with its edge painted, so that each figure I looked upon shimmered back at me from inside its bright pink or orange or blue everchanging outline, part now, it seemed, along with my far larger reflection, of that last version of her dream, them and me all pasted onto those old tenement windows, so that I kept looking, looking. Looking for precisely that one exact window, where moon and sun past and present and future could be located, thinking that if I could find it, if I could recover it, from where it circulated endlessly on the subway, circulated endlessly by the side of the train, I could yet recover something, change something, of what had happened or what had been, as my reflected hand touched the glass, as if to reach for the moon past the sunlit orange brick, and the dull interiors, only to always find walls, cracked or gleaming, light or dark, wallpapered living room or grease stained kitchen, with knickknacks or altars or magazine photos, or moving lines of cockroaches, or the fridge or the couch or the statue of Jesus or the Virgin Mary.

Because a time machine effect had started long before, it always does, it did with you, it did with Jeanpierre, the future moving into the past along with the train the plane the car, toward some dreadful or beautiful moment of conception that I seem neither able to change nor prevent, the way I knew even with you that it was there and that its name was Laura, Laura, Laura, Laura, waiting for the moment of the appearance of the conception of the concept of Laura. That could now be a new hysteresis of Laura, a new discontinuity, it's always there, that desire for the moment that can fold back on itself differently to unmake or remake the meaning of Laura Laura Laura Laura, clackety clack Laura Laura Laura Laura the sound of the wheels against the track, Laura Laura Laura Laura as the past and future rushed to meet until I was convinced that I would meet the Laura of so many years before, as I moved from timeless and idyllic river front to a dingier and older city.

Only the heaviness of my body had already told me that it was not that famous science fiction opportunity to skew it all, to go back into the past to make one small move that might change it, the aliens might have given me the gift of time travel, but not the ability to do it all over, I had only been invited to watch, to let it go by, the past running before my eyes just like the windows, just like a movie on an airplane, the roaring of the jets, the clackety clack of the drive wheels, the film before the projector light the videotape moving over the head, all of it inexorably to the same destination, the same conclusion. Events inevitably unresolved and just as inevitably terminated in a world in which I did not participate, in which no one any longer participated, but whose results, whose catastrophes we might still map as the points etched themselves onto the present.

With my emotions strangely orchestrated, apart from me the way they were in the moment that I hugged her the night I gave you the skirt, or even in the plane looking down, the way travel suspends you, so that I often feel myself to be the person I would see from time to time tenuously superimposed on the scenery by the particular refraction of the moment, a transparent Alma with trees in her, or clouds or fields or sun or moon or neon signs or bricks or even a second face, dull or shouting from a billboard, glamorous or housewifely, interchangeable persons interchangeable words interchangeable roles, my own emotions as muffled, as far away as the landscape.

Worse than usual this time because I could watch the orchestration, the slowing down the speeding up the modulations in the piece, the series of events taking place as if I were part of a work of art, which I suppose I was in a way. At that moment her most recent work, the performance piece of the best friend brought home at last, a work not so much radical as traditional, even classical, properly proportioned and segmented, with the sense of rhythm and interval her visual work had always had. From the first soft weeping and Jeanpierre's coming over and taking the phone from my hand and getting the details.
—I guess it's time to go back again, he said, sighing.

To the making of arrangements and his constant coming to comfort me, trying to figure out if it would be all right if I would be all right as he rubbed my hair and told me all the planes were full, an air strike or what I don't remember. Then a brief interval of sleep or dream a fall into jumbled images, a reassembling of the minimal coherence of the world. Then the sequences in which I board the train, hugging Jeanpierre and the children goodbye as if I were leaving for a war, looking at them with the kind of longing that knows nothing will be the same again. Then watching the outside from the isolation of my roomette, in an alternation between weeping and silent tears, spaced with occasional visits to the still existent dining car or observation deck. Though mostly I stayed away from the other passengers so that I could savour it all, sucking on the slow tragedy of my mourning, noting my feelings and how the glass separated me from my feelings, yet let them occur. Tears and the shadows of trees tears and the shadows of buildings tears and people moving inside windows tears and people leaning out to shout to each other above the rattling of the train. Tears and the train going down, the tunnel mouth gaping.

We sank down under Park Avenue. There was just one glimpse of the neat bushes behind their little fences, so pretty above us, the ones we would travel below as the sound of the train was muffled for the rich, to leave them with only the vibrations working their way up from underground. Without doubt the hum of security, like the refrigerator for so many of us, it was that train that had made so many of them rich, the grandparents of the rich girls with whom Laura and I had gone to school, I even realized in the dark that we were passing under the old school as we rumbled and rattled and smoked, and my reflection took on substance against the dark of the background, only grey pillars and tail tracks occasionally visible, then in the dark and the shadows one small deserted station where for a moment I thought I could see her waiting for the train her design project hanging in the bag from her hand, and I knew where I was.

Back in New York. Not home, but here, this place a place I could feel, a reality that fit me: that I could feel this place at last.

As the light and heat of that spring moving into summer seemed to echo and refract and become the same as the summer moving into fall of the time I left, reality continuing to fold in on itself now faster and faster, tighter and tighter, now at last, twisted to become one of her works, her catastrophes. Discontinuous. With only the big stitches of memory to sew it back together, to shape this elliptic or parabolic or swallowtail or cusp, it would be impossible to know which with so many realities tumbling over each other, or even if the mathematical shape of this moment had reached beyond an elementary catastrophe to some yet undefined complexity. Only it was not as if I had encountered the hysteresis, that unknown point of generation, but became instead the place of discontinuation, my point leaving the knotted surface of its Thomian plane to float, discontinued, in a place beyond cause and effect or even time, where all events took place at once together and thundering, multiplying each other until I put my hands over my ears, and closed my eyes tight: reality at last, too loud too loud, too bright too bright.

This reality from which Laura

had been excised. A white grub dug up from the dirt of the city and placed under glass high in her hospital room. Its fierce dark mandibulae still opening and closing as it fought for some sign of familiar substance in its bright new world. The way her eyes did against the whiteness of her skin and robe. Still burning fierce, startling, almost terrifying against her helplessness. The billowing sheets with their wrinkles so like the swollen white body of the grub, incapable of any action but digestion and waiting.

While I stood there looking at her, comparing that emaciated body with my memories of our time together and all the photographs she or my mother had sent, of openings and performances and vacations by the sea and parties late at night, then of the other fewer memories I had of her from that week when she had patted my already swollen body. And I was horrified, and put my hand to my mouth thinking what a long time it had been.

As she smiled and took my hand, the same gesture she had always had but more desperate somehow, the way she looked around before she spoke. Not of warriors and secret agents and Amazons, but of aliens who communicated with her through the radio and the records on the stereo, searing secret messages into their grooves, codes onto her magnetic tape, so that if I wanted to, she would let me hear them too, yes, she really wanted me to hear them too, as soon as she got out she would help me to hear them too.

And I could go with her and be her lieutenant the way I had always been and we could go together to do the work assigned her. To walk the streets of SoHo and the docks in the light of dawn and the Brooklyn Bridge at sunset to identify those who were still left, the very few who had not yet been made into robots.

It all seemed so trite and so awful, so absolutely grade 'B'. I don't know whether science fiction or horror. Except that it wouldn't have had enough depth to make even a bad psychological thriller, not the way she talked right then. Not even when I tried to add in, to flesh it out, memories of all we had shared.

In our fantasies under the forsythia so recently in bloom, or at the ocean, the Hamptons or Coney Island, or even what I had witnessed that last summer among the bedbugs, all of it so full of loving and longing and wanting the world and herself and me and Sandro to be other. All of it gone. What I had seen, what all the critics saw, what the artworld thirsted for as she worked out that hungry vision of hers piece by piece, its catastrophes and near catastrophes and triumphs, visible even in the photographs, the postcards, of the work she sent me, but which was absent now. What I couldn't find any trace of as I searched and searched her face, listened to her voice.

Not the way it had been, but as you heard it, high somehow and whiny. So that for a moment I thought that maybe it was she who was the robot, a cheap repetitive mechanism repeating and repeating from inside the shell of her body the dialogue of a very bad script.

And then as I watched her I was reminded of a grub again, its clacking mandibles, a white hemlock grub, the kind they say you can survive on in the bush in winter, that Jeanpierre will eat, I think it must be some kind of macho ritual derived from a government survival manual, not quite initiation but close to it, of the, Hey man, I can take anything variety. Always done with a bottle of beer in the other hand, as he picks the grub up by the mandibles with a wide demonstrative gesture, and bites off the body, while I look away, examining the beautiful sculpted patterns the creatures have made in the central cores of the trees they have gnawed their way through, pulling that enormous body behind them with their six tiny legs, not harming the flow of sap but weakening the tree until it falls in a storm. While I found myself asking if that's what she had done, hungry as she had always been, ravenous to get it all.

If perhaps in my absence she hadn't gnawed her way through all the world, consuming and consuming, her eyes devouring the white bag behind her swelling, as down went the apartment and the studio and her parents' place and SoHo and West Egg and East Hampton and 57th Street and the Gods on Olympus and the Hudson River and the Museum of Modern Art and the Atlantic Ocean cetaceans crustaceans cephalopods and nautili until she reached her own mind: digesting everything until the tree of life was blown over in the next cosmic breeze and her world of nourishment was gone and now only the aliens were left.

The aliens and me. Alone in that sterile room.

Or maybe I was one of them. Like the bumper stickers say (what I certainly felt): JUST VISITING THIS PLANET.

Until the nurse came in and said she needed rest.
—Mrs. Yurasic should have her rest now, she said, using Sandro's last name, not Laura's own. An act of protection or possession I didn't know, but it was obviously the name she'd been signed in under. Laura had made a joke of it as I stood by her bed staring, as a way to invite me to sit down, imitating the nurse who had looked into the room so chirpily bright when she said:
—Friend to see you, Mrs. Yurasic? How very nice.

While Laura turned toward me where I still stood staring.
—That's what they all say, she said in a whisper: Mrs. Yurasic, Mrs. Yur-a-sic, a sick sick woman, yr a sick woman Mrs. Yurasic, a sick sick woman, and then she laughed.

And even if the laugh went up too high, still it was her. It was her humour, and I knew the hemlock grub in the bed was my friend. Even if the next thing she said was about alien spacecraft and the secret messages she could read, even over the Muzak in the common room they used to try to jam the signals, it didn't matter that they didn't want her to understand, or that they fed her the pills. Even if she was a sick sick woman: still she knew.

I obeyed
the nurse when she told me to leave. When she told Laura to get her rest. And I took mine, sitting shaking in a small deli, until I came back for the evening visit. And found her dull, even her eyes muted, the grub dead, the pupils wide and dark like the sun in eclipse.

And all her words were apologies.
—I'm sorry about earlier really sorry, I guess I really am Mrs. You're-a-sick, there's no question about that, one sick sick lady, huh? she would say and giggle, her mouth covered by a hand, her eyes shaded, in her favourite gesture to mean: Oh how stupid of me what have I done, that she had developed in high school. The one that pulled the

pinkie of her right hand down as far as her left nostril, her left hand covering the mouth and chin.

While I would try to catch her eyes, the way I had always done, cajoling her into letting me see them, into letting herself look at me, with the way I walked around the bed and bent my head sideways to catch a glimpse, as I looked and looked for that spark that fire that was her, that had still been there earlier, however reduced, and found no spark at all, only the wrinkled sheets. With my mind asking itself over and over: How did they do it? How? How did they break her? So completely break her.

What had it been to finally push her over the edge. The cosmic wind that took down the tree. What was it? Not that had pushed her into insanity, but into this terrible disloyalty to her madness, to her voices and her vision: this obscenely calm acquiescence.

Until I even started to wish that she would tell me once more of the alien spacecraft, how the codes they broadcast to her by FM radio were formed; or repeat the part about how they wouldn't get it out of her, no more than her name rank and cereal boxtop, she would never be responsible for doing anything to hamper the development of the Greater Galactic Conspiracy for the Betterment of Sentient Life, or GGC for short.

Because no matter how trite her psychotic episode in the soap opera of life, still it had to be better than this giggling apology for normalcy, like a commercial for psycho-tranquillizers:

Nothing Ends Aliens like Thorazine, The *Real* Ghost Buster. Try it. And compare the results.

I apologized then too, because I couldn't stay, even if I'd planned to. – I'msorryIcouldn'tgetheresoonerI'msorryIhavetoleavenowIhavetocall-homeoneofthekidsissick, all run together like that, before I left quickly, smiling my way past the nurses as my mind cursed everyone who hadn't warned me.

–Anything is better than this, anything at all, I repeated out loud. Any thing, any place, any place at all. Better than this, better than this, BETTER THAN THIS. A goldfish bowl in your head better than this. In a litany to go with the clenching and unclenching of my fists all the way down the hospital corridors onto the elevators and out onto the streets where I could let go. And the tears would flow, where nobody would look at me and I wouldn't look at anybody. And I could remember. Who she had been. And how I had loved her.

I walked along one of those quiet Village
streets outside St. Vincent's, West 12th Street or maybe West 11th, on the edge of the tourist area, all full of brownstones and quiet and passersby hurrying from the subway to the action. Who walk almost at a run past the house where years ago there had been that famous fire, the house the Weatherpeople blew up the winter Laura met Sandro, at least I think it was then, not the year before, or the year after. I remember being there, I'm sure I was, I didn't just see it in the papers, and I don't think it was high school, that new and unfamiliar kind of tourism.

Because there'd been the atmosphere too. It wasn't all personal that terrible frenzy that dominated my last year in New York. It wasn't all Lilac, or even Sandro, that made the future seem a dark hole (in the ground or the universe, who knows) into which we alternately danced our way and were driven moaning. Toward what seemed then an inevitable apocalypse worthy of making anyone dream of alien spaceships. Who might attempt a planetary rescue, if the robots hadn't already taken over.

Or at the very least to make anyone indulge in that radical chic so common among the students that wound up at our apartment. The ones who bragged about meeting one or another of the Weatherpeople and went around the midtown area looking at the buildings. Where they worked summers or part-time or had worked once or their parents still did, lifting their arms up from their waists and splitting their hands apart and saying:

—BOOM, what about that one, why don't they get that one, it would be easy enough to get that one.

While Lilac, it's hard to tell why, whether it was something she did for Sandro, her first adventure into theatre/performance, or the precursor to her astronomy text, bought herself a Vietnamese dictionary. And would stand at the window for their benefit, or even out on the fire escape as if declaiming to the multitudes instead of the humid twilight, trying out words. Mostly names as far as I could tell, Ngoc or Phan or Trinh or Nguyen, making them very long, and probably terribly mispronounced: Neeeegoooooc Puuhaaaaan Treeennhuh Neeeegyewennnnnn, turning back to tell us it was there, she was sure it was there, if only she could find it. Not yet the word, the design that would call the ship, but the sound, the combination, the one that would bring it all down.
—It will. It will.

The word to make the revolution, the one, the exact word. She was sure it was there. While we all laughed. Howling and cackling until she did too, once she'd recovered her breath, falling onto the bed among the bedbugs. While a shiver once more ran up my arm goose flesh broke out all over my body.

It didn't matter whether I was in the living room laughing with them, or in my own room trying to sleep. It was then I too would pray for rescue.

The way
I did as I walked. For our rescue, her rescue, everybody's rescue. For that place that was better than this. Though, of course, the atmosphere of horror, at least the old horror, was gone as I walked past that house, I couldn't feel my way back to then, I still can't. I don't know if anybody can, even the statements of the Weatherpeople as they find their way above ground seem so mild or even bewildered: We know how we reasoned, the situation in retrospect seems as desperate as ever, but we still don't know why we talked like that, they say.

So that maybe it would be better if you were here, standing across the bedroom and we could do it as part of those drama therapy exercises you do, trying to get inside it, the feel of it, the late sixties to mid-seventies, Canada the United States the world, events resolved or unresolved blooming like bombs, parading their catastrophic discontinuities, the way they still do, and did then again as I walked down that street. Except that the only catastrophe that I had left, the only ghost that walked with me as I walked by that house, was the one I had brought with me from the hospital, the ghost of Laura past, something that I could not take beyond the personal. For all that she was brought forward from that era too, the folds in my time would not include anything beyond her, I could not feel history trailing behind her like the tail of a comet, as the events like points continued to drop from one topographical surface onto another, and there was no way I could find the womb-space, the hysteresis that had formed them, that had pushed her to where she was. There was just Laura, Alma and Laura, gastropods, cephalopods, bivalves and Laura; and the forsythia in the little front yards, where I had dropped onto this new plane, just past their bloom.

Into that time that had already changed, not the way any of us had wanted or dreamed or even imagined with terror, but still a lot by then, Nixon had long since quit and Saigon had fallen and the boys were home or with us in Canada, it must have been the Carter years of tranquilizing the liberal malaise, or maybe even the early Reagan years of charming the conservative complacency, when Rambo refought the war and won. When nothing but the personal could possibly seem on the edge of horror or chaos or mutation. With the large lump sum of humanity, me you Sandro all of us, continuing to eat and sleep its way into the future, glorious and full, locked in the hemlock we continued to carve out, pushed forward by our insatiable alienated hunger, nothing perturbing the smooth surface of our catastrophe, the folds the cliffs the edges the involutions and convolutions, all invisible from where we crawled. Even as we formed them ourselves, with our sharp ever-moving teeth.

Resilience was all. And so lovely besides. With the calm and wonderful dense summer evening with its leftover light leaving the sky still blue, while the orange street lights did not let the leaves darken to grey but left them in green, a greener green, like the detergents that get your clothes a whiter white, in a perfect synthetic Magritte, or maybe a biodegradable one. While the smells that always seem to intensify just after the sun sets, and with emotional difficulty too, did stop time, that personal time anyway, to form a kind of cocoon of permanence, like the circular myth time they say doesn't end.

Even if it's only later that you remember those moments, like an anthropologist returning to linear time to record a ritual. As you say:
–Ah, yes, dogshit, leaves and dogshit, I remember leaves and dogshit, the smell of springtime in New York resonating with the year Laura finally went crazy.

The traditional tranquillizing smell of the better neighbourhoods where you can always meet people walking their dogs. Though maybe it's gotten a bit better now with pooperscooper laws, I certainly don't remember the smell from when we were there, though it's true that was later in the season. So maybe it's gone from our lives forever that smell of peace, of organic elegance. Almost beautiful. To make me shrug my shoulders up high and down to relax them, and slow my pace, and breathe it in, and try to be one of them. Tentatively holding out my hand as if pooch were on the end of my leash, while I tried to find it, that same dogshit on the air upper middle class tranquility.

I almost made it.

Almost. Until I

turned down 6th Avenue. And all irony and elegance and even thoughtfulness was ripped away. By a sudden mob of people around the hot dog stands and the head shops and the imported clothes boutiques, everyone come to see the real New York or a part of New York that might seem real, each one anxious and energetic and on the lookout, to get something out of it, whatever it was, even the dopers who were stoned to the eyeballs trying to find it, NOW, NOW, this had to be just one terrific trip, more the Coney Island than the Village of my childhood: only more avid.

So that it wasn't my last summer or that crack-up summer or the first summer after I met Lilac or any other summer in particular, not even the summer that it was, not nostalgia or recollection or memories of childhood or lilacs or Vietnamese dictionaries or aliens but just the mandibles clacking open and shut the saliva dripping the tentacles pushing food into every species of mouth or digestive opening I had ever imagined the caterpillar moving over the leaf gobbling green in front and shitting out green behind. A multicoloured eat and be eaten as everyone jostled and leapt and crept and crawled over the surface of experience fighting not just for a little room on the surface of the planet a particular cell in the hive of human culture but trying to get the right one the perfect one the one you were supposed to have the one that would make everything different the one that would make life meaningful or bearable, THE EXPERIENCE, THE EXPERIENCE, THE

EXPERIENCE, the one that always came in capital letters, or maybe it was bright neon colours flashing on and off to guarantee each taker it was his or her turn at the action, to get fame or fortune or laid or stoned or just an eyeful. Of others about to get laid or stoned the drag queens screaming falsetto obscenities at each other outside one or another gay bar the bar dykes in their black leather studded jackets necking on the corners altogether tongue-in-cheek or tongues in one another's cheeks just to shock the tourists in their buses as you could imagine the tour guide saying: And ladies and gentlemen, very special for you tonight a rare Village bird, there right on the corner...

With all that energy expended just to be able to say it was worth it. That making money Monday to Friday in crowded cubicles or quitting your job to do this full-time was worth it. Like taking pictures home or even a tee-shirt saying my husband wife partner girlfriend boyfriend spouse son daughter second cousin significant other did New York/ Greenwich Village/SoHo and all I got was this lousy tee-shirt: taking something home to be the envy of their friends, even at the end of the subway line.

And all of them in different colours and all of them in a hurry, even the slow slow slow ones, palsied or stoned or drunk or disabled, in some sort of psychological rush to GET THERE. While I just walked. And tried to get nowhere at all. Walking and crying with no idea where I was going until I mutated. A science fiction shape changer who left the crowd to become part of the scenery.

Like an Indian boutique or an ice cream parlour, a painted punker or an elderly beatnik or a baglady or a dyke on a Harley, part of what you come to New York to see as the tears just streamed down my face and I kind of staggered or lurched from side to side. With movements whose efficacy in keeping people away I'd never comprehended in all the years I'd lived in the city.

While I could hear them whispering behind me, saying things as they nudged each other, I'm sure they nudged each other, until: Oh wow, the perverse thought crossed my mind, I have to admit it crossed my mind: I've made it too, I said to myself: Just like Laura. I'm a performance artist.

Because I was suddenly aware that they must see it that way, the great 'they' I was no longer a part of. Not a theatre of confrontation or even participation but the continuation of the Great Theatre of Alienation, a.k.a. the Theatre of Life. In which I was set apart, absolutely separated, and not by the edge of the stage, of the theatre lights, but by my emotion.

My lack of control made me part of the spectacle of New York as I performed for them the drama of my tears. Which they obediently consumed. While I could hear them saying, a kind of applause for the value of my act, Look, look, a crazy person, completely fried, I wonder what's wrong, what she's taken, that one's over the edge, you haven't really been to New York until you see one like that, yesterday I saw a black man singing lullabies to a white doll the day before a woman dressed in every style since 1912 each one on top of the other: this city is full of 'em.

I'm sure not one among the onlookers imagined that I had come straight from the psychiatric ward at St. Vincent's. Or that what I mourned was the mind of a friend. Because not one of them would catch my eye. Or ask me a question.

What frightened me so much we might be doing too when we came. That in my worst moments I could think I brought you to hide behind so that I too could smirk and giggle and laugh at pain and do New York. So that maybe even as a part of me examined the minute interstices of her clothes as we hugged and another thought of how best to orchestrate the gesture, there was yet another cynical piece looking on thinking it was making your New York experience for you, giving you your crazy lady. A crazy lady for Thorne, I might even have thought, and even if it wasn't true, even though I knew it wasn't true, the fear would return icy in my gut: that night's fear, that last summer's fear, the fear that lasted that whole return trip: that I was just another consumable, ready to be consumed.

And it doesn't matter how willingly you met my gaze, how tenderly you held me, those moments when the fear came on, you would frighten me. And maybe that's why I couldn't tell you this story. Really tell you about her, about Laura.

And that night for the first time I remember I came to hate the street, being on the street, the life of the street, and passionately cursed it. Until I would have loved to be rich, with sherpas or coolies or slaves or servants of any stripe that could be called upon, by the kind that is always called a Somebody: whose greater claim upon the world even the street would recognize. Who could command all its demons into silence. Or at the very least a cab.

Which is why it suddenly seemed so logical, so complete and so perfect how they had gotten her, not discontinuous or catastrophic at all, but just like any calculated curve, perfectly definable in just one formula, or mechanically linked and perfectly articulated, joint by joint piece by piece, one step following another in a breakdown, or perhaps a breakout, that could just about be diagrammed, a perfect story come perfect circle, three hundred and sixty degrees to its ending, so that you might even ask yourself if you stood with me in the street, how there could have been any other as the passersby looked at you without ever changing expression or meeting your eye.

  I even started to grin, a terrible perverse grin, that must have made me look crazier still. Especially as the emotion built up in me, a red to yellow pain moving out from my organs in small explosions one after another, orgasmic explosions like the ones Jeanpierre sets in the earth: making my breathing come quicker and quicker like in labour.

Following a method no classes had ever taught me anything of, and previous experience very little, obeying the rule I had just discovered for mourning breathing: blow it off to decrease the pain in abdomen and chest, uhh uhh uhh, blow blow blow. But through the nose so that no one is given the pleasure of grooving on your moans, I would not give that much to the onlookers, gathered in groups now, I think they were, to look at me, though perhaps it was street musicians.

Because the crescendo of my breathing rose until I could hear music, and not just someone's ghetto blaster, that was one of the new developments since I'd left, the sound emanating from one point, but more like the music of the spheres, something I could feel surrounding me echoing in and swelling my head, inside and outside at once, close and very far away, disembodied, like the whirring motors of an alien space ship I could almost feel descending just as I could feel her walking down these same streets as the same onlookers gathered in groups to look at her.

It's exactly what they must have done for her last performance. When she had done what the group had asked her to do, what they had all planned together, out of the studio and into the street again, only it wasn't just a performance this time where she would do something while others looked on. It was her attempt to make contact with those who looked on, to find out who they were and why as all those artworld people followed at a distance in solemn groups and said nothing. Just took in and noted down and documented, as Laura went from person to person, innocent or compromised bystander, whoever was there, alone or in couples or in groups, families and friends and tour groups who she stopped, even the children: to look at each one. Deeply into the eyes. Deeper and deeper. And on and on. Like any dimestore hypnotist or street corner crazy person. The kind that make parents grab their kids' hands and hurry them by.

While she would start to say:
—Hello, in a very soft voice, opening her hands: What is it that you want, can you specify exactly what you want?

Her words overwhelmed me as I walked, the story my mother had told me. As the tears streamed down my face, and I would not look at any of the onlookers, I had no questions. I didn't want to know what they wanted, I didn't want to know anything at all about them as I obeyed the intake of breath, the one that pulls the back of the neck into the sky, ah, ah, ah, ah, ah, the chest rising with the breath I could neither stop nor control, the diaphragm up and out, ah ah ah ah ah, then moaned or whistled between the teeth like the urge to push, PUSH NOW PUSH, push it all out now, PUSH, the body urging as the mind says no not now: stop now.

Hold on now, blow it off now, don't stop breathing to push now, as I walked into the park and grabbed a tree ah ah ah ah ah the way I had Jeanpierre during transition breathing, relieved at the solidity of him the way he had stood as if rooted his coarse tweed jacket rough like the bark of the tree, ah ah ah ah ah, here where I could do it where no one would stop me from doing my body's bidding, like when you're finally allowed to grab the handgrips in front of the stirrups on an old style delivery table and rise up off the bed ah ah ah ahunh and stop breathing to push, PUSH, that's good now, PUSH, my nails pressed into the sooty bark.

Until pushing into that tree I started to talk to that tree ah ah ah ahunh, ah ah ah ahunh, as I watched her in my mind as she walked down that street. Her question spoken over and over.

With those people from the art community falling further and further behind, after all, it had lost its interest, this constant repetition. It had been different in the studio, different with the group around doing different things to distract them, and her just passing among the art-world audience over and over: What is it that you want, what is it that you want?

After all you could look at the rest of the show you didn't have to just look at her, or look at her only when she came up to you, it was an interesting treat those eyes boring into yours. Not boring at all that boring gaze that gaze boring into you, somebody even quipped, but the special eyes of Laura Mack, your own Laura Mack original and they didn't know, of course, how could they, that she practiced it hour after hour even when she was alone with Sandro or alone with the group: What is it that you want, what is it that you want?

It was different here, out on the street she didn't look at you she looked at them and they didn't care, they didn't even know her eyes were interesting and maybe they were frightened. But it wasn't enough to make an interesting experience, maybe an interesting document,

maybe, if she was lucky, but it was a bit much to do this hour after hour, without even a video camera, a tape recorder, something to catch the nuances of expression, on the faces or in the voices, it was a bit much to expect that everyone would write down their impressions and send them to her, an experiment in multiplicity she had called it, in polyvocality, as many voices as there are wants, even if it wasn't the ones she spoke to – she had long since run out of cards to hand them – who would write in. Which didn't matter really, it's just that it was getting late, they had to go, all of them had to go, she must understand that they had to go, she'd said it would just last until one o'clock when the lunchtime rush was off the streets, and they took her arm and they asked her:
–Laura, isn't it time to quit, Laura you said you would quit now, Laura.
And she had replied:
–Yes, yes, quit now, quit, yes, of course. Quit now.

Then she had gone back to it.
–What is it that you want, can you tell me exactly what it is that you want?

Until finally when they had shaken her shoulder or grabbed her hand and said: Isn't it time to quit now Laura, she had just turned to all of them with their aching feet in their high heels or their boots or their runners and she had said:
–What is it that you want? Can you specify exactly what you want?

And at first they had laughed, they thought it was a joke, that the joke was on them. But then they had shrugged, even if it was a joke, they were tired, and it didn't feel good to be part of a joke that was on them.
So they left. And I could see them leaving, drifting away, as she walked on.
–What is it that you want, can you tell me exactly what you want?

And it was somewhere in there that she entered the subway. That she started to walk along the platform and to speak to each person in turn, even to grab their arms and try to look into their eyes. And maybe what she had seen there was their fear and maybe it was just their incomprehension but what she heard back was:

—You are nothing, nothing. We want you to be nothing.

Which was maybe like the fetus that was birthing itself off the Tchelichew world tree into the void, no mother to pick it up and carry it; or like the larva that had finally eaten itself to the surface of the plant but could not remember, its genes affected by pesticides, how to cocoon and learn to fly, or even to crawl. Or maybe it was just like a runaway truck, a runaway spaceship, the motor going faster and faster as it encountered less and less resistance, until the truck would fly off the road or into a tree, the spaceship disintegrate.

But whatever it was, there must have been a moment, perhaps the exact same moment that the one particular person, the one who made the call had turned away, when she had chosen for that disintegration, and slipped unnoticed off the topographical plane into the discontinuous space of her catastrophe. And let, not her design assignment but herself, be whipped away into the long dark tunnel. While that person had said, to himself, and then to those on the other end of the line, not:
—This woman is interesting, what a good question, I've never thought about that, not for a while anyway, she must be an artist.

But:
—Hey, you meet all kinds, what a nutty thing to say, and in the subway too, this woman must be crazy.

And then he had said, to himself or maybe to the woman next to him, firmer now:
—This woman is crazy. We must do something, this woman is crazy. For her own good we must do something, we should call the cops this woman is crazy.

And it had echoed, all down the subway platform:
—The cops before she can hurt herself this woman is crazy.

And the cops had come and they had moved through the crowd to reach the platform's edge where she stood one step from falling with her own empty space about her, and she had turned to look deep into their permanently adolescent faces. And perhaps this time she had seen the void that awaited or perhaps it was only the blue of the uniform on another young man, but it was her turn to shiver before she went on with it, her eyes boring deep deep the words repeated, whispered this time, as if she already knew the nature of this authority:

—Tell me what you want, do you know what you want, tell me exactly what you want.

Until they had answered, this time she had been answered.

—To take you somewhere to see some people. Dear. They had said.

—To see someone who will understand your problem. Dear. What it is that you need.

And she had gone with them talking the while to meet the psychiatrist in his white hospital coat with the pen in his pocket. That he took out after he sat her down so that when she said:

—What is that you want? he had given it to her and asked her to make a drawing.

Then when she had made one, controlled and beautiful, as all her drawings were always controlled and beautiful he had looked at it and not even noted that he was in possession of a Laura Mack original.

He just said: Aha, as if he already knew. What it was that she needed if not what she wanted. And he had replaced the pen in his pocket and smiled as she smiled again:

—Is this what you want, exactly what is it that you want?

And he had said:

—To know what day it is, my dear, exactly the day's date, my dear, what is today's date, my dear, of what month and of what year.

Repeating the question until she smiled and shrugged and said:

—Is that what you want, is that really what you want?

While he went on to ask if she had wished to kill herself and what it meant not to cry over spilled milk, and she had answered:

—It means what you want, exactly what you want, what exactly do you want? and she had burst out laughing.

Then while she laughed and laughed and said:

—What you want exactly what you want, he had finally answered.

And he had said:

—I want you to relax, my dear, while we arrange for your room my dear and contact your family my dear.

And for you to never cry over spilled milk.

Never ever cry over spilled milk while she laughed and laughed until for a moment she was serious.

−Spilled blood, she said, spilled blood? Never cry over spilled blood?
And he had put his hand on her arm and said:
−Try to calm down my dear, we will give you something to calm you down my dear. That is exactly what we want.

And then the orderlies had come and they had taken her arms and she had looked at them and she had said:
−What is it that you want, can you tell me precisely what you want?
And they had said:
−To give you this needle my dear, you need this needle my dear. And when you have had this needle my dear, you will look around you my dear, and you will know precisely what we want.

They had given her a needle and a robe, a white white robe. And she had put on the robe the white white robe and she had laughed again a hollow hollow laugh and as soon as they left she had gotten down from the bed and she had spun around, and spun and spun.

With the robe billowing out around her, spinning like you spun in that skirt, spinning and spinning. Pure white and spinning. No dense blue no coloured ribbons no colour at all, except before her eyes. Where there was red and yellow and palest purple and green like leaves in newest bloom as all of it mixed together.

Together and together and together, all those colours coming together all of us coming together, the way she had always imagined us, until she could become us: she saw us she was us. All of us and what we wanted.

And ritual and theatre and performance and the Great Goddess and the alien spaceship and the Amazon Queen and the intergalactic agent and the child of the spring in her white gown ready to be wed to the corn king and all she had read and all she had done and all she had painted and sculpted and performed and written: all of it together. Catastrophic and changed and united and exactly what she wanted until she fell down.

The pill took effect and she fell down. No ecstatic trance but just the shattering of her equilibrium. The first sense to go as she tried to grab the floor but slipped instead into a sleep without dreams and they came back in. And lifted her onto the bed and she woke to tell them.

To tell my mother to tell Sandro to tell the shrink to tell the nurse to tell the orderlies to tell me. As she looked away and down and at the sheets and the bedclothes and her robe which she squeezed till her knuckles turned white:

— I am sorry. So very sorry. I have never known what I wanted.

While I listened to her say it again and again her eyes all dry and tranquillized:

Oh, Alma, I am so sorry. I have never known what I wanted. As I watched her face and my hands tried to reach out and encountered instead the tree and held onto it tight listening to the grubs inside it move, as my breath caught and held: Ah ah Hah haHah. Until the breath finally subsided as the words were born:

— No, no, you, you, how could you, you you, let this happen to you, you you, you of all of us, not you, you you, please Goddess, not you, Athena Artemis Aphrodite, Hera, Demeter, Persephone, Ix Chel, Blood Woman, Coatlicue, Mother Kali, not you, how could you let it.

And then almost screaming, my face tight to the bark:

— Why did I ever leave you?

FADED COTTON

I knew
the
to
quest

answer
that
ion

even as I asked it. While all the reasons I had left her weighed my inarticulate body down as I sluggishly detached myself from the tree and still snuffling wiped my eyes and nose, smearing my face with the black soil from beneath the tree and the equally black city soot that had settled on the bark. Each action slowed as, passive and unconscious, I made myself into, with my clothes in disarray as I staggered toward the subway, even more than I had been before, a nightmare image of the insane loose upon the streets.

Yet there was something I had recovered in just that determination, in that body that moved like an automaton toward a pay phone and the subway, with the need to pull the answer to that question up out of the discontinuous morass of my pain allowing me once more some kind of distance from that hurt, that for one moment I had lost as I rushed into the park. Because however dishevelled I looked I was still able to look back with equally curious tourist eyes at those who stared at me, even smiling at them if they stared too long, so that they looked quickly away.

And I knew that there was something I had won.

I ducked quickly into a pay phone to change back into my not so secret identity of suburban housewife and mother, the one who needed a quick fix of daily life, my daily life, easily achieved through a quick call to Jeanpierre and the kids, with telephone huggies and kissies and little Amber who would only listen, just a chortle on the other end, while Jason told me baby René didn't feel too well, and Jeanpierre echoed that, giving me all the details of what was going on with the family before I got to tell him how upsetting it had all been, with my responsible young wife voice contradicting the clothes and the tear-streaked face he couldn't see, as I repeated, how terribly difficult.
—Yes, dear, it shouldn't surprise you but yes, she's cracked, that's right, completely bonkers, alien voices in the internal p.a. system, and everything. Unbelievable.

Words spoken while I breathed deep. Almost as if I could feel the fresh air so far away, nestle my face into the clean diapers we still hung out on the line so the sun could kill the last of the ammonia bacteria, repeated daily complacency better than doing New York any day, contentment like a cat basking in the sun better than the drama of a crazy best friend intent on seeking out new life and new civilizations.

Though it would still be hard to leave. Even after so many days in which my body followed out the trajectory on which it had been set, as my mind tried to turn around, to see if there was yet any way to make my bargain with Hell, if not with death, to bring her with me.

Only Hell would not yield her up. Anymore than it would Baldur. And as for the creatures of the earth, even the denizens of the artworld would no longer pledge to her. Nor did I have the keys to Hell's gates. And when at last they opened, I was afraid to enter. I had followed her many places, but I had already told her I would not search for her where she had gone. Nor even let her dream me.

Which is perhaps what sent me back, even that last time with you. Not that I wanted to know anymore why I had left her, but to see if there was something, somehow, left of her, that I could bring with me. Some concrete city totem perhaps, akin to her constructions, made with teeth and nails and blood and cloth and lines and figures and sewn and patched and glued together out of past and present and future, a story perhaps, her story, the one I have become obsessed with, like a fish swimming in its goldfish bowl, around and around, to create that place where her spirit could rest.

So that sometimes I would even see it as a dance. Something you could put together, I did that sometimes as we walked, Thorne, after you two met. Thinking of a dance for Laura, a story dance. That you could do around and around, in catastrophic steps, with her work appearing projected on a stage set like a subway platform. Where your steps could create that resting place, and maybe I could rescue her dream and bring her back.

Something
I could not make happen, no matter how hard I tried, in those fourteen days I was there. When even finding her was like being part of a magician's act, a now you see your friend, now you don't, as she would disappear and reappear before my eyes, no contact ever really made. And each thing I did, each decision to act, to take my life into my hands to make it move,

just twisted back on me, on itself, an illusion, or maze or Mobius strip. Leaving me in the exact same place, not in possession of one of her constructions, but still inside one, a point, pained and perplexed and motionless, or moved only by the energies around me, buffeted perhaps, as I once more let all the discontinuities assault me, my self, my body, each day more passive, each day more dull, with all of it as far beyond my control as it had ever been. Until, the same bitter taste in my mouth, or at the back of my throat like semen, I once more had to flee.

Especially after moving from my mother's to the hospital to the Village to SoHo to little purchases for the kids to little moments in the sun, to that last day when I met her at her parent's apartment. Alone. Within hours of her release.

We sat in the living room of her parents' apartment, the place the same as it had always been, so that I would find myself at intervals thinking that yes, time had turned back, that now was my opportunity to see if I could make things different, my past had at last been given back to me, to shape anew, here in the jungle of Lilac's mother's knickknacks.

Because, to compensate herself for the loss of her community, Alicia had built a living room wonderland just like any of the other women would in the old Italian area down near Union Street. With a profusion of delicate porcelain dolls in porcelain lace mostly, Virgins and ladies and saints and shepherdesses, but a share of porcelain roses as well, with the plastic flowers in cut glass vases held to a minimum, along with one or another form of animal or lodging. While the smaller creatures stood in precise formation inside dark wood cabinets with glass doors, the larger lounged about more or less at random on all available surfaces; all of them from those magnificent Italian knickknack shops whose overfilled storefronts are as available on Bloor Street as in Brooklyn. Or they were gifts from Laura's maternal grandmother, or some great aunt who still lived in the old country, what Laura's mother still called the old country, though she'd barely been born there.

Each one required a good hand with the dust cloth, and constant whistling while she worked. Tunes from the opera, perhaps, Alicia did love opera, it was her favourite art, the kind of theatre she would have preferred Laura to be in, she always said so. As she dusted roses in the shelter of those other roses that covered the walls in three shades of flattened pink with equally pink ribbons outlined in black on a ground grown brown either from age or a kind of genteel antiquing.

There were only a few squares to break up the constant movement of the flowers, the jostling of shape against shape, with framed photographs of the family, from grandfathers and mothers on down, and some early portraits Laura had done, in charcoal or conté crayon, sepia or sanguine, with their paper (it was the newsprint always used in life class), faded to the same colour as the walls, only behind glass. With one of them a flattened but voluptuous nude reminiscent of Picasso's blue period, the most adventurous work in the house, allowed on the wall only because nudes, as opposed to naked women, were obviously in good taste. Like classical music. Or opera.

There wasn't any of Laura's newer work present, nor for that matter any of her father's taste, except maybe the one Van Gogh print, one of a workman, or peasant, I can't quite visualize it, except that it's an older man looking down at his hands. It was the mother's colours but the father's social consciousness, kind of what had brought them together in the first place: her attachment to his romantic brightness, the high colour in his speech and love of cause; his attraction to her abnegation, her solidity and her class.

It did surprise me that none of Laura's other stuff had made it there, not the extreme stuff of course; if she could have, she would have avoided even telling them about that. But at the very least I expected one of the smaller works from the time when she had decided to re-vindicate her mother's taste together with Tchelichew, taking up the taste of her mother's lost community the way Judy Chicago did her seamstresses, maybe because she felt that she had grown up without one, in a sort of never-never land of Italian cooking and union organizing. Though she would never say if her father had been with the Communist Party, if that as much as the accident was the reason he could no longer find work, a pattern of 'not today, not for you' until he gave up and retreated to the bars, driving her mother out of the home to that job at the Brooklyn Heights Library.

Alicia had trained years before to be a librarian, someone in her family thought a good girl needed something to fall back on, and then not done anything with it. She felt terribly inadequate there on the Heights but she always said she met a lot of interesting people. As she carefully put each book back and made the children be quiet before she read stories aloud to them in her second generation voice, and watched *Nanook of the North* and other early documentary on Wednesday nights. And made herself at home, I met her there, no matter what she said: with so many different items, and each one in its place.

Though the organization of books and movies and children and stories and holidays around her was by no means as original as the one Alicia utilized in her living room, nor, even with the Dewey decimal system, as complex. Because it was true what Lilac said, secretly at first, or in those funny fits of temper she would have when only I was present, at sleepovers or when we walked through the park, or later when we would be in the apartment together, when something would be triggered and she would think of the girls at that school or the ladies in front of the paintings at the Modern, or even some of her teachers at the art school, and she would say:
–Those people, you know. Those girls those women those boys those men, I could never invite them home, never, not into my mother's living room. They'd die, they would, faint dead away, turn up their noses, break something, spit on the floor, laugh at her, laugh at her. THEY WOULD LAUGH AT HER.

Sometimes her voice would grow increasingly bitter so you could hardly shake her out of it, while others she would start to laugh herself. It would seem suddenly funny, as she told me how she'd known I was different because I hadn't said anything the first time I'd come over, though she'd been scared about what I would do, coming from Central

Park West and all. She repeated that for years, she even said it that last time, before she became angry again herself.

– You just tried to get into it, Alma, it was so beautiful, you just tried to understand what it was all about.

Though the truth of the matter is I had loved the knickknacks, I was just young enough to love froth and frill and what was then called femininity, to marvel at each thin porcelain petticoat with the holes in it to simulate lace. I was in full rebellion against my mother's starkness, her whites and blacks and large open spaces that would only tolerate complication when she could call it folk art, like for the totems or that skirt, or the one Panamanian *mola* on the wall.

I knew my mother's taste was good, impeccable in fact, she spent so much time emphasizing it, that I could never criticize. I just picked up Alicia's pieces and ran my hands along them and fantasized myself into a world just that small and precious. Though I would never say so to Laura. I don't know why I didn't dare add that place to our secret spaces, our agents and our Amazons and our forsythia and our magic animals, but I never did. Though I would agree with her when she needed my solidarity on the subject, then and later, it had a million ways of expressing itself, from a firm: Those girls are such snobs, to a tentative: Minimalism misses a lot.

And I did agree, it took no pushing, I would even try to argue her along that path, to convince her there really was some form of taste, no matter how absurd by the bauhaus standards she had to absorb in art school or from the houses of the rich, in her mother's rococo *horror vacui*. Because the filling up of that already small apartment with ever smaller and smaller spaces did fulfill some real human need.

Later Laura took to calling them rhythmic intervals and spoke of their power to seduce and entwine, to grow and remake, defending the energy field of the rhythmic interval with examples from Islamic, Indian and Mexican art. Then, when feminism would no longer allow for feminine to be a synonym for weak the way it was in so many of the textbooks she read for art history, they became Fecund Feminine Fomentations (They really do seem to breed, she wrote me), or Ferociously Fabulous Female Formulations, trying through alliteration to gain their effect in words. While on the canvas or paper, or in her constructions, she tried to imitate the intervals in her mother's apartment, while assigning them, along with Alma, some kind of originary status in the way she worked. In her love of the convoluted, her desire to live in Thomian space.

And it's true the wallpaper did always echo in the torn paper bags that she used, its printed roses in the dull red blue brown pink of her blood totems. With the sharper edges of the brighter items on the tables or the Van Gogh on the wall resonating in the sharp bright plastic edges of her catastrophes, some of them even trying for the sordid semi-melted texture of the plastic flowers. With that living room present in almost all the colour combinations she would choose, especially for her resolved events. All those pinks and purples with pale green surrounds brought into an intense repetition that would almost turn your stomach while informing you that nothing at all was resolved.

Which is probably exactly what her mother's living room would have told you too, if you caught it off guard. Or if it caught you. Because it would force your equilibrium into a baroque vertigo, making your mind acknowledge that life's little pieces never did quite fit together. They were just never quite the right size. The jigsaw puzzles never would be continuous. They weren't all in the same series, or even made by the same company.

There was a new addition to the room this time though. That took up enough space to tell me time had indeed passed, that warned me of how little could be changed. Its sordid statement far too clear.

Behind the couch her parents slept on was one of those Mexican rugs that surely inhabit a million working class homes throughout North America, even the homes of recent immigrants from the south, a popularized if not a truly popular art, something you could buy off a cart in a shopping mall or out of the back of a van or pickup truck in a mall parking lot, that's where they sell them in Calgary south on MacLeod Trail. With plaster planters too, distributed around the van the way you might outside your door or even for a ficus or bougainvillea in your living room, while the van itself is festooned with all sorts of cows and horses and roses and bullfights, or, for that matter, some famous painting like the *Mona Lisa*. Which, on black velvet or woven into one of these rugs, in the apartment of one of Lilac's old artworld friends could have been very camp, since it would seem that anything with the *Mona Lisa* is camp. So that Jeanpierre could wear the one I gave him just about anywhere and not be laughed at. It's on a bolo tie for when we dress western.

This one though, still a Leonardo, was *The Last Supper*, which always gets taken far more seriously. Whether or not anyone making those rugs up, patterning them or weaving them, would know that its composition is supposed to represent perfection, still the colours are always serious, serious, serious, no matter how badly done. And obviously her parents, even if neither one of them spent much time in church, took the image seriously too, probably for very different reasons, giving it the place of honour where the print of Van Gogh flowers that Lilac had so loved once hung. So that between her murmurs, her moans and groans looking at it, I heard her say:
– They know themselves well, my parents do. This is perfect for them. All cold and dark and dull.

Because it was put together in dull greens and greys with two-tone beige flesh and a too sharp black outline, like old interior enamel paint, in a mechanical weave by numbers which makes even roses look like enlarged velvet petit point. So that I could understand why she would say:
– It's a black hole, they've hung up a black hole. To make sure no energy will again escape this room. Because no matter how strangely crazy it might have sounded to say such a thing back in the white confines of the hospital, you could see it here. How there was truly nothing to that thing, too much nothing, how it took away from the room, sucked the energy from it, so that you noticed the shabbiness, the chips and scratches on things, rather than the care. The way the knickknacks made you do.

Because that image didn't have the power to enrich anything, not the way so many of the knickknacks enriched each other. Even surrounded by such playful figures it refused its occupants permission to come out and play, or even intermingle. It remained flat instead. Flat, flat, flat, like a badly reproduced postcard that becomes a memory of a memory of a memory, a sign of a sign of a sign. The kind that springs up in front of the eyes when you finally get there, wherever there is, Greenwich Village or Lake Louise, and makes you look out at the mountains or the sea or a ruin or a cathedral or a stoned out street singer or a market woman selling her wares, and instead of seeing them, say to yourself, Look, I'm here, I'm enjoying myself, I've done it, this is where I'm supposed to be.

The mind writing the back of the postcard even when it hasn't bought it yet, because you've been told by all the brochures that this will be a thrilling new experience, the trip of a lifetime, just the way this black hole of a rug was a lecture about what you ought to like if not believe in, not the old tourism of word of mouth and rubbing shoulders, but the new imperative mode of advertising literature, self help books, even university course descriptions, like a circus hypnotist, You will love this and see that, go here and enjoy there, become successful learn a lot, recommend this recommend that recommend us to your friends your relatives your acquaintances your pets, you are sleepy you are sleepy you are very very sleepy.

So sleepy that, if this rug were any example, when it comes to art it would seem that you weren't even supposed to notice how much you the poor or even middle are called upon to admire what the rich can possess, even when those possessions are works of popular or even high art that were stolen from you or from your ancestors or from your culture in the first place; for all I know Alicia's great great great great great great grandmother's second cousin twice removed's great aunt cleaned Leonardo's studio or mixed his pigments or did his actual painting or gave him his ideas the way I gave mine to Laura.

Because the rich are always reproducing what they own, or selling just one piece of it into a museum saying they want to give the poor the culture they are deprived of, even when it is they who have deprived the poor, or just the different to make them poor, like robbing the potlatch gifts of the B.C. natives to try to make them into good punctual thrifty Protestant workers who will be willing to mechanically reproduce for others instead of creating for themselves. Or they just imitate the survival culture of those they have already deprived, wearing their clothes and listening to their music, adopting their slang, the way they did Laura's, then selling it back, to give the stolen original more and more value.

Or it's maybe just some entrepreneur trying to get rich, like the guy leaning against the van, paying his own lip service to the taste of the rich, sometimes tastefully and sometimes not.

Or sometimes like that rug; where nothing of the original remains except its outline, its signature. And the admiration for its name, its reputation as high culture. So that this artifact on the wall could not even represent an attachment to that painting, like the photo reproduction of the Van Gogh had, a love of its texture, but just the worst, I could see it in her face, of what Lilac had always feared. What she had fought so strongly against.

– We have nothing, the rug said, nothing at all except the images of the images of the images, the dregs that you offer us to buy. For which we give in exchange our constant admiration, our alienation from ourselves, until we are as grey as this painting.

So that it became yet another incarnation of her terrible nightmare of never being real, never being present. Because that's what kept her banging on the doors of the rich, to allow them without her ever acknowledging it, the privilege of validating her, them and the critics who serve them, putting price tags on the art they own, the art she made, even if her art itself seemed to challenge their reality.

It would not even have surprised me to hear her say in her voice from years before:

– Maybe that's how I should do another version of my dream, with the windows and the moon phases woven in, maybe I could even get the factory to weave in a pull cord. Or to speak of doing black velvet collage catastrophes, how the galleries would love them.

Only she remained silent now. Silent and shaking her head. Perhaps wondering who had given it to them. Whose quick trip to Tijuana it had been that had ended with that gift. Someone coming back to say, We thought you would love this. After all your daughter is a famous artist.

While her parents had given it pride of place. And thus, unconsciously, betrayed even that sensibility she had come to consider – or at least say in the articles – was their greatest gift to her. So that now I could see how that painting, which might seem to them a nice addition, even an appreciative one, to her on her homecoming, would take on an increasing negative value for her, as if in her parents' turning their backs on what she had considered themselves whether they ever did or not, the whole world had turned its back on Laura Mack, the Laura Mack she had built, and all that Laura Mack had tried to vindicate. While all she had left to push back against it was that flat angry voice. Speaking again now:

—They've betrayed me.

—God, how they continue to betray me.

The only problem is that I didn't know who she meant. If it was her parents or the doctors or Sandro or her brother and sister, or me or the rich or the artworld. Or if it really was the rug, or at least something she saw symbolized in the rug, that made her fear that everything she had ever believed had betrayed her.

Because I think that the rug was also telling her how flat she had become, a reflection of a reflection of a reflection of what she had meant to be, another sign of a sign of a sign only more literal: the one hung on her. And the label recently changed from Artist to Crazy Person. So that it didn't matter, perhaps she felt then it had never really mattered, what she had meant to mean. It was all the same, the rug, the knick-knacks, her work, the Van Gogh print, her self. That sign, that label, like the price tags on all the work owned by the rich, whether auctioned off at Sotheby's or in reproduction out of the back of a van, had made her a collectible, a consumable. And where that sign had always resisted her meaning, it now overwhelmed it. So that what she realized standing there might be that it had become permanent, that she had been drugged and flattened, made less than what she was, completely disconnected and permanently branded with the sign of the other. In a universe from which her position as subject had been excised, where her point floated, discontinuous, unable to move from inside its own hysteresis. So that none of this was any longer a decoration, or a choice. She had been marked, branded, in a way she must have felt she could never recover from. Especially with that superstition about madness, well grounded enough, I think, in social practice, so alive in her family. So that her voice held a very special terror as her words echoed

in the garden of that room. Where everyone and everything was Judas, not just the man offering the kiss to Christ.
—They've all betrayed me. All of them. She said again.

If her psychiatrist had been there he might have thought it paranoid, but this part at least seemed normal to me, certainly within the normal limits of who she had always been, especially right then, this obsessive sense of betrayal. I could easily see her point about the way her parents had insisted on giving her back her old room, the room where they'd been sleeping since she'd left, moving themselves back onto the old convertible under *The Last Supper* rug, the place where they'd slept throughout her childhood. And I didn't think it was generosity on her parents' part either, or even what they would interpret as such.

They didn't do it because they thought she needed the space for her recovery, I don't think they've ever believed she could recover. Nor for that matter did they think of the time in the hospital as a breakdown so much as the moment she chose to admit how crazy she was. They knew she had to be kept apart; they had even sent all the things that could be salvaged from her studio directly into storage. Except for some clothes and one or two very old paintings and the oak lamp her father had carved. As if everything else she owned could be contagious, and not just with bedbugs.

Which meant that if she stayed in the living room, so openly among them, then those things she had done would be much easier to pass on into the entire family life. Pushing it drastically off its centre.

It seemed to come out of the
blue. Or maybe it was out of the green/black of that painting, the way she still stared at it and stared at it, as if through it she could fathom her parents' betrayal. Or everyone's. Because the next thing she said was:
—They can't make me go back to him. You know. They can't.

And then the head came back down, the chin stopped pointing at Jesus, or maybe it was Judas. As she hugged herself with her arms and turned toward me where I stood almost behind her, staring too.

−He didn't tell you either, did he? she said. All this time you've spent together during visiting hours at the hospital and I bet he never mentioned it. He tries to pretend it's one of my delusions, that everything will be all right now that I'm out. We will be the happy couple. Again. The happy theatre group the happy commune. All of us together again. But we've been separated for months. Months. He went back to the old apartment with the others, and I kept the studio, he kept the commune and I kept the studio. Me, alone, he didn't tell you did he?

I will admit the sneaky edge of paranoia had crept back into her voice, the same tone she had used in the hospital to tell me to Shshsh, to please be quiet, if we listened carefully we could hear the broadcast. At the same time as she warned me not to tell anyone we were listening.

With this sounding only slightly more real, as she looked around in that same obvious way, as if for spies in a childhood game or TV sitcom, waiting a moment before she went on:
−I didn't want to tell you when I was in there.

From the way she looked around I thought that maybe she believed there might still be electronic listening devices inside the plastic roses, or the Queen of the May, or the Virgin of Fatima. But what she said was very sensible. The way we all feel about our parents.
−It's hard to talk about here, I can feel their presence. Especially mother's, in all these things.

And she had smiled and picked up a perfect porcelain rose. And she had caressed it. As if to change through that action whatever ill will those objects might have picked up and broadcast from her words.

−**They won't tell you**. But that's why my parents closed my studio. They say they want me to rest but they really want to force me to go back. They know it will be impossible for me to stay here very long. That there are too many of us. There always have been.

I didn't know, from how she caressed that rose, if her 'us' included only the family, or all the room's porcelain denizens as well.
−But they don't understand, she said. And once more I didn't know who she meant. Not with the way she kept on rubbing.

— But no matter what any of them say, I won't go back. *I'll go back to the hospital first.*

I just stared at her. My stomach sicker and sicker with that warm nauseous feeling you get so often when you're really sad, I'm sure you've felt it, Thorne: a mourning sickness.

A mourning stomach, you could call it. With the lump in my throat to match, and the hand hidden behind me as I still tried to concentrate on that painting, clenching and unclenching. To know that she had left him.

She had left Sandro.

And no one had told me.

At that moment he

parents' cruelty

in trying to force her back seemed almost unimaginable. That now when she needed them, they should put on such pressure.

I shook my head to clear it, standing there behind her, as once more she looked at the wall. Then found myself wanting to scream. Or sweep my arm across one of the tables. Or punch through the glass of a cabinet. Especially as I remembered what they had put her through when they'd found out about him.

On a weekend Sandro had taken her to some sort of drama conference, or important theatre workshop. Something he was participating in. So she could see him in action I suppose, only I can't remember what it was. Or even how her parents found out that she was away.

A missed appointment of some sort, I believe, with her sister maybe, for Laura to take her somewhere. Then when Laura didn't show up the kid squealed, and the calls started. And I couldn't produce Laura. Nor remember where she was to try to get a call through. Not even the name of the conference.

I'd just figured thank god and a quiet weekend and turned the rest of it off. Yes, Laura, no Laura, it should be interesting Laura, while I ached for the time by myself.

Nothing jogged my memory. Not even when her father called in a rage at three o'clock in the morning to storm at me, asking me how I could call myself her friend and not even know where she was, in fact not even cover for her. I wasn't even smart enough or loyal enough to cover for her, that's what she got for hanging out with people like me. Snobs and worse than snobs, he knew about my mother and her pretentious intellectual ass-licking bourgeois ways. What he didn't know was how I could live in the same house with Laura and not treat her better. What was it I said she was, my *best friend*? I didn't have any rights to friends, much less a best one, I didn't even know what a friend was.

Then when that got no answer – he really did seem to think I knew and he could browbeat or cajole me into telling him, because anyone who really was her friend would be able to reach her, would be able to tell her parents where to reach her – he went on to blaming me. And this time it was for leading her astray or down the garden path or some such, because she must be up to the same whorish tricks I'd learned from my mother.

Which was when he hung up and called my mother instead, they knew each other as parents at the high school, to tell her off for being a whore of an intellectual snob or an intellectual snob of a whore it's hard to remember, because it was obvious that what my mother did with her intellectual friends was whore. Drink and whore whore and drink, this was the man who spent half his evenings in the bars talking, asking her how much she would get for a piece, and if she got more if she sold her daughter.
– Is that what you think you're preparing my daughter for? Well my daughter's better than that, he screamed. She's no courtesan to whore to the rich, she's not *puta*. Not like you, or your daughter, *puta, puta, puta*.

I think that's the word he used, my mother said he'd used the Italian word for whore when I finally spoke to her, though I don't know if she wasn't confusing it with the little Spanish, she would always ask for the swear words, she'd learned when she went to New Mexico that summer, and checked out on the streets below.

It was probably one of the few Italian words he'd have learned too, as far as that goes, probably not from his wife but from his father-in-law's friends, or maybe from his father-in-law, the guy had probably called Alicia that for marrying Mack, there'd apparently been a lot of problems.

Of which I think Laura was the most immediate product, though she never said that. It's just that the first of the other two children wasn't born for six years, probably due to what Alicia learned after leaving her family. The whole incident sort of funny in any case, that word popping onto his tongue.

Right before my mother, at least that's how she tells it, said:
– *Really*, Mr. Mack.

A perfect comment, or at least accent, for a New York intellectual whore, and hung up. To call me. To find out what the hell was going on. Only I wasn't answering right then.

Convinced it was him.

Then when
I decided to answer again at seven, hoping it was Laura, I got the mother instead. And I don't know where she came up with the stuff she was into, this isolated woman who should have been part of a neighbourhood gossip network, who had given all that up to run off with her husband, the big union organizer from out there somewhere, south or west, to share his unrealized, perhaps unrealizable, dreams of a better life for her for him for them for her class and his, and to try to pass them on unclearly to her oldest child. If she had thought it up on her own, or it came from the books that came and went from the library. Or the lives of the women who came in, she had established some sort of network there, even if she seemed a combination of maid and poor relation when they went out for coffee, and talked of their daughters who were away in school. Which would let her talk about her oldest with the scholarship to an exclusive private school, and now to university, and how bright and talented she was. Or maybe it was from the little tidbits of gossip, positioned each in its place like her knickknacks, that would

still filter down from Union Street through a couple of her childhood friends who still stayed in touch. I know it wasn't the TV. They didn't have one yet.

But it had somehow gotten into Alicia's head, I guess it had happened to Mrs. Calabrese or Mrs. Arnovsky or Mrs. O'Brien or Mrs. Friedman or Mrs. Jones or Mrs. Thomas with at least one of their daughters. Getting pregnant by that young man, we thought he was so responsible, from such a good family, she went to see for the weekend at Harvard. Or knocked up by that no good married motorcycle mechanic, he tries it on with all the girls, how could she have believed he would divorce his wife, and her already with a bun in the oven, a good churchgoing woman, such a lovely wedding too, the bride in white the bridesmaids in pink, down on Tompkins Place. But Mrs. Mack was convinced that Laura had to leave town for a quick abortion.

They weren't legal back then of course. You didn't go to New York for an abortion you left it. And that was the worst thing that could happen. Because she knew the other stories too, the terrible conditions the unclean instruments the less clean men, the unsafe chemicals the old coat hangers the fainting in pools of blood. And she was a practical woman, possible physical damage was far more important than any act against a distant God. Which was what started her crying.
– Please Alma please, Mia Alma please. Stop her, call her, you must know where she's gone, tell me. Tell me. I'll talk to her, I will, Alma, please. I'll talk her out of it, I will. Just tell me she hasn't done anything to herself, please say she hasn't done anything to herself. That she hasn't had time yet to do anything to herself.

So that I actually did. I said:
– Mrs. Mack I'm sure she hasn't done anything to herself.

I was still unsure what that anything could be, committing suicide or sleeping with a man or driving without a license or getting secretly married in front of a rural justice of the peace. One just didn't say the big word out loud back then, not in the circles that woman ran in, or just observed. Although maybe it whispered through the pages of some of the books, the romances or the pseudo-scientific tomes on adolescent nymphomania the neighbourhood housewives took out of the library, aaaaaborrrshun, aaaaaaborrrrshun, aaaaborrrrrrrrrrrshn, a wind in the text. While in dialogue it would stay the same as for her, it was just: doing something to yourself.

I really couldn't figure it out. At least until I noticed my words had produced no effect. That Mrs. Mack was continuing.
—Promise me, promise me, promise me. She hasn't, she hasn't; that she hasn't. Done anything. She hasn't done anything. To herself. She hasn't done anything to herself. Promisemethatshe hasntharmedherself.

Alma, I'd rather have twins ...

And it was only then that I knew.

And I just repeated what I had said to her father before he had become so outraged that I couldn't get a word in. I told her that many of the students had left for the weekend, that it was something important. Not directly in her department, not specifically art, but drama. Drama. DRAMA. Something to do with old-fashioned agit-prop style street theatre, maybe Mr. Mack would have enjoyed it. And yes, I was quite sure that was all it was: a conference.

Not an abor, not an abuh, not an abr, not an aa: not doing something to herself.

I don't
know to this day how they found out the exact truth. If it was Laura making too many promises to the sister and not coming through, building on an already large enough resentment, so that when Elena did go to a play with Laura and Sandro she told the parents about it later, pretending to herself, she was only twelve or so after all, that it was the natural thing to do. After all, her brilliant older sister couldn't have anything to hide.

Or if it was a more calm cool and collected sifting of information out of what little I had told them. Maybe that thing about street theatre had been combined with a couple of well placed calls to the drama department at the university. Then followed with a couple of better placed ones to the apartment, using some ruse or another to catch him off guard, to get him to say who he was.

But pretty soon it wasn't twins they would rather have, it was a daughter who wasn't a whore after all they had done for her. A whore who lives in a whorehouse, with my mother still the Madam, even if she would seldom cross the Bridge. While they barred Laura from their house, and especially from seeing her sister, who snuck out to see Laura anyway, it made her feel important to participate in her sister's dramatic and sordid life, even if she might have caused the blow-up upon whose results she reported with avid glee. How her father screamed at her mother that he'd known this would happen when they'd sent Laura to that ritzy school, he'd known how she would learn those whorish and decadent ways.

With the mother replying that it was his fault, his, his, his and his alone. He was the union man and the socialist, she knew what socialists believed in, all that free love, her family had warned her about him. All that she had wanted was for her daughter to be special, she had enough strikes against her being born early the way she was, he was the one who had thrown her to the lions, he was the one who had wanted her to be different, to not be like other neighbourhood kids.

And he would reply:

—Then why that school why that one?

Alicia had wanted it the moment she had heard about it, the moment his friend had suggested it. Laura could have gone to Music and Art, to Performing Arts, to Hunter, to a public school for the talented members of the working class. But no, it had to be that snotty place on the Upper East Side, it had to be that. Alicia was too romantic, she hadn't believed in her daughter's talent just that Laura would make a better match if she went there, those girls would introduce her to some rich guy, so that Alicia could brag of it, get back in touch with the old ladies in the old neighbourhood and brag about it, that was all.

Since when did the sons of the bosses do anything with the daughters of the workers besides knock them up, didn't she know it was just like the old country, her father could tell her that, the only way a girl from the people got close to a rich man was to become his whore.

And then Alicia would burst into tears.

—**All I wanted** was a good girl, a good girl and a white wedding, she would say: At least I still have Elena, my little Elena.

Who would be busy pretending not to hear. As they would start off again, over and over the same territory: I wanted a better life for her, I only wanted a better life for her, what do you mean a better life for her, you mean a decadent life for her, I wanted her to show them, what we can do, what we can do, the downtrodden, the working class, I never meant to fill her with ideas.

Until they would finally agree: they should never have sent her to that school. Much less let her sleep over at my house, much less let her meet my mother much less let her move in with me. As if we hadn't gotten the apartment together. As if she hadn't needed the space to work.

That, or one of them would turn and leave the room.

I guess it was hard on them. Though lord knows it would get harder, much harder, with all that black leather and interviews, before she came back home. After all, when they had talked about how she would be an artist, a great artist, how she would show all those people who thought they were better than she was, better than they were, better than the workers; they had meant opera, the ballet. Even those strange abstract paintings like Picasso had done, after all he'd been in the French Communist Party, or was it the Spanish, would have been all right. Though they would both have preferred something along the lines of Ben Shahn or Van Gogh or Diego Rivera, something pretty or of obvious social content, a compromise between Alicia's knickknacks and Mack's consciousness. With nothing ever able to explain performing in strange open empty lofts with lampshades on her head, or making prints of parts of her anatomy her mother wouldn't even mention.

I do remember that period of time. Vividly once I think about it. How even though Laura would laugh when she told me about the various goings on, her voice would be hollow. Hollow and rasping. Not quite as dead as when you met her, but already like the wind across the dunes. The terribly tired voice of a creature that knows it has been dealt a mortal blow.

She kept repeating to me how, yes, she could have expected that of her mother, her mother was like that, old country Italian after all. But not her father, not him, he was different. He'd always been interested in her ideas while her mother just said: Yes, dear, if it pleases you dear. Just as she must have to the patrons at the library, continuing to bring them books. Or to dress Laura. In that style so out of old movies or older dreams. Her father was the one who would talk to her, tell her things. He was modern, a socialist, just like Sandro.

And she would sigh and continue to try on new clothes in front of the mirror, because it was then, exactly then in fact, that her wardrobe really changed. That she came to belong to the house or the artworld or to Sandro, or even to Thursday nights. Because she was proving something to them, her fellow students or other artworld hangers-on, who would then become her chorus and her audience.

After all, she couldn't perform for her family anymore, the way she had always done, this had been too much, it was too explicit, they had made it very clear that they had already stood up and left the theatre. Just the way so many people, trained in traditional theatre, would always leave Sandro's ritual work or her performances, sometimes even the way her parents had, with their hands over the younger children's eyes. Or ears.

That was when she got herself the black leather jacket, maybe the same one or maybe an earlier version, though still without its painting. Sandro would bring her things then too, and even some of the Thursday night guests. Though I would not.

I don't know why. I had always brought her little presents, and it wasn't an expensive transition, purchased mostly out of the secondhand stores. It was just one I somehow didn't want to participate in. Another choice I didn't know I was making. Even as she tried, taking energy from the clothes, the meetings, the presents, to push life energy into the new being, the new self she was growing with its equally new rumbling sexy voice. Which did emerge almost that instant now that I think about it. Right after she got back from that weekend. Maybe on Monday morning.

Out of one of the workshops, I thought at the time. But it was the self that had decided it might as well be hung for a sheep as for a lamb. A great big specifically female ewe. The kind the shepherds are always after.

She would use that voice to call me out from the kitchen or from my room, especially nights when a certain touch of the whine had entered her words as she said to all present:
– But my faaather, he's a ssssoooocialist.
  When Sandro would quickly slap her down. That one never worked with him.
– Yes, like half the socialists in the old country, he would say. And the communists too, glancing over at Laura to see if that word got a rise out of her, if he could determine whether or not her father was or had ever been a member of the Communist Party.
– Even the anarchists and especially the union men, every last one of them believes in free love until you get hold of one of their daughters.
  And he would laugh and pat her possessively, and she would know it was time to practice the new self rather than bemoan the old one. As she called me, the voice lower than before, and slow, as if chewing on something infinitely sweet.
– Oh, Alma, Ah, Aalma, she would call. Come tell them.

She would want me to come sit with them, if I wasn't already, or to just peek out from wherever I was, the kitchen with the coffee or my own room with my thoughts, to offer up that anecdote about her mother, about how she had told me she would rather have twins. Because Laura wanted to give her answer, to tell them what she had said when I'd told her, to serve it up to her new audience, trying to look at me just the way she had at that moment.
  To the side, and out from under her brows. With just that wonderful perverse childishness that always made me laugh, no matter how sad or angry I was. The look with which she had baptized the Great Turd. That had sealed our friendship, again and again, making it primordial. Us against the world, first and foremost, before parents or Sandro or groups on Thursday nights.

Only the second time she repeated her remark it was no longer to me, and though I was there reflected behind her in the mirror, she did not see me, but just studied herself as she narrowed her eyes and French inhaled her cigarette. While my hand reached out to her, tried to reach across the glass, my hand opening and closing, with a wrenching sense of letting go, my face showing it, as she must have seen herself in the subway window the train pulling away, almost a vertigo, as something of her was lost to me, I could feel it, see it, in this feeding of her new self, her new voice, against the fear of her own loss.

And something more with each repetition, like those infinite reflections in the mirror that even if they go on forever, slowly fade, just as the painting the specific painting, that was Leonardo da Vinci's painting of *The Last Supper*, each stroke of the brush as he concentrated on it, that specific thing disappears behind all its reproductions. Just as I could see her fading away from me, as she went over that brief dialogue time and time again. Then yet again in the living room. Each version showing off a more accomplished streetwalkerliness to strut the whore her father had called her.
– Why didn't you tell her to get laid? She would say and wink.
– That's what I told Alma, you know. If my mother would rather have twins, well that's the obvious thing isn't it? She should get laid. Alma should have told her to get laid.

Why don't you get laid, Alicia in Wonderland? That's what Alma should have said. Exactly what Alma should have said.

And she would roar.

It was the first time I'd heard her use that expression. Although with each successive telling it rolled off her tongue with more ease. While the laugh held more and more resonance.

Until it came to be her trademark.

Her parents
finally did find a way to blow Sandro's cool. They threatened to go to the University with it. To accuse him of moral turpitude I think it was. I don't think it

was having sex with a student that was the problem, but going to live with her out of wedlock. But it meant he had to go have it out with the father.

For all he would laugh about that scene later, I think he really enjoyed playing the role. I can still imagine him twirling his moustache as he knocked back his drinks. Maybe they even arranged to meet in the bar so as not to stain the house, woman's pure province, with his presence. The virile seducer brought to justice to restore the young woman's honour, the honour of the clan, something similar to what the father himself must have gone through with the mother's male relatives, only over homemade wine.

As Sandro promised to take care of their daughter, to give her a place in his life, a very special place. Although he, and he said he was quite up front about his lack of belief in the bonds of holy matrimony, would commit himself to no more. And maybe then they went on to talk about women, how you can't live with them or without them but their two were exceptions, obviously not the ones they looked over entering the bar. Or maybe it was politics, what young people want these days and whether or not they understand class struggle, or even believe in class. Or maybe it was the war. What was to be done about the war.

With Sandro feeling he had handled the old man really well, twisted him around his finger to be exact. Which must have been true, at least in part, because afterwards the telephone assaults finally stopped, and our address became officially his. Though it wasn't until they married years later, with a license registered at City Hall and a strange anarchist ceremony the only elements still attesting to Sandro's convictions, that they were allowed into the house as a couple. Or that they would be invited to family dinners at which the other children were present. Though I don't think it could have been many, since that phase only lasted months.

I still think that was the reason they wouldn't let her occupy that living room. It was the spectre of immorality more than madness that was dictating their actions. Or perhaps her immorality was her madness, I don't know. Especially with her threatening to do it again. To break those bonds of holy matrimony so recently taken on, and family harmony too, however inharmonious they had always been.

They must have been terrified of her becoming a centrepiece. Lying around, a strange hybrid in her secondhand flowered housedresses. As if some alien horticulturist had crossed the gold rimmed rose bedecked hand painted soup tureen and the old rabbit eared black and white TV her parents had finally had given to them: a homemade science fiction movie when she was off the tranks, and a soap opera when she was on them.

While her laugh at that precise moment as she looked at that hanging *Last Supper* carpet was neither one. Not the adolescent psycho-tranked giggle everyone on the ward had seemed to have, nor that rumbling thick sensual laughter she had taken on with Sandro and adversity.

She had suddenly gone back. To the first time I had met her or to the first time she had said it to me, open and spontaneous, that thing about telling her mother to get laid. And it was so much a child's laugh, knowing but still childish, once more the kid with the perverse grin and the even more perverse sense of humour, and the gleam in its eye of course, that I wanted to hug her and welcome her home. While her voice lost all its whine and all its paranoia as she suddenly said, a complete change:
– The invasion of the shepherds.

Then repeated it.

– **The invasion of** the shepherds gone to defend their Saviour.

And she moved, before I could stop her, to take a couple of figurines, an eighteenth century pastoral style shepherdess in one hand, the shepherd in the other, and place them on the back of the couch.
– Come on, Alma, she said waving to me: We must liberate the Apostles from where they're being held hostage, along with several hundred colourblind women, in a Mexican sweatshop.

I started to laugh too. Covering my mouth with my hand, sure for a moment that the past couple of weeks really had been no more than an episode, an unusual episode, almost a dream. And that whatever secret message that rug contained, maybe to her father the union organizer, betrayal or not, it had brought the old Laura back.

I wanted to join her. It seemed so right. What I could see coming. That she would try to balance her mother's knickknacks one on top of the other, until shepherds and princesses and Fairy Godmothers and roses would rise up in triangular formation toward that rug, in their invasion designed to give their Saviour dimension. And then there would be her parents coming in, casually slamming the door behind them, the groceries still in their hands, while all those figurines crashed to the ground, a brilliant multicoloured multidimensional catastrophe. And whatever followed, followed: a hollow vengeance against us all.

Myself included.

Because I wouldn't just be a pimp to her whore, now I would be egging her on in the only thing worse than prostitution, this madness that she insisted on disgracing them with, so that it would be right back to the hospital for her. But I didn't want to stop her either. I liked that vision of a concrete intervention in Alicia's wonderland complete with her parents' entrance. And besides, who wanted to be the one to have to say:
— Now Laura do you really think you should … ? the way all the nurses had, as if talking to a seven-year-old child.

Only in the end I couldn't let it happen. Even to stand by and watch. I couldn't do that to her. To us. The mother in me won out. I had to be responsible. So I used another technique, from that same repertoire the nurses use, probably equally condescending, just less noticeable, and at least designed to save both our hides. The one I use with my children, the one they recommend in all the books on parenting. When the little dears fixate on something dangerous, like electrical outlets or hot water faucets, or even borrowing the car, don't yell and scream and slap them around, offer them something else instead.

Which meant I found myself taking the lord and lady in peasant costume out of her hands, and clapping my hands together, just the way I had always responded to her perverse child self, and offering her the roof.
— Come on Laura, I said. Let's go up on the roof. The way we used to. It's a beautiful day.

It was. I hadn'

ied about that.

Beautiful the way the weather had been for the whole two weeks. What makes that trip truly surreal in retrospect, New York horror not on a grey, but on a bright, ground.

Because I kept thinking the weather should make me feel better. That was the other reason I invited her up there. I kept thinking the sharp edge of the light could somehow cut through to the swelling pain in my chest and abdomen, that it could release it somehow, like lancing a boil, let it ooze out into the clear air, where it could drain away, until I could relax.

And once more ignore the knowledge that when she'd said that they'd betrayed her, the statement should really have been made in second person, singular or plural, it wouldn't have mattered, but it should have been:

—You. You. All of you. You've betrayed me.

Alma. You've betrayed me.

Sandro had kept calling that whole time. Called or met me at the hospital. Even that first night when I'd walked out of Mrs. You're-a-sick's room for the first time, there was Mr. You're-a-sick waiting by the elevators. And even if I wouldn't go out on the town with him, but insisted on coming right back to the hospital where I would see her in her tranquillized state, still I let him take me out to a deli for a brief dinner, the way he would again and again, for drinks or lunch or supper or coffee.

So that I had come to know all his favourite hangouts within walking distance of the hospital, even long walking distance, through SoHo and almost as far south as the fish market. We had gone in for long slow walks too. To put some colour back into our world after so much grey and white, faces and coats, we said, and laughed. Though we usually ended up in the brown and grey of one or another of his favourite bars, rather than looking out across the orange/blue reflections on the polluted water that you loved so well.

He introduced me to a lot of his theatre and artworld friends who hung out in those places too, telling them I was Laura's best friend from school, Alma-in-from-Suburbia, he called me all in one breath as if it represented a peculiar heroic deed for me to be there, or as if I lived in Scarsdale, right north of the Bronx. While they would clap him on the shoulder or some such, and say something like: Getting better I hope? Or: Be herself again soon, you'll see.

And I would say: Which one?

And they would deign to laugh. Surprised, I guess, that Alma-in-from-Suburbia could talk, even to say something quite so lame; or know Mrs. You're-a-Sick at all. Because I would tell them about that name she had given herself too, it seemed to match. And besides, it made Sandro's moustache twitch.

Then, because I couldn't ask him, or even them, if he thought she had married him for his name, I would go on to say:
– Well, at least it wasn't all cliché. At least they didn't haul her off to Bellevue.

While they would keep on laughing. Just a trifle too loud, I thought, and often, they would wink at me. While Sandro would laugh too. Harder even than the rest. Trying to make up for the fact that he hadn't understood the comment the first time I'd made it. That he'd missed a New York nuance of quite such importance.

We had sat opposite each other in one of those fake ethnic delis in the Village that have now spread all over the world, or certainly North America, breeding and crossbreeding, Pied Pickles and Pumper Nicks and Pickle Havens and Heavenly Pickles and Bagels and Buns and Big Buns from Too Many Bagels and the Just Plain Bagel and the Bagel Itself and the Other Bagel and the Outer Bagel and the Bagel from Outer Space, real plants in the window instead of real food on the table. The food was plastic to go with the inevitable plastic rose or carnation, just one in contrast to all the philodendron or spider plant, in a molded plastic poured to resemble a cut crystal vase.

We certainly weren't impressing each other with our knowledge of authentic deli cuisine, it was just that this was within walking distance of St. Vincent's and Laura, and I was determined to get back to the hospital. Though I did ask him if Katz's was still there, to let him know I hadn't forgotten where I came from. Which is when I started thinking about the hospital, its location within one block of the subway, and how thank god the little men in white coats hadn't hauled her off to Bellevue, which, besides being a cliché, is two million miles from nowhere, or at least any form of public transportation. So that I said that to him, just for something to say that wasn't earnest, to add a little humour, twisted perhaps, but better than nothing.

—**At least it** wasn't Bellevue, I said. And he didn't understand.
—Bellevue? he replied as he let go of the hand he'd been holding while he sighed dramatically.

I laughed. And it felt like the first time I'd laughed in weeks. And I suppose it was cruel, all the relaxation so noticeable in that laugh, even my shoulders unknotting, to tell him I had realized he was still an outsider, still an interloper. I knew he didn't own this city, or this tragedy. It wasn't copyright.

Because all his mournfully sensuous pomposity was gone as he repeated, confused:

–What's wrong with Bellevue? Isn't it a good hospital?

As I laughed louder.
–Oh, I'm sorry, Sandro, no, no, I shouldn't laugh, it's probably not even funny, it's just, you know, and by then I was squeezing little tears out of the corners of my eyes:
–It's an expression, I said: The kind all New Yorkers use, especially as kids, we always said it as kids, Laura and I.

While I leaned on those words, my laugh wheezing to a stop to underline them: *as kids Laura and I*, then added my own deep sigh, as I wiped my eyes, not realizing it would just make him wish to possess me too, the way he always did all of her world. While I went on to explain.
–In New York, he belongs in Bellevue, or she for that matter, said with a bit of a giggle, is like saying he's nuts, crackers, bonkers, bats, got a bat in his belfry, both oars out of the water, some cards missing from the deck, is at the very least, well, a few fries short of a happy meal, you know, a bit of a space cadet. With a one-way ticket to the funny farm.

While all he could reply, as if he'd known all along, or hadn't heard, was:
–But why? I've always heard that the care is so good there. As he went on with his deep stare.

And I stared back, annoyed. Which didn't mean I didn't giggle about it again later, about how suave he was, and how pretentious. But *why*? The care is so good there, I would repeat to myself, mimicking his tone, and my belly would start to jiggle. At how he could overlook anything that might shake his mastery.

But I would kick myself too. Thinking about how I just should have told him, word by word, like for a kid, or the way so many people treat those who don't speak their language: Because. It's. The. New. York. State. Mental. Hospital. At. Bellevue. Not known for anything else. No matter how good the care is in the other departments. That's what it is, and that's all: our local funny farm. And we've propagated the expression all over the country. There. are. very. few. people. who. don't. know. that. when. you. say. Bellevue. you. mean. Bellevue. Psychiatric.

Although it did in fact surprise me that he didn't. After all his years in New York. That he'd somehow managed to pass it by, or not pay it any attention. It's a great one for showing you've done New York, there are people who know it, even in Calgary. Maybe you should keep it, Thorne. In case of need. At some boring party when some nut harasses you, all you'll have to do is yawn and look him in the eye and say:
— You should be in Bellevue.
  And when he says:
— Bellevue? Why should anyone be in Bellevue? If they're not from there, I mean?
— Oh, I'm sorry. You can say, as you yawn: Not that Bellevue. Not the one that's hometown to noted Alberta author Roberta Rees down in the Crowsnest. Not the mining town. I'm not talking about the Hillcrest Mine disaster here. Oh, no. I'm sorry. The New York hospital. Big general hospital actually, around East Twenty-third Street, down by the river. Known for its psychiatric ward. It's where they take you if you try to jump off the Brooklyn Bridge. It's an expression I thought you would know.
  And then you could smile your chomp the Big Apple smile. It would be a real coup.

The way I was for Sandro it seemed, despite my constant repetition of that remark, as he introduced me to all those people, or reintroduced me, helping me to recognize them. Because people came around who went back as far as those Thursday nights. Though mostly they were from Sandro's group, the ones who had worked with him for years, and with Laura too, when she moved out of what they all referred to as static visual art, with the first word said like a curse, or the noise you hear on the radio, into performance.

She had gone into it after I'd left. Moving gradually through the painting and the graphics, the sculptural reliefs and the collages, doing performances at her openings like just about everybody did, at least if you were part, or wanted to be part, of the avant garde. With the only unusual part of what Laura did, it's not so unusual anymore, not after Yoko and Laurie Anderson, the fact that she came to specialize in it, almost completely leaving the monumental catastrophic reliefs she had become known for. So that by the time she was hospitalized, along with one or another installation, some small drawings and postcards, she was just doing her performances. Mostly in her studio, she had a studio by then, where everybody who was anybody came, while Sandro played host.

And designer to her persona too or so I'm told, it would stand to reason with what I'd seen before I left; as well as doing a little scene design of his own for money, and directing the theatre/ritual/performance group that she too was part of, or adviser to, or something very central I never could figure out. Along with most of the people who came over to see Sandro and me, while we sat in whatever place it might be, who served the group in one capacity or another.

I never did understand whether it was they who had inspired her to abandon the art object, that was another of their words, or if it was she who had inspired Sandro to use the group to attempt the merger of performance and theatre. Because there is a difference, or so I'm told by all the ideologues of the artworld, as well as by the denizens of the bars, though perhaps they are much the same, who specialize in that kind of definition.

The recreation of ritual, he would call his work, with alternating pronunciations, whether it was re-creation or recreation, never quite clear, though it always did apparently involve the remaking of our participation in myth time, the re-marking of our position in sacred space, he used the same words Laura would, to allow us to become one with the sources of our creativity, reunite us with our more primitive selves, the atavistic parts that would lead us to the avatar, we had abolished in childhood. Through play as well as ritual, he said, making him toy with the idea of naming the group Play-Rites, or so he told me.

I get the impression too, without knowing quite from where, that there was also a lot of confrontation in it, and a lot of meanness. It might have been obvious enough from the conversation, so perhaps it was one of them who talked about the details, or even my mother one night at home. Though the most likely source is Our Toad, he was one who'd made it all the way from Thursday nights to the group, his real name was Danny something, it still is Danny for that matter but the last name has changed, he left for Hollywood soon after I saw him, and right now he's all over the world on the microwaves, you'd know him if you watched TV at all, Thorne, and from Sandro to sitcoms seems somehow right, with the boob tube a good match for the theatre of alienation, though it doesn't really go with his love of Artaud, that's where he got his nickname, that everyone still seemed to call him by, even in the bars.

The first night he came in, I even sprang up and shouted out: Our Toad and then stood there, arms at my sides, deadly embarrassed, even blushing, thinking I had let out one of those secret names from childhood or adolescence, that would make you kill and bury your friends in the backyard or at the bottom of the airshaft, for repeating.

Only he laughed. And came over to hug me, and said:
—Not to worry. Not a prince yet, Alma. And then, after winking, at someone at the table, I don't remember who, he even croaked, in his wonderful New York accent, as rich as Laura's, to prove it.

Because that's where the name came from, of course, and even if he could turn it on and off, changing accent at will as most actors can, back then he wouldn't concede anything to elegance or sophistication as most people will, including French final consonants, he was doing the working class hero number, though Laura's working class heroine always outdid him, so that Sartre was Saaatruh and Artaud was just that, Aahhtoad not Arrrtoe, the same way one would lay claim to a frog, and we all called him that: How's Our Toad tonight we said, and made jokes about whose toad he might be and whether or not any amount of kissing or necking or even heavy petting could turn him into a prince, until the name stuck, maybe it still sticks in Hollywood, because he was never Danny again, but just Our Toad. And to go with his name, crroak, crrroooaaak, as deep into the darker reaches as any of them.

So he would stand to reason as the one to talk about the chicken killing they had done, though apparently they never did get into any of the really heavy stuff, like the tearing off of heads with teeth that did happen in those years. Just a polite dipping of the fingers in the still warm blood, with the progression to rabbits quickly stopped by the authorities. All of it pretty typical more of time than of place, even that mean style that was so common then, that is probably still around, along with more up-to-date versions of cruelty to animals, human or otherwise, as far as it goes.

With a sexual side to the meanness too, that the women's movement hadn't contained yet, or forced underground or into a more equal opportunity nastiness. Like the admiration for that guy who called it performance when he masturbated behind the chairs in the theatre, with special glee if there were females present, a gutsy breakthrough to come all over the uptight ladies, even symbolically, ladies being by definition uptight and inhibited; women, I guess, something that much more earthy. So that even those women present, to prove themselves, would nod too, yes, yes, very innovative, the penis re-presents itself, as if it had ever been absent. Though in my suburban housewife cum, no pun intended, street kid sort of way, the only thing I could do as I listened to them was yawn and think: If you've seen one flasher you've seen them all.

And then when Sandro said, or maybe it was Our Toad, it seemed aimed at me, in some form of justification, as if the yeses from the other women just weren't enough, that Laura admired that too, I laughed out loud. Though I wouldn't elaborate why, even as they looked at me expectantly. I just waved my hand in front of my face the way you do sometimes when something is too funny for words, and giggling said: —I'm sure she did. I'm sure she did. And was content to seem stupid as I listened while they debated whether Sneeman's pulling words out of her vagina wasn't at least that much more radical, the birth of language in the cunt of the world. How Laura had loved that even more. And wished she'd done it herself.

Because even if I was tempted to tell them of our flashing sentinel, and mark him as the beginning of any thoughts Laura might have had on the presentation of the penis, just so they would know I could not only follow them, but do them one better, I could never bring myself to do it. And no matter how often one of them might suggest I write my "Early Laura Mack Memoirs", they even took turns titling them – *A Discontinuous Childhood*, or maybe it was *A Discontinued Childhood*, kept coming up – still, to tell them a story like that would have seemed already a violation. Of our most private relationship. Another betrayal before I was even accused. Used only to establish my supremacy – over them, and perhaps over her. The same kind of ownership I had always accused Sandro of. Something that could easily become an act of assault against the tranked out body in the hospital, a prayer for her early demise.

It all seemed just so theatrical. Even without that perfect anecdote of early perversity there was enough drama – and always enough lines – for the already large and interesting cast. With the old friend telling older stories leaning in to shape the golden mean while the suffering husband leaned back to suffer in silence right at centre stage to make those evenings seem at times almost ludicrous, though at least a form of comic relief. While at the same time, histrionic or not, Sandro really did seem to need support so much. On those walks or when he would look around the group of people so mournfully, even bewildered, until he would come to focus on me. After he stared the rest of them into silence.

So that there would always come a moment when all those people, or just the one or two of them we ran into, even Our Toad, would look at us and sigh, saying something about how they really hoped to see Laura back in action soon, though you could tell from their expressions they hardly expected it. And then ruefully they would add, their mouths downturned as they searched for the proper expression to affix to their words: Well, you two must have a lot to talk about, and the next thing you knew Sandro and I would be alone, just the way we'd been that first night in the deli.

Sitting surrounded by warm orange wallpaper with oranges printed on it, hands resting on the wood grain plastic that imitated the real wood trim, while he would take my hand and turn it over in his, and say: Oh, Alma, Alma, at regular intervals. So that I could almost think the sequence computer generated, while I stared in silence, and wondered how much we looked like tourists who had just been robbed of their American Express card. And I never did have the guts to ask directly: So, Sandro, what happened?

I would just occasionally murmur: It's terrible, terrible, as computer generated as he, until we were both finally finished with our slow and deliberate chewing. And we would leave and walk down to the river or to the subway where maybe he would start again.

Grabbing my hand. And telling me how desperate he was. As he talked about Laura and was she making progress and if progress could be made and what was going to happen to her and what was going to happen to him and what was going to happen to them and how I had no idea how difficult the past few months had been how hard they had been on him he loved her so much he really did I knew that didn't I?

–**You know how** much I love her don't you, Alma? he would say, and grab my hand if he wasn't already holding it; he didn't know what he was going to do. And maybe he did say something about how he was afraid she might leave him, he looked into her eyes and felt that she had already left, only he didn't know if it was her: The Laura *we* knew Alma, or her craziness. What he saw there reflected when he saw that emptiness, maybe it was just the drugs.

–God, I don't know I don't know, he would sob and shake his head as he held it with his hands: But you know I don't want her to leave, I would never want her to leave, I only want what's best for her, you know that don't you, Alma? Don't you?

And here the sobbing would start in earnest as he would moan about how maybe he wasn't the right man, maybe he wasn't a very good man, maybe he'd never been the man he should have been, maybe he wasn't the best man for her, but god, he'd like to be, he'd liked to be, he'd tried the best he knew how, I knew he loved her didn't I. And of course, there was no mention of how she had already left, much less of why. Something, like so much else, my mother had to tell me the night before I went home.

Maybe to start with I was smart enough to know that it was just a game, that's what I think now anyway, another way of making himself the centre, of making it all his tragedy not hers. Of pulling me into his web again, as surely as if I were lying on my bed behind the wall, or leaning out onto the fire escape as they talked or whimpered or moaned. Only it was so terribly convincing, him sobbing out loud in public like that, being the emotional, the vulnerable, the new European artistic man, that I really would rise, and go to his side. Especially if it was one of those bars with the benches along the wall, and I would take his head in my arms and hold it against my chest.

And truly, it must have been terrible to face. His role in her tragedy, or just her. Because he would have to know, even looking at the expressions on the faces of the people in the bars, that as far as they were concerned, Pygmalion had just turned into Doctor Frankenstein.

And the monster, or at least the monster I had seen that first night, and would see for nights after, that we would go to the bars to avoid – he'd left that first night after walking me back to the hospital, without doubt he'd seen her medicated before – was just as empty, just as mechanical, just as obtusely obedient, as any in the monster movies. So that maybe the truth is that he was just practicing a new role. One that would get him out of his position of culpability. He could be the kind and understanding, all-suffering husband who would stick with her through thick and thin. As he practiced sad-eyed and yearning looks in order to preside over a crazy person.

He obviously still considered her his, he wasn't going to deny his creation, after all, instead he would re-write the script. Now to be about how he had spent years trying to save her from herself. She had been signed in Mrs. Yurasic, after all, he might even have told the secretary that Laura Mack was just a *nom de plume*. Or told her it was the best way to remain incognito. While he thought about how to add having a crazy wife, or a wife who had gone crazy, to his c.v. Because it's not the worst thing in the world, it must be easily as fashionable as killing chickens, at least in the big cities, to keep a crazy for a pet. Especially a famous one.

If only he'd put it together right, and gotten her back, he could have had her do consultations. Or made her insanity part of a new kind of confrontational theatre. A *Close Encounters of the Third Kind with Ouija Board*. And recorded messages from outer space on your favourite rock tape.

Maybe she would have been better off, it's hard to know.

His group had done fairly well for itself, even if his need to compete with her had exaggerated his need to manipulate, to be one of the many Svengalis as well as Pygmalions of the artworld, with Our Toad and a lot of the rest of the group calling him the Magician. And there was the tension too that is always present in that whole scene, made much worse since he had to keep up with her, and stay on top.

Which meant talking faster and faster, the way he kept telling the critics he was moving toward a new synthesis, the apotheosis of confrontational theatre, he said, that would bring about a new form of collective ritual. And he would stress the word *collective*.

– We will come to share a vision a total reality a new comprehension, he would say.

He even got some of the critics to agree with him, especially since he had Lilac there, and put her more and more at the group's centre, brought her in more and more to be its den-mother earth-mother mother-goddess, its free female spirit, with the whole group performing at her studio sometimes, where she worked each day though she lived with them, backing her independent performances up. While she would work with them in small theatres, off-off-Broadway, or maybe it was off-off-off-Broadway: with a little bit more off they'd have been in the river, swimming in the polluted water.

Then the other thing they would do, far more refreshing than such a swim I'm sure, was to combine the two, the group and Lilac with equal billing for special performances at the exclusive parties on the Island. Where having your own Contact Rituals, I think that's what they called them, became almost as necessary as the right caterer.

So that she was at last a star out there in the Hamptons, the way she had always wanted. Finally in a long white dress rather than black leather. Only covered in blood, maybe pretend menstrual blood, I don't know, with her head covered in it too. I'm told she looked something like Sissy Spacek in the climactic scene in *Carrie*. If Sissy had only stuck her finger in an electric socket first to get the hair.

That's how I wound up on the

Island too. That and coming to trust him, imagining how difficult it must really have been. I told myself I had no reason to believe Laura had ever been any easier on him than she had on me. I would just remember how hard she could be, rather than how malleable she often was in his hands, thinking of how you were always either with her or against her. Whether that was in an argument in class or in a judgement on another person or in the precise position for the next alien landing or whatever it was that she had decided to take a position on, so that there was just no way of saying no.

I'm sorry but no. Not quite. I disagree. Not absolutely you understand but with this little detail different. Maybe they'll land in Chicago not New York, on 125th Street not 57th. There could be none of that. There was just no way. Not without yelling and screaming and recriminations, even the occasional broken dish, the locked bathroom, the slammed apartment door as she ran down the three stories to the street, the ranting call in the middle of the night, just like her father's: it was either all or nothing.

And I could imagine that Sandro had gone through exactly the same thing, so that I'd even started to identify with him, regarding him by then from a safer distance, along the bench or across the table. And I would really like that crooked little sad smile and the staring half closed eyes, and the European shrug followed by:
– But what am I to do?

It was hard on me, too, with Laura in the hospital. Those moments with Sandro became the few in which I could relax, the few in which I let my guard down, the few in which I felt I had a purpose in being in New York. Which is when I did the stupidest thing of all, something that I had never done before nor thought of doing: I came not only to trust him but to depend on him. Even on his perceptions of her. And on his stories.

Until I wouldn't mind anymore when he grabbed my hand and rubbed it on his face as if it were a lucky rabbit's foot or a Laura Mack totem, though I would take his hand away when it reached for breast or thigh, while tears would spring to my eyes when he told me that I should have been there for her, god he wished I'd been there, I should have been there when they needed me. I didn't even feel offended. Not even when he hugged me and kissed me goodbye. On the lips. I just told myself it was affection. And desperation. Just the way he said: We needed you.

Until I forgot to notice that 'we'. That he always said: When we needed you. Not when Laura did.

That's why I said: Sure, when he called that Thursday morning and told me that some of the people from the theatre group were going out on someone's houseboat to Fire Island later in the day. It was hardly the Hamptons but there'd be a Contact Ritual, and what the hell they were going to make it a long weekend.

– Nothing will happen over the weekend, Alma. Her parents will bring her back to their place on Sunday. And they'll want to have a while with her before you go over. You know that, Alma. They even said so. And if you come, you'll get to see us in action. Nothing big, we wouldn't all fit on the boat. But a little something you might enjoy.

And even my mother agreed. That I should go.

– **You're a big girl now**, Alma, she said. I'm sure you can deal with a situation like that. And it should be interesting. And here the eyebrows slowly rose: Very, very interesting.

– Knowing those people will help you understand more about what happened. But, and for a moment it was just like my weekend in the Hamptons or my summer with Daddy, this time the weekend on the bohemian houseboat: You'll have to tell me all about it. Absolutely all about it. Everything. What happens, and what you *think* about those people.

And now she winked, I hadn't told her how I'd been meeting them in the bars:

—I've never seen them in their natural habitat.

I didn't understand the possible significance of that remark until I got to the boat, moored in the 79th Street Marina, down toward the southern end of Riverside Drive, where all the super-boats in New York moor. I almost said park, you can see how close I got to boats as a kid, at least the cruising and sailing side of them.

Though I had once seen someone off at the Queen Elizabeth, I grew up when you still chose between the sea and air routes to Europe, if you were the lucky kind who got to go at all. I remember the liner, floors and floors of it, out of all proportion, I still see it as an endless stairway. Then there was always walking by the marina, boats more in proportion, though equally out of my reach, from Onassis's yacht on down.

I stood there on the dock that Thursday afternoon, almost the pigeon-toed gawker, and knew that whether or not this was part of the group's natural habitat, the fact that I would be a guest on the boat, and not a passerby, made it no longer a part of mine.

And only when Sandro came up from below decks, I think that's what you say, and he walked down the gangplank, everyone knows that term from pirate movies and Peter Pan, to where I stood stupidly holding onto my little bag, proud that my mother had at least instructed me in what shoes were suitable for walking on the deck, did I understand that his removing me from my own ecosystem could have some reason other than kindness.

While as he took my bag and swung it over his shoulder before taking both my hands and leading me placidly onto the boat, already swaying and off-balance, it occurred to me for the first time that he knew exactly what he was doing: whatever he was about to stage, it was all for me.

That the bars and the cafés had just served to soften me up, like some pimp breaking in a whore: that I had truly entered his territory now.

It did take me a while to realize what was going on. And it wasn't so much the group's natural habitat that impressed me, as watching them take on their protective coloration. Not that it was totally different, it was still that borderline between hip and punk that Sandro had taught Laura to adopt before punk had a name, that they always wore, it was just more exaggerated. More sequins more leather more Guatemalan cotton more starred berets more kaffiyehs more political tee-shirts more patchouli oil more Chinese silk more nineteenth century lace more Army surplus more heavy kohl more carmine lipstick more purple nail polish more rouge more powder more paint; and all of it mixed together in the most outrageous combinations, each one trying to outdo the next to cause an impression. To be so much the epitome of bohemian politically correct radical chic that the boat's owner would be sure to invite each one and even the whole group back, as well as tell his friends all about them. And him already an exotic in his own right.

The Captain and his Mates they called him, because all the young men he'd brought were involved with him in one way or another, were staying in his luxurious Brooklyn Heights townhouse at the very least, on what terms for each I don't really know. Although one of the guys was definitely the current wife.

And maybe you would tell me I shouldn't be so offhand about that, Thorne, since I haven't had a lot of exposure to the lifestyle in question, but I would just tell you that I know a wife when I see a wife, that's a lifestyle I do have a lot of experience with. And it doesn't really matter if it's a straight wife or an artwife or the gay wife to a gay television personality or disc jockey, I don't remember which: a wife is a wife.

And this particular husband was way up there, the six figure income type, even back then, and really into roles, that was obvious too, or maybe it was just power, or maybe certain kinds of roles follow from the love of a certain kind of power, that's a theoretical question I still don't much want to answer, but there was the big boat and the fast car and the bigger house and the wives to live there, more of a harem than most guys even get to imagine, and he wasn't letting go of any of it. He made sure the whole time everyone knew exactly who owned whom, and who was under short-term contract.

Though he did it with a great deal of style and panache, and charm too as far as it goes, giving us all part of his concentration as if it were a marvellous gift, from a man who was definitely the Emperor of all he surveyed. Even if a bit of a secret one, because he definitely was not out of the closet, no Gay Rights marches for him, that would be too threatening to the income. And the power in the entertainment world that brought the steady stream of starry-eyed young men to his house to be manoeuvred as he saw fit.

With Sandro his only peer. Or perhaps just not of his court, more a lesser lord from another realm, who must be treated with respect though not deference. This was definitely not Sandro's first time on the boat, and he'd probably visited the townhouse often enough as well, it was within walking distance of the old apartment, as well as of Laura's parents, so maybe they would go over there after family dinner, it's the sort of thing they might have found amusing. Two such totally different ways of life, one for the main course and the other for dessert, Sandro might even have done a ritual there, with the way he and a couple of the other guys seemed perfectly comfortable, even envious, talking with Manny of his domestic arrangements, while Manny would turn to Sandro and tell him how happy he was that the group was finally going to do one of its 'little numbers' out on the Island, it would be so adorable, and he would clap Sandro on the back as Sandro grimaced, but took the blow.

Just stood there and took it.

We passed down the river and under the Narrows bridge and out through the harbour within the beautiful pastel cocoon of a perfect New York twilight, the kind you and I only got to watch from the shore, sitting on those wood deck chairs at Pier 16, as afternoon turned to evening. While from the boat we watched city turn to country too, muted blues giving way to brighter greens, the flow of cars and urban noise to the steady slap of water, the flight and call of birds. We even saw snowy egrets coming to tree themselves for the night, like flashes of cloud, after we entered the inland passage to Fire Island, and the water calmed to glass.

With only the western orange that seemed to go on forever shared between one landscape and the next, each one rendered a flat backdrop by the evening mist, with us the actors at centre stage, keeping up our self-centred conversations, while the stagehands of the boat's steady progress changed the stage sets behind us from the lead of buildings to the green of forest or brush or low-growing poison ivy to the empty horizon of the open sea. And all of it confused in my mind with the things I listened to, as people came and went.

Though perhaps I did make a mistake in thinking I was just the audience, that I could just watch, that I could never be dragged into the middle of it all, even if I knew that was just what the group specialized in: making the audience participate. I didn't even notice who was piloting or even how much booze was consumed, or grass smoked either, whether by the people out on deck or the person at the helm or by me. I just let it all go by. And noted only that the little hits of amyl nitrate hung around people's necks in vials didn't start until we had safely docked, when I demurred saying I suffered cardiac arrhythmia. It sounded good and I had once, the day Jeanpierre and I married. When I was so anxiety stricken I couldn't see.

—Try not to do this too often, the doctor had said and winked as he checked me out, I'd been desperate and I couldn't understand it. I still don't. Nothing like that has happened to me before or since.

But I didn't tell them about that, it would have been too much of a victory for Sandro. Nor was I very nervous, I probably should have been but I wasn't, I'd had too much of something too, booze or grass or the ocean. Or days in the hospital with Laura. So I just laughed, that kind of stoned out laughter which makes everything a lie, and continued flying high and showing it.

Another boat pulled alongside. And there was a sudden flurry on board, a sudden wakefulness, even a wariness, an energy that you could feel immediate and electric in your body, something I thought at first due to the size of the newcomer, with us suddenly so small. I thought it brought out the hunting instincts like sharks going for a lone whale, then learned as I was finally taken aside, they had asked Sandro first, I'm sure I heard, She won't mind Sandro, will she? long before I was asked directly, that it was the boat of an 'uncool' higher-up, from whatever network it was our Captain worked for. And I was being called upon to become our Captain's date.

—You don't mind Alma, do you? someone finally inquired: Being the Captain's date?

After all, it was bad enough to be caught docked at Cherry Grove, Fire Island's gay hangout since before I was born, with Cherry Grove jokes introducing me, and most young New Yorkers, into the facts of life and homophobia. Though it didn't affect me quite as much as it did others, I was one of the few kids I knew who was aware of having met homosexuals, my mother always had too many gay theatre people around for me to be shocked by gay men, even at their most outrageous, though she did explain it in a whisper. And kind of spell it out with her voice ho-mo-seck-shooal, as if it were a disease. Which she of course thought it was, like so many other things in those Freudian days, being an ambitious woman among them. So that she would kind of say something about the tragedy of their lives, and how they couldn't help it. But, speaking of gay couples she knew, they did give each other so much support, and besides, gay men made such good friends. But in this case, docked where we were, it was obvious we would have to make some kind of compensation.

I was picked because I was the straightest looking person in the bunch, in all senses of the word, a perfect choice to bill and coo over the Captain. It was actually rather fun to fulfill the role, I'd had a pretty long vacation from wifeliness, so I enjoyed the extra alertness needed to dash in and out to bring him his drinks and look at him with big eyes while slipping into the background, noting other people's needs and expectations as well, to remember exactly how that role was played. Because I will still do it sometimes for Jeanpierre, the little woman pushing her man ahead act that seems so necessary at those company cocktail parties, for all involved, with its talk full of the exchange of recipes and admiration.

So that I would arrive every few minutes in the galley where the young man whose role I had taken over was stashed fixing the drinks just the way his lover wanted them, allowing the Captain to compliment me without making any sour faces when I arrived on deck; while in the galley the two of us would look at each other, role transcending gender, touching hands and bursting into laughter, while I would invite him out to flirt with Sandro, since I thought Sandro's reputation beyond possible harm.

—Oh, what fun it is to swap men, he even said, giggling. We should try it tonight.

While I didn't even bother to contradict him. Not realizing how prophetic my silence might be. Or that touching his hand and raising my eyebrows in the open laughter of that wifely moment would turn out to be the most fun I would have that whole trip.

By the
time that act of the play was over, it was rather late, and, I was convinced, time for the curtain to go down. In a darkened theatre, where only the town's lights and the stars were left to give us light. The last thing I was hoping for was an encore. When Sandro came over to consult with the Captain about the cabin arrangements, and to start a whole new drama. Even if I was still there draped over the Captain's leg, stuck in the role or too tired to move. But definitely ready to call it quits.

I only fully woke, and sat suddenly up, when Sandro touched my shoulder and said, it was obvious that I hadn't been understanding a word they were saying:
—Alma, listen, I'm sorry. But apparently there aren't enough cabins. The Captain here just kind of assumed you were with me.

Then as I just stared at him, more unbelieving now than uncomprehending, he went on, a strange rhythm, speeding up and slowing down, as if he had to guide me over the bumps, make them less than what they were.

—And well, I suppose we could move you in with Clea, and Marvin could come in with me. But, well, you know, they were, I guess, lookingforthistimetogether. And well, you understand, therearetwobunksinourcabin. Or I could take on Our Toad. Only he's bunking with Michael. So that wouldn't do you any good anyway. Besides, we've known each other a long time. Certainly itwouldbebetterthan a stranger. It wouldn't be like wehadtobein the same bed. Totally platonic thewayweare and all.

So that you could almost have thought him embarrassed. Until he winked. And raised one brow. And I knew that I was totally trapped, in this test of my aplomb. There was no way to stay sophisticated and refuse.

Two bunks. Men and women stay in the same room all the time.

But when I said yes I must admit I knew exactly what it would mean. It even gave me a little bit of a thrill. To know that I would be led away, bound by my own good manners, overcome by his superior manipulation, swept away by a need to be cool. While this rolling houseboat and its close cabins as white as my nun's cell in our old apartment, would be my gothic mansion, and my own best friend the mad lady in the attic of all our minds.

Which doesn't mean that I didn't convince myself in the fifteen seconds between his proposition and my reply, that it would be exactly the way he had said: totally platonic. It was that I noticed, not only the way my eyes sought his eyes, but the rush of anticipatory excitement, of pleasure, in my lower abdomen, right above my pelvic bone, when our eyes did meet. With that feeling that said: this is the new thing. This is the excitement.

It is very hard to

alk about what

happened next. Even to imagine talking about it. To find a way of imagining how I would say it, how I would enter the topic. How I could tell you about walking down those narrow stairs below decks, how I now kept my eyes off him, and turned my back as I hurried into my rather matronly, and just a little too heavy, checked cotton flannel nightgown, refusing to believe the messages my body was sending me, what they meant, even as, just on cue, he came up behind me and clasped my naked shoulders before I could finish putting on the nightgown.

Clasped my shoulders and turned me around. And took the nightgown off my arms. Then stepped back a moment as he looked at me. And murmured something about my rich body, my rich mother's body. How beautiful it was.

While I tried to laugh at him.

I've always been passable but never beautiful, Thorne. You and Jeanpierre are the only people to call me beautiful, who could make me believe it. And neither of you ever meant physically. And I certainly wasn't then.

Two months after quitting nursing with my sagging breasts, their Montgomery's tubercles still so prominent on the areolae that they seemed secondary nipples, the whole apparatus aimed downward

and ready to squirt, a bit like an udder I thought, or those multibreasted statues of Juno, my belly back in shape, but barely, I was a walking disaster area. So that I did really want to say, cold and laid back:
– Oh Sandro cool it, or even: Rich? Are you trying to compare me to an upside down ice cream sundae or a Guernsey cow?

But for all I wanted to snort and laugh, and maybe even offer him a tit, not the way you might a lover but the way you do a baby, I couldn't do it. I found myself pulling my shoulders back to force my breasts more upright, and shivering. Which turned into a spasm that shook my whole body, as my breath caught when he put his hand on my belly where my stretch marks are, and repeated it.
– So beautiful. And then said: Oh Alma, you're the one who nurtured us all. Oh, Alma.

And then he asked me if I wouldn't, please, if I wouldn't, just lie with him for a while. It was so hard, seeing me and thinking of Laura, it was so hard.
– Alma, I don't want to be alone, he said.

And I said:
– Yes. Nurturant again: Yes.
– Yes of course Sandro, and took his face between my hands, and repeated it, almost tearful.
– Yes, it has been so hard. Yes.

And it wouldn't be the only yes I would say that evening either.

So that
I suppose I could start: Well, Thorne, did you ever sleep with your best friend's man? Or woman, it wouldn't matter, just something you did that you could never figure out how it happened; you were stoned you had wanted him/her for the longest time and you couldn't admit it much less figure out why, you were challenged and your groin ached and everyone around you kept saying what are friends for anyway? Sex is just that, sex, it's a gesture, and besides you did it for her for your friend, it was just a way of getting closer?

Because that really is what I told myself then, when I wasn't denying what was happening altogether. When I wasn't telling myself that I would do just what he said, lie next to him and give him some comfort, he did need comfort, he wasn't the terrible ogre I had once thought him; the same things I had told myself on the benches of those bars, it really had been so hard, and he really did love her, even I had seen that, even the summer I had left, he had loved her so much and now she was probably lost to us both, and what was wrong with a little comfort.

Though I in no way doubted, not in that part of my mind that measures and that thinks, what would happen once I consented even to enter his bed. But that was comfort too, even as the kisses started as we snuggled together and I pretended it was for both of us and for her too: that it would work, that it would mean something. As the wet between my legs grew.

The wet that had been there even before the kisses were placed, first on my back and then along my hairline while he whispered:

–Turn around please turn around. Turn around I just want to feel your body your warm body your beautiful body, your warm nurturing mother's body, Alma who nurtured us.

A constant barrage until I did turn around, attempting to hold him the way I would a child the way I had tried in the restaurant, while he responded by kissing my face and my eyes his hands coming to my breast, at first yes, just the way a child's hand, the baby's hand as it nurses comes to the mother's breast, unconscious and grabbing while the baby feeds. Only his hand would become delicate and appreciative, no longer the child but the child in the man who knows where the child has fed, so tentative so thankful, so gratified, as if I really were a treasure, just touching them like a baby's mouth when it searches, the terrible or beautiful rolling of lover into mother into lover into mother into lover into mother that seems to fuel so much of our image of womanhood, a trap or a release it is hard to know, in that moment before man or baby's mouth clamps on and demands, the milk of the mother of the lover, so much that has not been given him, becoming punishing and hard, and conscious. But in that moment so gentle that I felt the letdown reflex.

And thought for a moment that I really was about to give him milk, the phrase: the milk of human kindness, appearing for a moment in my mind, as I distracted myself both away and into the moment thinking how strange it was, how we don't recognize what those words mean, after so many years of formula feeding, of denial of the breast as other than erotic toy, that not even La Leche League has done anything to stop its amputation, with its conversion into nurturant tool, separating it just as much from us, in its objectification you might say, Thorne. Just as I thought, well, that milk, it's not exactly from Elsie the cow or even Alpha Dairies, at the same time as I made a bet with myself that there's no one in the English-speaking world who sees a dripping tit, much less a baby's, or even an older person's, mouth clamping over it, when he hears that phrase, almost wanting to giggle and ask Sandro about it. It might have been one way to interrupt his no longer babylike determination: Well, Sandro, I could have said: Have you ever thought of the meaning of that phrase, 'the milk of human kindness', if you're not careful in a moment I might be giving you the milk of human kindness, and I could have giggled, it would have been a perfect antidote to his sipping. Except that I was liking it, that moment when I let him sip on me physically as well as emotionally, feeling myself give, give like a mother, give, so that I neither sputtered nor giggled nor said any of that to him, even as he said, with a kind of chuckle:

—Alma Mater, Alma, our Mother.

Although that comment did at least bring me back down to earth enough to make the one remark I think I was to say of my own volition in that whole encounter:

—Our Mother who is not exactly in Heaven, Sandro, don't joke, I said. Because I had started to respond, even as he said, almost serious, his voice no longer pleading:

—But I mean it Alma, you *did* nurture us all. You were very important to us. And besides, what could be a better image of the Mother of Heaven, than mother and lover rolled into one? And you did nurture us, Alma, he repeated. You did. Even if ... and suddenly he looked away. Thinking perhaps of what had never happened. Or that I had left. And I thought right then, that the encounter was over.

I closed my eyes. And found that instead of relief, or the sense of calm the mother feels after nursing, the calm I wanted, what I felt was longing. His myth-making had started to nurture me and I wanted to incarnate for him his myth of Alma the One Who Left and return, a heroine or a goddess, at last to set things straight. Only straight was to enter his version. Fulfill his story. As I was overwhelmed by a sense ... of incompletion, a terrible sadness, a sorrow, that went beyond frustrated lust, that sense of horniness that you have to finish off on your own, to a mourning for so many moments left unfulfilled, even unlooked at, as if there were a road we should take together that we never had, that in fact we never could, if only to see where it did lead, and I found myself wanting to say that to him: Oh Sandro, I'm sorry Sandro, that we couldn't go that road together Sandro, drawing out the melodrama.

All I managed, his face between my hands again, the hairs of his moustache tickling at my palms was:
—Oh, Sandro. Because his name was like a trigger. On hearing it he started again.
—Please, Alma, oh Alma, please, he said. Please, then please again please. While I squeezed my legs together against the wetness between them, still wanting to deny it, as: Oh, Alma, he said, again and again: Please.

Until I allowed him to inch his hand between my thighs, and then to part them, slowly letting go of the energy that held them together like a great huff of breath, or the way you learn to relax, on cue, each part each muscle, against the tensions of labour, all the muscles of my legs relaxing, to accommodate that hand, and then to allow him to open them and to turn me completely onto my back, feeling myself melting into the bed, as he moved on top and into me, and started the ride, the long long ride. As he said:
—Oh God, Alma, take me home. Take me home.

And I remember thinking, like a title for a cartoon, the last rebellion of my rational mind, in the same place as the 'milk of human kindness' had appeared, for the kind of cartoon you might see in *Playboy* or *Penthouse*, a last defense against my pleasure, my desire, drawing myself in that space as one of those cartoon women while Sandro moved to his position on top: "Saddled up the cowboy remembers that a good horse always remembers its way home". So that I shook my head a moment, feeling the moustache, and imagining him with boots on.

It is what I thought while I let him
ride. Not the part about cowboys or boots, but that at last I was going home. That finally the opportunity had been given. That here was my chance to go back, to make the past again. While I lay there in the good old missionary position and like a nineteenth century lady, did not move. Certainly didn't carry him off at a gallop. Though I was loose, very loose.

A loose woman, with the labour relaxation complete, as legs apart I did feel the sensuousness of myself opening. Letting the arms the hands the feet the fingers the toes tingle and relax, the tongue the lips inside his mouth tingle and relax, as I tried to forget, not my pain but my pleasure, my ecstatic longing, or at least to place it on some transcendent plane. Convert it into an act of worship, of sympathetic magic, for her, for Laura. There on her hospital bed, as he said over and over:
— Be with me be with me, moaning and moving, moaning and moving, in and out and from side to side, repeating:
— I need you I need you oh so bad, between the thrusts as I quickly came and then did again, repeated orgasms, but silent. Silent and soft and gentle and so inside myself that he didn't even know as I let myself melt and I came. And I didn't tell him and I bit his tongue and I came.

Home to Laura. Home to Laura. My mind repeating: I'm coming home to Laura. Home to Laura. Home to Laura, to the rhythm of his thrusts.

Home to Laura.

While in that moment of transcendence, because it was that, a moment without time or boundaries, a moment when even the white walls of the cabin, so like the white walls of Laura's room, would dissolve, I let my mind remake that last summer. Because that is what I wanted, to have it all again, and to have it different, to reweave it again as he brought me again toward a secret ecstasy, behind the cell walls of my silence, as I had so often been behind the walls, the white walls, of my tiny bedroom.

While all he would do whenever we were alone in the apartment during the day was try to catch my hand the way he had in those restaurants, those bars and cafés, only so much less subtle. As he breathed on me, looking slightly down, as if his anxious panting breath contained something miraculous to send Sleeping Beauty to sleep, to make her forget the morality she had held as long as she could remember. The axiom of conduct that says that whatever else you do, whether you do it in the road or on the roof or in large groups, you still don't sleep with your best friend's man.

And the line wasn't: I need you, we need you. It was far simpler far more straightforward. Because back then he didn't need anything. He was successful and she wasn't and he was the teacher though not yet the Magician; and he was from Europe and he had travelled and he brought culture and he talked of history. As if it were all his personal gift, his very personal, and very important gift to us, and all he wanted from me was to get to know me better. The way he must have been saying to all and sundry since his arrival: I must get to know you, get to know your country, better. Repeating it over and over.

Every day it seemed sometimes until I was afraid to be alone with him because I knew I would have to listen to it.

– I really want to get to know you better, in the kitchen.

– We must try to get to know each other better, in Laura's small studio.

– Laura says I must get to know you better, Alma, in the middle room that still contained the desk I never worked on.

– Laura would appreciate it if we got to know each other better, in the living room among the bedbugs.

Until he would back me to the corner of my own room and stand in the doorway, never quite daring to enter. Or perhaps knowing that it would force me out my own door into the hall. As he went on and on, I this and Laura that, until one day he said again:
– Laura would love it if we got to know each other better.

And I laughed at him and said, my anger blooming:
– Then why don't you ask her to join us.

He didn't laugh with me. Or even get angry at my literal mindedness. He pulled me to him. Literally pulled, very dramatic, a scene from the early movies: the hero or villain, it doesn't seem to much matter, bent over the heroine his arms behind her as if he can totally surround her, while she almost swoons, her head thrown back.

Only I didn't bend my head back, even when he pushed at my hair, as if to force the gesture. I still tried to look straight at his chest, to somehow change that act, it was too much what one would expect of the ideal lover Laura and I had always imagined, the one I didn't want him to be. Although that gesture made it obvious enough why she had fallen for him: cheap romances combined with Achilles after the battle.

Win or lose, but after the battle. When the brave warrior could push his prize, whether the daughter of a priest or the Amazon Queen herself, roughly onto the bed or the pallet or whatever they slept on in those tents in the *Iliad* (surely not army cots with beetles), just the way Sandro threw me dramatically onto the bed, and followed me, bringing my hand down to his prick, hard already, but still in his pants.

This next part is harder even than

talking about what happened on the boat. Maybe the boat is only hard because it connects to this: the incident that doesn't bear thinking about. Even if I understand well enough why it happened, I still recoil from repeating it. Even standing here, I have an old suit of Jeanpierre's in my hands now, Thorne, my mind rebels at going over it. Like a finger refusing to touch a sore, or the way I twisted the toilet paper over my thumb that afternoon in the apartment, looking only obliquely at how the knife had split the flesh and dug into the bone. That stops me too from repeating the details of this other afternoon. From visualizing them. From looking that scene, that I can see so clearly in my dreams, squarely in my mind's eye.

Though I think I will try this time, there might be some good in it, to face that encounter. With no decorations, or even little asides, to see that incident with all my faculties. So that I will try again to actually say it, maybe that way I can reduce it to reasonable proportions, to that adolescent faux pas I've always believed it to be, even if I could not make my feelings concur. The kind of thing you shouldn't do but that always seems to happen anyway, even if you know very well that you shouldn't sleep with your best friend's man, still life and literature are full of it, including how you get the giggles twenty years later thinking about it or do it once more for old times' sake and laughing still or do it with her instead laughing harder, after the divorce or twenty years of successful marriage or interesting screwing around, or change of sexual preference, it doesn't seem to matter, but you laugh and laugh louder and louder, no harm done.

And I'm not even sure I feel so very bad about that part of it, the act itself, that first act, so full of some strange and sordid petty vengeance. Though I know I don't like to think of myself like that. I still think the problem is in all the events that one act let loose, the future that it definitely changed, a true hysteresis of a true discontinuity, the one that sent this one small point that was me hurtling out into the space that was Canada and the north and a series of homes and cities and children, only to land again on the boat, on the roof next to her, in a reality so changed and still somehow the same that there was no doubting it was the same loop in space even as I dug my nails into Sandro's back and heard him whisper:
—Be with me Alma, be with me. That's right, Alma, I've waited so long be with me. When I finally let my body respond.

263

So I'll just go over that act, that afternoon, now. Slow and easy and not too fast, or even loose, the way I tried to pretend back then I was with men, though the reality was far more quick and awkward. Probably the way this will sound, more true to the facts of that afternoon in any case, even if I had already had some experience.

Stuff that I had never told Laura about because it was just too sordid, the typical apartment couch while the family is out, New York's own version of the back seat of the car, with only one truly traditional Volkswagen on a Jersey highway thrown in, the kind where even in back you almost wind up fucking the gear shift lever, and maybe too there'd been something in the stacks of the library my year at college, though I can't remember what section we picked. With all of it more than anything a kind of relief, comic relief really, from the stress of my so serious commitment to Laura's genius; or even just plain relief that I could do it, get rid of my virginity and be normal and attract men, at least for that most basic of functions. Which amounted to a series of not terribly skillful hand and blowjobs, three or four uncomfortable screws, with two or three even more uncomfortable young men, the kind Laura and I would always make stammer and blush over dinner, even before she underwent her transformation.

So I could hardly admit to doing it with one of *them*, or try to explain how I felt I had to do it, even if that was the sort of thing you could read about even back at the time, certainly in *The Bell Jar* if not *The Group*, how I needed to end my possession of this most uncomfortable thing called virginity with its strange ceremonial nature that seemed to call a halt to the flow of experience, obsess you with sex or with love or with combining sex and love in a way that would make you think your body a special gift to a man and not your own at all. That had made me say, I won't I won't, I won't do that; and take the plunge.

Even if I didn't want Laura to know. Not even that I thought that way. She was true to the romantic tradition.

She was keeping hers as a treasure.

And not for any husband. At least she denied it was for any husband, she kept saying she didn't want to be husbanded. It would be a gift to the gods, to the goddess, to the spirits of earth and wind and life, that sort of thing.

It sounded marvellously pure, and perfect: the pure sacrifice that would bring as pure a pleasure. The kind of larger than life thing she was always into, perhaps her first version of the perfect victim, the perfect mirror, the perfect receptacle. Guarding a treasure in a way that would let her, I think she thought this, continue to be a treasure herself. Her family's treasure, the way she had always been, not just any loose woman. Because even if she hadn't kept it for a husband, or for holy matrimony, still she would have kept it for the most perfect man, the most perfect lover, she could find. With that image of herself, still held in some recess of her mind, even when the family went crazy on her. Because she knew, despite how it looked or how she dressed, just how pure and right, how worshipful, her acts had been. How somehow *right*.

And yet totally free. Truly free. The way she had always thought her father believed in freedom.

She would speak often of how he would arrive. Not Prince Charming, but her Demon Lover. How he would incarnate the arrival of Dionysus and the harvest, the playing of the pipes of Pan to make her come and dance to his fecund tune. As he would come in triumphal march to make changes, this someone that she always talked about as her male half, her other side, her *daemon*. But never her partner, never her friend.

— Never what you are Alma, never my soul, he will never be my soul, she said; even as we went around the apartment preparing the ceremony for him.

When we filled the living room with incense and exotic flowers, and I helped bathe her in that funny deep tub in the kitchen with the fancy oils she had bought just for the occasion.

— He's come, he's come to me, she repeated while I laughed and agreed.

— Yes, yes, I said and washed her back, and didn't believe a word.

It was easier to believe the man in the park was Achilles standing watch than that such men truly existed, much less that our exotic dinner guest was one of them. But I went along. Like everything else with her: it was fun. Believing in that mythic life was fun. And it made me feel special.

Even if the Queen's tub was surrounded by kitchen utensils, and last night's dirty dishes, the ones I still had to wash before the *daemon*'s arrival.

That's why I carefully kneaded my fingers into her shoulders, as I said:
— Tonight the Queen prepares to accept the Warrior.

And then I washed the dishes and went up to my mother's for dinner. Where I washed them again. Or maybe that was the time I went for the night. I've forgotten on what excuse. Though I think, you know how good my mother is at this, she may very well have guessed.

—Soon it will be your turn and we will prepare for you, the two of us would giggle later, the way I imagine two girls in some older more traditional culture might, as they prepare to meet the husband they have never seen, for the act they have often imagined. Which assured me that Laura truly thought me unsullied before Jeanpierre, and made it impossible to ever tell her any different.

I couldn't say that the shieldbearer to the Queen hardly needed such ceremony, that all she needed was drunken tavern lovers like any good soldier. Like most mistresses when asked about their servants' morals, she would have been convinced that hers was the exception to all those terrible things they always say about the lower orders, as perhaps Sir Galahad thought of the morality of his page: Laura was convinced that I too was awaiting the Demon. That I must prepare myself for the Demon Lover as part of our partnership. And of course, that is the servant's part of this bargain: I never told her any different.

And, I guess, in the end, my more sordid encounters had indeed prepared me for what was to come: the servant's eye view of the household. At least of the master.

And looking at him I would feel in myself sometimes that rising wave I had always satisfied so peremptorily, as if it were a craving for ice cream or chocolate, getting it over quickly with a lover or with my hand, sighing, washing, and back to business. Only with Sandro it was so unwanted that it made me furious. Because of course I wanted him. Sometimes I think you always do: just because she was his.

And this time on the bed that desire was so strong, and I was so horny. From sneaking around the apartment they had booby trapped with their moans and their groans and their smells. And their smiles too. With the looks that passed between them.

I remember coming in once and going to make a cup of tea, only to find them balling in the bathtub.
—Oh hi, Alma, Laura said, while they kept going.
As if they expected me to just turn my back and put the kettle on.

There is
no doubt the place was mined. There were little bombs of sexual energy placed in the most obscure corners, that might go off any time and hit me in the groin, even as I snuck out the private entrance I had made myself.

I wouldn't even bother to use the skeleton key: the only thing around the place you couldn't replace for fifteen dollars at a secondhand store was that energy of theirs. It was something you could come to long for, even to lust after the secret feel of it, while you hated yourself for that longing. Feeling it always under the skin like the vaguely painful itch of a mosquito bite, so common for me that summer, that you had scratched again and again until it bled, the pain and the pleasure and the guilt mixing, until I would spend days avoiding the rest of the house. Avoiding what it would remind me of.

By the middle of the summer I was eating my breakfast and even lunch at a small restaurant around the corner most of the time, while I would spend a lot of time walking into Brooklyn Heights and along the Promenade that overlooks the harbour, or even across the Brooklyn Bridge, the way we walked that day we went to get the crabs, when I talked that little bit to you about her.

Because I couldn't avoid their space when I was cleaning, I wound up doing less and less of that, and when I did, it was usually when they'd both gone out. Which made me feel more and more like a maid, not so much because I did the work as because I invaded the space of another, and gathered a secret unspoken knowledge of her, always of her, she was my mistress as he would never be my master, not even master of the house, as I would find the stained sheets still wet tossed onto the floor, or her underwear hung over a lamp, until nothing about the place seemed mine anymore. Not even the things I had brought or bought, not even when I made supper with the utensils my mother had given us that she would then sometimes come over to cheerfully try out. Still I was the one who worried in the background, while they made her their guest.

–**Are you using** the blender, dear, she would call and ask, then volunteer to show us a wonderful recipe. Checking up on me was what it really was, and what she found caused her to raise an eyebrow more than once.
–Really, dear, this is disgusting, she would say eyeing the bloodstains: You must do something about it. Which really meant, it was something that just could not be said, you never say anything terribly negative about a friend's young man, not out loud, but Sandro, Sandro, it meant: You must do something about Sandro.

And I could not tell her it was not my place. That I could only whisper in the mistress's ear, but it was no longer my place in this household, to command.

Though I'm sure she saw it. The new reticence in my fingers, even in my eyes, as they avoided hers. Until there came a time when she had turned to him and raised the other eyebrow as well, and they had stood across the filthy living room opposite each other eyebrows raised in duelling formation.
–Don't think my daughter is your servant, young man, she said. Putting into those last two words all of Sandro's failures as well as his failings, all the things he had failed to do, implying all the things he never would. Mother at her most trenchant, as good as the time she had just that wee bit too much wine and asked him what he did all day when he wasn't pulling his prick, then called the next day to apologize. And told me to pass it on to Sandro. She shouldn't be vulgar she said. She should have said: Masturbate.

What really must have driven Dad crackers, while Sandro just stood there practically shaking. And I saw it. I saw it.

And I laughed inside. Laughed and laughed and fixed it in my mind, rubbing over it like smearing fixer on an old black and white Polaroid. So that I could keep that image in some special place, that image of him cowed before my mother just the way I was so often cowed before her. Or him. So that anytime he would call a woman a bitch or a cow or a cunt I would remember, and laugh inside, picking up my picture of Sandro Cowed Before Alma's Mother's Eyebrows, until I finally felt immune.

Only I never was. I knew that well enough as he pushed me onto the bed. Well enough again that weekend years later. Though maybe it did have something to do with why he wanted me. That through me he could bring under control what my mother had done to him. That I was still too much out on the edge of the space he had created. Still too much Laura's loyal friend and my mother's daughter. Because I had sat cowed watching them, too. And he needed the whole place under his control.

Though maybe he never needed a reason. It was just that I was there. To tame.

The way
he was trying to do as he held me against those same wrinkled and sex filled sheets, while all that anger and desire gave rise to a rebellion in me that refused the romance and the melodrama of his gestures, the way I would not be able to refuse his obvious need on the boat, and push him back off me. Because I found myself, and I really could not tell you what possessed me. What sudden rage, against him, against her, against me, fuelled that gesture. But after I levered his one leg out from between mine where it was rubbing, I did not run from him but surprised myself by turning to catch hold of his belt with one hand while I lowered his fly with the other.

All that I can say is that I knew that gesture was in me: that it did not surprise me. That something in me said, Yes. This is the right one. This one will bring my anger to climax. My hands choosing this way to do it.

What I

pulled from his pants was something I would never have believed occurred in nature. It was narrow at the bottom and wider toward the top like that famous statue of the goat in the Museum of Modern Art with its enormous cock and balls, that I would always kind of tiptoe around as a kid, and later with Laura, again and again, both of us looking and looking at that phallus entity which we would never dare approach too closely, licking our lips just like our sentry in the park.

While we would giggle and elbow each other in the ribs, just the way I had earlier protected myself by hiding behind my mother's skirt then peeking out. Even into late adolescence we were more afraid of what others might think to watch girls or young women staring fixedly in some form of phallic worship, than any patriarchal terror of the thing itself, any This Then Shall Be Thy Master. Which leaves me still thinking that copping a quick feel, or maybe a more longer lasting one, rubbing it up and down, would probably make a better performance than a guy masturbating in a theatre. It would certainly go further toward breaking through to the central problem contained in that uptight sense of propriety. In that turning away of the face like for so many things women don't find out, or words so many still pretend never to have heard, even about their own bodies, much less the other sex's: I've never even known that statue's author. The ladies have already had enough done to them, thank you, between flashers and rapists and child molesters and verbal misogyny and pornography and advertising and incest, even the women have, that they hardly need to pay to see another one hiding out behind the chairs, since each day is just an opportunity for more of the same. And gratis too. So that what we still have to do, I think, or perhaps repeat doing every day, is take our destiny into our own hands. And one of those too, I guess, if we really want one.

Though it wasn't really apparent whether I did or not, at least that one, when I got to look that same phallus's demonic power in the face that afternoon. And almost giggled. It did make him so perfect for her purposes. For a moment I even tried to remember if I had ever seen his feet, if he did indeed have cloven hooves. Up to that moment

I hadn't thought that penises were an organ subject to much variation, except maybe in length, guys have always talked about that, reporting always, though I've never seen it, on someone who had to strap it to his leg, I don't know if it's true, or just the way they reinforce their own feelings of inadequacy.

I was sure that all penises must be quite evenly cylindrical, the human kind anyway, and my limited groping had done nothing to disabuse me of that impression, there was only one, even I could tell the difference, with a very slight curve. Which would make them, except, of course, for the one end, much like sausages, or pickles, or miniature flagpoles you could run something up to see if it got saluted: all the old jokes. Cardboard toilet paper, or paper towel if you're really into length, tubes, with a mushroom on one end, whose volume except for that would correspond easily to formula: pi times the radius squared times the height and – Eureka – you've got an erect penis.

That's why the one in my hand seemed as definitely fetishistic as that goat, especially uncircumcised, something I had never come across either, they weren't very popular back then, although I haven't put my own sons through the operation, since it's much more well thought of now, if there are no religious reasons, not to. I pulled back the foreskin, more in an absent-minded gesture to check if it was really real, than to attempt to further stimulate him, wondering at the beauty of its proportions, how it coordinated so well with his bone structure, a big man, Sandro, big bones and the big boner, hands in proportion to face like the David of Michelangelo.

Only with the equipment David should have had, that Michelangelo at a different historical moment might have preferred to give him, though who knows, maybe the great man was hung up on the infantile. Though I'm sure he would have loved its delicate colour, certainly Raphael would have, or Tintoretto or Rubens, a pale blue as much like a mandrill's ass hair or a lady's eyeshadow as like marble, the colour you will see sometimes around a truly pale skinned person's eyes, though Sandro's own face was more the sallow yellow pallor of the northern European or Slavic night person, the shadows around his eyes more a burnt umber, like great brown bruises, his tawny blonde the kind that matches hair and skin and eyes.

Maybe that swollen thing was his body's only blue, except for some veins on his arms, but swollen like that and surrounded by the straight reddish blonde pubic hair, much straighter and blonder than the hair on his head or in his moustache, and going pinkish toward the head, the scene before me was very much a pastel variation on the three primary colours that Laura was just getting into right then, placing them on her totemic backdrops, graph paper or paper bags or dried blood. Only in this case the bedbug bloodstains formed a background, and the pastels I held in my hand were the fore, so much gentler than her primaries, and all of it beautifully decorative really.

I have always been quite surprised that Laura in her heyday didn't make more of that phallic totem, I always thought that one day I would receive in the mail, whether as criticism or celebration I don't know, some kind of brilliant print of Sandro's cock, perhaps even twisted into one of her catastrophic knots. I know that I wouldn't have been able to resist it, that's the element I would have used over and over.

For ages it would pop into my mind at the oddest moments, when I wouldn't know whether to giggle or to cry, thinking how it could have been yet another kind of breakthrough in feminine imagery: molded in polyester resin and light pastel tints it would have made the colour field dildo of the decade.

I was pulled up on one elbow and just kind of staring at it, and lord knows now what thoughts really ran through my mind in that moment of examination, or what look was on my face. Or his either for that matter, beyond the dilated nostrils of the evenly controlled breathing I could hear, the stillness of his waiting. For the moment when I would finish pushing the foreskin back and come up onto my knees to be able to cup my other hand over its head and feel the little viscous drop of semen with my thumb as it would appear.

And then, of course, what more natural ceremony for the phallic vase in all its righteous glory than to move off the bed down onto my knees once more. Pulling the covers and the bedbugs with me to tuck them under my knees while I bowed my head to its comeliness and licked around its edge.

While he tried to sit up and undo my blouse.

It would have been the right move I suppose, if this had been a romantic encounter. Except that all that cloth was a shield for the wielding of my anger, making me push his hand away to stop him from touching my breasts. This act of getting to know each other better was to be a very one-sided affair, even if he did manage to bring one foot in, there between my legs, up the peasant skirt that I often wore into the restaurant. Where I was due in half an hour.

He got to move the foot up and down against my underwear while I did my work on him, up and down and around and the tongue and the tongue and the tongue. With him just kind of breathing as I looked at the so much smaller base of his prick like a flower's stem growing out of that sparse straight hair that peeked around the metal of the zipper, thinking ridiculously enough of whether flowers were indeed phallic symbols or symbols of the vulva or maybe a little bit of both and how maybe Laura should try to figure it out, maybe she should take that on, along with the rest of her work, the way Judy Chicago finally did, making a decision for the female.

Thoughts I intermixed with a run through of my program for the day, who would be on and who would be at which station and would I have to hostess again and how many customers would we have and how much would they tip and would there be any crises. Preparing my personality, or better my impersonality, for the evening ahead the way I always did, hardly noticing what I did anymore than I would had I been brushing my teeth, consciousness completely separate from the movements of my hand, the taste in my mouth when. His foot stiffens against me and his hand grabs onto my hair, and all the muscles I can see, the flat ones of his belly where his shirt has come untucked, his forearm against the bed, the unseen foot between my legs, go into tension.

And then there's the tremble, that funny little one men have, and the rough intake of breath without outcry, and he's holding my head down with one hand and coming into my mouth, before I can withdraw. Not the way the others had, letting me take it in my hand, or using a kerchief or their own. But pulling down hard on my hair, his hips lifting to push deep into my mouth, where the blue line of the urethra, I can feel it moving. In spasm from base to tip, where my hand my mouth covers it.

I still remember that bitter goodbye taste. Even on the evening we spent at Pier 16 in our deck chairs (we had come to love that place) I could taste it. As I felt the pull of the lights and the air and the water, so like the nights on the fire escape, although the view was better, there over to Brooklyn. With the yellow lights and the traffic moving while I felt that acute longing that I always feel looking into city buildings, all the layers of life past and present breathing in the brick and stone and metal and wood, all the things that we will never know, the stories we will never hear, the dreams realized and unrealized; and then the harbour opening out toward the sea, toward silence and voicelessness and first nurturance, the poisoned ocean aching with her burden of life, so that I felt her call in the pit of my stomach, and insisted that we go down, closer to the water for all its pollution, and we went down over to the seaport and sat on the old wood of the pier, and looked directly into the polluted water, and I shivered and you put your arm around me, and I sighed, and said:
–I lived right over there, you know.
–Yes, you told me. You answered.
  And I shivered again. And I remembered it all.

Though it would never have occurred to me to look up Sandro. To see how he's getting on, or if the group is functioning. It was just his taste and his smell in the salt and flour and creosote of that evening. And in the dead fish too, from the Fulton Fish Market, still New York's major fish market and active by midnight, that refused to move from right next door to Pier 16, even for the tourists. So that you can still smell it, and even, if you want to the way we did, sneak in and look at all that shining silvered flesh, gleaming at us under the neon. Though his colours were there too, not in the dead pilot fish the way they are sometimes in Kensington Market in Toronto, in the Portuguese markets with fish from the Canary Islands, but in the lights, on the buildings and the bridge, yellow and blue, and moving away.

—Goodbye, goodbye, they said, the way the taste in my mouth had said it: Goodbye, goodbye. As if some huge barrier had been broken or crossed, like reaching a continental divide and looking down on the immensity of a different watershed, you know that feeling, Thorne, you've commented on it, when we drove once, out to the Shushwap or down to Radium, and you talked about how you can feel the divide coming before you're there, even when you're mountaineering skiing. Then when you come up into the last pass you know it, you just know it. And then the world opens.

And then you're headed down.

I dribbled some of the semen back
out along his cock and watched it flow down into his hair. Then suddenly dizzy, I found I had to hold onto his pants. There was red and yellow dancing before my eyes and even he was a whole new landscape that told me somehow that something new had started. That I was on the other side now. And that I had intended it, felt myself moving there, that I had seen it coming: in more ways than one.

With the scene and that feeling, I can still see it sometimes, exactly as it was, the brass zipper, the dark denim, the withering bottle, the few tendrils of hair, the grey bloodstained wall like cloudy sky behind, just felt and logged in, the scene's power acknowledged only in the wordless image, because all the words in my mind were idle ones. Thoughts whose specificity I would never be able to recall, containing nothing about the trajectory of this act at all, about where it might aim me in its role of catastrophic hysteresis in what would soon become the discontinuity of my life.

My only regret in that moment was that I couldn't see his balls. Because I wondered what the balls would be like that partnered a prick like that one. An answer I would only find on the boat, as if that is what I had come back for, an answer to that question imagined for years, whether they would be blue or purple, and downy like a mandrill's, with pink or purple fur growing about, my imaginings became quite surrealistic, even converting his really quite ordinary, if a little straight, pubic hair, into those amazing mandrill colours that would match his cock the way the randiness of those monkeys that always grabbed their own for us in the Central Park Zoo, sending Laura and me off into gales of laughter, seemed to match his desire, or if that part of his anatomy at least, was really quite normal.

His cock started to go limp as I said goodbye to it, moving my fingers across it, auscultating almost, as if there were a secret there that only a doctor could find. While my anger stiffened me, rising again, a second erection out of the centre of my overwhelming though unnamed feelings. That pulled me to my feet right from my centre line, the middle of my head, like a puppet on a string, a balloon or condom or penis or rubber doll inflating, only with a terrible urge to spit into his face, all the rest of the come that hadn't already seeped out. So that I had to concentrate on slowly smoothing my skirt to restrain that impulse.

Because I no longer knew who I was angry at: him or myself. I just knew that it was me, me, me who had made that choice, whatever choice it was. Me who had gone up and across that pass, into that new watershed. In anger or desperation or longing it didn't matter. Still: it was me. Even if my statement had only been a grudging and sulky: You want it so badly, here, take it. His cock pulling my mouth into the expression of a pouting baby. Still.

The decision was mine. And the catastrophe.

I did manage to conserve some minimum of the sexual etiquette they would talk of on the boat, sex was still all etiquette that summer, not safety. Maybe it was even the last summer you could say the word sex without the word safe before it, when Acquired Immune Deficiency Syndrome was already a syndrome but not yet a disease, just something that seemed to mostly happen to gay men while tongues clucked, and wagged, and said it was just the inevitable breakdown of the body through the abuse of a promiscuous life style. The same way they always talk about promiscuous women abusing their sexual organs, but mostly their vaginas, with a great deal of medical time over the years dedicated to the discovery of the exact point at which great use becomes abuse, and if getting paid for it makes any difference. Though the general idea seems to be, that no matter how abusive the penetrating penis may be, still its use can never be abused, that is the job of the mucosa, anal or vaginal, or bucal for that matter, I suppose, that receives it.

An idea that's still around it would seem, at least in the straight community, I notice that around the school. All those debates about condoms or no condoms, at least in the Senior if not the Junior Highs, and tee-shirts with slogans like 'Cover Me I'm Going In', with sex an intrusion like a raid in a cop show, maybe *Dirty Hairy*, who knows. While the anti-condom side still marshals arguments against the possibility of heterosexual AIDS, despite the greatest spread of the virus in recent years being in that area, it still being god's vengeance on gay men. But with much the same attitude toward the act itself, making remarks like, 'statistically it would be almost impossible for a man to pick up AIDS from a heterosexual partner', meaning a woman I suppose, not another heterosexual man. While I will sit there in shock, thinking to myself, besides how it's a great argument in favour of lesbianism coupled with artificial insemination, it being far closer to impossible – though not absolutely impossible which is important enough – for a woman to pick up AIDS from a homosexual partner, assuming again that to be a *homosexual* female and not a gay man out for a lark, because I always thought the purpose of the condom was to protect the partner, male or female gay or straight. So it's interesting. The legend of Penis, the Super Warrior, in need of no armour, at least when attacking the female of the species, still goes on.

Which wasn't of course, condoms or no condoms safe or unsafe sex, the kind of thing they would talk about, though rumour has it, through my mother, though I'm not quite sure, that the owner of the boat has since died of AIDS, with all his money protecting him no more than it did Rock Hudson. And whatever fantasies they still secretly held, they certainly never mentioned the penis as weapon, though it was certainly a tool, whether of pleasure or manipulation never seemed quite clear. Because they were into an etiquette of what they thought of as equality, with the only concern how you, female or male, straight or gay or bi or undecided, could get laid as much as possible and still not treat your partner like complete shit, though who knows what they all really would do in practice, as each one nodded in accord with the idea that all things sexual were possible and even good, the heads of the women from the commune going up and down as quickly as the men's. With any little bit of S&M that precluded permanent bodily harm, or ripping off a piece right under your current partner's nose, as good as anything else, as long as you were polite.

Which meant not leaving your partner completely in the lurch, if she or he didn't want to watch or even participate, you had to at least make sure other minimal needs were met, maybe the long tall drink and a hit of something, some cool music or calling a cab to take them home from the party, with maybe even a suggestion as to who might be available to share the bed when they got there, so that you would always be careful to make them comfortable and at ease. Or at least make it impossible for them to say they weren't comfortable and at ease and enjoying themselves, before you went into the head for a quick bit of head, or the kitchen to do it on the counter or out into the woods to do it on the moss, or along the sandy beach among the dunes, with Fire Island presenting its own particular problems in those terms, they assured me, a lot of this did seem staged for my benefit, though I'm not sure whoever said this didn't mean it as a warning to any of us who hadn't been there before, at least they said they'd seen it happen.

You had to be very careful that the piece of the wild you picked for your wild piece wasn't among the poison ivy they said, because almost all the green on Fire Island, on the entire sand spit, is poison ivy, with boardwalks running between. So that hospitalizable disasters had happened more than once, hands grabbing at the greenery and then wandering off into one or another available orifice, with all of them winking at each other, sometimes it seemed almost a kind of initiation rite, maybe someone in the group would like to dance with a crown of poison ivy, someone who was immune, of course, around their head? —So, if anyone has any ideas, the voice continued: Just ask for a bed, or if your group's too large for a cabin, and here there was much laughter: Do it on the deck. See just how much you can rock the boat. And then, if you get seasick, there's miles of beach: just don't share it with any plant life.

I had nodded as I listened to all of this, trying to imagine how Laura would have handled the situation, if she would have agreed, or just nodded in agreement in order not to disagree and appear gauche and unsophisticated. Or if she might have felt by the time she got onto that boat, in possession of enough power to take advantage of whatever sexual rewards were offered, feeling herself, at least metaphorically, on the fucker side. She might have had her own groupies by then, there was no way I could tell.

Though I couldn't imagine her doing less than letting it slip off her leather jacket shell, easing her way among the contradictions with her throaty laugh, because she would certainly never let herself be considered a prude. So I wouldn't let myself be considered one either, even if it has always seemed to me, condoms or no condoms, then or now, that this much vaunted new sexual freedom still has a way of coming to always contain a fucker and a fuckee. Something that you've said too, that this one can't be the one women have been fighting for. Though it's hard to know which one is. I don't want to go back to the old puritanism either, where sexually active women live in one or another form of guilt or terror. Though maybe this freedom, at least the way they drew it, like Linda Lovelace's life, amounts to the same thing.

I just smiled my most polite smile and tried to hold on, looking as sophisticated as my mother would have wanted me to be, after all there was no telling how much of it was meant to get at me. So I emitted no

'ohs' of shock, or squeaked out comments that the voice is always too high for.
—How could you think that's all *right*?, or: What about those young *people*? What happens to *them*? the voice always rising querulous at the end.

As they went on to speak of trips to certain very exclusive bordellos, where there were teenage, very young teenage, though no prepubescent as far as I could figure out, prostitutes. Who loved it apparently, they said that without being asked.
—Oh, they've found their chosen life those kids, they're absolutely insatiable. And they don't have to think about anything. They just get to screw their brains out. Get high and fuck, fuck and get high. Can you think of a better life?

As they were driven by the huge and uninhibited appetites for sex, and quality drugs I believe, that puberty had given them, that puberty would have given all of us, if we could just be free enough to recognize it. I think Sandro said that, because I know there was one point or another in there that he winked at me. To tell me that I could be insatiable too.

That's when I should have turned and said:
—Oh, as long as we're on the subject, what exactly *are* you supposed to do when you give someone a blowjob? Do you smile and swallow? Or just let it kind of subtly dribble out of the corner of your mouth? Are you supposed to comment on the taste? What if it's terrible and you want to gag? Can you do that and then apologize? Or if you decide you don't like him after all, can you spit it in his face?

In a tone that might indicate it was all a matter for Miss Manners, like knowing to eat asparagus tips with your fingers. Dear Miss Manners: Is it proper decorum to wipe the back of your hand across your mouth after you swallow semen?

That was what I finally did, in an act of defiance after swallowing hard, the taste so salty and aptly named, semen sea-man, and bitter too in the back of the mouth, like algae filled water. I did it for my own pride I think, after all I'd swallowed his, just the way those dreadful ads for Bob's Burgers used to remind me, Swallow Our Pride, they would say from the billboards, so that every time I saw them I would emit a sound between a giggle and a croak.

It would have been nice to say it though. And to smile over at him from where I sat perched near the rail, with my voice a little high, and bouncing, aiming my shoulders at him, the way we all do so often when we're flirting. At least it would have saved me from thinking he was on my side the way I did right then, and from thinking he had always had her good in mind, and from trusting him so much. Though I don't think it would have stopped what happened later, still, it would have made it happen in another dimension, continuing another reality.

Instead I smiled and just kind of nodded, maybe we are all insatiable, who knows, that's what the pornography propaganda keeps telling us, and maybe it's true, if we really could just make sex ecstatic, a true and open, a promiscuous celebration. It's possible that my smile may even have seemed a come-on, what made them all think I had already consented, as I looked back over to the water and tried to pretend that I was just too into the trip to really pay close attention.

Laura might have handled all that innuendo that way too, looking away into sea or brush, thinking of the concrete movements her hands had made in the plastic arts as well as in the art of love. The scenery might have been the most interesting thing to her. Conversations like this might have been boring to her by then.

I'm sure that's why one of them remarked to another, loud enough to let me know it was a compliment I was supposed to hear:
— You see, one said: She *is* like Laura. Just like Laura used to say. You remember: Alma is my twin, she said.
— That's right. Laura could never take her eyes off the scenery either. How the unchanging changes, the continuous discontinues, she always said.

Only with me

it was the discontinuous continuing. Even if I didn't know it yet. Even if it would be some hours still before I got to hear his voice following me again. Always to get in the last word, twisting something he had said previously, something that seemed perfectly innocent, into triumph. Or letting circumstances do it for him.

The way his voice came from behind me that day in the apartment, as I walked back into my room to get the sweater I had left. I would need it for the air conditioning at work, god knows it was hot enough out.
– You can stay. You can. Just this once you can miss work, Sandro said as I threaded my way through last night's dirty glasses and the coffee cups I had been emerging from my room to clean when he pulled me to him. Slow and sexy that voice was supposed to be; slow and sexy and pleading, with an undertone of command, of gift.

Then when I turned back, I must have had some response in mind, I saw that he was rubbing his prick, the way he would on the boat. Like a promise, his fingers running over it:
– We should get to know each other more, much much more.
 Then he had continued, believing I'm sure that it had truly pleased me, that his come tasted of wine or roses, as if offering me a great bargain:
– I can give you four orgasms in the time it will take you to get to work on the subway.
 And he smiled while he slowly took his hand off it long enough to pat the bed next to him.
– C'mon Alma, stay, he said with a strange laugh, the bomb he had placed inside me, the kind that go off after they hit, a kind of psychological anti-personnel weapon, what he uses in his theatre work, finally detonating.
– We could surprise Laura.

I did gag then. Totally unmannerly, totally against all the decorum if not dignity I was trying to maintain. I just couldn't help it. There was the slow rising cold along my arm, and then a lot of saliva in my mouth and then I was gagging. So that I ran into the kitchen with the nausea rising from the pit of my stomach to engulf my body until I didn't care if he heard while I spit and choked and gagged and rinsed out my mouth and threw water on my face and wiped it dry and hurried down the stairs and to work; the wet between my thighs leaking through my panties to nag at me, a terrible criticism.

 Salty, like secret tears.

The same wet that would nag at me all the way down to Laura's house that Sunday afternoon after I got back from my weekend on the boat. No matter what I tried to tell myself about the connective value of my act. Only it would be much worse then, mixed the way it would be with his come. That I would tell myself was a gift for her, the gift I had not stayed that afternoon to give. Only once more I would have it explode on me, like all of Sandro's gifts, tearing at my insides this time, as I followed her up the stairs onto the roof.

  He kept saying that he loved her. That as soon as she was well enough she would be home with him. That I should stay until then. But she had already left. Before the hospital.

When I got to wor

after leaving the

apartment that afternoon, I found myself trying so hard to escape the bitter taste in my mouth, the salty wetness between my legs, that instead of being depressed the way I might have expected, I was giddy and outgoing, and far more talkative with customers and colleagues alike, one of the other waitresses even asked me what I was on. Then, when a bunch of young men came into the restaurant late in the evening, all flirtatious and foreign sounding and nice, I flirted back. Until they invited me for a drink at a disco when I got off.

And I picked out for my own the sweetest and darkest of them. A man with chocolate hair and large fresh wintergreen eyes and a way of looking at things around him, slightly secret and delicate and scared, that said he thought the world might explode if he touched it.

While his friends went for the women at the bar, women I thought far more glamorous, I concentrated on him and on my drinks, hoping that just my concentration would hold him, would make it work, would let those hands explode me. Until in the end he invited me back to his place, just as I had wanted, a cheap furnished apartment with no individual taste to measure him by, where I screwed him and screwed him, with hardly any foreplay, hardly any mouth work at all, the two of us a miracle of enthusiasm and lack of technique, just hands and eyes and sticking it in, that straight thick proper sausage of a cock with the thick curly hair under it, with me just saying something like, Give it to me baby the way I thought I was supposed to, while he replied, Oh baby baby, and then something incomprehensible in French the way I guess he thought Americans would appreciate.

Until he screwed me dry, and there was only a vague rawness left in my flesh and in my mind. And the next day one hell of a hangover. With no regrets.

Or at least none that involved him.

I left in the morning without even finding out his name. Thinking, of course, that I would never see him again. That was how those things were supposed to work. Barroom romances were supposed to leave you lonely. Quickly. He was supposed to brag about you to his friends. Not come around again.

Only he appeared alone in the restaurant the next evening and told me his name and asked for mine, and insisted on taking me for another ride, sitting me up this time on top of that thickness of him, while I pushed and shoved and moaned and groaned. And even if the pink flesh that took him in was swollen from soreness as much as from arousal, still I laughed a lot and kissed him more and watched the sunrise out his window.

And that's when I knew that I had not only climbed to the top of the pass but come down the other side, and walked into the forest of his eyes and of his body and that I could hide there if I wanted. As I did for years. As perhaps I still do.

Because that barroom encounter was Jeanpierre. Down for a summer in New York on the money he had made in the north, before going back to school to finish his course. Where he had learned seismology, and to chart the rhythms of the earth, with the dynamite. 'Le dinamateur' they would call him in French, that was his job. But I loved the title. It's my favourite of all the titles he has ever had. Of all the jobs he has ever done. The one I still call him by, in the kitchen or in bed, or during a fight.

The one that still seems peculiarly apt. Because there must have been something in my desperation, in my wanting, that moved him, the way he moved me. Because he said later, laughing of course, one can hardly use that kind of metaphor without laughing, and even then only in bed, with his hand on my belly, that I was the blasting cap for the dynamite inside him.

−Of course, I giggled and answered: You're the one with the stick. But then, in his job, I asked, wasn't I supposed be the earth? A perfect earth mother. The one with the holes in it? As ridiculous a bedroom conversation as any one might wish to imagine. The kind of thing, like those fond nicknames one develops, that would turn your cheeks crimson, or worse, if anyone else found out.

Only he refused to keep joking. He looked away out the window toward the city lights and the pale lilac horizon of late twilight or early dawn, we spent so much time in bed that it's hard to recall, I was even missing time at work for the first time since I'd started, and he said that he had known it from the very first time we met, from the first moment we had looked at each other.

There was something in me that wanted him, he said, that wanted *him*. I was the first woman who had ever just wanted him, reaching out to make him explode with the force, the beauty, of that wanting.

So that I have never had the guts to tell him that what I saw was the vulnerable sweetness of his face. And that what he felt was the groaning earthquake of my betrayal.

By then I had walked too far into the bush. Away from the pinnacle of Laura and of Sandro. And besides, I needed him so much. Him and our brief and repeated animal couplings. And the marvel in his eyes, the appreciation.

As if the gift I so imperfectly gave him through my body was so pure and so special, like one of those new maps he is forever making, as we would move together each day further into what they always call virgin territory. With him the mapmaker and me the map. And above all that he came back to take me with him. That he gave me some place to go.

So that I wouldn't have to face Sandro. Or deal with the two of them. Not even in the morning.

It was hard right then. After what had happened. What I had done. Very hard to go home. Harder listening. And hardest of all that mixture of horniness and hatred, when I did. What Sandro would comment on in his cabin as he played with my breast, my defeat consummated, that he could always feel me there, concentrated behind that wall, wanting it, wanting it, wanting him.

–Did you masturbate while you listened, Alma, he said, lowering his hand to my crotch, placing it in the tangled wet hairs.

–Yes, Sandro, I answered, licking my lips, the heroine of the romance, conquered and obedient.

Only I didn't tell him it had helped make Jeanpierre perfect. How it had honed his fresh beauty. As we drove the horniness out of me, night after night of hard driving. Like running a marathon. And loving every inch of the road. Every sound, every sight, every smell, every taste, every minute every movement every second every secretion of it.

Until that afternoon toward the end of the summer when Laura came into my room.

I was sitting on my bed in my underwear wondering

what I would wear that evening for work, and what I could add to it to meet Jeanpierre at a nightclub after. I was yawning too, I was so tired, even as she started to speak, her full blonde body blocking my door.

She was in her underwear too, but not because she was changing, summer days she liked to lounge around like that, declaring that the neighbours couldn't see in because it was so much darker inside than out, and anyway who cared. Her round moon face looking down at me as her voice made its flat statement while filling with a strange vibrating power, even through its evenness of tone, a resonance that stopped my yawn before it had neared its completion.

—You are not coming home, she said.

I wanted to answer, defiant and adolescent, almost sulky, I could feel the pout playing at the corners of my lips: How would you know, anyway. You're so busy with him.

But I knew that she knew. As much as Sandro. She could feel me too. And more than that, I could feel the knowledge licking at me, arousing terror, I was suddenly sure as I looked at her that she needed my presence there, in my small cell, to listen to her cries. To take in the oceanic pullings of her, to be her nun and her priestess and her priesthood, counting not my rosary but the small circular strokes of my finger against my clitoris as I masturbated to her rhythms, to the sound of her triumph and her need of him. Her voice knew all that, and wanted it.

—Uuuuhhn, was all I could answer when I heard that voice.

And saw in her eyes the need for all that tension and attention, oblique but sure, there since he'd moved in with us. As if my drinking them in, their outcries, their utterances, their smallest mouselike squeaks, their tidal ebbs and flows, at such close range, were a necessary hidden seismic equipment of the kind Jeanpierre would use to chart the movements caused by the charges he had laid, that would tell him the nature of the surrounding earth. As perhaps my silent presence told them theirs. As important as Sandro doing it to her: me listening.

She pointed to the floor
in front of her and told me to come to her with a sudden broad smile. And I shivered.

With a shudder that ran all the way up my hands to my shoulders. Only I still felt safe enough sitting on my own bed, safe in my own territory, that I did manage to smile back, a pale reflection.

She moved forward then and took both my hands and led me unresisting, I didn't know to resist, into their bedroom and sat me down on the edge of their bed, just, I swear, where I had knelt before Sandro.

Only she knelt before me.

I thought for a moment she would either challenge me for doing it: Right here Alma, right here! or forgive me. She would tell me that what I had done with Sandro was not a reason not to come home, that she understood. Or maybe she didn't but I should come home anyway. And my hands started to shake as I felt a terrible sorrow rising, the same sorrow I would feel on the roof as we walked over to the tar papered incline above the tin cornice and lay down.

I was close to tears as I awaited her verdict there among the smells and the carcasses and the dirty dishes, trying to shrink down while she knelt high up on her knees so that her face was above mine, while she squeezed my hands. It's to give me comfort I thought, the stern comfort of a mother about to tell the child to take her medicine, a teacher about to give a bad grade, a boss about to give a painful reprimand.

Or a commanding officer. She was once more my commanding officer, about to give this reluctant recruit a necessary message.

About loyalty perhaps, I didn't know.

In a way I guess it was. Because she said, my hands still firmly held in hers:

–I do not know who he is, but he is not worthy of you.

Her words measured as if what she said were a foregone conclusion. As if I must already know.

Perhaps I should have been relieved. Perhaps I should have sighed and thought: At least there's that, at least she doesn't know.

Only instead of diminishing, my fear increased. My fear and something I can't explain, if it was in the set of her body or in the smells arising from the mattress or in my sex worn cunt or in my memory, but it was suddenly worse than with Sandro, the wet there between my legs to have us both so close and so near naked by that bed in tableau. To make me hide my trembling hands in the sheets, and break my eyes away from hers, to try to retreat from the precipice I suddenly found myself looking over, the precipice in her eyes, that invited everywhere and nowhere, not a watershed but a cliff, a catastrophe, completely unexpected.

I shook my head and let her take my hands again as I maintained my eyes against the bloodstained wall. Examining each one like some people do water stains, to find some hidden image or meaning. As I tried not to feel her. Her eyes on me. Those eyes that had gone beyond searching to finding. Those eyes that knew. The ones they had to kill with the tranquilizers to take from them that essence of knowing. The way the drugs took her smile, and tore it apart, and made it drift on the wind, too vague for her face.

Her what do you want eyes, that already had the answer. Penetrating to the centre. Of bedrock or of earth. Fluid rock or earth: her magma eyes.
—But he's like me, I said. My voice small and mouselike. Hardly the defense I wanted, but it was all I could think of. Then in the moment that I said it, nibbling around its edge, I knew that it was true.
—He's like me. I repeated.

Strangely enough, when I said it, she relaxed. The tension leaving her body and her arms, as she sat back, her thighs pressed onto her calves. Her breath letting out and a smile finally curving her lips.

She smiled because she knew. She already knew. Not my words but what that tiny voice had said: that whoever he was like and whoever or wherever he belonged, he didn't have the power in him to take me away. She smiled because she was still sure that I was hers. That I always would be. As perhaps I always have been.

291

It made her smile and joke. Suddenly gone childish. But childish like a child. A real and playful child. The way she would be for one moment again as she lifted that porcelain shepherd in her mother's living room to wield in the service of its Saviour, or in that one instant before I fell on my knees to hug her at my mother's.

Only that time she let go of my hands and smiling and childish spoke, patting the side of her face then, as if she wished to lean forward and do the same to mine, crinkling up the corners of her eyes.
– No. Lady, you mistake yourself. He cannot be like you. You are the heroine. You are the Amazon warrior.

And then her hands came to my shoulders. Still the commanding officer to the new recruit. As if sizing me up, a hard grip, to fully enter into the game, like so many of our games, feeling me under her hands.
– You have a mission, she announced. Shaking me to apprise me of it.
– You have a mission. And the consort of the Amazon must be worthy.

It was perfect. That combination of joke and of seriousness. To give an exact meaning to her play. To tell me of her belief in my role in her destiny. Because that's what it was, not a belief in my own. So that my body leaned toward her while my mind recoiled. And my eyes saw Jeanpierre in the bloodstains.

To what purpose I don't know, but I almost told her who he was and that I wanted to go with him. That my mission with her was over. Only I couldn't. Not even say: I have come to love that man. Or just: You're wrong. Because still: her eyes held me.

My confusion made me take her hands from my shoulders and get up and turn from her, pacing five steps, each one determined and measured by the rules of the game, before I turned back. Almost twenty years old and still playing this game. And still enjoying it. Because I could leave the desperation of the moment for the ritual magnitude of our own myth time, to feel the power of the fantasy I had always loved: the fantasy with its kernel of truth. As I bowed.
– My lady Queen, I said: I am but your shieldbearer. And the ways of this war I do not know.

– Then bear my shield, she answered, standing too now, a regal gesture, pointing to the place where it was my turn to go to my knees on the floor.

I did so. And in proper fealty, I touched my head to the rug, and I put it all back onto her. The betrayal I had felt.

– I cannot, Great Queen, I said: Bear the shield of one who has chosen another in her stead.

It was interesting that even then she did not break out of the game, that all of our personal drama could take place as easily on that plane, on that stage, as on any other. Without any pause, even for a moment, for her to relax her shoulders. Or open her mouth or let her fingers flex.

She just stood there. And she was my Queen.

With the regal posture and the direct gaze and that ability she had only let slip in that final performance, the facility at reading her audience, at drawing in the other participants, that would make her the darling of the performance circuit, especially the feminist performance circuit. That would never seem ridiculous despite the lack of glamour in her girl next door looks, her rounded cheeks, her full body, her pouty lips or the too frizzy dirty blonde hair. Slimy/frightening maybe in secondhand sequins or black leather, but never ridiculous.

Any more than she was ridiculous to me as I stood, caught there, unable to leave the game myself, a suppliant subject. As her slightly raised upper lip made me marshal unspoken elements to justify myself.

To say: Yes, and, But, and, Look, and, Please, My Queen.

Just a brief time out. An Intermission before we go on. To redefine my character. I'm not comfortable in the role you've chosen for me, can't you see that I just can't act it well. I've never even been able to stand centre stage to say my lines, and I can't marshal the drama, surely you've seen that. Whether it's a major or a minor character I'm supposed to play, I'm still only the comic relief: the slapstick part of the work that entertains the lower orders. There is nothing noble in me, even my delusions. I'm Sancho Panza, not Don Quixote, not even Dulcinea, not any king or queen or princess, active or passive or in-between, gentle or sweet or fierce or regal, or an Amazon. Not any of them.

I'm just the one who walked behind, I wanted to tell her, the cook and camp follower who polished the armour and entertained the warriors, the one they finally let go back to her village. That even the Queen Hippolyta would let go back to her village, once the Queen's shield had been shined.

She could become a barmaid or a waitress or a whore. Just the way I was. At least one of the above. And she could tell stories of the war, the way I would for years, tales of my tour of duty in Bohemian Countercultural Postmodern New York. And she could tell of the Queen and of her battles, while she watched the world go by, and the children in their dirty nightshirts as they did their tasks.

And she could laugh again, a different laugh. At stupid things, not frames of reference or discontinuous space or alien landings, but at sitcoms or lightbulb jokes or first run movies.

Or being tickled. The way Jeanpierre and I did, or you and I, muffling it a bit, when we laughed and hunkered down, there between the sheets.

I was a sidekick not a partner. That's what I wanted to tell her. That I had always been her sidekick, whether among the forsythia or the lilac or the beetles or the bedbugs. Even Sandro had noticed that. And the girls in school. And my mother.

Only I knew she wouldn't want to understand. Even as the plaintive whine rose in my throat to start me on my way, I knew I shouldn't do it. There was no reason to. She would just urge me back by telling me how wonderful, how important, how essential, I was. At least to her. How she couldn't do any of it without me. The way she did in her letters. Talking of how her '*Alma*' was what moved her into the future. Trying to bring me back. Or to believe I wanted to come.

I got up and I turned away from her as she looked at me. And I picked something up, I don't remember what it was, just that with my gesture I did what I had to do: I took it upon myself to briefly change my character in the game.

I was no longer the foot soldier called upon to explain herself to her captain, but another lady, another courtier, another gossip, another juggler another jester at the Queen's court. Who would form our dialogue into another favourite teenage pastime, all that who likes who likes what does what with whom, as the lady-in-waiting said to her Queen what neither I nor the foot soldier had ever wanted to say.

– And Sandro, I said, my back still turned: I suppose he's worthy?

I waited for the gasp behind me. Or sigh or growl or outrush of air, the angry protest, the hand clawing into my back while the words would come all together in a rush, the way it always used to be when we fought.

Only it didn't.

I heard a laugh. But not the one that signalled the end of the game, the one that would leave us lying on the ground together, giggling and giddy as time resumed its continuous course along its Cartesian co-ordinates, and we looked around us and we knew the world for what it was and we felt the earth and rubbed our fingers through the forsythia and we looked at the sky and we giggled.

This regal laugh accepted the change but continued the game, showing that she was satisfied to be at court now too. As the Queen drew herself up, to laugh in a manner befitting her rank and privilege: calculating and deep and magnanimous.

And above all, since the Queen may do as the Queen decides, even as she lectures her lady-in-waiting on gossiping too much of her affairs, slightly bawdy.

Powerful and bawdy. Far more so than the laugh she practiced for Thursday nights, than the one she used to tell her stories. The one she would use to call me into the room: Alma, oh Alma, tell them about my mother.

And this laugh called to me far more. I might have claimed I'd never heard it before, except she would know I had. It was the most special laugh of all: the one she retained in her mouth for Sandro.

The one that bubbled deep in her throat, that she played with, to let him know she played, that must call him into her, to echo around his tongue, around his oversized cock, the way it would around her words. A laugh that spoke to a power deep inside her, that invited you in so that you might never come out: except transformed.

And utterly hers. As it would forever bubble around you and define you as it arose out of some source deeper even than the laugh that became her trademark, that was talked of and written about. And worshipped. A laugh that embodied in that moment everything I was afraid of. Even as I was called to the altar of Laura. My Laura.

As the hairs rose on my arms and the back of my neck, and my body filled with fear and heat. Cold and warm together to think that she would laugh that laugh for me. Because it made me wet again, far wetter now than I had ever been; with Sandro, or with Jeanpierre. Or with so many nights of listening to them as I silently rubbed myself to sleep.

I was full of a terrified liquid waiting no longer just between my thighs but in all my body, flowing from its centre behind my pubic bone to fill me up. To harden my nipples and liquefy even my elbows and my knees so that I could not move until the tidal wave reached my throat, my mouth suddenly rich with saliva.

Only the taste was of Sandro's sacrament, bitter on my tongue.

She moved

behind me. Her steps falling from toe to heel the way you might imagine an ancient warrior queen would walk as she came up behind me to breathe over my shoulder. And she placed her hands on my waist, and she spoke.
– It is not Sandro's to be worthy or to be unworthy, she said, a rumbling whisper in my ear. He is not the husband to the queen, but the consort: the priest of the temple. Sandro incarnates Dionysus. And he is a teacher.

And then came that laugh again. So close that I shivered.
– He teaches me many things, I heard.

And I would swear, without truly knowing if it happened, there was so much tension in my body, that she licked my ear, flashing her tongue quickly inside it, as if demonstrating that teaching.

—The things gods teach, she said. Many worthy things, that the Queen could teach her shieldbearer.

And at that her hands started down my body, across my hips. Moving in time to her laughter. The laughter that made her a stranger to me despite all our years of childish erotic games. That made me suddenly wish to yell at her. To turn and to scream and to slap her face and to call her names.

Cunt. **Cunt**. I wanted to shout. Not: Whore! the way her father had, but: Cunt. Cunt.

Because only a cunt could laugh like that. Surely it must have been that: her cunt laughing. From deep inside her to deep inside me, cunt to cunt or womb to womb, the fecund feminine of her calling out to pull me in like that. To make me wish to fall into that morass of bedbugs and ejaculate, into the smells of sex and blood and insanity and love and exaltation and sleepless nights and new depths to any or all experience, as I stood there her hands on my body my body aching to join them, to call out.

Cunt cunt, a cry of exultant longing not a curse, a word of most profound blessing even as I tried to focus on Jeanpierre's eyes to stop myself from jumping in, from drowning in that sea, from turning around to move forever out from my solitary room from his solitary suite to meet them in the depths, in that secret place only she could call me to, so much deeper, so much more profound, so much more my world, my mystery, than Sandro's overly obvious so ostentatious blue bottle monolith. Even if he should guard our flower-strewn lair the way our sentry once had.

With his cock no mighty sword but a mere instrument of prayer, the way I saw it right then before my eyes as she spoke his name.

When suddenly my skin went raw and my mind too. With a sunburn pain from floating too long on a bright sea whose depths I would not enter. While the wetness from her laugh was the

Hampton undertow pulling at me, scraping my skin and getting inside my bathing suit, rubbing me with all the little rocks that I could hear rolling around in her throat.

I felt terribly and deeply hurt. As I took her hands from my hips and turned around it was no longer fear that moved me, but pain. They both knew. They both knew. They both knew. A pulsating sign going off and on. I even questioned in my mind whether they had planned it. All of it, even Sandro's constantly voiced need to get to know me. While knowing that they knew turned the longing in my body to an unvoiced scream.

Because she had not come to challenge me about Jeanpierre. The challenge was to make it come to this. To see me willingly give him up because I would want, once I understood the nature of the invitation, more than anything else, to be with them in the way that they wanted to be with each other. That I could share now as well as witness.

Only she wanted me to say it: what they both knew.

That's why I stilled myself. Physically willed myself, my trembling hands, my hot groin, into stillness. Like a rock on the shore. A huge and distant rock. Willed to rise out of that current. Apart from the pebbles already turning to sand in her throat.

Because I was furious too. At how they both thought they could play with me: with who I had always been to her.

All the time I had spent in that room, sneaking in and out as I isolated myself in horny listening, was not a favour she appreciated, that I would one day be thanked for, the way she had thanked me those first nights I had spent at my mother's.

—Thank you Alma for giving me this space, she would say, and I would feel noble because I was giving her that place to develop with her man, what I was sure we had both thought of at one time as the proper future for us. What it was still costing me so much to let her have: the life of the couple.

And now I found that it had been a trial for me. In which I could prove my loyalty or my purity or my worthiness: my abnegation. Like the trial a warrior might have to pass through to show her dedication to her sovereign, her goddess, in preparation for love and battle. The trial of the knight who must spend a last night in the church before the Holy Grail while all manner of demons and impure thoughts and finally beautiful women come to seduce him and are refused. While he without doubt remains hard all night, hard and trying to think of England, or whatever, just the way I had stayed so wet.

Where in the end what was imagined for me was a garden of sensual delights, once my loyalty, silent behind that white wall, staring out that window, was proved.

I had not been strong enough. That is what she was telling me: that I had not been strong enough for that trial, for that trap. That obstacle course of ejaculate and bedbugs that she had made me run. As she stood behind me now, telling me it did not matter to her, that I had failed the test, still she would give me one last chance, even if I had broken and run, at the first opportunity, into the arms of the Prince of Winter.

Who had swooped down from the north for me as I knelt at her sexual altar all warm and wet and waiting, so angry and so lonely and so confused in that new space she had made in our house, that new white walled back room celibate's temple cell, that I did not know when he came laughing into the restaurant with his friends, that it was not him I should have been waiting for. The one who covers the earth with cold, who freezes the moment into stillness and calculates its impact, while laughing into his parka hood.

Because I had come to want that. In all this turbulence, this discontinuity, I wanted that still and calculable moment. It was all I had wished for even as I snuck in to change that afternoon: not the walls of my cell but the walls of my own mind. A mind that would command my body. Even in pleasure.

Where the seismologist, not the earth, would dictate the moments of the explosion, its proportions and its scale. Even if they were small, even if he was small, small and proud and unworthy, that's what she had called him. With his penis sinking into me as his charges sank into the earth.

While he laughed with his comrades, I am sure he has done that, about us both. The earth and me. It was obvious in the way he looked at me the nights we drank with them, love out of the corners of his eyes, as if he could not admit to so deep a passion in their presence.

That was really a good one, wasn't it? he might say to cover up. After all, he'd gotten just the response he'd wanted, received just the right data, from the moving needles of the seismograph or the whistle of my breath, my moving hips. With the gall to think he mapped the true ramifications of our explosions, of our orgasms, that he could sit apart from them, as he would say it.

Ah, that one, yes. That was very good, she is very good, you know the kind, three thrusts and she goes crazy, did I ever stick it to her, that one really worked, we got just the data the pleasure we needed.

Yet even if I could hear those imagined conversations, ringing true in my mind, it was still so easy, with her breathing down my neck, to imagine like an oasis the clear beauty in him. To see instead of the coarse male bonding laughter, the awkward movements of his hands, the stupefied eagerness of his eyes and his smile.

It was far easier to wish to be refreshed in the dense forest of his eyes than to wish to deal with that sordid hot apartment and what I could see in Laura's gaze, rising and rising and rising from the greatest depths, what I was sure would be in mine, if I would only look. What had always been between us, that neither one had ever wished to acknowledge, not just desire, but our unconscious knowledge that we could be whole. That we could be everything. The unity of everything. That we could stop time. Together.

I recapitulated the brief time I had spent with Jeanpierre, taking up my one weapon against her and against Sandro, against the siren song of their moans and of their groans, tying myself to the image of him, of his breath sighing out as we finished. When I would watch his hands, the two hands, one on his belly and one on mine. As if measuring the waves, the infinitesimal aftershocks of pleasure, to know how to calculate their impact.

Then lighting a cigarette to say that what had just happened would always be enough, without looking any further, without having to make any of it into giant world-shaking theories of discontinuity and catastrophe. Or permanent mystic unity. Not the cunt not the womb not the earth not the hysteresis, but looking at me again as if that would be more than enough, the raw data and its measure more than enough, as he would run his hands over me again and close his eyes. While my body would shake and tense where his hand had passed, the rippling response to the charge he had set, there right there, and he would smile, and close his eyes, making a map of those waves, my body the earth moving.

Then from his distance he would form that map into knowledge. So that I could see myself, the map of me, its insides still terra incognita, mysterious but unimportant. While its outlines, there right there, its limits and its limitations, its boundaries, became exposed for all to acknowledge.

Including me. Because I had come to want nothing more. No closer approach to the mysteries.

Which is why, I think, throughout that encounter, whether she knelt before me and tried to recover my hands, or circled her arms about my waist to make that invitation to follow her, as I had always followed her, into depths without maps or even outlines, where she would explore while I tried to make sense, the cook and bottle washer and sidekick and shieldbearer and log keeper on the journey of our two in one self, I suddenly found myself understanding Jeanpierre so well, especially as he would stand, overlooking the tundra.

I remembered

our explorations, Laura's and mine, Laura's with me following, a perfect sherpa except that I didn't know the way up the mountain, only the way out to Coney Island. And I understood suddenly what it could mean to know that your worship, your adoration of something, is the only creation, the only source of creativity, you have in you. That you will never be the earth, fecund and catastrophic, much less feel that you are a new earth, rising into self-consciousness, to reach and name, from the inside out, new limits of experience.

Because all you can be is the preplanned worship of the earth, and by no means always a benign worship, just a repeated pattern of touching and making and loving and eating and breaking and killing and mourning over and over, planned for you long before, each word or line or symbol already used, like baroque emblems or Chinese ideographs, or pieces of traditional religions. So that you would never have to look back, or perhaps even want to, to try to systematize your acts yourself, to make a new system, or even to analyze what system it is your worship, your love, fits into. What ends it finally serves.

Just as Jeanpierre finds it impossible to look back, and surely does not want to, from the window of his office, to try to see beyond the city, beyond his pleasure in the data he has gathered, his joy in his time spent in the bush, to what it has meant over the years, all his explorations, for the places he has loved. That others like him have loved and killed. Or at least helped make room for the armies, the machines, of death. For the tundra or the great river basins or the rainforest.

While I would not look either. It must have been that day I decided not to look. At the meaning, not of what, but of how, we explored. Of what our inability to articulate our worship in any way differently from all of the common places, all the clichés, could mean. And in his worship of my body, what those images of femininity or motherhood could mean for the female, for our place, our bodies' place, in the world. Because even as he would always look upon me, as beautiful as worthy as magnificent, the way nobody ever had, I would be different too. Essentially different. At least my body would. As different as an insect or a houseplant or a mineral deposit.

And I would feel the same. Taught as I was from early on to think of my body as different from me, most women are, if they are allowed a self beyond the body at all, and it certainly went with the territory I grew up in. Where you were allowed to have both a mind and a body but the mind was one gender and the body another. So that now I would come to regard the body I had been gifted with as a magnificent tool the two of us could use together, two male buddies exploring the feminine earth.

Which is, strangely enough, what I think has made it such a pleasure to have children with him, to have his hands always with me, inside and out, the best possible father on the delivery table for Jason and René, by our own bed for Amber, as he would watch all the functions of my body, whether in nursing or orgasm, and of my pleasure. With that same expression in his eyes as I saw the first time we got out of a plane when he took me north, that look, squinting but wide-eyed, of love and worship.

The look of a lover, yes, of a lover. An uncomprehending and anxious lover. Until I took it on too, looking out across prairie or bush or tundra or even in a mirror. The way I had once looked at each new drawing, each new plan, each new construction, Laura would produce.

Only now I realize it's always been a little bit too much like looking at pornography and getting horny, all those oohs and aaahs for landscapes and large cocks, with a special quick Beautiful for the moment the sun shatters a cloud, a particularly sharp moan for the opening of a wet pussy.

And never without its many layers of mediation, never simply present in its passion. There is always a subliminal message. Some strange tale of unacknowledged degradation. That keeps us in our place. Worshipping. Without ecstasy. Through repeating the words of the liturgy or of the classroom. But beautiful around our eyes. Our anxious mouths. Our edgy wanting. Beautiful.

And inherently unworthy.

What I already knew as I held her hands in mine, and squeezed them, ever so briefly, while holding them out from my side, from both our sides, as I said, letting the cold wind in to blow in my voice.
—Then it is I, my Queen, who am not worthy.

I turned and left the room. Going out through the apartment door, just as I had done with Sandro. And two weeks later I left with Jeanpierre. Almost without seeing her. Though I could feel her eyes, her eyes and my mother's eyes. Following me. Angry. Almost colder than my own.

And what I would never have imagined was that already she was not my Queen but his Messenger. That she called me to her already for him.

I wish that I could

end this story there.

I often do. When I tell it in my mind. It is my abridged version. The easier more conventional one. With me going off with that Prince. Short and sweet to the moment of parting. With all of us, or each of us, living happily ever after. In our separate worlds. It was easy enough to keep through the years of the postcards and telephone calls, and to fight to keep, even through that terrible return. Which I told myself was merely catastrophic, an accident, gratuitous. Something that had nothing to do with me. Or with the essential storyline, the plot. Something from the outside, something that would never be written, something without true meaning. A non-event. Or series of them. As I suppressed all the necessary and terrible information. That made a story of its own. A new narrative or metanarrative. That I refused to face.

And it does make a well-rounded story, abridged this way. Even if I put in that final scene, it could still be construed as noble. At least in Freudian terms. My mother would certainly love it. It might even be the one she tells to herself. With its giving up of potential adolescent homosexuality for adult heterosexual love, perhaps even for vaginal orgasms, and the ownership of the phallus in the birth of babies.

A story in which I could firmly refuse Laura, for both our sakes, and for the future. In which I might even let myself screw Sandro right there on the bed, his Dionysian cock reconciling me with my femininity.

So that I would know I had to go out into the world to find one of my own. After all, I could not share hers, even if she invited me.

I could make the skirt the centre of that story too, and say that when I left that day, it was the last time I saw it unfaded. That it was on that day I took it back to my mother's and she lent it to her friend who threw it into the washer. It may even be the way it happened. Not just the way I have taught myself to remember it: first the rejection, the parting, and then that fading.

I could add something about how it seemed to me for the longest while that nothing, not even that skirt, could vibrate with colour away from her. That long swinging skirt in all its colours could be the symbol of an adolescent purity, the kind of girlish friendship, that must always end with initiation into the rites of womanhood. As I would bear children while her star, replete with its explorations of new depths of feminine experience, would keep ascending. With the two of us turning our backs, not on each other, but on the bright colours of our adolescent infatuation, to enter the more restricted palette of adulthood.

Even after madness it might work. It could be a sort of high art bodice ripper, a postmodern *Valley of the Dolls*: one gets famous one goes home one overdoses one cracks up. A typical story of our time, even if it would have to be contained in just two characters: the high price of success the glories of home. Especially for women.

It would be perfect for the laundromat, a *Cosmo* condensed novel for the place where all those stories are read and told. Or tarted up a bit it might make *Vanity Fair*. So that once I got my own washer I could still tell it to the wives as they helped me in the kitchen after executive dinners, mentioning my friend who had appeared in *Vogue* before she went crazy.

It would make us all marvellously smug. Especially if I talked about how I was struggling to write about it. But if I did that I would have to talk about how I discovered the skirt in my closet as I packed, and how I wept over it alone. I wouldn't be able to go to our women's group, to try to learn what it really meant, or give the skirt to you.

And that's too important. More important than all the stories I have ever told myself, for me, or for her. Even if I have to see the sordid parts through to the end. With neither bittersweet parting nor triumphant return.

Instead there will be Sandro on the boat, and Laura on the roof, and me begging you now to understand how I thought I was doing it for her: how that could be.

How I could grab his back and push my fingernails into his flesh as I thrust up toward him, thinking to end it. That this was it that it had finished, that I would fake it this time and it would be over, that he wasn't at all as great as I'd thought he'd be, this grass wasn't greener even if I breathed hard, panting breathing like in labour, panting breathing that catches and holds, catches and holds, holding for the increase in pleasure caused by the thrust in, or for the push out. Out out, as the instinct to bear down realizes itself, when ready or not you will bear down, you will you will, as in that moment the rhythm reversed itself, just as he came down off his straightened elbows, in a well executed push-up, like the kind where the guy claps in the middle, in mid-stride.

Only he didn't clap, he kissed me on the end of the nose, as if it were a reward, his voice lighter suddenly in the way he said:
—Please. With more of a tone of thank you before he went back to his concentration, as if he were working so hard. Until suddenly his breathing was like labour breathing too, or Jeanpierre accompanying me in labour breathing, in transition breathing, holding me up the two of us together almost breathing in each other's mouths like Inuit mouth music, only instead of one two three huh, it was:
—Please be with me, Please be with me, give yourself, give yourself, all of you, all of you, he said until I was suddenly up there holding on to him and thrusting back and moaning and groaning. Though there was no writhing, the rest of my body was still, concentrated in my cunt, as: Oh oh oh ohhhh, Sandro ohhhh, I repeated, just the way he told me to say it.
—Say, *Now* Alma, *now*. Now for me Alma now.
 And I was there.
—Now Sandro Now Sandro Now Sandro, aaahh aaahh.

And I must have come. I must have. Though what I felt was that I had given birth. That I was back once more in the delivery room of my baby son's birth, when I had moaned and groaned and finally thrust him free. When it was the Tchelichew placental tree of Laura and I bursting. When what looked back at me was her, birthed and free and whole.

Only this time it was me. And what was around me was no longer the white cabin but a bright pulsating placenta, the red before my eyes imposed on the cabin wall, the cabin and me inside the cabin and Sandro inside the cabin and me inside the womb and me pushing and me moving down, down and down and down and out and out, oh oh oh oh, still holding him and sobbing inside the red as I looked out again out and down and it was me I was holding. Me on the delivery table, me between my hands me at my breast, me looking down on me holding Sandro, me looking down on that dreadful red guilt, moving outward, outward, because she was not there.

And I knew that she was supposed to be there. That I was supposed to share this with her, with my twin, it was for her, for my twin: only she was not there. She was not there the way she had not been on her bed, as I gasped and my nails dug thoughtless into his back and the formless placenta, the purple red liverlike guilt rose up around me and flowed with me, out from my body and into my body with him ebbing and flowing in my body with him moving out now finally out from my body his come flowing from between my legs until I was me again. Just me.

As I finally took my hands from where they held his shoulder blades and hugged myself with them, and felt it there, in the room with us, that afterbirth of love and guilt. With its smell of sea and semen, its texture like a still warm rabbit skin held in the hand that does not hold the skinning knife, its suffocating stillness like placental failure. As our placenta, Laura's and mine, the hysteresis of whatever catastrophic shape it had taken as we tried to feed in the womb of the universe, had failed us.

And all of it, there present in that cabin, love and guilt and freedom and willing slavery, so terrible and intertwined. And my body so full with it, so sharp so high so on edge so horny, that he just brushed his hand over my cunt, over the wet pubic hair, and I felt the spasms of orgasm once more take my body. And Sandro laughed, triumphant, as the tears came to my eyes. With an image of Laura white on white in her hospital bed.

Reversing
when I closed my eyes, to blue on blue black the way I would see her on the roof. Her dark jeans and dark shirt spread out against the black tar paper as she lay face upward and eyes closed against the unusually bright sun, just the white of face and hands echoing the light. She wouldn't take off her heavy cotton flannel shirt even after we had walked over to the incline, the way she often had, leaving herself in tee-shirt or bra.
– Don't I look like one of those paperback covers, she would say, long before she had almost become one, pulling her shoulders back and arching her spine to push her breasts forward as she winked at me: *Sultry Nights in the City* or something.

While I would giggle at her alliteration and tell her she needed a cigarette hanging from her mouth, something she could never do, which would make her pout, making the pose more perfect, because that was what the girls did anyway. So I don't know if that afternoon her sudden modesty was a new-found shyness, a fear of showing her skinny body, or something about the drugs.

We were lying just where the tar paper slanted upward toward the front edge of the building, lifting up over the tin cornice, the ones that from a distance you think might be stone, just the way the tin ceilings so common in that era of house are supposed to look like plaster, the ones that have garnered their own plastic imitations now, and show themselves in new trendy restaurants, certainly all over North America, I can think of at least two in Calgary. When Lilac was growing up, they were still the symbol of ultimate poverty, her parents had one in their kitchen though nowhere else. While my mother's building still has the real thing, lovely complex stucco leaves and branches and even faces along the ceiling of its lobby, while Jeanpierre and I have only the most recent imitation of all, aluminum siding designed to look like wood, complete with the knots.

Which were stylish once too among the newer middle class, though now they're just common, with the look-alike vinyls the easiest cheapest way to go. There was a time I could have joked with Lilac, maybe you would laugh at it too, a bitter laugh like hers, about how they might be trendy some day too, maybe when all the artists are living in suburban bungalows and all the wood is gone, after all the rainforests are cut down, B.C. and the Amazon clear-cut logged, who knows.

—It is so strange how these things come around, we might say in our sophisticated So-fee-a voices.

Though it seems stranger even still how people like Laura have helped create those trends, as the artists who come from the poor start by celebrating their heritage against all odds, until pretty soon the rich must have one of whatever it was too, followed in descending order by the upper middle then the lower middle, though seldom by the poor themselves as they try their hardest to get away from whatever it was, unless it has been so long that collective memory has faded.

I doubt those recycled ceilings could ever have filled her with anything other than a poignant sorrow, perhaps she could have done sad pale constructions on their tiles, collaging in elements of social realism, perhaps in pastel porcelain like Alicia's knickknacks, the broken bottles of the whisky consumed under them, the bandages full of ointments from her father's accident, the twisted spaghetti and old vegetables of her mother's pain. Though the roof itself, for both of us, was always a source of freedom, and of great joy. It was another one of those places where we came to play, with play exactly the right word, it was one of the secret places she one day decided to show me, the way I showed her the old wrought iron elevator shafts in my building, though the forsythia was something we discovered together, that neither one of us had had before.

I'm sure you've seen that kind of elevator shaft in the movies, the ones where the elevator is a cage and you can see through it, even if you don't remember the one in my mother's building which looks out to the stairs that surround it to make one large well, elevator and stairs, terribly unsafe in case of fire when you think about it, but I don't think anyone did back when it was built. With its windows on each floor, and between floors as well, the kind you notice sometimes in old buildings when you look at them from the outside, with one row of windows offset from the others and the shadows of the stairs drawn across them by the lights in the stairwell, the glass sometimes opaque and reinforced with chicken wire, a sight I always find sad somehow. Even if I don't remember how we would push ourselves out into the window casings to slip from floor to floor, while we looked down never thinking it possible to break the windows and fall out, concentrated as we were on the elevator.

Which became, with all its creakings and groanings, the whines of the greasy old cables as they would start to move, the bumps each time the cage stopped, some monstrous apparition. Out of myth or future it didn't matter. It was our duty to paralyze it with magic or space rays, or just by breaking the secret codes, as we pressed the button on one floor then slipped down one or two, or even ran up, a real risk in that since the elevator wasn't automatic, and the elevator operator was about to get very very angry.

— Kids kids, he would shout: I know who's doing this.

Though I don't think he ever did really, he must have thought it was some tough boys from other apartments, maybe even from another building, at least it was never mentioned to my mother. While we just kept running, in the sure knowledge that we had to get to a certain place before the monster stopped if the world was to be saved. Which it would be sometimes. Though often not. What with the way we would break down and giggle, rendering ourselves unable to complete our assigned mission.

Which would happen on the roof as well. Though there the monsters were less specific. As the Amazon warriors or secret agents climbed from roof to roof along her block, with each roof a slightly different shade of tar paper, even one made of tar with pebbles laid deep on top so that you could throw them over and listen to them hit the sidewalk. And enough levels that we always did feel a little bit daring as we climbed up or down, leaping or giving each other a hand up the three to six foot differences in height.

We would always stop short of trying to jump where there were gaps between the buildings, that was for the movies, or those slum-based potboilers whose covers but not whose actions Laura would so boldly imitate. The truth is we did read them for the dirty parts, somewhere in the *Sultry City* someone's sister was always being initiated by the gang leader, books definitely one or two steps below *Walk on the Wild Side* or *Concrete Jungle*. And farther away than that from the real hoods a few blocks away in the real Red Hook, who we avoided as best we could.

They weren't for Amazon warriors whose territory we had known full well, at least back then, was the world of pretense and fantasy. Playing tough with the real thing, leaps through space with the nearest earth six storeys below a switchblade in hand, or playing sweet hot mama to some gang leader with acne who we were sure would kiss no better than the rich kids on the Island, was not our style. We never did dare the real pit. On the discontinuous roof of our real physical world when the point left one plane to land upon another the softness of the landing was never guaranteed. And besides, the gaps were as often as not full of garbage. Which meant we always turned back, without a word to each other, when the gap confronted us.

Although often we would reach out our hands, and hold them and swing them, our toes over the edge. Or we would put our arms around each other, and laughing, retreat. Even that day I think we approached the incline with our arms about each other, it certainly would have been the natural thing to do. Even if we didn't move from roof to roof at all. Not even down the two foot jump onto the roof next door. The Thorazine had so changed her sense of balance, and recent pregnancy mine, that we were not up to any sudden movements.
– Oh, let's take the sun, we had said instead in our imitate the rich bitches way, nudging each other and giggling, entering that other fantasy that could still be safely indulged in, where we were high up a cliff at a seaside resort, and the incline was either clean white sand or deck chairs, depending on what we'd worn and if we'd brought suntan lotion or towels. Because the asphalt on that section of the roof, with its angle, could be counted on to hold the sun and then give it back to you

as you lay, so that you would be warm on belly and back like a snake on a rock, the way I watched her snuggling down, rubbing her shoulders against its warmth. Though it was only me who chose, before I settled onto my elbow, to look at the street below.

—Oh, Alma, I can't do that anymore, Laura said. I just can't look down.

She collapsed onto her back instead and chose to look into the sun. Until I told her to close her eyes. I looked at the activity you could always see below, staring at the passersby one moment for old times' sake. Sometimes, in our younger days, we would even shout something, though mostly we just enjoyed the flowers in their window boxes, mostly along the second storeys, on some blocks you could move along the fronts of buildings at that level going from ledge to ledge to stoop to ledge to ledge to stoop. Especially if you crossed into the Heights where the really elegant brownstones are, though there were only a couple like that on the other side of the street below us.

While along the other edge of the roof, if I turned to look toward my feet, I could see the ginkgo trees just peaking over the edge, growing up wild and untrimmed and bigger than most ginkgo trees, from the back yard her family was allowed to use together with the other families in the building. Though nobody had managed to make a garden there. Or even a lawn. It was just a patch of brown soil and crab grass, and a variety of bashed up children's toys, depending on the current age of those in the building. And of course, the laundry hanging out at each floor, pushed out by those squeaky pulleys that on sunny days make all the back yards all the way along the block look from the roof like quilts, brighter even than the skirt at its brightest, during the few hours of sun the yards would receive.

—**Picturesque, isn't it**? I said while I looked at her, just the way I always did.

—Yes, how *mah*vellously quaint, she answered, exactly on cue. And we both laughed a minute. Until she took my hand. And our eyes caught.

—Alma, I'm so glad you came, she said. So very glad.

And I felt that I was falling. Even as my whole body filled now to bursting with the terrible purple red agony I had felt in the pit of my stomach since the moment she told me she had left Sandro.
—But you don't know what I've done, I wanted to say. You don't know.

While I heard Sandro's voice layered over hers as he said what he had repeated so often that weekend, up to so short a time before.
—Thank you Alma, thank you.

And I was once more back in that cabin. Even the sky I looked into with her turning red on me like the placental walls of that room. Where Sandro had lit a cigarette and leaned back and taken a long deep breath, before he reached over and nestled his hand into me, far into me, as if his hand had always belonged there, playing with me again, determined I guess to give me at least the four orgasms he had promised so long before, because his gesture seemed so much that of the landlord taking final possession of property acquired in some remote past. That he had always thought of as there, waiting for him to realize its potential.
—That was a wonderful coming home present, Alma, he said. And laughed. Then repeated her exact words: Alma, I'm so glad you came. Laughing harder. As if it were such a wonderful pun. As he hugged me. Affectionate, like a little boy.

—**Thank you, thank you**, he kept repeating, as if I had given him an ice cream or a new toy: I know that was just for me, just for me. Oh God Alma thank you.

As his hand went in out and around, mixing our substances together then leading his hand up to my mouth to get me to kiss his fingers, to lick them round and round.
—Thank you Alma thank you as I sucked on their tips until he had laughed some more and he was hard again, and he lifted me on top of him and he laughed and moaned and groaned and said:
—Say my name, say my name, over and over and over.

And I did just the way she had, over and over just the way she had, remembering the sound of her voice, two voices already superimposed, only it was mine over hers, and hers so clear, so clear and triumphant the way it had been then, so animated and rich, as I wriggled and I moaned and I groaned and I moved into the richness of it, listening to her voice, the beauty of her voice, until I was far far away trying to find her. Wandering some unbounded space some unknown territory as the sensations in my body grew and I repeated his name in her voice searching with it for where my twin had gone, where perhaps we both were, I have no way of knowing, perhaps he was looking for her too in the rhythms of my voice, the rhythms he asked me for, bringing her back to him through her words in my body, calling to her through me, so that perhaps it is still true that we both searched out the firstborn twin, daughter and child, to see if the two could be reunited inside the voice of the sea.

Because I said all the things he told me to, I did. Every word in every tone with every howl and every moan that I remembered. Only I could not come again, no matter how much I tried, and I tried and tried, I really did. I wanted so much to find that moment again, when I could be myself and her at once, when I could birth us both again, I wanted to get there and to be there, to be there forever. And I couldn't do it.

I couldn't get there no matter how I moaned and groaned and struggled there on top until he had come again and rolled me off, laughing. To hold me away from him and study me, until he said:
—I've waited so long for this. So long. And he licked his lips as he stared at me. Not at my body this time, but looking me in the eyes, my eyes that held his. Though I do not know this time what they told him, if they were empty or full, steady or wandering, only that his gaze no longer seemed capable of pouring into me in a direct line along the optic nerve to my cunt.

While he seemed to find enough there to nurture his smile, inflating the way it did to cover his face, as he ran one finger down my body.
—You see, I always knew you wanted it. Just the way she did. So much. No one ever wanted it so much. God, you're just like her.

He had stopped a moment then to lick his lips, as if he were listening to her voice, just the way I had. Perhaps he was thinking of how he might get her back, even perhaps of how he might use me to get her back, or how he could keep the two of us.

Because he spoke, echoing my thoughts, even the images in my mind, far too closely:
—You are twins, he said, as he traced his fingers along what he had decided to call my motherlush body.
—Twins.

And somehow when he said it I felt violated.

As he leaned back, his hands behind his head, and went on.
—You are so alike, you see, Alma, so alike, yet opposites. Not Gemini but Pisces.

And suddenly he was off into a lecture on astrology. On how he used, 'the old principles' he called them, a lot in his work.
—You know how Pisces is always portrayed, Alma, he said, the fish pulling in two different directions, but still attached. Well, there's a reason for that. In Pisces the ocean pulls in two directions, inside one person. But for the two of you, it's still like that, she told me all about it you know, all your adolescent fantasies, how you were blood sisters and kissed and became each other, where was it Alma? under the lilacs or the roses, I don't remember, a very New York bush she said it was, just like hers, a very New York bush, or yours, no matter how much you try to run away, and he moved his hand along the top of my very wet pubic hair, and he laughed and my sense of violation increased, the same sense I felt as I looked at her on the roof, that he had turned me inside out, that I was inside out, the Tchelichew tree, my veins my arteries exposed directly to the world. And he would not let me cover myself, not even with the sheet.
—Oh, Alma, I want to look at you, he said: Now that I finally can. Only the fact was that he looked at the ceiling. It was just knowing I was there. Exposed. At his side. The way I felt on the roof I would be exposed forever.
—She said you always thought of yourselves as one person, a two in one person, incomplete one without the other. She said it quite recently in

fact: If only Alma were here so I could be complete, she said. Well that's what Pisces is, Alma, the two fish pulling along the line that has caught them. Well, I want to be that line, Alma, I always have: that umbilicus. You know now that I could do it well.

And he smiled yet again. His widest, his hungriest, smile.
– You are so beautiful. Both, so very very beautiful. Two such beautiful fish. And his teeth glinted, a shark now, as he went on: And you do swim around it, around it and around it, you both like it so much. This so much. And he touched his limp prick, and kind of waved it at me.
– You see, you want it so much. The way you tried to tell me you didn't. And you did, Alma. You see. You did. And after you made me wait so long.

And he sighed here, and leaned back against the cabin wall, his hands behind his head.
– It would have been so much simpler if you hadn't made me wait. If you'd let me be your umbilicus back then, this be your umbilicus. And he reached over and took my hand and put it on his prick.
– If you had known what you wanted. So much simpler.

And he'd started to rub that odd cock of his. To rub it with my hand, and then as mine fell away, twisting to face me, exactly as she would on the roof, on her side, one hand behind her head, one tucked between her legs, only his hand did not tuck, anymore than it had when I turned around in the apartment, it still moved feeling what was there, rubbing it and pulling back the foreskin, while his eyes crinkled up and he laughed some more, and I couldn't take my eyes off it as he said:
– But perhaps it is better this way. You here again, and so full. With so much motherhood in you. I'm glad we've finally done it, Alma, that we've gotten to know each other better. And I bet it's better for you now.

You'd take it again, I know you would. Any way I told you to.

As he said that he changed. His eyes narrowed and there was no more Please, no more Thank you. Just his bitter knowing laugh, the one he had tried to teach her, but that always reminded me of my mother, coming from deep inside his chest. As if life was always inside out, the way I felt inside out.
– I know it's not like that for you always, Alma. Now is it?

319

I fled then. With his words bringing a new explosion inside me, a CO_2 cartridge going off somewhere in my wet groin that seemed to inflate me down to the ends of my fingers, the same anger I'd felt in the living room for this man who thought he knew me, who thought he could use his cock to control me, making my arms pop out from my sides as I seemed to unfold yet again, quickly getting up to pull on my nightgown, to get out onto the deck before the expanding gas reached the back of my throat. As I moved quickly out of the cabin, with its door so much like the door of an airplane latrine, our cabin suddenly feeling so much like a latrine, as I ran to the rail. And this time I did not labour my words but vomited them. Truly seasick, I vomited them.

—You're right Sandro, I yelled into the wind. You're right. It wasn't for you. It wasn't for you at all. It was never for you. Not even now. It was for her. Always for her. It was her voice behind the wall, her voice calling me to rejoin her. It was her. Always calling me. Not you. Not that thing between your legs. Never.

That's what I wanted to tell her about as we lay on the roof. About what he had said and about the Pisces twins and about how he had fooled me. I guess because she seemed so normal then. Whatever it is we mean by normal. Her old self perhaps, with her giggling about the shepherds and her arm around me, her lying so close to me, languid on the roof. It would have been so easy to think it had all just been a nervous breakdown: You know, the stress of the breakup and all.

I could hear myself, I could hear her, saying that, a yawn in the voice: Why yes, my dear, a nervous breakdown, the stress of the breakup and all, I was back on my feet pretty quick though, and a wink. It was certainly what I wanted, and I could almost believe it right then, that she would be up and moving fast enough, taking the artworld by storm once more.

While I felt those Pisces twins as I lay opposite her, stretched out on my elbow, while she lay on her back, taking the sun. And I imagined I could smell them too, the fish the ocean, in my cunt. In Sandro's come still oozing out from between my legs, and I wanted to share my secret, I don't know why. If it was to make Sandro more an umbilicus than ever and thus bind us more strongly, bringing both anchor and nourishment, while we would still float free and forever in the ocean of ourselves, of our one self. Or to make him more fully present so that we could then exorcise him, through dissecting him, perhaps even consuming him, as baby praying mantises do on hatching the headless body of their father, to thus become fully separate, fully freely birthed, two fish women swimming in a greater mother ocean, out of the net and in the world.

Where we could grow up to be the fully separated and mature selves we were meant to be. And we could look at each other across the distance between us, and measure that distance exactly. And love each other as mature and healthy individuals, as we were meant to do. Another psychiatrist's dream, not terribly Freudian this time, but the one I most fervently wished at that moment could come true. Just as I invented scenarios in which somehow, now that she was single, she could immigrate to Canada, or I, somehow freed, could spend more time in New York. While I dreamed of how our having shared Sandro would somehow help to realize this new re-unified relationship, because there is a mystery in it, a connection, in that sharing of a partner, that always makes you think such sharing will make you whole. Just as somehow in some place you seem always to want your best friend's partner. While the logic follows, of course, that if the sharing completes your union, then what more the talking of it, a kind of magic sexual cannibalism, a sharing of bodily fluids through a third person akin somehow to our bloodsistership, in which the best of the other partners your shared partner has experienced is taken into the self – the reason, some say, men like to share women, though not often the mothers of their children, no matter what great buddies, they do not seem to want to see each other in their sons – while now, I thought it would free us of him, take that umbilicus forever out from between us. As I fell deeper and deeper into the same erotic reverie I had felt those years before, her hands on my shoulders, and I prepared myself

to go forward, now that Dionysus had taught us both all we would ever need to know of him. Or perhaps it was simply a childish wish to share a secret as I reached out with my free hand to her, and stroked her arm.
—Sandro, I began tentatively: Sandro.

—Yes, Sandro. I said. Sandro. Slowly gaining speed: He's been talking to me all week, telling me things, feeling sorry for himself, but never that, never. It was just an assumption. That you were together. That you would get back together. And that he needed comfort. Because it was so hard on him. After all, I'm sure he does love you. And it has been hard on him. Seeing you like this.

And I took a breath.

—I went with him, you know, I said. And knew I had reached the crossroads. Though I still didn't know if I would say: To the bar, or on the boat, or to bed. But I was ready to go on. To tell her how I had believed him. The way I never had before. And how I had finally done it. Given him the comfort he had always wanted from me. The comfort he had always said would seal us together, the three of us. And I wanted to tell her how wrong I had been. And maybe her too, about all of it. And I thought I might explain about the Pisces twins, about how he saw us. And whatever my need for confession, inscribed in the belief that the truth will always make us free, if also very uncomfortable, I will swear that it was still not to achieve any kind of victory over her that I began to explain. In fact, I wanted her to explain it back to me, to make it all right, I thought she could explicate it, it's the sort of thing she could do so well, once she had the first thread.

I even found myself awaiting that explanation, to find out who we really were, to once more be apprised, the way I had so often been, with baited breath, of my function in the universe. While tangling and untangling the skein she would be drawn into talking about her future work.

I even thought it would help. Immensely, in fact. After all at the hospital she had never mentioned her work. I was sure this would get that going. And speed the cure.

Only she spoke first. Before I could go on. And she laughed.

– Oh, yes. Sandro, she said. He's a great one for comfort, Sandro is. And he still thinks he's the centre of my life.

And then her voice broke.

– Only I've fooled him, I have. I met the cutest boys in the hospital.

And the laugh rose to a high-pitched giggle, the kind giggling gaggles of girls had possessed on the sitcoms of our adolescence, something that had never been part of her. That cancelled out all the laughs I had ever heard come out of that mouth, the free young spirit, the throaty femme fatale, my open-hearted friend, all cancelled by one giggle as she went on.

– Really, Alma, I've fooled him. There was the cutest boy with red hair. You have no idea.

She looked suddenly trapped. Moving her head back and forth just once, shaking it as if to clear it of something she did not understand. As she went on describing him. How tall he was with his red hair sticking up, how he even blushed when he approached her. And brought her flowers he had picked himself, just once from the hospital grounds, when he was awkward and tripped over his feet, as spastic as any adolescent, and as gawky, an image that made her giggle again. Only a little more shrill.

Caught out. She knew she had been caught out. As she stopped for a second again, and this time looked around, while I knew that in that brief moment she could see it too: How this time she had truly been sent into a parallel universe. That the drugs kept displacing them all back to high school.

And for a moment I wanted to make a joke, a long and silly one, something about a sitcom cum romance in a mental hospital where the patients had to check out the compatibility of their voices, she talked about that too, how he'd tried to kill himself and heard voices, heard voices too, I think she said, so that it could be like all those sitcoms with the new stepfamilies, blended families I think they call them, only they would be families of voices, you could even call this one: *A Very Special Blend.*

I thought she might still find it funny. Only when I looked into her eyes to say it, I could not go on.

What I
saw in that moment, that one aching moment, was terror. Such a fierce terror was in her eyes as she looked at me across the very few inches of the space between us, that my throat went numb. When she curled up further, and tucked both arms now, deep between her legs. As if the alien spaceship were her body and she its prisoner and she was being dragged away she knew not where. Except that this was a last goodbye. And not just to me. But to the entire world that she had known.

Her voice stopped. Although the giggle still hung on the air. Where it would stay, a cawing shadow, the whole afternoon. But there was just no way for me to go on anymore. Or reason either. Even as I continued to reach out my hand. To stroke her arm over and over, to comfort some small part of me even if I knew there was no genie in the bottle of her body that could bring the Laura I had known once more within my reach. Nothing I could do to bring that beached fish back into the ocean. Nothing any longer that I could say, about Sandro or about art or about the day, or about us: nothing to bring her back and place her here.

Nothing.

She was gone. The

vay she had been gone that whole weekend. That whole two weeks. Just as Our Toad had tried to tell me, walking up behind me on the boat, as I finished vomiting my words out into the heavy humid sea air. That it would not matter how hard I should try to find her inside her own body inside the white hospital gown, or inside my body inside Sandro's bed as his cock his fingers his tongue explored the me I wanted so much to make into her. None of it mattered: she was gone.

In words so strong I could only deny them. And let them push me back to Sandro, to my hunt for her, so that even as I rebelled, still Sandro's prophecy came true: I had gone back, and taken it any way he told me to. In a weekend not just of one explosive sexual mistake, but of the same one repeated and repeated, being let go and reeled back in, a masochist's or a romantic's dream, in a weekend consecrated to going to gay bars and balling Sandro and watching a bodybuilding contest and balling Sandro and seeing Fire Island's finest drag queens give the prizes and balling Sandro and listening to more conversations about sexuality and all its variants and balling Sandro and walking by the shore watching the scallops with their mantles of bright blue eyes and balling Sandro and lying on the beach half buried in sand and balling Sandro and participating in his ritual and balling Sandro and swimming in the ocean and balling Sandro and watching the world through my salty eyelashes and balling Sandro and getting high on the boat and balling Sandro. While the more I did it the less time I spent in my own body the more time I spent trying to find her, the lost twin, trying to be her, the lost twin, even as I came and came and came, the lost twin, I would feel my way into her body the nuances of what she must have felt, the lost twin, as on purpose or by accident he told me more of their relationship, and of her plans and of their dreams and of their rituals and of her performances and of the group and of its future as I felt her moans and her groans arising in my throat through the walls, now in my mouth now in my chest now in my cunt, echoing as he told me how she had always imagined I would come back I would come back I would come back and his hand or his cock would tease me to orgasm as he told me how I would share in their triumphs in all their triumphs: All our triumphs all of them, Alma, he would say, until after his own orgasm once more deflated, in the trough before starting again, he would say:

– I just hope it isn't too late.

And I kept thinking he meant for her to make a comeback, for her to recover, just the way I wanted her to make a comeback, to recover, the way for a moment on the roof I could believe, even with what she had told me of the breakup, that my acts of sympathetic magic on the boat, had brought her back had made her present there, present at last for me, present again. So that I never imagined he meant for the two of them, that it wasn't too late for the two of them, because I had come to believe in the two of them, as my body came to feel her body more and more as I came to believe more and more that yes, it was possible, that yes, she could come back. And I consecrated myself more fervently to finding her, to ending his sudden stillness his sudden sadness by bringing him back to erection, licking him then biting him then climbing on, as I took it upon myself to search for her again as I fucked him and fucked him, active and hungry and wanting as I felt her body more and more in the waves outside the cabin or in the waves that banged against my chest as I rode them to the shore where the sand scratched my belly or they caught me with the salt and my hair still in my eyes and scrabbled me around until I came up panting for breath or they ground me into the sand the way Sandro ground me into the bed, the way I returned the favour all salty and sweaty and exhausted with saying yes to him yes to her yes to the ocean yes to them yes to the burning sun yes yes yes as I repeatedly went out on my quest sped on by the rhythms of his body of my body thrusting back at him thrusting myself out into that space in which I could find her my legs wrapped around him, and thrusting thrusting, beating at myself like the waves at him like the waves to beat back Our Toad's voice Our Toad's words until we finally emerged from our long goodbye below decks into the crisp bright sun where even the buildings and the woodgrain on the piers had shadows as we approached the dock.

And it was a perfect day like so many perfect days the way it would still be a perfect day there on the roof with her for that one instant even if he had fooled me and the red terror was in my gut and his smell between my legs still it was a perfect day even if she was as dark as the sun was bright still she was there with me and I reached out to her just as I had reached out to him that one last time when I turned to him suddenly back in a strange city all pristine and perfect and clean and I said:
– God Sandro, it's a Van Gogh day.

Only by the time my hand reached the dark cloth of her arm, I could see the shadow. The shadow that had been there, the shadow I had known to be there, no matter what I told myself, the shadow so clear in Our Toad's voice, clearer still in her giggle, that shadow, cawing, croaking. One of Magritte's stone crows flying through the grey air, casting its shadow upon her body.

I had
heard his footsteps behind me. And thought they were Sandro's. That Sandro had followed me. Only when I turned it was other teeth gleaming in the little light from the shore as Our Toad approached the railing.

At first I was relieved. I didn't want to face Sandro again. At least that's what I thought. Until Our Toad started to speak.
– It's hard, Alma, isn't it? he said.
– Uh huh, I answered without turning toward him. My attention only

partly there. Just enough for him to dash in, to lock on target. And to say it. That one thing I did not wish to hear.

—She's gone, Alma, he said. Gone. Laura's gone. Shit, you know.

And there was a pause there, a pause I can still feel, and felt more profoundly still, there on the roof, the stone crow flying over her, stopped like in Magritte's painting, stopped in that moment. So that her body congealed, became other, and I knew in the image that I saw, that it no longer mattered how bright the day, how complex and colourful the world, because all our world was grey, all our world the colour of Our Toad's voice, an old disembodied radio voice. While we were no longer simple Pisces twins, but Magritte fish/women.

Another favourite icon along with the stone crows and *The Empire of Light* the street that was both night and day, or the woman who was a fragmented pyramid with the sky in cubes behind her. The one Laura had imagined imitating for the last unrealized version of her dream. All of them images of time stopped, that one too an image of time stopped, of evolution stopped, of the moment of catastrophe. Only in these grey/brown pictures of the beach, at least that is how I remember them, there is not even the sweetness the freshness of the blue or green to make you wish to stay in that moment, but the captured instant of claustrophobia, of awakening from nightmare that can only bring wish for escape. Looking at those beached creatures who are not mermaids but quite the opposite, another image that had surfaced sometimes through the years as I made love or nursed, a creature with a fish's head and a woman's lower body, its separate legs and without doubt its salty cunt oozing the ocean even as my cunt oozed Sandro's ocean, crawling with its microorganisms, its plankton, as I lay on the roof beside Laura, or stood still looking into the night my back turned to Our Toad, my mouth opening and closing as he spoke, my mind starting to drown, in that image full of silence and sacrifice and isolation: the beaching of the human species.

Which was exactly what I saw as I looked from Laura to my feet from my body to Laura because she was in those dull colours too, fish dark and widemouthed with that empty smile, like a bottom dwelling catfish without the whiskers, because those fish never have whiskers either. As it became obvious to me why I should have jumped over the side of the boat even as Our Toad's arms came around my arms, to surround me from the back because he was so much taller, why I should have done anything to escape the impact of his words, that would acquire more and more power as I looked at her.

—She really should have killed herself, he said. And it echoed across the water.

—That was the only correct ending.

And I knew on the roof suddenly that Sandro had not fooled me, that I had only fooled myself, and that it could no longer matter. Whether or not we were the Pisces twins, whether or not he was the rope, the umbilicus the ocean the river the semen the milky way between us. He could never have been my lifeline to let me continue on my search for her. Because there on the roof, I finally had to understand. And try to keep the tears from welling out of my eyes as I watched her.

While to Our Toad I had only replied:

—What do you mean? as hoarse as any bullfrog, my staring eyes bulging out, as big as any toad.

—What do you mean? repeated. As he hugged his arms more closely around my shoulders to protect me from the blow of his own words.

—**I thought you knew**, Alma, he said. In fact I was sure of it. I thought that was why you left. To let her do what she had to do.

And I guess he heard my breathing then, how laboured it was, because he went on.

—You do know this isn't the way it should have gone, Alma. You do know that. It's the wrong script. She failed at the end, don't you see. Only it couldn't even save her. Because no matter which way it went, death or crack-up, it would still be over. Laura Mack is over. God, Alma, she's gone. Gone from among us. And his hands gripped hard on the rails.

—It's tragic really. How her will failed at the end. And worse to see her now. Less than half herself. Such a terrible failure. His rising voice aimed at the stage of the night.

—Her life is no longer exemplary to anyone.

331

And the worst of it, that now, on the roof, I should hear her giggle, and hear his voice, and almost, I should believe it.

Though then, what he noticed was my shock. My silence. Even in the dark how I turned to stare at him. Because he chose to go on. His voice starting to carry emotion, now, persuasive emotion. That stone crow cawing out the terrible resonant overblown emotion of the professional actor, the way they can channel it, the way Our Toad actually does in his little serious work, Vietnam vets and that sort of thing.
—You know I mean nothing against her, Alma. Any more than you ever did. Even when you ran away.

Then modulating his voice to soft and full, as if it could eat the whole boat, he went on:
—God she was beautiful. She's the most beautiful person, the most brilliant person, I've ever known, Alma. You know that, don't you? And you could hear the voice, sweet and vibrant, unctuous and consuming, waiting to eat. There was already too much saliva produced into the mouth. It was the tone I imagine the critics used, days they lauded her, and said things so close to what he was saying:
—She was so easy to love. You do know how much I loved her, don't you. So easy to follow. I wanted to follow her to the ends of the earth. To the end of the world. I wanted to go there with her. To say goodbye. To bring back her message. That's what I thought I was doing. Maybe we all did. But she missed her cue.

God, how could she?

I was sick then. A terrible nausea rising in my stomach. And a redness like weeping.

And worse for me. That the only thing that should occur to me to do to maintain any control, any power at all in the situation, as he rubbed my arm as if to comfort me, was to ask for an explanation. To make him an invitation to continue.
—Our Toad, I think you'd better explain, I said. Because I certainly wasn't going to break down and cry.

I just wish he hadn't. Really I do. Because the worst of it was how much sense he made, that he kept making, even as I pushed the words away with my orgasms. Until I would come to have to watch her, watch her. As his plot, his story line, etched itself onto that frightened shell before me and it suddenly made such terrible beautiful sense to cry out against her being like this. No matter what the consequences. Even her death. To say that this person so reduced could not have been the climax, or the ending. Not this. Never.

Even my own story as he told it back to me was lovely. It was no longer sordid and life-size, a Cinderella among the bedbugs, the artwife of Cobble Hill. It was monumental. Perhaps even a blockbuster, a legend. Better, let me tell you, Thorne, than I could do. And with its overtones of sexuality it made me horny again, oh, yes, he was into that too, enough for a moment to make me think of trying it, indulging in that sexual sophistication they had all been speaking so much about: I wanted to let him talk me into bed.

With his own personal Our Toadian theatre of cruelty, that he was developing for my benefit, beating me into the conspiracy of memory that would become the bed he intended us to share, letting me become part of his vision, his version, better by far than my bodice-ripping *Valley of the Dolls*, this *Alma Does the Commune*, like *Debbie Does Dallas*. He even told me how beautiful I was, echoing Sandro, how they had all thought that. How I had been the centre of the house.

–**You knew her** so well. And you were so charming and self-contained in your knowledge. You had her, he said.
– The way none of the rest of us ever could. Not even the Magician, not even Sandro. And you showed it so much in your Cheshire cat smile, in the way you walked around that apartment, the way you made it circle around you with your cooking and cleaning and tossing your little remarks over your shoulders along with your hair, and he touched my hair, falling down my back the way Sandro had left it: While flicking your head, and your ass, and here he laughed and lowered his hand to

my thigh. His intentions suddenly far clearer than his voice, for all its overtones, now made undertones as well, and undertows.

– As if you were above us all, and the hand moved up: Because you had her, you had her.

Christ, I wanted you then, Alma. I wanted you. I thought that if I could have you, I would have the key to her. The one even Sandro couldn't get. But he wanted you too, Alma, didn't he? While you were keeping yourself pure. Pure for her.

He never had you. Sandro never had you, did he Alma? Not before this weekend. Now that she's gone. That's another way I know it's true. You never would have done this if she were here. Even in spirit. You would have been with her.

That's true Alma, isn't it? Tell me it's true. Tell me he never had you.

And I did. Assent seemed to be the essence of the day.

– **No, he never** had me, I whispered, even using Our Toad's terms. Lying even to myself, because really, the more I look at it now, the truth is, Sandro had had me all along. While I was hooked then on Our Toad's line, on his story, his version, like a fly on his sticky amphibian tongue, his digestive eloquence. I even told him I had done Sandro only for Laura. As a form of prayer.

And he laughed. Deep in his throat. Savouring the gift. His hand still moving.

– You must be a beautiful prayer, Alma, he said. And I could feel it. All over my body. A new horniness starting. For all of them. Like reflexive Kugel exercises. The vagina tightening.

– I used to get hard watching you. We all did. Hard or wet. And shallow in the throat now, he giggled.

– We even made bets, though that was mostly the guys, on who would finally get you. And by now his hand brushed my wet pubic hair. And my breath came harsh. My nostrils flaring.

– And then you left. You just left.

– **I never met** Jeanpierre, he said. But then, it never mattered. At first I thought he must be extraordinary. To take you away from her. From us. But then I became convinced that it didn't matter who he was. He was just a means.

You had understood. You had left to allow her to do what her destiny dictated. What her knowledge dictated. You had given her a great gift. Like Judas gave Christ.

Like Judas gave Christ, he repeated. And here his voice was a whisper.

—**Oh don't tell** me you didn't know, Alma. Don't tell me that, he said, feeling, I'm sure, the sudden stiffness in my body, the way my jaw clenched, threatening to ruin the mood.

—Oh, my little Judas, you must have, I'm sure. Somewhere inside, you must have. And he turned me to him just a little more with his free hand, so that he could touch my cheek. And then brush it lightly across my breast. With what appeared to be great tenderness. As the other hand pushed upward again, just a tiny bit, so I could feel it with the edge of my labia. And once more there was the rapid intake of breath.

That satisfied him.

—You're the one who cleared the way, he said smiling: To her perfection. To her perfection.

He sighed then. And the hand moved back down. Just as I yearned to push my cunt onto it, to fist and finger fuck it, all of it, he became contemplative. He had teased me enough I guess. That he thought he had me hooked. That his words could tie me there, an image of submission moaning and groaning in his mind, please, please, fuck me, fuck over me fuck me over, please yes, now, now, please. As he could make me wait and wait, his story taking him over like a black leather fantasy. That I was only a part of, a small part of: his captive audience.

Maybe it was only then, as his eyes went blank, moving up into his head, that I clearly remembered him. That I could see him in that room among the bloodstains in the same pose, always looking up, always his large eyes, green irises sheltered in the forest of his lashes, pupils enlarged, with the whites along the bottom gleaming. As he melded everything together, like making a hamburger patty, solid and continuous, no matter what theories of chaos or discontinuity it contained,

seamless and smooth, even in its consistency. When he wouldn't look at us either, but just at the ceiling or the floor, once his theory took him. At the same time as I could feel him feeling us up, kneading us with his words. Until I said to Laura:
– Despite his drama, he really is a toad. He's so cold, so slimy. Can you imagine kissing him?

And she had giggled. And told me how all his words would stick to you, worse than the clutter in her mother's living room. All sticky and covered with dust. It would be hard to breathe like that, she said. Before she became serious. Mature in her judgement. And told me he was Sandro's best student. And everyone else's. Absolutely brilliant, she said. But she agreed. There was no amount of kissing that would turn him into a Prince.
– Certainly not your Prince, Alma, she said. To make sure I understood. Then told me how he only wanted us around to give his theories validity. As an audience. All of us.
– Except for you, I said. But that only annoyed her. It was better to be audience than raw material she said, her hands swinging. As usual so terribly prophetic. Prophetic and unknowing all at once. A terrible flash of insight said with her most calculating laugh. Her tongue, not in her cheek, but over under her teeth, feeling its way there. The annoyance only in the speed of her voice.
– At least then, you don't get eaten alive.

Digested.

His hand had become a dead fish on my thigh as he went to it. He had even forgotten the little gestures of sexual interest to keep me aroused now that he was sure he had me hooked, his words infinitely more fascinating than the world around him. Even the reality of finally having me. I was just another element to add to his airless universe; his perfect story of his perfect victim. The one before me on the roof. The one that should not be there.

As I listened to him trying to combine Artaud and Genet, Godard's *Weekend* and Antonioni's *Zabriskie Point* and Costa-Gavras's *Z*, for its elements of ritual sacrifice, plus whichever movie it was that Passolini did on the gospel; starting back there in the era we had shared, with Marat and Sade and *Marat/Sade*, Weiss and Brooks and what they had done to, or was it for, theatre now that Brecht and Artaud were dead. All the substance of our Thursday nights combined with all those movies made and plays presented since those long evenings had ended for me, names I have easily let drift away, along with countless others mentioned to me by countless others, forgotten since the birth of my children ended my cinephilia, forcing me toward the live entertainment of friends, at a party a class or the group, evenings I do go out.

Something the VCR and a little more time are slowly giving back to me, only that night I missed them all, whether they were first-run foreign films or far more obscure European and even Oriental theorists, sources found in recent papers on the meaning of Japanese *Nō* theatre, even his own criticism of Zen. People I could shrug about without endangering my credibility as more than vegetable *mater*, at the same time as I heard names I'm sure I should have known, that twigged something in the back of my mind, a small twinge of anxiety in the stomach, books and works of theatre and art, critics and films and modern dance works, names that I might have seen mentioned in some Sunday supplement or other, as I had to acknowledge how great a toll motherhood had taken on my intellectual life, all that energy absorbed into the daily, the plotline of the family and the familiar.

So that I became dizzy, I couldn't even tell how well he was doing, if the system he was inventing was at least internally consistent, something I can usually tell, and sometimes comment on. Only I couldn't, not with that esoteric and eclectic stew, that by the end had included a combination of various theories of the goddess religions, of ritual sacrifice and sympathetic magic, along with modern performance, gender identity and pansexuality.

Though I do remember quite clearly the special kudos for the West German performance artist, that was more than a simple twinge of the gut, it was a kick that made me momentarily nauseous, who had cut off his prick piece by piece, slice by slice, while a friend took pictures; then proceeded on with other various parts of his body until it finally killed him, he was all bandages by then. While I can't remember if Our Toad's principal admiration was for the man who did the gradual and literal erasure of the self, starting with his sex, or the one who documented it. I don't know which Our Toad considered more brave. Or if maybe he hadn't somehow wanted, or even thought he could have fulfilled, if only she'd just selected the correct course, the right ending, that documentarian's role in Laura's apotheosis of victimization.

Then after a long and dizzying while it did come down to the classics. And more than any the crucifixion and *The Story of O*. What some fundamentalists would probably find a quite satanic combination, as might many anti-pornography activists, but which was perfect for his purposes. As he spoke of the brilliant sacrifice of self, the allowing the self to become the cup that runneth over, that takes in all until it is overwhelmed into non-being, the way the crucified Jesus opened his arms or a woman does her legs. Yes: the way the female body takes in the male. Becoming other in being herself. The vessel that encompasses the world or the spermatozoa or whatever it is that has been given in order to transform, to move beyond consciousness, to birth that which has never before been seen. Which would somehow, I don't think I quite got this part, be nonetheless the same. As one person would be reflected in the other, but perfected, so that he can at last understand himself. And he did say he. Although with someone like Our Toad it's always hard to tell if he means the generic he or the specific he. I think he would still use those terms. In which you and I are men, as part of mankind. But whoever he (whichever he or she he truly meant) was, he was to discover who he could be. The best that he could be. Perhaps even through seeing the worst. In the victim's martyrdom.
—What she did, Alma, what she did. What she intended all along. All along. It was what she meant to be, Alma: the perfect vessel, she'd already started when you were with us, you remember all those cunt-prints. That was their real intent. To mirror her so that she could become the perfect mirror, who is yet an imperfect one. The one in the hall of mirrors who lets us see ourselves as we really are. The womb that will take us in again only to transform us. She couldn't have children the way you did, she wanted them you know, Alma, because she needed to have us. All of us. And to let us have her: the perfect victim who in letting us act upon her, and he did say her (she

was not mankind), who in taking the imprint of our acts, makes us look at those acts. And take responsibility for them.

To change.

Change.

—**She was** the sacrificial victim. Like Christ, like 'O'. The one who makes change possible. She talked about that, Alma. She talked about it a lot. When you were still here she had already begun to talk about that. You must remember, Alma.

By the end she didn't just talk, either. She knew. That she had to do it. Look at people until they saw themselves. Obey them until they understood their orders. She was really into things like that. She must have talked to you about it. Written letters to you about it. I was sure that was why you'd left. To clear her way.

And he had shaken his head, confused.

—You must have seen that she couldn't do it with you around. That you impeded her becoming a perfect mirror. Because she could only see you. And he started to speed up again. Regaining his rhythm.

—So you released her to all of us. To keep and nurture her. To be nurtured by her. As she came into the truth of her art. That magnificent art. Those sacrificial catastrophic blood totems which showed her the way. To her performance. To her last performance.

What should have been her last performance.

He turned from me. And grabbed the railing of the boat. Tight. So that his knuckles shone white. At least I remember them that way. Even if I could hardly see.

—Only she couldn't do it. To complete it she had to force them to dance her to the edge of the platform, in front of the oncoming train. To complete that trajectory, that catastrophe, she had to die. She had to kill herself. If that was the role she wanted, she had to take responsibility for it. Just as we would have to take responsibility for seeing her. So she had to die. She had to.

She just had to kill herself. She just had to. It was the only way to make them see. Make them understand what their real intentions are.

And now he banged the railing with his fist.

—Their real intentions. Toward her toward us toward the whole planet.

He was crying.

Our Toad was crying.

—To be the perfect mirror the perfect victim, the perfect mirror, she had to die. There was no other way.

And he turned back to me, and he grabbed me, and he kissed me. Harsh and abrupt, with no sensuality left in it, only drama. Drama and power.

—Oh Judas, Judas, my little Judas, it will be worse for her like this.

And the words Judas, JudasJudasJudas, echoed there, as they would on the roof, in the giggle, in the shadow, in Sandro's come, in my mind, in my footsteps, in my words, over and over, as if with his kiss he had not betrayed, but named me. Until I do remember that moment as if it were in Alicia's living room too, but not so much cluttered among the knickknacks of his words as contained inside that painting on the wall: everything all grey and green and soggy with his words. Only instead of Christ, Laura is there at the centre, and as I reach in to pass on to her my Judas kiss, Our Toad's hand reaches beneath my nightgown brushing my labia as he seals us all within that moment like flies in olive green amber. While back on the roof, looking at her and rubbing her arm, I knew that in this at least he was right: that it was worse, worse than I can yet imagine.

As that look of fear on her face told me that this last long performance had in fact hardly yet begun.

It was only there

sitting on the roof

looking over at her, that I began in my mind all the arguments against his terrible cannibalism, his desire not to be consumed and changed by her, but to consume and then excrete her, Our Turd, to bring her back to our world in his story, so much less than what she was. Though the arguments I felt arising in my mind even then were not so much against his conspicuous consumption, but just to ask him, please, please, in this compelling tale: Please to change the ending.

Because he was right, just the way he said: she was the story of our times. So that even the way he told it was far better than the Freudian fantasy I had told myself in Mother's voice after I'd left, my personal soap opera. It was no small domestic drama this, but a magnificent epic. So full of evocative elements.
– Do you remember the Vietnamese dictionary, Alma? he asked. How she would recite it out the window, how she said the word was there, the word to bring this all down, the one word, you do remember Alma, don't you? Well think about that Alma, *The War and the Word and America*, think about it. What a wonderful story, Alma. Maybe if she'd just gone through with it to the end, just maybe. Maybe the word would have been there. Maybe it would have happened. Even now, maybe it could all change.

343

And he sighed. As if he meant it. As if he could still want it: that change.

I listened
to that resonant voice in my mind as I watched her on the roof, heard the vibration of its compelling tension, its sense of narrative necessity, and I argued with it. Point by point I argued. Though I did leave the beginning much the same. He had done well by me, and he did well by her, reciting all the things I should think of.

It was beautiful how he constructed his story. How he built it up, layer on layer. With all her questions and her catastrophes and her performances, her what is it you want, and her this is what I need, her female fomentations and her feminine fecundities, all the things that she had been up to that moment. Until I am sure that now when he tells that same story to whoever will listen, building it and building it, *The War and The Word and America*, finding an audience to listen to his early adventures in Off-Off-Off-Off-Broadway: God it was so far off it was over the bridge in Brooklyn, with bedbugs, he might even say, he builds into it every element he has heard about since, I am sure he asks around, I know he occasionally calls my mother. So that, in his attempts not to keep her, but to keep the story, alive, it must by now include her attempts at rearranging the library and the welfare system, her killing and framing of Mandy, and her talks with the aliens, that he builds inexorably toward the same climax he built for me, with a story for each set of eyes that she looks into along the subway platform as he tells and retells it.

The tale of the beautiful sparkling artist who exemplified our America, the free spirit he wanted to follow everywhere. Except that at the last minute he couldn't, he was too weak, you can imagine that too, how he would describe himself standing by the subway entrance, afraid to go down, afraid to face what he would have to come to know down there. So that he would miss the dramatic moment, where it would all come together, Thorne, with madness and the Vietnamese dictionary and the infinite rearranged library and the desire to reflect all our victims to be all our victims coalescing into one final catastrophe as she would look into the last set of eyes and those eyes would at last see themselves for what they were. And in that moment reach salvation or Nirvana or some other alien parallel or tangent universe. While in the ecstasy of apotheosis the hands would reach out to hold her to hug her to caress her to call her by her name of saviour or bodhisattva or whatever other name there might be, Artemis or Athena some name for wisdom in the Great Mother, but something. Only to find that she had sprung away in that instant.

So that he, so that she, in caressing her, in grabbing at her, shoved. Instead, in ecstasy, shoved. Just in that moment when the train would break onto the platform announcing itself with its hollow echo its wind the way those trains always do, its bright lights catching her in their beam, the sound augmenting to a great whoosh, as she, as he, as that person would be transformed. That one person who at last *knew*, that person would still be reaching out, reaching out, while Laura would reach back, a Chagall figure flying through the air, one who would know exactly where she was going, though the gesture would be hard to decipher, would it be intentional or accidental, or suddenly inside some catastrophic universe in which accident and intent combine, to become necessity, or a banana peel, the last absurd gesture; discontinuous and profound, as her point would leave its plane, just as she broke through just as they started to understand. When there she would be, gratuitous and lovely, flying through the air all the notes of all the wants of all those she had asked, written at that very moment and pinned to her clothes, or flying down the subway entrance after her through some hole in space and time, would coalesce into a map of the world. The living planet. With all the wants of all its species, all its creatures. Just as she would fall. And the last person to look at her would see in her eyes, in their round orbs, the earth floating in space, among a myriad of stars, and pulling the hand back she/he would retreat from the edge of the platform, forever changed. And he/she would turn to the rest and know they had not seen. And would weep, while all the rest would scream. As the crucifix/train would bring itself to a halt.

And it would be over. The Free Spirit of Laura Mack over. And perhaps the world would be saved. Or a small part of it. Our Toad's view of it perhaps. The way he turned to me and, spreading his arm out against the starry sky behind the boat's railing, as at a giant screen, said:

—That's the way it should have been, Alma, don't you see it? Right before your eyes. Don't you?

And I did.

Of course I did. That's why I found myself going on with it. Telling his story to myself as I watched her. In debate with him. No, Our Toad, change this. Yes, Our Toad, the first part's okay but alter that, she really meant something just a little bit different when she said the other. I'd take out the part about the bedbugs and include instead the cockroaches, the ones that ran over her face right before the end, whose antennae were in communication with the spaceship. Certainly, Our Toad, I hadn't known about that, but please yes, you should know to include this, and remember, if you need more material there is always the jacket, and the mussels of course, and the ocean.

I would go on, imagining him in front of me, adding and subtracting and even multiplying and dividing elements, juxtaposing them and equating them and balancing them in the air, until finally I would always let myself come down to the ending, or almost to the ending. When I too would walk out onto the subway platform, when I would say to him in my mind: Well, no.

This part too, this part: we could change it just a little. You see, if you look at it closely, very closely now, this death at the end that you've got written in here, well, it's probably unnecessary. Even, perhaps, well, a wee bit melodramatic, don't you think? The story would probably be far more effective if the end wasn't made definite, you know, you could make it an absorption, well, not really directly into Heaven by a chorus of Angels, but maybe onto the alien spaceship by the aliens who, well if it were a movie, they could just look like angels.

And she'd be wearing that skirt see, oh, you don't remember about the skirt, well it would be the best thing for her costume, you could even pin some of those cards to it, and have it all flowing, sort of like El Greco's Assumption of the Virgin. Only all those lines in it, those ribbons, they would be like a New York subway map that could slowly transform into your map of the world, and you could have really deep dramatic music, but very modern, that would start when the light would change, no, not the light at the end of the tunnel, or the light of the train. No, *all* the lighting, it would become just that much more ethereal, the way it always is in dream sequences so you can't tell if something has really happened or not, so we wouldn't know if that one person had reached apotheosis or even if the police, you could have a nice crewcut pair of them running down the stairs in slow motion, if they had made it in time to restrain her, it would all be unclear, but at least it would be left open. And finally my true motivations would show, you know, for her to come back.

With word from the aliens or from god or the goddess or from somewhere, and then I would pull out my high card, after all, it was myths for our time we were talking about wasn't it, and that's what all those tales do, they never really get closed off, the idea is to make ready for the return of the hero, isn't it, whether it's Christ or Buddha or King Arthur or General MacArthur or Tecumseh or Joan of Arc or Quetzalcoatl, or even the Virgin of Guadalupe, isn't that what they all say, that they will return? So why shouldn't Laura, really, wouldn't that be good enough, better even, just the way the shell across from me, still concealed that, the possibility of return, spoke to the possibility of return, that my Laura could still return there, well that would be all right, wouldn't it.

And I found myself breathing hard, trying to keep up with my racing mind, even as I could hear Our Toad's counterarguments, that it just wouldn't be stark enough, just wouldn't be good enough or tragic enough or real enough: I want it real, Alma, real, world-changing gutsy. Or maybe it would even be, ballsy, real ballsy, I could hear him say that in my mind, he did say it once, I'm sure of it, when I interrupted him to ask in the tiniest voice for her return, hammering his fist on the railing, before he would go on to tell me how, yes, maybe the spirit could come back, maybe that spirit always does come back, maybe we were just lucky to know one of its incarnations, but that spirit, you know that spirit, it could never incarnate in the same body twice.

And maybe that was the problem, maybe that body was the problem, the body always the problem, like Jesus when he asks God the Father why he has been betrayed. So that maybe the body, the sensuous body, god she had such a sensuous body, maybe the body wouldn't let her go, maybe it just wouldn't. Because she was a woman, you know, so much a woman, so much part of *this world* as a woman. Maybe that was it, her greatest virtue yet her greatest burden, that femaleness that takes in the world, only maybe once she'd taken it in, even as a perfect victim she couldn't let it go. So that even if she'd used that body to understand the other to reach new heights of spirituality and sacrifice, still, still. When it came to the final one, the final act, the final sacrifice, that all-encompassing body, it wouldn't let the world go, it wouldn't let her go, let the spirit go, it just wouldn't. And that's when that spirit incarnate in her, that spirit had to leave the body behind. But with that body still here, it couldn't enter another one.

– Oh, Alma, Alma, it's so awful, so terrifying, because that spirit is gone now, and her body is so empty now that maybe it won't be able to come back at all. Maybe we've seen the last of it, maybe our world is on its own now.

But the fact would remain, it will remain, that she had made a mistake, a terrible mistake. With the body betraying the spirit like that, but still: this was not the ending. This could not be the ending. And he will cry in my mind again, he still does, Thorne, I could hear him as I walked with you along the Promenade, hear him still intervening in this story I wish to tell you as I pack. So that even now I feel I must interrupt this telling to start in again: with new and better arguments.

Sometimes
I will appeal to the new spirit of magic realism, of absurd abundance, after all she had that abundance in her work. That it is just that abundance that will allow us to make her story into a new absurdist remake of one of those legends of the spirit wanderer, a cross between Don Quixote and the Buddha. So that he was right that we could imply she'd been a messenger all along, and what better time than now for a return in the feminine, the return of the feminine, you could even say, after all, everybody is saying that,

even apologists for patriarchy think it's time for the feminine to come back, and besides, she was known for that, wasn't she? All those new heights and depths of female experience in all those articles so what vehicle could be more perfect for bringing back the feminine and what better reason not to have to destroy her body, or even her whole mind, no matter what he said.

And it is usually then that I will remember the dream, I remembered it there on the roof, and I will say to him:

—But the dream, Our Toad, you've forgotten the dream, surely she told you about the dream.

And I will tell him that there is no better place for the return of the feminine than to her bed, that the bed can be both a symbol of her gender and her sexuality, even a symbol of the birthing she never did in the flesh. So that the writhing sheets she always saw from such a distance as empty, the moon and sun at the same position in the sky, will suddenly and always call to her, wherever she is, and she will come, to become female and embodied and catastrophic all at once, always there and always not there, the woman who is, yet *qui n'existe pas*, surely that would be perfect, wouldn't it.

And then to connect it even more, well, he did remember that the last version of the dream, he did know this didn't he, that she'd lost it on the subway? And the earlier ones were torn and pasted into her first Thomian totems? So what a perfect catastrophic loop, that even if she was meant to leave our world at that moment as he said, still she wouldn't be able to leave that version of the dream behind, but had to come back for it – and back for it and back for it and back for it. So that the dream itself, that empty bed or even chair she searches out, could symbolize the world's need for the incarnation of the feminine, so long missing from our midst in a male dominated, or did the people who talked like that say patrivalent, society, and how because there was so little of it, that incarnation, she must come back to make it present, looping back into the system at various points, like the dream fragments she had collaged into her totems, so that there could be sightings. And maybe, instead of being shoved in front of the train, she would be dragged along the platform by the train leaving, by the wrist, by the hand that holds onto the dream, the dream of the return of the feminine.

That she will then know was precisely what she wanted, and what perhaps the eyes of that last young man – or young woman, I'm not sure which is the best way to play that, the masculine recognizing the feminine or woman recognizing herself – wanted as well. As she will look at him or her, not on the platform, but through the glass of the door, the way I always imagined her looking at me. And both will know this is what the world needed.

So in that ending sequence we could have her dragged away, once more that skirt, now a map, flying. Billowing out until it took up the whole entrance to the tunnel. And then later when the police would look for the body it wouldn't be there. And we'd have instead a brief look at her wandering, trying to read that suddenly faded skirt that was frog map and subway map and world map and catastrophic collage, in the subway tunnels, trying to figure out where next she would encounter the dream. At what station or along what route. Where next she would have to heal the planet.

So that later those sightings, localized at first, you know, would spread to different parts of the world. Places where tragic things were about to happen or just kept happening, things that would affect the whole earth – things like that – I will always want to say. The Amazon jungle or the B.C. rainforest, or the Exxon Valdez, or Chernobyl, or something. Whatever has happened to the environment that year that is particularly awful. Or, perhaps too, the planet's genocidal wars. And as for her body, the body we all knew, well, she could just drop by to inhabit it, every once in a while. To say hello. Wish you were here. The way she will sometimes seem to.

I'm sure you can understand why I still do that. Make my desperate attempts at different endings, just as I did there on the roof, until I am carried away. And not exactly by angels myself. But by the story, just as he had been, while my breathing will become no longer desperate but calm, my eyes no longer searching, but just wandering without much attention placed on what they see, the way his had always wandered in the apartment, or that night on the boat. So that on the roof, the conversation I was having with her, the few moments her attention would return to me, became like a conversation I might still have in the laundromat – at the campsite if not at home, now that I have a washing machine – hellos and goodbyes and how are the kids, spoken between paragraphs of the latest potboiler or mystery or *Chatelaine*.

Because the plot I was making in my mind started to take over, that still happens, but right then it was something that had never happened to me before, wresting substance, not so much from her as from the pain I felt at seeing her like that, as I concocted more and more outlandish stories, anything that would render her, not so much discontinuous as to be continued. And right then, it was not the dream I remembered, but the girl Jeanpierre and I had met once, it wasn't the Amazon, I've never been there, though Jeanpierre has at least been in Brazil. It was Mexico, the lowland jungle that borders the Guatemalan Petén, not quite as symbolic as the Amazon but truly as difficult, as catastrophic, a place.

And though back then the problems were in Guatemala, with absolutely no possibility of flying in to Tikal, the Maya city with the highest pyramids, the same problems now have moved into Mexico, or not moved so much as manifested themselves, they've always been there just not so right in your tourist face, the way they are now exactly where we were in Chiapas. Something we always do know just that little bit about, through the years of information coming to us in the mail as we buy off our guilt through Oxfam. And somehow somewhere in that area there always seems to be another attempt taking place among the many in the five hundred years since the arrival of Columbus, to exterminate the last of the descendants of the Maya, in whatever country it is they find themselves. Whether it is in order to take their land, for mineral rights in Guatemala in the eighties, nickel mostly if I remember, or to run cattle as it is in the zone near Palenque.

Which, at least, is not the kind of thing where Jeanpierre could get invited to do the seismic studies.

Though it would make a wonderful place to put Laura. Because she could wander there with her astronomy text, the Maya were great astronomers, that's part of what I learned on that trip, making that

Mesoamerican border space even better than the Amazon. Though it would be easy enough for Laura's trails to be so discontinuous that she could appear and disappear. So she could do the Amazon as well. Then reappear the way this girl seemed to. Though she carried no books at all. Not even to guide her.

All she had was a monkey. Who sat on her shoulder as she sat in the Temple of the Magician at Palenque. That's not the tall pyramid that has the incredible tombstone at the bottom, in a kind of low relief carving I'm sure Laura would have loved, a combination of lazy elegance and acute *horror vacui*, but the temple in the middle of the site that leads up into a three storey square tower, that gives a view out the pastel plain toward the ocean. Or, if you turn, back into the green and blue intensity of the jungle.

Jeanpierre
and I had flown in from coastal Cancun over the low scrub brush of the Yucatan, a limestone plateau with little surface soil and no surface water, too much like the north, really, if not for his liking then for him to be surprised by when we went to Chichén Itzá and Uxmal, so that we had decided to come into the real jungle for a few days, settling for Palenque and a chartered Cessna into Bonampak, where the only extant, and barely extant at that, Maya murals are. Though, in the end, even that territory with its trees over a hundred feet tall, seemed terribly familiar to him, mostly from the B.C. rainforest, and then there was the pilot who kept losing the landing strip as he circled to come in. The only difference, obvious when we reached the ground, was that all the trees were covered in vines.

Then, when we got back to Palenque, and travelled out from our hotel to the old Maya city, really far more beautiful than Bonampak where the jungle is more extraordinary than the ruins with how it overgrows everything, we met this skinny young American sitting in the middle of the tower in lotus position with a monkey on her shoulder who claimed she had seen us go and return.

—I have seen you look upon the old gods in awe, and rejoice for the captive who awaits his sacrifice, she said in dark sepulchral tones.

Part of me wanted to giggle, though the part that won out huddled closer to Jeanpierre and let her skin crawl. While Jeanpierre tried as casually as possible to ask questions, since he was obviously surprised too, after all how had she known we had been looking upon the brilliance of that painting, the languid languishing captive as beautiful and willing a sacrifice as anyone on the boat could have wanted to have his wicked will of, including Our Toad. Still, we didn't think she had seen the plane take off or land, or had any other way of knowing we were on it. Only it didn't seem to matter, even if it was clairvoyance it seemed to mean so very little.

It seemed to diminish rather than expand us to be included in her world, as she would feed fruit to the monkey and laugh when it shit on her bare shoulder. She was wearing an aged Indian print cotton skirt and a girl's undershirt that showed her small pointed breasts, which were really little more than nipple and areola, while she gradually told us in a voice as flat and pastel as the plain, of how she had been there for months, it was just so Far OUT, being here like this. All she did was walk, from place to place to place, though all the roads did not lead to Rome, she had said and giggled, or even to El Dorado. That was the one remark that made me think she had known something before giving it up for her seemingly permanent walk-about, talking of that golden city the Conquistadors had searched for. Still she did go from one village to another, where the villagers would always feed her, and when they didn't, well, she could always pick fruit. Like the kind she was feeding to the monkey, who shit on her shoulder again. As she continued to giggle.

And I suppose there always are so many of them, the pilot certainly seemed to think so, shrugging a glorious Latin shrug when asked, just that slightly sarcastic and sophisticated and looking down his nose, not at all your stereotypical mañana Mexican – but then so few are – even as he searched for words to describe how there were at least one or two a year, the kind always in search of good dope – magic mushrooms seemed to be the specialty of the place, another link with B.C. – or the perfect moment, ancient religions or a warm tropical lover.

To live in the now, or among the truly natural, the truly primitive, they used to always say, with tribal the new code word if you are striving to be politically correct, though how the remnants of one of the world's true urban civilizations could be described that way, I'll never know, while in any case, whether it's deep tribal or true primitive, it's still the same one Sandro always wanted and talked so much about, that he supposed to be at our core, that would speak to our intuition and our spontaneity. While not any of them will ever take into account there in the Maya territory, or anywhere else, the human reality that surrounds them. The energy and brilliance and years that had gone into the monumental art of those ruins, the glyphs thought out over centuries brushed onto paper and inscribed in stone, or even the daily passing on from generation to generation of what was left after the conquest when the books had all been burned, of the systems of numbers and agriculture and medicine and child-rearing, never seeing that difficult and painful and ebullient living as history. Much less apply such a concept to the shamanic systems of the Inuit or the Yanomama to see them as the fruit of – what would you call it – not civilization with its privileging of city, but culture. All that sacred space and myth time Laura would talk about – and you, too, Thorne, you had that in common – finding its place, its history, in the concrete or the oral. While instead, this girl, just like Sandro, just like all of them would pay lip service to living in the present. Created for them by someone else's past. Invisible, like the servants of the rich. The sherpas conquering Everest.

While the past this girl had succumbed to would doubtless be her own, her own the pain or horror or stress or ecstasy or drugs, that made her trade that previous life for the permanent present tense without past or future, as others would on the streets of the Bowery, or Marrakech, or Laura among the subways and the cockroaches, stuck finally in their own vision, or the vision others had told them they should have, a postcard mantra they could repeat and repeat, just as Laura does.

With the greater complexity and profundity of her expression serving only to entrap her further rather than to free her, a spider in her own catastrophic web, as discontinuities and epiphanies and being here now turn into being nowhere ever. Just as that girl would go round and round, from village to village and fruit tree to fruit tree, because the villagers in that area do feed those people. They are the fools of god or of the mother earth, and the least that they deserve are her provisions. So that maybe the girl does at least have a symbolic function in that culture, as well as a cautionary one in her own.

Though what I wanted

to do right then was follow Jeanpierre's lead. Become a typical tourist or travel researcher with my ever more detailed and perky questions: Well, which fruit was good and which villages kindest and where did she sleep at night when she was on the trail and wasn't she afraid of snakes or maybe jaguars – I'm sure there are still jaguars – or if not snakes or jaguars or even small poisonous tree frogs or even toads, tree toads, small poisonous sneaky little tree toads, poisonous even to the touch, then maybe of never being able to speak to anyone ever again in a language that she knew, because I knew she wasn't learning theirs.

Only looking at her, I realized she was afraid of nothing. If the fear I would see pass over Laura's face that afternoon had ever passed over hers, then it had passed for her a long time before. And that as far as language went, there was no longer any language spoken anywhere that was any longer truly comprehensible to her: not as we might understand it.

So that what I did do was not ask questions or even talk at all. But turn my back on the jungle and look out over the changing twilight colours above the plain, so like the twilight colours out my mother's window that night we said goodbye to Laura. And then go back to our motel, the only one with air-conditioning in the town, where the power failed and it was Brooklyn summer heat again and I was sick, for no reason I have ever been able to discern, just sick, vomiting the fruit I'd eaten, bright tropical colours coming out my mouth to match the monkey's shit on the girl's shoulder.

And maybe it was that Laura's last postcard had already come in the mail, the one with the jungle on it, or maybe it was something else in our space/time discontinuum I still don't understand. But when I think of that day I am sure I saw Laura's future, this girl a catastrophic echo of what was yet to come. In her smile, in the sense of what her smile had once been, or even in how she brushed the monkey shit off her shoulder the way Laura once had the bedbugs off her bed, there was something that warned me. That I would remember again on the roof as I avoided Laura's eyes just as I had the girl's, and memorized instead the plain, its colours now as pale as Alicia's knickknacks. As I let that girl and Laura become one in my mind, let her somehow take my place as twin, or become our triplet, as I debated with Our Toad in silence.

Though maybe this too is a changing of the past to fit present knowledge. Maybe I saw nothing of any of that on that day in the tower, experienced no hair-raising shiver of premonition, of parallel universes colliding, of time enfolding, but just the usual, even if brief, grief for present potential lost, the fear that is always there of what it means to go too far. And throwing up was just throwing up. Something in the water or the fruit or the heat. Though I am sure that for some reason I did start to speak of Laura with Jeanpierre that night, as we fled from our overheated room to the village square to watch kids play soccer in the village schoolyard, something about how some visions exclude so much more of the world than they include, no matter how brilliant. While on the roof I did suddenly see them as one and the same, the dark tunnel of those two sets of eyes like the subway tunnel of Laura's performance, so that I imagined a tunnel connecting them somehow, and then that there were more, and that they could exchange places, even bodies, moving through some sort of hysteresis of discontinuous time.

And I started to play with it, how that would work, making the pieces move around a game board in my mind until I hardly heard Laura with her small complaints or larger cosmic demands, hardly saw her anymore at all, in fact, but just wove and rewove that story. As Our Toad must weave and reweave his, as Penelope must have the tapestry on her loom.

It would have been perfect for Laura. It still would be. That tragicomic position between now and never. And the truth is I love it still. Love it best. With its need for a semiotics more complex than the infinite library of Jorge Luis Borges – much less the one in Brooklyn Heights that Laura tried to rearrange – but a closed system of fruit and of pathways nonetheless. So that I will see it sometimes, see her sometimes, as I take my morning coffee fresh from the camp stove perched on the picnic table at our campsite, to walk the marked trails of the B.C. highland, their red trail markers glinting in the dappled sun, so like sunlight along the clear if unmarked trails of the Maya lowland, summer camping trip sloppy, as the morning warms and I find myself with my polarfleece tied about my old jeans, my shoulders in my tank top now bare to the sun, so that I imagine them the shoulders of that girl, with her pet monkey perched there, and I brush away the leaves or spider webs like monkey shit and laugh her hollow laugh, and suddenly it's true.

She and I and Laura are a troop of interchangeable hers, interchangeable bodies, and it's then I name us, name her, Earthchild America, to make a more perfect version of Our Toad's *The War, The Word and America*. While in this version the feminine spirit, in search of the dream of true incarnation, could drop into interchangeable, though usually pain-racked, bodies, as so many of us do into makeup and into costumes, calming them a moment the way we still our faces before the mirror, then leave again.

To enter the jungle where she could come with a small red tent that would feel like being on the inside of a heart if not of the womb, that she had carried hidden somewhere when she had fallen from the platform. Together with her astronomy text and a pad on which she could write love letters to her Alma. Who in this version would not be her childhood friend, but the last set of eyes she had seen upon the platform.

And there would be bugs, of course. The tent would fill with bugs. The way our apartment had with bedbugs. Or her parents' old army tent had with beetles. Only this time it would be beautiful multicoloured tropical bugs that would leap up and fall to earth, leap up and fall to earth, never flying, despite their loveliness. Though I would not have her eat them, as Jeanpierre would the hemlock grubs, not even the fruit, the way that girl and her monkey did, but survive instead on cosmic emanations. While she would sit and write, or perhaps draw, with her coloured markers. Version after version of the dream. Attempting to calculate the exact place the exact room the exact tunnel the exact wrinkled sheet for her next entry into it. Sketches and scribblings which would, of course, also be love letters and maps of the aliens' trajectories. That could hint at the story of her discontinuous and catastrophic existence, with side trips into other wanderers – who would be and not be her – entered through the tunnels, the mirrors, of their eyes. Allowing her to move through yet other places, other times.

With each piece of correspondence more abstract, each paragraph less comprehensible, each picture less strictly readable, as they would contain more and more the full round circles of the ideograms of the Maya, but more idiosyncratic in how they bring language and image together. Until they would involve themselves only with number, the beautiful Maya numbers with their base of five, until she would forsake language and even image altogether, and the numbers would default to zero, the Maya too invented zero – one of the few cultures that ever did – and she would send blank pages, the white sheets of her dream place perfect now and unwrinkled, until the supplies would run out and there was nothing more to send. When she would at last have found the word that would change the world.

Or the piece of paper.

While the one who had followed her, taken in by that look, there on the subway platform, wanting once more to see herself as she truly was – and it would be a she in this version, this a woman's story – would receive those last empty pages and weep, sure that they contained a message, instructions to go to a place, that only the truly pure of heart could see. Not one so compromised as she would be in her dealings with the earth. Though perhaps she could go to her husband or to his friends or to her own, and challenge them about their lives, letting those blank pages finally tell them who they really are.

So that it would be beautiful, that would be the most important thing of all, that it be beautiful, the way I kept trying to make it on the roof, the way I try it still, each version more and more beautiful, more and more complex, putting in and taking out and trying on different incidents and intents and characters just as Our Toad had done, my tapestry of Laura the spirit of the jungle woven and rewoven to resemble those brilliant complicated Oaxacan and Guatemalan weavings their tradition millennia old, I saw for the first time on that trip, woven and embroidered and painted, layer upon layer, with some left on the loom for the tourists to hang on the wall, perhaps next to a cheaper blanket version of the last supper, though never, the way I did, to take down and weave again.

A perfect incomplete and discontinuous covering, whether to protect me or to protect her I do not know, or perhaps, just to protect that shell that once was her from that one last final closure Our Toad so desired, as I saw less and less of the real Laura in front of me, my Magritte fish/woman tumbled on her side, perhaps even less and less of the real Laura of my memory, as I wove and unwove and rewove that precise if not concise story. And if I am like Penelope in my weaving, then it is not to avoid my suitors but my grief, the acknowledgement of my loss. Telling it still just so I can tell myself it is not over, that it is still possible: that someone can still be parachuted in to occupy that shell.

Which is

what I wanted to say on the boat, that we really didn't have to close the book on her, finish it, have closure, we really didn't have to close her, did we?

While all I managed to say was: No. With my hand held in front of me.
— No.

The story finally too much.
— No. Our Toad. No.

As I pushed him away, and walked toward the stairs. My sense of violation doubled now, by his intellectual S&M, his attempt to open me up with a can opener so that then he might have me. Even if it was only to enter the fantasy. Tied and bound by his words, to watch him beat off to them, in hungry longing. Until even Sandro's commands seemed better, his overblown mastery that allowed me no real place at all. But at least, I thought, left me alone to continue my search.

Even as Our Toad's voice followed me. To let me know that he had had me long enough to never let me go. That I would always be with him. Part of this fantasy. As his story would be part of my life.

– Don't be a sentimentalist, Alma, he said. You know better than that. You always did. I never expected this of you. That you could be like this. And there was a harsh intake of breath. Before he continued, the voice higher.

– I'm sorry, Alma, sorry. But I understand. Why you can't face it either. It must have been hard for Judas too. To be brave.

And then as I started down, he spoke again. The strange manipulative warmth back in his voice. As if he could wrap me in it, and then with it watch what Sandro and I would do together.

– Be careful of the Magician, Alma, he said. Don't count on him. His is a world of illusion. He will not aid you in your quest. But help you lose the way.

And then, the terrible sound of sobs, louder and louder, tearing through his stoned out laughter.

The problem is

could never write

it that way, Thorne. The way Our Toad wanted. Or even the way I often have told it in my mind to reply to him. I don't know how long I've known that, maybe I knew it all along, but I know that I've known it since I met you. That it would betray some knowledge you gave me the first time you smiled. And I am so sick of being Judas.

Though I am sure I could use it to satisfy her. Or her ghost. That wandering spirit. The way she comes to me in dreams and asks me to. Now that I have started those courses at the university, compulsively signing up for writing courses and women's studies courses, when really, I still intend to finally get my degree in something else. Maybe still, after all this time, in anthropology.

She comes to tell me, sitting on that funny old-fashioned oak bench in my mother's foyer, the one with the mirror and the beautifully carved back, and the storage space under the seat where my mother keeps old sweaters and old books, how I must write her story. Write her right story, she says. Write her right story right.

Sitting there all school girl proper the way she looked that first day of class when I thought I would never like her, as the hall on either side elongates and elongates into infinity, and I see her image again and again in the mirror although there is no other mirror to reflect it back, except the little peephole in my mother's door, while she takes out a book that is not her astronomy text but one of those beautiful bound journals they sell in expensive stationery stores, and she looks at her notes, and she tells me how I must do it, how I must do it now. Or even, how I am doing it wrong. How I must do it some other way. Write her right story right now. Even if, really, I have not even started it yet. If, perhaps, I never will.

Though, I am sure, this is the version that dream presence must like best of all. The way it would satisfy all the rules in those courses, too. Just the way her work always satisfied her teachers. And went so far beyond them. *The War, The Word and America* with its scope and beauty of the kind she always claimed for herself, it could go beyond them too, replete, just as Our Toad said it would be, with all its tales for our time.

I could even add her consciousness into the bingo games I go to for my sons' hockey clubs, I think of that sometimes as I'm standing there amid the smoke, looking around at all the faces. Or later, preoccupied, my feet tired, as I must pick up all the used cards from among the candy wrappers and old Coke cans, the chips and paper cups, the empty plastic bingo ink containers with their felt tips to stamp circles onto the cards, while I sweep up the already stamped and soggy paper, all multicoloured into my arms, and I hug them to me replete with their smell of ink, and I start to think again as the Maya did, of numbers and of systems.

While all those dots become topological points in my mind, and the papers I hold become the catastrophes themselves, crumpled much beyond the elementary seven of our four dimensions, to make me think it must be emotion, nothing less, that has added the extra coordinates. The anger or pain or joy of the successful or unsuccessful player, the exhaustion of those of us who must clean the smokefilled hall at the end, changing time and space with sudden irrevocable movements of our hands, as we gather and squeeze the paper. While I contemplate what Laura once could have done with them, I even see her there sometimes, running around to pick up all the paper in some mysterious order that respects the energy contained in each piece, that she could rip and tear and reform, perhaps until it changed the nature of the known universe.

Even if in reality, such bingo prints would in the end be no more colourful than the menstrual prints she once made. All those cheap dyes would fade too to brown at the first exposure to sun, for all the avid enthusiasm of those sets of eyes watching, of hands touching, moving from the cards to the small china figures that are brought to the bingo hall for good luck, to the bin where the numbers roll around on their balls until one falls out and is transmitted on the closed circuit TV. That she might be sure was not closed at all but broadcast direct to or from the alien spaceship, while the cards and the cries of Bingo! would be another form of answer, or of worship, that those privy to the secret life of numbers could understand. A cone of power accidentally or deliberately raised, that she would pick up and twist and change, the act of collage her favourite magic forming act, that she could laugh over. So that sometimes, in the bingo palaces, empty or full, I can hear her laughter. As the tears cloud my eyes.

Which I tell the other mothers, if any of them notice, catch me standing there, staring a minute, off into space, are due to the smoke, combined with a terribly tiring day, as I breathe deeply a moment, and think about how I might get my degree in psychology after all. How, if I went on, I might do some kind of thesis on, the Interior Organizing System, I could call it, its role in madness and in art, or in some strange combination of the two.

As I think of her catastrophes and her astronomies, and the cute red-haired boy in the hospital of whom she spoke to me on the roof, who besides bringing her flowers had the whole world, its beginning and its end, organized in terms of the numbers on the license plates of the cars that followed and somehow controlled him, working it out with calculations in his mind that I for one could never do. While so many works of art enclose the same kind of system, with secrets, verbal or spatial or numerical or numerological, woven into text or image, until conceptual art that contains only number series will take up notebook after notebook and wall after wall at Castelli's, to great critical acclaim.

To make me wonder sometimes if it isn't that secret system that organizes or holds the energy of the work in such a way as to make it go beyond the simple world of sign or of design, into that of transcendence, of excess. Because art does do that for us whether we wish to admit it or not, wish to call it by some other name, it is still one of the moments of ecstatic connection. Of going beyond. Whether beyond is the ethereal or the embodied. Just like ritual, even the ritual that Sandro did on Fire Island, impoverished as it must have been compared to the religious rituals of those who truly believe, but with the system he'd designed, no matter what I choose to think of him, or where its elements originated, holding and broadcasting energy all the same.

So that it's when I think about that, the wondrous ability to connect, that I wonder how in the end she could have become so totally disconnected, where it was that she stopped being able to weave a world that we could all, if not understand, at least enter. And when I get back to that, my hand is once more in my mouth and the tears in my eyes, and I think that I will get my degree in geology or chemistry, and follow Jeanpierre into some simpler science, some simpler system. Or just forget it and stay home. Or get a job as a cashier.

And I take my hand out of my mouth to stuff all the old crumpled papers into the large green garbage bags that I haul out to the dumpster, throwing them up and over in a long curving arc, or I go back to selling lucky tens. And as I move I fold myself back into the fantasy, with its degrees in ecology and its narrator who will feel the spirit's commanding presence among the bingo cards and the cries of Bingo! until she falls into a deeper reverie than I ever do and she remembers that woman's eyes. And suddenly she is walking through the jungle with Earthchild America, or, perhaps I should call her, Americas, all the Americas, from the beginning of Maya time, as I remember all the small stories, or longer adventures, that could be fit into the frame of the narrator's reverie, whether originating in dream or memory or broadcast from the alien spaceship never made clear, as she would work the bingo to collect money for Friends of the Earth.

Such a lovely postmodern picaresque, it would be hard to imagine a vehicle more perfect. As the narrator would absently attempt to straighten out only one crumpled up bingo card, not knowing that through doing it, she would seal Earthchild's fate. Changing the doors in the discontinuous space in which she wandered, making it impossible for Earthchild to ever know where the doors all were, that she could have used to make her rendezvous, as slowly slowly, the narrator, now deep in her storyteller's trance would continue to flatten out that paper, now ironing it with her hand, only to find that – unknown to its owner, or perhaps all those coloured circles had rearranged themselves, the points had jumped the catastrophic gaps – that paper did contain a bingo after all.

At the same time as Earthchild America, forever frustrated at finding the changing door, would make more and more collages, more and more totems, from different and various parts of her anatomy, and the anatomy of the day, that further and further compressed what America really was, into its own cosmic blood totems, until, stuck in SoHo unable to reach the nourishment of her ship, or even her jungle home, she would start wandering from person to person, asking them one after the other, what it was they really wanted, to see if understanding that, knowing that, would help her find the door that would catapult her back, or at least make her comfortable, in her new role, being one of them. Which would set the final act in motion.

To end the terrible and terrifying and illuminating adventures of Earthchild America. If only for the moment. As they would come full circle. As she would see the narrator's eyes on the platform or inside the subway car, feel the dream in her hand and feel it ripped away, fly through the air knocked off the platform or dragged down it unable to let go, Chagall figure and subway map and hot Chinook wind and green plastic garbage bag and faded cotton skirt at once, glinting in the pink lights of a suburban street. As my hand thrusts up, the way that last hand would thrust her, or attempt to grab on, as the leftovers of the bingo, the ashes and cigarette butts and papers and empty bottles fly into a grey black dumpster, dull and metallic, so like an onrushing train. And disappear into it, so like the gaping mouth of a tunnel.

Our Toad's version or mine. The catastrophe finally a Mobius strip.

Only in the end it is simply a story, an internal monologue, like all the other fantasies, science fiction or mystery or adventure, Freudian or Jungian or Lacanian, pop psychology texts or mass market magazines, that anyone could find herself running through her mind to pass the time. With each version farther and farther away from the book or article that originated it or the Laura Mack that I knew, neutralizing her more and more even as it lionizes her, distilling her into a finer and finer vintage to be more easily consumed, without aftertaste or hangover.

So that if I do ever wish to impress my fellow students or my professors, or even a potential publisher, with a picaresque, then surely the outline of that story you told to me, the one I have dubbed in my mind, *The Pícaro of Winnipeg*, surely that would do much better. And even if it would never be a vehicle for her, still it would be wonderful to tell the story of that young artist, recently graduated from art school, come down to the Big Apple to seek his fortune, exemplifying so many, from urban centres and suburbs and towns and villages and farms and slums around the world, even Queens. Or Brooklyn. Like Laura. The one matching element which might let me use Laura as the trigger, the catalyst, as she so often wanted to be a catalyst, in what happened to him. The discontinuous work of Laura Mack what led him to take up performance. Bloody performance, because her work was also so full of blood.

Though I might not tell the story from his point of view at all, but tell it instead from the point of view of the girl who followed him, now a postmodern *Perils of Colleen*, like one of those medieval or romantic or gothic tales of the woman who must face all, perils and temptations, perhaps even the devil himself, to regain her man. Captive in some prison, among infidels. So that she could even visit those brothels Sandro's friends on the boat spoke of, that would put together whatever fantasy you could pay for, with whatever age of man or woman girl or boy, including being a prisoner in a Sultan's Harem. Where she might even be able to discover and differentiate – what better temptation for a modern woman to have to face and overcome – between eroticism and pornography, maintaining her true positive sexuality rather than her purity, in order not to lose her man to the vile degraded temptresses he must face within that place. That could be one among many marvellous metaphors and metonymies to invent, though none could be so good as those in the story itself.

I don't know where you heard it. You never said that. If you knew the man's girlfriend or the man himself, or just a friend of theirs. Or if there's a circuit you happen to be on, like being a member of a book club, that hears those stories passed around.

When you told it to me, I didn't ask myself if it would fit into a picaresque, I don't think I knew about picaresques then, or even if it would add to the constantly revised story in my mind. That I did work on so often those days we walked around New York, using what we saw, the light and the shadows and the colours for texture, though only before you met her. Afterwards, my story seemed a travesty. Which has hardly stopped me from going back to it. Again. And yet again.

While with yours, the only thing that passed through my mind was how wonderful it would have been, in the bars and cafés of that previous trip, over those endless beers or coffees, to have had that story as ammunition. It would have been so nice to be able to lean back, Alma not only from Suburbia but from Canada, to tell them about not Nanook, but *Candide* of the North. *Colleen of Canada*. And to have been able to laugh, with them or against them it wouldn't matter, but as funny as: Bellevue, at least it wasn't Bellevue.

Or maybe funnier, the way the two of us knocked shoulders as we laughed and looked up, it was a magnificent story, on such a glorious day, all blue and red, the sky and the bricks, just like it was the whole weekend on the boat. Only with you there was no pain, not then. There was just the brief shadow that passed over, the Magritte crow or the last cool tang of spring, the winter inside the bright of the day, to make me sure I wanted to bring up none of this, that I would not want to stop us laughing, or top your story. I wanted you to have the best New York performance artist story, so funny and bitter, with all its strange symbolism mixed in.

We even sang a chorus of *I've Been Bathed in the Blood of the Lamb*, with our arms around each other, as people stared and we passed over from SoHo into the South Village, the part they used to call Little Italy, for a cappuccino. Where, sitting outside and looking at the old tenements, full of a human history we could palpate with our eyes, I listened to more details of how that wet behind the ears young man had further wet his ears with blood, when the German performance group, I'm sure you said they were West Germans, from the same place as the man who'd cut off his prick, asked him to lie down and have lamb's blood poured all over him, whether because lamb's blood was symbolic, or because it was all they could get, who knows.

With the only problem the fact that the blood was contaminated, probably with some simple bacteria that's in everything, the one that causes hamburger disease maybe, except this time it leaked into his ear. And resulted in some kind of fulminating brain infection that brought him, brave art crusader, to death's door.

Which he did not enter, of course. That is the moment for the entrance of the brave and troubled sweetheart, as she will follow him, through perils she was always too sensible to seek out, the artwife to the rescue. Though truly a courageous and independent woman, and, for that matter, an artist in her own right. Since, to pay her way down, she would get herself into a show of Canadian art at the 49th Parallel Gallery, a food art show to be exact, as soon as she heard about what he'd come down with.

So that between visits to the hospital, in his case I think it really was Bellevue, though not the psych ward, and transferring his health insurance down from Manitoba, and bringing him flowers and small treats as he got better, and all those other responsible details she chose to take care of, she visited the studios of his artworld friends. Which would mean that in the story she too could be influenced by Laura Mack, just as he could join Sandro's group. And maybe Colleen could clean Laura's studio, since Colleen at least needed a bright clean space. Where she could take all day to cook herself up a turkey, working in a fit of temper over a long, I am sure it would be hot, afternoon, like so many on which I cooked for Laura and for Sandro.

As she would roast her fowl golden brown with butter and freshly grown savory herbs, then crucify it on a large, tinfoil covered, cardboard cross. While right in the opening of its empty chest cavity, the story of a different 'O', a different emptiness, a perfect mark, if not a perfect victim, she placed his picture. A little oval cameo like the open mouth of a startled heroine, of just the right size and proportions. After which she hurried him back to Winnipeg to tend his garden, while she, without doubt, tended his career. Probably both of theirs. I think she was that kind of heroine. She was definitely no fool, God's or anyone else's.

With the turkey the only victim as the public would laugh, and proceed not just to the puncturing, but to the carving up of its sides. While in the story Our Toad told me, that I have revised and polished, woven and unwoven again and again, the return of the feminine is only the return of the Mad Muse, and Laura is just another version of the unattainable female spirit, the one who, in her epiphanies, even Jacques Lacan claimed not to know or understand. That the men still chase, endlessly, endlessly, saint and martyr and virgin and nymphomaniac, claiming they will never be as good as her, in her purity or her sexuality, her insatiable appetite or her disciplined self-sacrifice, her depravity or her deprivation. Never, not ever, even with great effort, as close to the Earth, or to God, or to spirituality, as she is by nature. With only the greatest of Saints or Masters surpassing the most natural and unthinking of women.

The woman the sixties tried to exemplify again and again, the woman we all tried to be as we came of age on the cusp of the seventies, the natural spiritual intuitive woman, who accepted her femininity even if that meant accepting male versions of it, in sex or in the home. With Laura trying harder than any, even as she moved beyond the simpler definitions into the hardest female role of all. The one that was seen as her feminism, because of her affirmation of the feminine, as she still tried harder and harder to be that mirage that all could follow. With all her power and all her knowledge and all her vision, still coming back to that, to that one image, in which in order to realize herself she would have to annihilate herself, because she would have to go the limit, not merely define it the way men so often can.

Though not always. They do not always escape self-annihilation. Though often they feminize themselves to achieve it, still speaking as if annihilation were the nature of the female, by taking on the literal or metaphoric elimination rather than exaltation of their manhood – our West German friend with his politely sliced and documented prick a prime example of a fate the boy from Winnipeg escaped – as they attempt to keep pace with the spiritual with the holy with the absent with the intuitive with the right brain with the Mad Muse.

With the other more usual, holding onto that manhood, literally or figuratively, as they exalt the phallus or the testicles or the voice they believe exudes from there like semen, saying that they speak her because she cannot speak herself, knowing her at last in the insightful intuition of their art as she cannot know herself. While she goes on, living it out, living it out, in the centre of her life or her body, acting or singing or performing or cooking or cleaning or bearing children or blows, more and more voiceless as her voicelessness becomes the symbol of her purity, her saintliness her spirituality her profundity her femininity her victimization: that purity which should make us all realize exactly who we are and why no one should be a victim.

Only it never does. We just want to use her more, take up more and more of her energy mold her into more and more of our stories, swallow her down excrete her out, complete her annihilation for her. As like Laura she keeps trying and trying not only within her art but within her life which men have told us for so long is, along with her children, woman's only real art, not to see it to voice it to imagine it, that unity and purity and sacrifice without boundaries, that last complete letting go, or even to come back from it, to visit it temporarily then return to tell of it, a great explorer, but to incarnate it absolutely, because she must *be* it, that is her nature. Not to do or to have but to be, like Laura spinning further and further and further out, crying look at me, look at me, have I done it yet, have I done it, am I there yet am I there, spinning faster and faster and gathering more and more voices, until, even if she could not do what had to be done, obliterate herself completely, body and all, as Our Toad said, still she did disembody, destined for whatever place it was she had to go, that left her body so empty.

And by now, I think, we should all like our heroines more down to earth, if not more earthy than that. It is time to let the Sibyls leave the mysteries, at least long enough to speak in their own voices. To take a load off, play a bingo, have a cup of coffee, and gossip for a while. To tell us what they know directly, without intermediaries, gods or great male artists, priests or drugs. To do their own naming, their own imaging, if only of the turkeys they are roasting. And of how to season them, the recipes quite precise.

Because there is nothing, for all the scope and beauty of the story, that could entice me to use Laura, any version of her, no matter how close to her truth, the truth she wanted to be hers, to tell that story again: to become the Pied Piper of PoMo SoHo. Because if I were to write Laura's story as that postmodern pilgrimage, with *The War, the Word and America*, starting in that moment, my historical moment, that *Vanity Fair* calls: "when Postmodern New York was just coming out of the lofts", I would just be another pimp, even if for a far more interesting, even visionary, string of girls. As I would entice yet another young woman, or young women, along that path that Laura took, find some other desperate and even brilliant innocent, willing still to incarnate that horrifying idea, or ideal, of the female. The male's most perfect version of topological catastrophe, just the one Laura predicted, there at her entrance, when she made those prints, the discontinuous interface, the self-devouring cunt, the absent fullness, as she absorbs herself into silence, into annihilation, into her own echoing cave.

And besides, I for one have learned long since, the group helped teach me this, that it is not a word that will end any war or change the world, or even the face of Our Toad's, much less the Maya's, America. But many words, and far more work. Not one individual's ecstatic experience but a far more limited and triter thing. With its infinitely repeated acts, committed by severely flawed people, who have cared enough to move or to be moved, as imperfect in their victories as in their victimization.

The story I will finally tell will be far more diminished and ugly, then, just as it was. Lacking always so wide and brilliant a scope, no Pynchon or Rushdie or Marquez or Allende or Morante, to take on all of a moment in history or even all of a history with their mad beauty, their quarries and their butterflies and their self-diapering babies and their green-haired beauties, their falls from airplanes or from grace, there will be left instead only the tiny madness to which the breadth of her vision was reduced. A perfect small woman's novel, the kind, against all the evidence, we are still known for. With its one postmodern moment, her small but continued postponement of full closure standing at its centre, more a piece of social than of magic realism, the sordid terror in that one fact that stands unmovable against the force of all the versions all the readings all the tellings, that one fact that should not be, and is. And is. And is. And was. And will be. Her still staring blank-eyed off into that space none of us can enter.

While she will continue to shrink in terror deep into the shell of her body as she did throughout those last hours that I watched her on the roof, or as she will huddle over her astronomy text, her giggle still echoing across the sky those years later as we watch her. As she will shrink and expand, surfacing ever more briefly, the train leaving more quickly, the bed standing more empty, as were her eyes. As finally that afternoon she did transform yet again. From that Magritte fish/woman, to the female echo of just that Kienholz construction we had gone to those years before. With her arms tucked between her legs the way the old man's were, her head no longer a fish, but the goldfish swimming now within her head, the goldfish bowl of her mind, as she curled around her defeated body. Black on black on the asphalt roof as she had been white on white in her hospital bed. Gone at last to that place I told her I would never follow.

While I also know, even as that image of her will still appear to me, in dreams or as I sit watching our aquarium, the one that delights my daughter so, that if the story could be just for her, or if there were even the least hope that in its telling, I could, if not save her, then at least transport her, to that place she was sure the old man had really gone, that place she spoke of, so sure that it existed, that place that is better than this, BETTER THAN THIS, BETTER THAN THIS, then I would continue to tell it. And, even, I would commit it to paper. The way still, in my mind, even if I can no longer believe in Our Toad's cannibalism, or even my own, in our appropriation of her voice to save ourselves from the impact of her life, I do continue to tell it, in laundromat or bingo parlour or walking through the woods. In hopes that it can in some strange and remote way connect me with her. The way I can still believe sometimes that when I dream her, telling me to tell her story this way, or that, that really, in some true sense she is there with me. As I believe too, that I see her sometimes, echoing in some street person's eyes, one who carries a doll, the way that young black man we saw down on the Mall did, or pushes a shopping cart up to a dumpster, or an empty baby carriage down the street.

So that when I see that, I try it again. To make myself another small fish, her Pisces twin, that swims with her in that closed ocean of her mind. And as I enter those other eyes to swim with her I take her far away, from the streets that she inhabits and she walks, retrieving her from her alien spaceship, so that we are together in the jungle with her ancient Maya astronomy text. Where maybe I let her help the survivors build a spaceship to escape the coming days, a spatial catastrophic ark, all beautiful Maya numbers and round New York subway balloon letters. While she stays behind to remind us, and to be exemplary, and I let her once more be perfect and pure, as she always wanted: the mirror of the earth, if not the aliens' video remote, moving through her green world in silent criticism of us all. Politically correct and ecologically sound, a spirit of place, or better perhaps, of displacement.

Until the last tree falls.

While on that afternoon on the roof, in the end, I looked over at her terrified. Forgetting all sense of guilt or of betrayal, no longer caring if I was Judas or the Adulteress. Forgetting Sandro's come and Our Toad's words and the Tchelichew tree. The scar on my thumb and the brilliance of her work. Her hands on my shoulders, her lips against my lips. Thinking only that if I did not leave, get up and leave right then, leave and go back to my mother's right then, organize myself to get back to my husband and children right then, I would not become another goldfish in her bowl, or even stay her Pisces twin, but that I would be that one figure, that one figment of her imagination, I had told her I would never be. Suspended above the beaten old man on the lower bunk, the one enclosed in the bubble of thought. And that she would not enter my dreams, but instead forever dream me.

Dream me.

I heaved myself heavily up onto my feet, and left her there alone on the roof. Forgetting even the possible danger in such an act as I severed at last our umbilical cord, to move into another dark moment of discontinuity, even of terror. Toward an ending, already faded like the skirt, that when I learned it I thought would silence me forever. No matter what words I should say in the noisy cacophony of my mind. While in that moment it is a shorter chorus that will guide me across the tar paper of the roof and direct me down the stairs, the words taking over my mind and pacing themselves to my steps as I move into the future.

One two three four my feet will go: horseshoe crabs hermit crabs king crabs eels, sea slugs sea urchins sea cucumbers squid, manta rays sting rays hammerhead sharks, octopi nautili arctic char, cetaceans crustaceans annelid worms, gastropods tetrapods humpback whales, sunfish sailfish swordfish skates, porgies flounders big mouth bass, guppies swordtails bettas neons, rainbow trout brown trout brook trout salmon, horseshoe crabs hermit crabs sea slugs Laura, manta rays sting rays flounders Laura, octopi nautili cuttlefish Laura, sea slugs sea horses mussels Laura, scallops brook trout red snapper Laura, Laura Laura Laura Laura.

Laura Laura Laura Laura.

Laura Laura Laura Laura.

TIME

Cepha
gastro
tetrap

opods,
pods,
ods,
Laura.

The words will keep repeating. Cetaceans, crustaceans, blowfish, Laura. Until finally I will stand at my mother's door to compose my face, twisting the jaw fiercely in what could appear to be a yawn, trying to relax the muscles enough to be able to come up with a reasonable semblance of a smile, before I silence the repeating voice as I turn my key in the lock, and open the door shouting:
— Mother, I'm home.

And pretty soon I will be in a deep hot bath, washing away the weekend with my hands, digging deep into all the crevices of my shipwrecked body; then pretty soon again after that I will be sitting with my mother over wine trying to wash away the implications of the weekend with the cheerful plastic scrubbing of my voice much as I had its signs on my body with my mother's harsh new loofah sponge. As I run the stories I have rehearsed over and over past my mother, much like a projector passing a movie, or a VCR a tape, with all the energy going into the mechanism of making the film go by the light at a certain speed, or the magnetic tape over the head, almost with the same mechanical buzzing or whupping in the too-controlled intonations of my voice as it proceeds inexorably onward, until she will shut it down quite abruptly.
— A rough time? she will say. And I will know, as my voice breaks and I look at the wall, that I have not fooled her.

And with me shut down she will take it over, all that I have said suddenly a very different gift from the unique wrapped and sealed present I'll think I've given her, plastic and unbreakable, like a family Christmas video sent through the mail, maybe with a title like Fire Island Body Builders. Because she will be able to take it back apart, or perhaps more to dissolve it, until it becomes a river, an irrigation channel, changeable but open to direction. The new information I have given her, with my wonderful eyes she will call them, my powers of observation thankfully not frozen by the frozen north, eddying and flowing and backing up and stagnating, together with opinions and observations of her own generated over the years.

So that it will seem a desultory trip down river at first, almost worthy of one of those songs about a lazy hazy day in summer, because certainly as I drink more wine a certain haze will set in, and it will seem so much more comfortable than running my own film by her, so afraid the emotion might show as my mind works the projector, that I will even squirm and sink my shoulders back into the couch. As I watch all the flotsam and jetsam eddy by the raft she has constructed me, with statements about how she didn't want to prejudice me against Sandro following admiration for my stories about the boat, my delicious travelogue she will say as she licks her lips, and tells me how it was what she expected, exactly what she expected, with a twinkle to the eye and another sip of wine, as she will bring in her favourite theories of the bohemian demimonde, generated by writers from Sand through Colette to Nin.

—You must read her diaries dear, they *do* say so much about it.

This world into which she has folded herself for as long as I have memory of her theories of the world, of something beyond what were her hugs, or perhaps the housekeeper's, that's difficult to know, an image of herself that she always liked better than any that could be propagated by: Those spinsterish Englishwomen, meaning everyone from the Brontës to Woolf. Or even today's magazines, whether *Ms.* or *Cosmopolitan*, where sex between consenting adults is a matter always for either jokes or hygiene, even your affairs diagrammed for you so as to have least effect on your obviously successful career or, for that matter, your happy marriage; replaced by a tragic and adventurous world, where men could admit to mistresses and women to pain, and even if they could not switch from one side of the fence to the other the way the men who used them could, respectable by day and whores by night, or the other way around, still they were allowed, not romance, but a little bit of the true romantic, the derring-do of outsize acts that might lead to personal tragedy rather than personal failure.

So that always she would fall back into that position, that world, and lecture me from it, as if it were a place she had a right to occupy, so that even that night she would let out the occasional well-constructed warship, destroyer or P.T. boat, from those coordinates, each one moving out from its mooring through the raising and lowering drawbridges of her eyebrows. Which meant that between stories of doctors bringing in diaphragms sewn into the lining of their trenchcoats: Ah for the real cloak and dagger, in the days when contraception was illegal in New York, and no one would dream of a legal abortion, at best of a safe one, a story she retold that night with you, that I know you love as much as I do, Thorne, shots would be fired in my direction about how she at least had not run away so quickly to maternity. And the suburbs she will say, the way I did. Speaking instead of the experience that she has had and her knowledge of the world, as I will occasionally lean forward or snuggle further back, trying to ride out the eddies or the rapids.

Or come to a halt suddenly in the backwaters to look around, reminded suddenly of the boat ride, how I had stared and stared, trying to figure out where we were, if there was any sign that could connect this world seen from the edge to the world inland with all its constructions, its roadways, so that now I will say to myself, not just where am I but where are we going, because this time I will have no idea, even of the destination. Though it won't really worry me, there's no destination I think she can take me to that will hurt more than what I have already seen and endured, so that I will be as happy refilling our wine glasses as I was serving drinks to the Captain, knowing I am along for the ride.

And as far as the people from the commune coming to see her is concerned, a smile will play about my lips as she mentions that, almost gloats over it actually, because, well, I'm sure I'm in for a good time now, certainly an amusing one. Without doubt, I'll find myself thinking, they've given her the best bohemia she's ever had. And if she's done so well with the bohemias of the imagination, what will she do with this?

So it will seem a great giggle as she says:

—What I'm trying to get at, honey, is that I've been around long enough to understand. To read between the lines. Even if mostly I didn't have to. Even if mostly they told me.

It was mostly baths and showers they came for, with the water pressure so bad in their place they had no alternative. And she was deeply convinced that they stayed on to talk, only as what they imagined to be a reward for her, the lonely divorcee whose daughter had once been Laura's best friend. Or that was it at first.

Though later it turned around. The bath or shower was the excuse, and the talking was something they just needed to do.

Just needed to do, she will repeat. Looking at me closely and saying: The way we all need to talk sometimes, honey, her hand going over mine, to hint that she knows there is more to my story, if I will just be like those other people, who after all didn't run away to suburbia, and just spill the beans to her, the way she says:

—They came here and just spilled the beans, spilled the beans. A look of pride on her face, of cat who just ate the canary – or artworld doyenne who just swallowed all the gossip in SoHo – pride.

While here I will just sigh a little, and let her have her day. Because even if it bothers me a bit, maybe it even makes me jealous, I don't know, but I have to admit it's true, my mother is one of those women, who without being maternal at all, still makes a perfect confidante. The kind of woman who would have made some man, for all I know she did, a great mistress, or several for that matter: a perfect *saloniere*.

Which is what that living room could have been. At least from the way she described them. Draped on the furniture or admiring the prints or the little sculptures, talking about the colour scheme, the way even Laura would do, in love with the bourgeois order if not splendor, because Laura came too of course, though never Sandro, to eat the things in the apartment up with her eyes. And besides that, and here my mother's gloating will increase, her hand rub up and down on her wine glass to rub it in:

—I guess with you gone, she still needed a womanly ear, she will say. And I was the next best thing.

She would appear, always tired, always looking like she needed a rest more than a bath. And sometimes, after asking about you, she always asked about you, she would just sit here and cry.

But she never told me directly, not in so many words. Not the way the others did.

And I will sit there wondering what it was Laura cried over, surely it couldn't be the jades she would rub, the prints she would admire, maybe just the stress of life, not being able to get off the roller coaster, it will be hard to tell among the amusing anecdotes, about how Laura would come there to practice her act for the houses of the rich, because Mother had been sure for the longest time that it was some sort of act.

She would ask Laura if she liked one of the jades, which were, in fact, worth so much less than the art Laura could by then, if not afford, trade for, and Laura would turn and start to speak, not of her like or dislike, but of how she could feel the strength of the carver, or maybe it was the Pleistocene upheaval as the rock was born, or the last person who had touched the stone, or even its relationship to the magnetic field of the earth or the cosmic energies of alien civilizations. Speaking in such stentorian tones that my mother really would giggle, especially since soon after that Laura would turn toward her, and volunteer to read her horoscope or her palm. So that my mother felt she had no alternative but to believe that Laura was playing a part, even as she spoke in the same tones about the aliens, as if everyone who lived south of 14th Street, much less Houston, must have participated in sightings. Everyone who was anyone knew the aliens were due back any day now, so that Laura was lucky to be their agent.

—Secret or literary is hard to tell, my mother will say, and I will laugh too, as she goes on to tell me how she thought it a form of protective coloration, the aliens and those voices Laura heard, a phonier than thou pose among all the phony poses the members of that community adopt, with Laura having to stay ahead of the pack, always ahead of the pack. After all she was the one who was either plumbing new depths or rising to new heights.

Because Laura was always under tremendous pressure to show new and unusual conclusions, so why not new life forms if not new civilizations? While between giggles my mother will describe how she always thought it a form of mental prestidigitation, a vaudeville act of now you see the spaceship now you don't, with all of it just to wangle more invitations to exclusive parties, because, well, after all.

—You know I just think the world of Laura, honey. And her talent. But she always was a climber.

I will jump to alert status then. I always will, no matter how often it happens. Even now, when she reminisces. When we both know that whether it is along the parapets of high art or into the castles of high society, Laura will never social climb again. Walls maybe. But that's about it.

Still I will be outraged. And offended. And defensive. The way I was then. Because I cannot stand that tone of dismissal. That says it was amusing all along, and just so predictable, anyway.

So that bristling, I will rush in without thinking. Spilling myself off the raft and into the current. Telling her how Laura deserved whatever little fame she had achieved. My voice a projector out of control now, becoming faster and faster like any engine revving up, as it rises to a whine. Until finally the film breaks, only to continue spinning in the projector, hitting various parts, whump bung zip pok, fast slow slow fast, as I say:

— Youofallpeopleknowhowmuch Laura'salwaysputinto her work.

As I begin a long lecture that will include all the things my mother has already known so long, as she will just sit back and smile at me. Readying the big guns, or waiting to rescue me from drowning, it's hard to know. As I will tell her how those people in the Hamptons always treat people like Laura, the ones who bring them their thrills, in real life adventure or art or drugs or kinky sex, as entertainers. As prosssssstitutes.

— Sowhoareyoutobesurprised ifLauragottobecourt jester?

The point will somehow be the obvious one about how if you can't keep up your side of the bargain, and in the end Laura certainly couldn't, well then, well then, well then, you'll just get abandoned in those depths you're plumbing without oxygen or a lifeline, in fact, those people would even walk away from the air pump if anything more interesting seemed to be happening on deck. The way they wandered away from that last performance, and how, without the audience, the video cameras following her on the streets, the specific frame for her actions, she was just one more crazy lady.

— One more crazy lady.

Because once it isn't art, definitely art, the kind that has, or whose creator has, a price tag, then it doesn't matter what else you do. She could spray paint anything she wanted on the walls of the city, or even of their country houses and it would just be graffiti and they would just call the cops. And as for the aging hooker persona, the madwoman persona, the baglady persona, they would just be the baglady the aging hooker, the madwoman. The madwoman: her own mother's nightmare. —Haven'tweall seen that? Haven'twehaven'twe? Isn'tshestill living it? Isn'tsheisn'tshe? Rightnow? Atthisvery MOMENT? Somewhere? InBrooklyn?

While Mother will look

at me. Amused. The teacher look again, her hand fidgeting on the sofa arm, almost as if it has a pencil in it, she can slowly tap on the desk, as she waits for the impassioned, but wrong, student, the one who has fallen into the trap of emotion, to stop, to finish, to calm down. The one for whom she has such sympathy.

And she will go back to her previous speculations, happy it would seem that at least one salvo has hit home. Feeling, I guess, that with me off the raft and in the water, now she has total control. Because she will go on. Her hand reaching out to pat mine again.

—**Of course, honey**. I know that. I didn't mean to denigrate Laura. We all know how hard she's worked. And like I said, no one would deny the immensity of her talent.

But is that what you think? Is that what you think happened? Just that? Oh, honey. You underestimate your friend. Laura thrived on that contradiction. On that energy. Oh, no. That getting in touch with the public. That's the stuff that probably kept her sane. Or at least functionally insane, for the longest time. It was something a lot more personal than that which brought her down. Hasn't anyone even given you a hint? Sandro? That Toad person? But of course, they would want to keep you in the dark.

And I will almost hear her say it too, Alma from Suburbia. Too innocent now to deal with the big city. With the downfall of her friend. As Mother will go on, paralyzing me in the sweetness of her smile. The river honey now, a viscous slower substance.

—It was something very private. Very private indeed.

And I will begin to be afraid then, knowing that there is no use struggling, that I might drown in this honey if I find no way to come up for air. As I try to remember my drownproofing, that the point is to relax, and get your head above water.

Which will prove, at least for the moment, easier than I could have hoped. Floating in this river will be a lot like watching television. Because this biography of hers will have all the elements. Ones I can add to the story I am writing for, or against, Our Toad in my mind. Or leave up to her, for the moment, to write, since her story would certainly be as good as anything Our Toad could come up with for prime time. One of those stylish docudramas. A mini-series or even a pilot for an evening soap, her own *Midnight Cowboy* serialized over the weeks, its storyline like so many I have been avoiding, but perfect on its own terms, the kind that tell you they are inviting you, just you, into a special world, one you will otherwise never come to know, and that it's just as downright sordid as you ever imagined. But you will now get to imagine it more and more completely, and cluck your tongue, or masturbate, or do them both at once, depending on your frame of mind.

I might even be able to tell it that way myself if I had the skill. And a desire to make the best seller list. Make this a kind of biographical memoir with lots of dirt. It would certainly make it easier, with the decision about what to put in and what to leave out already decided by prurience and what sells, and the constant going over and over the chosen details, not just an editorial necessity but a way of achieving numbness, a way of making myself not care so much.

So that I wouldn't get sidetracked the way I always do, out of the plot and into the texture, into trying to feel her again, trying to feel that time again, with a hand touching a forsythia blossom or a cheek rubbing a faded skirt, an eye contemplating a bloody painting, a thumbnail crushing a bedbug, a mouth kissing an uplifted face.

Only when I find out what my mother has chosen for her climactic moment, replete with exact details, which jade Laura picked up and how she ran her fingers over it and held it up to her cheek, what words she picked and how she looked away and out the window, I will want to giggle myself. It's more perfect than I could have imagined, a prime time or even a daytime soap, the kind you watch as you clean, your mind half there, though better perhaps for a bodice-ripper in the laundromat, you could get better details that way, of the crime of sexuality, that must inevitably be punished. Leaving out the adolescent friendship, we are once more in *Valley of the Dolls*, with tears in the corners of the eyes to acknowledge how that adventurous high artworld would never live up to the comforts of home, even if you could get off on watching it. Because after all, you could see how it had destroyed that poor woman, that Laura Mack. Lord knows, with her talent she could have had a better life than that. And a better man. And still made it out of the slums. If she just hadn't been so ambitious.

So you can understand why she did it can't you, in circumstances like those. But the poor thing, and late too by the time she'd made up her mind, that she would have to have the abortion. A second trimester abortion.

And all I will want to say at first is, thinking of Alicia, and of the baby at home:
—Oh, Mother, I'd rather have twins.

Even as she tells me how technical Laura was at first when she told her. How difficult it had been to make up her mind, how awful it was, how sorry she was that it was so late, but now that she had reached a decision she knew she had to do it. Abortion was the answer.

And Laura had started to cry.

And my mother will repeat the rest of that conversation. Phrase by phrase, pause by pause, moment by moment, question by question

and sip by sip of her wine. As if it were a very delicious dessert, as if she just had to impart to me the full flavour, to make sure I could see the moral of the story, the reason she just had to tell me, as still replete with hidden meaning her voice will say over and over, slowly very slowly:
–*Laura* was going to have an *abortion*.
An abortion.

Only it just won't compute, it won't, my desire to giggle and the intent look on my mother's face, and Laura's, without doubt, very real pain. No matter how often my mind runs quickly through the facts of the case, and tries to make a balance, a meaning, out of them. It won't compute it won't, not with the facts I have. So that it's like when you jam a computer's memory, asking the wrong questions, perhaps in the wrong categories, the flow of data gradually slowing down, until there's hardly anything coming in at all, each calculation very slow now, because of the overload. So that once again, I will be sitting there. Perhaps my mouth will have, the muscles unnoticed by my mental calculations, dropped open. My face without doubt a complete blank as I sit there staring at my mother, as she will repeat, each word very long:
–Laauurrraa waaaaas going to haaaaaave aaaaaaann aboorrrrtion, and then again to make sure I'd gotten it, with a great space between each one: Laura   said   she   was   going to   have   an   abortion.

Because, after all, who the hell hasn't had an abortion?
Or decided not to have an abortion. Or been afraid she might have to have an abortion. Or helped someone else, in the days before the Supreme Court decision, days that threaten their return, to have an abortion. Collecting money or names or places or going to hold her hand. While asking herself, at the very least, since there must be someone out there who is so careful about contraception or so definitely sterile that she's never worried, what she would do in her friend's place, or in the place of the woman on the program she is watching, the book she is reading, would she too, or even he too, if he can make that leap of the imagination, have an abortion? (Anaborshun. Annnnnaborshn.)
There's even a certain heroism in that. Abortion was always high adventure and risk and drama. People snuck across State lines, doctors faking mental health reports, braver ones just performing them in their

offices. While if you were the one who could do it, who could safely turn it around, make all the arrangements, you were a heroine (annnaborshn, annnnnnnaborshn), and the centre of a gossip network too, or part of one, your name becoming the answer to the question, who ya gonna call? even if you didn't know the people anymore, a network that stretched back to our high school days, though there, at least the richer girls from our school, if something like that happened, and it was rumoured to more than once, flew off to Puerto Rico. With at least one Caribbean vacation chalked up not to the desire to scuba dive, but to the need to have someone hunt a different prey in the coral depths of the student's body. So that the people of our name rank and television serial will always have that word floating somewhere in the back of the mind or bobbing to the surface of it. Anaborshun. Annnnnnnnaborshn.

It had obviously even popped into Alicia's mind that once, though quickly answered with the word: twins.

So if Laura'd finally had to do it so many years after Alicia declared her desire for twins and her father called her a whore, well, I found myself thinking, it's even legal now. So what's the big deal: anenema, anathema, anabaptist, annodomini, anancephaly, anaborshn.

That all the weight should fall onto that one word, my mother repeating: aaan aaabbooorrrshuuunnn.

Until my anger will become scathing, bordering on ridicule, as I wish to ask my mother whether that is what they do in this great bohemia she's been building in her mind with all the true confessions that come all the time to her apartment. Down there South of Houston in that world they have abortions? The great headline that has been washing around in her mouth with her wine is: Famous Bohemian Artworld New York Sophisticate Gets Abortion?

Only all I will do is repeat what she has said, an edge to my voice, a get on with it implicit in my words. Each word enunciated clearly like a language lesson:

—Laura. told. you. she. was. going. to. have. aannnn. aaabboor-rrrshun? While I will try to taste each word to see if I can grasp any further meaning that way. Then say it faster to see if that will help, as compressed as possible. Just: anaborshn?

Only even as my words come out all clipped and hard, new memories will come rushing in, and I will gasp. And briefly put my hands over my eyes. As my mother will stare fixedly at me, with that eager teacher look again, the one that will not give the bright student the answer but eagerly awaits how she will put the answer together for herself.

While I will want to give her the raspberry, only I won't be able to. Not with tears in my eyes. It would just turn out a blubbery pout. So that, finally going down a third time into the honey, I know I will not give her the pleasure of my defeat.

I look away. Trying to appear only tired, as I try to piece it all together. And remember.

It was such a pe

ect, if accidental,

gesture. Putting that postcard with its baby carriage there on top of the images of the wedding that had finally taken place such a short time before. One image bright and multicoloured and evocative over many images in the typical vague black and white of newspaper photographs, already fading. For all that even the text in *The Village Voice* said that it was the event of the season.

With everybody there, ab*solut*ely everybody, my mother would write me, though what I will remember is how eager Laura had been to have me down, how she'd called and cajoled me, for the first time in months, with repeated choruses that said: Now's the time, Alma. Now's the time. A tune she'd given up on years before.

—Come on, Alma, she said: Everybody will be there. And I want them all to meet you and Jeanpierre, and the kids especially the kids, oh, Alma, bring the kids.

Some you'll know and some you won't, some from the last trip and some from the commune and some from Thursday nights, but I want to see the kids, it's time for me to see the kids, oh Alma.

Repeating and repeating. I've never seen your kids, I want to see your kids, oh, Alma.

So that I did actually think it. That she and Sandro were finally thinking of having kids, especially with that invitation they sent. A small print of hers, and the words: A Resolved Event Years in the Making. I even giggled to myself, looking at Amber pouring water from glass to glass and onto the table, that maybe they could call their first: Mobile Discontinuity.

Only I really did feel that I was too far away to make the baby travel that far. I know everyone says it's easy, but I don't like to travel with them when they're very young. That's why I left Jason with my mother-in-law even that one time we came down.

Which is how Jeanpierre and I, and the kids too for that matter, missed what was supposed to have been an incredible celebration. Apparently there were lots of smaller people there, and clowns for them, and even an acrobat, because a lot of that crowd were having kids then, and dressing them as dramatically as they did, those pictures were the first time I ever saw kids under ten in black leather. As well as Andy Warhol, dressed idem, who was there too, with god knows who all else, but that photo was in *The Village Voice* too.

Along with a lovely take of a hansom cab coming to pick up the happy couple, to take them for one night to the Plaza, now I believe the Westin Plaza, but still a quintessential New York that most New Yorkers never get to know. Because even today it's still only for the very rich or the high priced hookers hired by them, or maybe someone with a million frequent flier points.

Sandro had even managed to mention the hookers in an interview, winking and telling the reporters he knew all about the patterns of social and sexual perversion at the Plaza because a student of his was driving one of those cabs part-time, the one that picked the happy couple up, in fact. He'd told Sandro once in class, that besides being able to get a look at the best and highest priced tail in New York, when you were on that job you even had to protect the tail of the horses. Because there were those few perverts who came to molest the mares, lifting tails up to smell under them, and to stick in fingers.

While I thought it a perfect story to tell on his wedding night, my mother sent that clipping too. I even remember asking myself if that comment could once more inspire Laura to greater heights or depths, especially within the masturbatory performance art of the period, leading perhaps to a series of Mare's Nests, to go with the Menstrual Moments. Her life might even have been tangled enough to combine the two.

While Sandro had also designed a special ritual. With elements from old fertility rites, or at least his version of them, patched together with very modern odes to freedom, sexual and otherwise, that nonetheless contained an announcement at its end about how the happy couple would stop staying with the rest of the commune and live just the two of them in their own little Mare's Nest, her studio where the party was taking place.

And then to get that postcard. And to stand there looking at it, as I stood there with my knife, looking up at my bulletin board where I had hastily punched it over the wedding photos so that I could look at it as I prepared the fish for dinner. Previously frozen as most fish is that we get out here, and smelling of salt and just a little of the sea and of decay, like putting our hands into those barrels to pull out the skates' eggs, and the shiny brown wrapping paper the fish had been wrapped in just up above the cutting board in my peripheral vision, as I made the careful one inch chunks for bouillabaisse, the shrimp and the scallops and the crab claws off on the table to one side with the vegetables, all on their brown paper too, and all of it like the newspapers that might have blown down the street she walked.

And all the colours combining even then to pull me into that small image. And to place me there once more as I will discover looking at my mother, that even if I do not know what it means, I have the last piece of the puzzle: that card in my eye, that image, with the eager hello on its back that I will soon find out was a goodbye. As I will sit, remembering it, and not the day it came but the day just past, all its bloody equally fish smelling memories, its boat and its harbour and its roof. Its Laura and its Sandro. Knowing that it was out of that image, combined somehow already on that night I had gotten sick in Palenque with the young American I had called Rima, that all my mental images of jungle paths had grown.

The colours were beautiful. Even the blue line so carefully drawn around her figure as she walked in her baglady layers of old old clothes with pages from magazines safety-pinned to them, her face already skinnier than I had known it.

Though I wasn't able to tell how much her makeup contributed to that, or her hair. It wasn't slick or greasy from lack of care the way it was when we saw her, but a perm added to the natural frizz, to become a blonde afro that matched perfectly the bug-eyed expression she wore, like a kid born with its hand in an electric socket, or a faded Raggedy Ann. Itself something you could have found along with the rest of the detritus, leaned up against one of those imposing buildings she looks at, with their huge metal doors stretching up into the air, the ones I had by moments found magnificent or frightening the few times I would walk through that area with her. Not SoHo, but among the warehouses under the Brooklyn Bridge, lofted too now, with a name I can't remember.

Since all those neighbourhoods acquire names once they get co-oped, or condoed, maybe it's even condomed, I can never remember that one either, at the same time as they lose their mystery. I'm not sure there are any areas left like that one used to be when I would walk there when I lived with her. The new container ports so much like large parking lots would never let loose the smell of moldy spice or mildewed coffee, they're far too self-contained to spill pieces of their contents, or let the old burlap, just the colour of my brown wrapping paper, from the bags the stevedores once had to handle, blow down the deserted street.

That neighbourhood was never light industry like SoHo. Though, when I was growing up, SoHo didn't have a name either, or maybe it was just the beginning of the Lower East Side, a kind of no-man's-land that was home to no one after five but the bums from the Bowery flaked out in doorways, and nightwatchmen. Though a city by day with its trucks and handcarts. You still see those sometimes, I'm sure you remember them, full of clothes or packages, adding to the effect of urban busyness, the wonderful changes in texture with even the little decorations along the facades adding to the sense of movement along the narrow streets, rivers of people flowing between the riverbeds of decorations and of windows, while the polluted water from the Hudson reaches out toward you with its smell of shit and creosote.

Just as the East River, really a branch of the Hudson, would have reached up to where she walked, I am quite sure I have the right neighbourhood, those buildings are just that much more monolithic, those facades that much plainer, that much tougher, to hide only the goods, not the painful days of the workers within them. Though the postcard didn't give a location, a street name or an address, and I never did get the chance or the time to ask, maybe there would have been the opportunity if I had made it, it just didn't seem like the right thing to do, accost her in her hospital bed, or even on the roof as I sat looking at her, with a bright opener like:
—Oh, I loved your last postcard. Where was it taken? As if I were just one of her admirers.

Besides, it was much too close to where we lay, and the day of so much the same quality as the one she had communicated, that I will get them mixed up in memory now, so that when I see myself approaching her house that afternoon, the blue line is around me, and the smell of old coffee beans enters my nostrils, the way maybe I did walk with her along that exact same street once, either in one of our excursions from our own apartment, under or over the Brooklyn Bridge, or even from her parents' place, when I was still welcome there for dinner.

So that memory still helps me to enter those blue and white sweeps of colour crayoned on with Pantone marker, the kind she showed me once when we lived together. They almost seemed a miracle to her then, made up for the design market true to print colour, so that you just marked them on and then they were printed, no colour separation necessary. She had swept pink and yellow over the buildings in bold strokes, with a kind of morass over her own figure in some form of burnt orange that gave a sense of desperation, as if she had sat there the marker in her fist going over it and over it like a kid does with black crayon when she's angry at the page or her parents. As she walks down that street straight on toward the viewer.

As she somehow managed to place herself, and it must be one of the spaces she has always inhabited, another eddy in time like Magritte's *Empire of Light*, squarely between those neighbourhoods as they had been in our childhoods, and their new art and money incarnations. Somehow pulling forward the cold metal under all that gentrified lofting, the terrible logic of what had once transformed the material but never the human, the city of light and light industry in terrible contrast, the commerce that ground down so many grinding at last to a halt, becoming just a comment on itself, the way so much of New York is now just a comment on its past, a giant sized Disney World of Commerce. While the image of the baglady that is her and that is not her, that is the baglady and the baglady commenting on the baglady is both image and caustic aside and a tourist sight you just must see, artist and baglady and madwoman and the old old pram that could once have held her, that same baglady or her, Laura.

From the days before the big change when white ladies of means went to Central Park or Riverside to discuss infant formula and feeding schedules and their children's first words while the black maids did the actual work, the care and the feeding and the pushing of the prams. What my mother must have done when she was still a lady of means and I was a kid, while Alicia would have pushed a slightly more used version, passed on from someone in the family, the big pram the flagship of pride and family life for the first born so that it would hardly matter if Laura was a girl as Alicia would push her down slightly narrower more aromatic streets and the neighbours who always sat on the stoops once designed for the dramatic entrance of ladies in long dresses would call to her or call her over or congratulate her as she walked her head held up her kerchief on her head the one she would still put on when I knew her just at the moment of passing across Atlantic Avenue back into what was then Red Hook and is now Cobble Hill, its name changed too, but that pram that one.

That was my pram and her pram and Alicia's pram and all the prams that our culture has traded for umbrella strollers and convertible strollers and car seats so that the pram she pushes contains only her pencils, collaged in, gigantic, outside of time. As she defines her moment, defines it perfectly. A last desperate act, from the days before the drugs stole her voice. And Donald Trump stole the voice of the city. To sell it. Just the way she did her work. So that it was perfect she should put it on a postcard. To add yet another layer of meaning to yet another image of New York. Having a Meaningful Time. Thinking of You.

Because however much may have been contained in the performance itself of the politics of that perambulating hysteresis that was lady of means and baglady, as it located itself in its causative moment outside of time, there was in that postcard, in its colours, more than any Magritte sense of timelessness, the timelessness contained in the hardbound children's books of the period, of that time before, of the time of our childhoods, that is *Goodnight Moon* and *Madeleine* with bowls of mush under yellow lamplights or the shadows of nurses long along the space between rows of beds, only filtered through Alicia's sensibility, the knickknacks and lace that must have decorated her pram that still decorated that living room. So that it is as if, no matter how difficult that moment was, still she had created in this particular catastrophe, a place of safety, an eddy in the discontinuous flow of time, like the beauty of those books that no matter how often they said 'Something is not right', no matter how many times they shut off the light, shutting the world down from colour to black and white, they still convinced you that the world was safe. Safe. At least that world between the covers, not of your bed, but of those books.

And in remembering that sense it was as though I had been punched in the gut, because I could see there, not just the safety, the desired safety, to accommodate her work, but in that pram, in that ceremony of exorcism, marking those buildings, making them known, making them safe, a space, a beautiful space, despite all the difficulty, in which to accommodate and shelter and teach, a child. And with such longing that I will say, still looking away, still seeing that card:
—But Laura was successful. And she likes children. She always has. More than I ever did before I had them. Why the hell would she have an abortion?

And I will lean back expecting no more than the lecture on creation and procreation, productivity and reproductivity, the lectures that brought me up, anatomy is destiny and the difference between children of the flesh and children of the mind or soul, how women have always had one and men the other and even when women have chosen for the other, they have mostly known that it is better not to try for both, and how Laura had decided that maybe birthing a baby just wouldn't allow her to keep birthing her own deep concepts from her mind, her creatures from unplumbed lagoons.

Though I will know it isn't as simple as that, as gender biased, or even as rational, even then I will know that. And besides, it could never be so simple a decision, even if you felt you might need to make it, it still wouldn't be so clear a this or that, yes or no, the way that for all I participated in the abortion network for years, I am still happy that I never had to have one. That all my pregnancies were wanted ones, and all my labours easy. So that for all I believe in Choice, it's still a choice I would never have wanted to make. And I can assure you that I don't say that because I've been converted by my mother-in-law, and come to believe that Life, with its capital letter, or ensoulment, or whatever, starts at conception.

That Ziggy the Zygote soon to be Alma or Laura or Thorne or Jason or Jeanpierre or Sandro the baby is any more than just a skin cell or a brain cell or any other kind of cell with its full complement of chromosomes, even if shaken out of two beings and recombined, that somehow gets the idea it can do it, stand up and be counted, differentiate itself in the nurturing space of the womb, C'mon do it, be a person now, Ziggy, we're behind you a hundred percent, for nine months anyway you get unconditional love to do your job in, or as close as we can get, if no crack or smack or thalidomide gets transported across the placental barrier to kick you in your still nonexistent teeth, so let's do it NOW. NOW. With a quick but supportive kick in the DNA or the cell barrier starting her off on her journey, to let that one cell not just replicate but become different kinds of units. So that whether the necessary support system goes on for the necessary five to nine months, or is terminated by accident saline the suction tube or the curette, I don't for one second believe that the magic moment, THIS IS A PERSON, occurs, soft violin music here, when two germ cells meet.

Yet I've always felt that the whole web of things, I think I tried to express this at the group once, depends at least in some small part on the sacred nature of the cosmic accident, perhaps, without being too facetious, the hysterical discontinuity, that there is something mystical in the fact of conception, in the fact that right now right here, there is the possibility of this being, THIS ONE, and no other. That is not tampered with lightly.

But the worst thing will be, that sitting there letting the pain take form, feeling the saline injection, the cramps, the white hospital gown the horror, I will remember that Laura shared those ideas with me, even, that she may have, in one of our endless discussions, planted them in my mind. That in some time in that last summer when we were once more roaring and slapping our thighs over Alicia's twins, when we stopped a moment and looked at each other, there may have been a terrible stillness, a what would you have done if... passing back and forth between us.

And that maybe she'd manifested how strongly she would try to avoid that moment. Because luck and birth and intuition and discontinuities were all of a piece. And if she expected for herself the luck of inspiration to know what to do, a pulling of the meaning of the moment out of something she could not at that moment herself understand, no matter how determined or overdetermined it might be, then how could she deny the divine inspiration, the determined moment, the resolved event of the goddess's will, the cosmic accident, chaos becoming order, at conception?

If you wish to rely on your own intuition then you must rely on the intuition of the universe. I will actually hear her say that. As if she were in the room. And I will become nauseous. Even as I will remember how she giggled when she spoke, even as she attempted to stare me down in absolute seriousness. Trying to make it once more, a joke. Even as I argued it was just her leftover Catholicism. I might even have said something about the Angel Gabriel.

Which is why I will be waiting in anger for my mother's next comment, even as she leans in to make it, sure that there is nothing she can say that will not be either a trivialization or a dramatization of Laura's pain, or possibly both at once. Sure again of how much better I know my friend than she ever will, because there is nothing in this children of the mind and children of the flesh that will encompass that pain, not even a caustic aside about how, well, honey, maybe, tragic as it was, it was the smartest move Laura could have made, even if it wrecked her. Still it probably showed she had the insight or the foresight to know, and I could just see the eyebrows rising for this one, that the only baby she would ever be able to take care of, and none too well, was herself. Which is what I am expecting even as Mother fixes me again with that measured look that tells the student she has finally given the right answer. The one that will allow the teacher to go on. Because she will lean in now. Really close. Don't-you-understand-that's-what-I've-been-trying-to-tell-you close, almost pushing me into the couch with the intentness of her look as she finally says it.
—Don't you understand that's what I've been trying to tell you? she will say.

And I will still wait. Between quizzical and angry. Only what comes next will not be anything like what I've been waiting for. Even as she prepares it with verbal drumrolls. As the quizzical part of my look overcomes the anger. This isn't Anaïs Nin at all. Or if it is, it's the Nin of the voyeur's peephole.

—**Didn't any of** them even give you a hint? she will say: Those people on the boat? That Toad person of yours? About what was going on? Haven't you gotten even a whiff of it?

And we will be back to that chorus. Like in the bars. That now Alma in from Suburbia is even too naïve to figure out what happened to her best friend. And the truth is, she will be right. If I'd really wanted to know I would have heard it. From both Sandro and Our Toad. But then I wasn't listening. Not for that.

—But then maybe they wouldn't want you to know, my mother will go on: Maybe you're the last person they would want to know. And she will continue to look at me, as I get more and more lost. Until finally she will say each word very long, as if I were low on English language skills:

—Itttt. Wassssss. Aaaaa. Realllllll. Commmmmmmmmune.

And when that gets her no further, I already knew it was a commune, a theatre commune, thank you, she will finally say, looking away, in exasperation or in modesty, or in embarrassment at being made to spell it out, who can say:

—They were all sleeping together, Alma. All of them.

And still looking away she will go on. All of it pouring out. Fast now.
—BecauseSandrowanted itthatway. That'swhattheyall told me. That Sandro orchestrated it all. He said that's what being a real commune meant. And he wanted her to go with all the men, so that he could have all the women.

And then looking back at me, her words down to a whisper, as if it were suddenly a secret, or someone else were there, it was she at the voyeur's peephole, she will say:

—I don't know exactly how they arranged it. They never told me that. If they took turns or if it was in groups. Or if it was both. You know group sex is almost respectable these days. Positively everybody, if you read the papers, is into it.

And then, because she knows there is no way to keep up the light tone she is trying for, a Ms. Manners of Bohemian Life, and definitely a Better Bohemia at that, if you are looking for the risqué, she will become very serious. Worried looking. Clinical.

—But I am sure that he sometimes watched. Sandro did. I'm sure that was part of the deal. And she will rap on her chair arm, as she leans back. As if it is all just too much.

—I am sure. Sure. I swear to it. Looking at me earnestly as if afraid I won't believe her. They even called him the Ringmaster, the Magician, things like that. And that was what it meant.

And I will shiver, hearing the words. Our Toad's warning echoing. While she continues.

—Laura would never say it that directly. But I guess I shouldn't have expected that. When she told me about the abortion, she just said: We're very modern, you know, very free, we have open relationships, things like that. She never told me Sandro dictated who everyone should have them with. They told me that, the rest of them. Especially that one guy, she will say flicking her hand at me like you do when you're giving away something you don't want: The one who was hung up on you, Your Toad.

And she will giggle again. A giggle that turns to a sigh.

—But, then again. At least Laura told me enough that I could ask the question. Without seeming totally out of line. Or betraying her friends. I still think she wanted me to find out, that she wanted to know she could talk to me about it, maybe even that you would come to know. Even if she could never admit that.

Who's the father, Laura? I said. Who's the father. And she picked up one of those jades in her hand. No, actually, and my mother will wave her hand: I think it was the totem, the animal hunting totem from the Southwest, the one with blood in the clay that she likes so much. And Laura turned it over and over, just the way you used to do with the jades when you'd done something wrong and didn't want to answer my question, while you would gather the best answer you could, or just make up your mind to speak, gathering your words together, which is what she was doing. And she didn't turn to face me when she said it, either. She just spoke to the totem.

And my mother will repeat what Laura said.

—I don't know. I don't know. That was her only answer.

And then when she had finally turned to face my mother, she looked her in the eye to say what must be said.

—One of them, Laura had said. One of the men in the commune.

My mother won't stop there either. She never does know when to stop. Though maybe it's that she mostly doesn't want to. Because I think she will know she has me nailed. Nailed so hard to the cross of my own pain, that to this day I will not know if that is what she wanted to have happen. If she will be conscious of each nail as she drives it in. To this turkey nailed to her cardboard cross. With Laura's portrait over her empty chest cavity.

—Apparently he'd been doing it for a long time, she will say. A long time. He never tried that with you, honey, did he? With the two of you?

And then she will say:

—God, I hope not.

And turn away. In some final modesty that does not wish to see me blush, or bite my lip to keep from screaming: No, no. And not in denial but in a terrible recognition, as I imagine she can smell the come between my legs even after I have bathed and douched and scraped at myself, smell me as I suddenly smell myself, in the cabin of the boat and among the bedbugs in our living room as I got up from before him or was sat down by her, when she told me how worthy I was, how worthy. And now I will not know of whom. Or how much Laura lied to me.

When she took me by the shoulders and made me want her. If that too, like her *Menstrual Moments*, had not been for him. And I would have been just another gift to tell him how much she loved him.

I will get up then. And I will walk over toward the window. And on the way I will pick up a jade, and strangle a sob, even as my mother's voice will keep on behind me.

—The women too, all of them together, the women too, Mother will say, speaking as if they had done it in a heap, so that I will want to say to her, cold and hard, in my best bitchy voice: And what about the men, did they do it too, all together, and were there daisy chains? Only I won't be able to do anything. When my voice finally comes out it will be the smallest harshest croak, without resonance or intonation.

—Christ, but that's an awful story.

An awful story.

It will seem like hours later when she speaks. Hours in which an unknown hand I only vaguely recognize as mine has touched and picked up each statue on the shelves by the window, dolphins and fish and mermaids and even the Inuit carved whale vertebra Jeanpierre and I sent her one Christmas to celebrate a promotion, rubbing and rubbing as if enough rubbing still might put this genie back into the bottle, leave me with another story. Any other story.

Until I will finally hear the voice behind me. Rubbing against me much as I must be rubbing the carvings. And I will not know how long it has been repeating. Or how long I will have been standing there. Or even how many statues my fingers will have covered.

—I'm sorry honey. She will say. I just thought you should know. I'm sorry.

But I know you're going to try to keep in touch with both of them. I'm sorry.

I just thought you should know. I'm sorry.

It's the kind of thing that's hard to keep to oneself. I'm sorry.

I thought that maybe it would help you understand. I'm sorry.

I'm sorry.

I'm sorry.

I'm sorry.

And then finally she will run down. And there will be an almost audible shrug behind me. And her voice when she speaks will be as hollow as mine.

—That's what it was really all about. The crisis. Even if it took a while to build up. I'm sure of it. Maybe it was even inevitable. Maybe if this hadn't happened something else would have. But I'm sure that's what triggered it. That's what made her lose touch. Or faith, really. With reality. The world. You know. It wasn't performances at all.

And she will sigh.

I will walk over to

the window then.

And I will look down. And I will knock my closed fist briefly against the gritty greyed radiator top. And then, almost without thinking, my voice as tired as it will be bitter, I will say.
—So that's it then. And I will shrug. Knowing, as I always have, that freedom only extends so far, and faith too.
—That's why she decided she didn't want it. Because she didn't know for sure that it was Sandro's. Well. So much for the communal life.

And in my next shrug, more powerful than the first, there will be contained my own sense that I have once more been played for the fool, that perhaps they are right. Alma is the pícara from Suburbia. The one who can never really quite get it, is never really able to figure out the purpose of her quest. Or even able to play the odds of such a sophisticated, or perhaps cruel, environment for her own gain, to attain anything at all from fame to fortune to comfort to true love. And my voice will become as sarcastic as my mother's, anger pushing it forward.
—I guess group sex is one thing. And group children quite another. And I will laugh, a harsh bark: It would have been so perfect. They could have designed a ritual for it. The Total Commune's first child.

While my mother will look closely at me. Finding my laughter disconcerting. Perhaps even hard to believe. As she looks for a way to go on. Because as she walks over toward me I will see, more in the lean of her body even than in her eyes, that there is more. And in the quick look full in my face, that tries to see whether my laughter is really a prelude to tears, I will read what she is about to say, and I will let her lead me unresisting back to the chair, and I will even wait as she goes to get us, not wine, but cognac.

—No, no, she will say as she sits down, occupying herself with the snifter and the bottle, I think to avoid my eyes: Laura seemed quite happy. She was even defensive when I asked that question. One of the men in the commune, she said. And then she added: the perfect father.

And even if she was a little spacey, I believed her. That she thought this was the right thing. That it was a magic moment, just like the magic moments of her work. She even tried to explain it to me in terms of numerology. And uttered in the same tones she usually reserved for trying to read my palm or the bumps on my head: This is the child of all we believe in.

But none of that mattered. What mattered was that she glowed, the way pregnant women are supposed to.

It will be my mother's turn to shrug and sigh before she goes on.
—No dear, it was Sandro. Even after he urged her into doing all those things. It was Sandro who wouldn't let her have a baby that he didn't know was his.

And here she will sniff at her cognac and look deep into the glass. As if it could tell her where to go next.
—At first Laura wouldn't do it. Have the abortion, I mean. She refused absolutely. And threw up in his face just those words she had used with me. How could he abort the child of all they believed in. Of all he had said he believed in for as long as she had known him. That when push came to shove he was as bad as her father.

That's what Your Toad said anyway. And though I don't know if Sandro called her a whore, I do know there were some pretty rough fights. She even showed up in public once with two black eyes. And casually said she'd asked Sandro to do it to match her black leather jacket.

But when she told him, when she told him she'd leave him first, that's what she said, that she'd leave him instead, he said he'd go to her parents. And tell them all about it. All about it all, I guess. And you know, they're already ashamed enough.

The upright, or uptight, librarian, and the staid disabled union organizer, my mother will call them because she never has been able to resist categorizing them, not since Mack called her a whore. Nor could she stop herself from giggling. Just a little, in its own way it was a darkly comic form of poetic justice, if only Laura'd had the strength to go through with it.

And besides we'd both reached that point where pain has just gone too far, and you can't stand it anymore, and even if you don't want it to, it starts to give way to gallows humour. So that you get giddy and laugh just to release the tension from your body, and then you can't stop laughing: the threat which will make us avoid each other's eyes in order to let her finish. Her voice already far too high, the way it so seldom is, she gets mistaken for a man on the phone, and still too near to cracking to risk eye contact. So that even if we will both know what is coming, it will still be hard for her to say:

—They were already ashamed enough. You can just imagine, Oh god, hee hee hoo hoo, with the pussy prints.

There will be a gasp then. Or maybe two, as we will both let go, giggling uncontrollably, the giggles mounting to gasps and to sobs, as we will wipe our hands across our faces to stop from crying, or maybe from throwing up, the way you can laugh or cry until you throw up.

Until finally she will move. She will lean forward again. And in that sudden silence, she will rustle.

—When she said her parents would never believe him, he said the papers would. And her parents would believe that, or at least be mortified by it, and after all her father was very sick now, she didn't want him to find out, did she?

And besides, Sandro said he thought it would be fun. Though I think it was for the money. Or the fame. Who knows. But he's always been like that, and I guess he didn't think it would hurt him. Men never do. Their sexual exploits.

He said he could just see it in print. Memoirs of well, or moderately well, known artist. To *The SoHo News* or maybe even *New York* magazine, or *The Voice*. I don't remember. But he kept threatening her. Browbeating her. And those black eyes weren't the first, or the last blows that fell.

But she did come here to tell me. And right then. She looked awful. Worse than she does now.

My mother will smile. A smile as wan as mine, spreading her hands out, over the snifter:
—The only thing I don't understand is why she ever reconciled with him. Why they got married. And left the commune. Maybe she did think she'd been too hard on him. After all, there aren't many men who could deal with that. No matter what they say. And I don't think they should have to either. But that's me.

Or maybe he made promises, about how it would be different. Maybe they even decided on monogamy, and meant to try again. But the crisis came too fast.

But she was beautiful when she was pregnant. She was. And she was making plans, lots of plans, and here there was another giggle: They would have been so much more interesting than that marriage ritual. Her pregnancy and birth pieces.

And we will both look at each other. Finally. Over our glasses. Long and warm and conspiratorial. Two women together. As we will say at the same time:
—Those I would like to have seen.

And we will laugh, looking into each other's eyes, with a warm but terrible sadness. And say, in turn now:
—Really I would have.
—Really I would have.

And our eyes will close slowly over our cognac as we will both try to imagine them. What Laura's pregnancy pieces could have been.

Only instead I will see what I saw brief moments before as I looked down at the park. Where there was a vague shadow moving, out of the comforting circle of the streetlight, so like the lamplight in *Goodnight Moon*, into the dark along the stone fence surrounding the park, going toward the entrance. The kind of image that later you cannot even be sure was there, but that becomes part of your thinking. So that even if the figure could never have been that of a lady with a pram, it was far too late for that, in hour and in era, it could have been a bag-lady with just such an old and disused carriage as Laura had pushed in her performance, or even the standard shopping cart whose shape would seem pram-like enough so far away. Or perhaps imagination, imagination all along, that had wanted someone somehow for just one moment to enjoy the safety of that light.

Though as I will sit there thinking of what I saw, I will feel that sense of time stopping, Magritte's *Empire of Light* again, or her postcard. Or the constant unwavering theatrical lighting of difficult memory or hallucination, the one I would recommend to Our Toad for the end of his story. And suddenly I will be with her.

Down there. A person pushing a carriage. So that for a moment I will not know who I am, if I am my mother pushing me to Riverside Park, or mother me pushing my children in their strollers through Calgary; or if I am Laura, looking out of her eyes into that world she has created. Except that it will not be the buildings that surround me, but the green of trees, tall and taller and leaning in toward me, like the buildings in her postcard, or the shadow of the nurse, in *Madeleine*. While I will remember that in that postcard Laura surrounded the buildings with a border of tropical plants, I am sure she did, in bright black outline drawing, not so much the round soft shapes of the Douanier Rousseau as the sharp-edged carnivorous jungle plants of the Cuban, Alfredo Lam. With colours filled in to match, what I had thought at the time to be a tribute to the places the produce stored in those warehouses originated. Cuba itself at one time, perhaps, but whose meaning and message my mind will now make into something different, what had perhaps called all those images of jungle pathways earlier into my mind: it is the shelter of the jungle, of her own jungle, a complex world of her own making, into which Laura pushes that pram.

Which will bring her suddenly to my side. To walk along, puffy with early pregnancy and with the piled up paper messages pinned to her clothes. In so many colours, taken from the pens inside that carriage, while my own small baby will ride wide-eyed in mine, looking out and cooing at the world while the two older children will cling to my carriage and eat candy apples that will melt onto their faces and their hands and their politely appliquéd little children's wear shirts from our nearby children's wear boutique. While her old pram will ride just there, proud next to our convertible stroller like a ship plowing its way through a rough sea, with one of my hands touching it, to keep it from running into me or mine, its crooked wheels just won't want to go straight along the bumpy jungle path. Because we will have left the pavement of the park and its more staid and proper trees, while I will look at all the myriad pens in her carriage, far more than those collaged onto the postcard, which she will take out one after the other, and mark not the walls, but the trees.

This is not art, this is not art, this is not art, the messages will say, the way they had in the postcard and in the performance that originated it, on building after building and note after note, that had marked the city and its warehouses, the storage houses of our past. With that message again and again: This is not art, this is not art, this is not art, just as she will mark her own body: This is not art this is not art this is not art, pinning that message again and again to what I will only know then is her enlarging abdomen.

In what is no longer an imitation of Magritte, who wrote again and again on his paintings of pipes or sky that these were indeed not either pipes or sky, but is her own last act of desperation. And assertion. Because it never has been art. The female body never has been art. Even if more than any other object art purveys the female body, still: This is not art this is not art this is not art. This is us this is us this is us. Even if in the end she could hardly be heard saying it: This is me this is me this is me; me and the child I carry this is me. Still it was there that last message, as clear as the voice I will always hear repeating again and again: What do you want, what do you want, what do you want? So much clearer than the voice that repeated: Say you want it, say you want it now, in so cruel a mockery of her who surely by then did not know what she wanted, or if she did could no longer let herself know. Until she finally had to articulate that hollow inside by asking others, by attempting to be their mirror, asking again and again until she would move into the subway and onto the ward and onto the drugs, because surely it was clear that this postcard was a goodbye.

And that it was not art it was not art it was not art, but a growing being inside her, to which she used her art to say that goodbye, that she was saying goodbye to that child. That this was her abortion performance, and the postcard a message that could be sent again and again to that world into which the child had gone. That Laura had built for it, a New York not exorcised of evil spirits, but recreated in the safe texture of those books read to her inside her mother's living room, which survives in the jungle plants, where the tiny defenseless spirit could be safe until such time as someone could return to nurture it.

While I watched the vision until I could smell it, until I could hear the traffic noises, until I could feel the pathway hard under my feet, through the cork of my Birkenstocks. And the warmth of her body next to mine, even under all those clothes, all that paper. Until we both seemed to glow, with the same golden roundness that seems to take me during pregnancy, my body the apple, my mind its stem, glowing for me and for her, until for a moment the room will seem to shake with laughter, with her pure open laughter, the way she had laughed the first years I had known her. And as I will listen to her laugh, laugh until tears come to my eyes, the light behind the vision will flash and go out, and I will be left still sitting in my chair, the tears in my eyes refracting the light into a rainbow of colours.

Only before that light goes out, I will swear to you, Thorne, that I will wave to her, and that she will wave back. As she will turn to push the baby carriage into that space she had made, the pram sliding away into the green jungle, and then all of it darkness.

Though my hand will reach out to the window, as if reaching out to her, and I will murmur: What would you have called her then, sure it was a her: What would you have called her, Rima or Sheena, which one, for the jungle?

And I will hear my mother respond behind me.
—What dear? she will say.
And to disguise my reverie I will answer, because I can't believe it, I just can't believe it, not with that postcard, the laughter in it, the laughter I had just heard, that this was how it had to be, that this was finally, the ending. And that it was true: it was not the Free Spirit of PoMo SoHo but Laura who would come no more to occupy that shell I had lain beside on the roof. Not to make art, or babies. So that I will say, disbelief still in my voice:
—Shit.
Shit. Just: Shit.

Before I
will walk out of the room and go into the bathroom where I will let the vomit that had been there all along behind the tears and the giggles rise up into my throat in order to throw up Sandro's words, all his words. The ones I had let myself hear again and again, until I came to believe them. Of love for her, and of wanting of me, and of possession of us both. The orchestration of my orgasms his hands going in and out, one from the front one from the back: You're like her, you're so like her, you want it so much, so much so much, while I pretended to be her and to want it. And came to want it so much being her, that I would betray her into his hands. Again and again. The way I had. Even listening through the wall. Judas and more than Judas. Again and again.

So that I will throw up and throw up and throw up, and this time I will surely know why, gagging on his words and spitting them out, the way I once had his come. Only this time I will know that I will never be clean again.

I will turn on the water to cover the noise so that my mother will not have to hear the sound of my desperation and without thinking I will once more get into the bath. Dirtier now than the last time I entered it, what could not be more than three hours before, while I will scrub and scrub and scrub with even more attention. Rubbing the flesh raw with heat and with pressure, and still I will not feel clean nor will my nausea subside, as I will touch myself. And wonder.

At him and at her and at the softness of the hard flesh. At his flesh and at mine and at hers as once more I will hear the moaning and the groaning of them together and I will not know if he beats her or pleasures her, or if it isn't him, if he isn't the one, who has truly never known what he's wanted.

Besides the power to hear his words, his name, his image, flow refracted out of female mouths and eyes. A harem of funhouse mirrors.

What is there always, perhaps, for the men of our culture. Who have been trained to want or even need the erasure of the mother, the first image of power, of power in the female, from the moment they see themselves reflected in her eyes, and know they are not her and can never be her. All that bearing of names and needing of names and carrying on of names and names of the father. Until they have convinced themselves that the beings that emerge from between our legs are just themselves created again: of them, and them only. That it is they who make them, and who insist on remaking them, limiting the possible knowledge of each child to their version, pushing each one into their language.

While our only job is to reflect them and to copy them and to clone them. Even for her, who moved through all those uncharted depths of female experience. Only to have them bear no more weight in the end than the accomplishments of a Victorian lady. As she became another muse. Another instrument: and an instrument only. Because she was denied in the end the power to make those depths present, to make them real: to make them rule. To speak them so that they could not be denied. Or manipulated. Or turned back against her. Until her freedom became her prison.

I will find myself sitting there then, floating dizzied by so much wine and cognac and bad bad news while each time I will open my eyes once more, the room will be spinning. And each time I close them I will watch again and again as she waves goodbye and follows the pram into her jungle. While Sandro watches her enraged, holding a small aborted creature, pulled, as if it had always grown there, from the bottle end of his malformed prick. Into which he attempts to but cannot breathe life, while for all he screams at her: Say you want it, say it, say it, still all she will do is wave, and move off, her body, and this time she is naked, still covered with that one message written in her menstrual blood: This is not art, this is not art, this is not art.

While Our Toad will stand by Sandro pulling his arm and saying: Let her go, man, let her go, don't you know she has to go all the way. That she came here TO GO ALL THE WAY. And the tears will run down his cheeks as he watches her move further and further along those pathways, and I will know that my story was right: that one I wrote in my mind there as I watched her lying on the overheated asphalt. Only it was not any secret place in the subway but this terrible moment that would allow her to transfer.

That it was the womb, the emptied womb, the unmade choice, the true hysteresis, that had set her out to wander. And it would not matter much whether it was abortion or pregnancy, sterility or fertility, that was forced upon her, it was that finally she too, was made, like so many women, to unchoose herself. Which is where at last she became the perfect victim, the historical victim, the hysterical victim. Never the one she meant, never the spirit of gift and sacrifice and mystical union, but of oppression and exploitation and isolation: of voicelessness.

So that it is not as a free spirit that she wanders that jungle. Because the free feminine spirit, the demi-goddess childwoman the Surrealists and so many others have worshipped is not a goddess at all, but a small and terrified, a beaten exile, her hollow fevered eyes those of starvation rather than ecstasy, an escaped labour camp victim, never allowed her own name her own voice, even the maturity of her own body. Who therefore chooses nothing. And perhaps nothingness. With the eternal feminine finally only a creature who hides from the world and from herself, so that all those places such a mystic would venture who is better than any man, represent not apotheosis but escape: the exile from the self she can never name. The only places that she can make better than this. Because even her body can never be her home, as her voice can never be her voice, as she wanders crying out for her spaceship, for the places she was meant to go, as at last she too deserts, as in that moment on the roof I had seen Laura desert in terror, just that body, that can no longer be hers, the flesh the temple of the spirit. The flesh, the spirit, one. Ready to encounter her demon lover.

I will hear then her words as she spoke them to me there on the roof, the only ones that had briefly penetrated the jungle greens of that story I was weaving for her like a blanket:
—Stay lady, stay, she had said. And once more, I heard that voice, and it pulled me, to be one last time, there inside our game.

And I had replied, in sudden wakeful panic. With the words I had been using for two weeks.
—My son, I had said: My son.

He's sick, I had said: He's sick. I must go, I had said: I must. Terrified that she could still be my Queen, and she could hold me.
—Then go you must, lady, she replied, the old smile playing about her lips.

And for one last time I had answered her, relieved that it could be so easy, that even the Queen could understand:
—Yes, my Queen, I had said, in my most acquiescent tone.

Only to hear her continue.
—But you must return. You will be the mother of our children.

The mother of our children.

And for one brief instant I would hear it: the command in her voice. Calling me. Chaining me. Even as I turned to her, incomprehension written on my face. My words unspoken.
—You know I am at your service, my Queen, I wished to say. But why, my Queen, why. Why is it in this that you would have me serve you.

I don't know if I will ever know what made it impossible for her to sustain the power of that command, if over the past weeks such a quizzical look as mine had been turned too often upon her, that it would alert her to danger and cause her to leave her body, but this time the change in her was instant. Even as I looked at her and before I could say a word, she turned back into the creature who understood not alien spacecrafts or Amazon warriors but cute redheaded boys. And she spoke as if she had never said the words that went before. And the hospital whine was already back in her voice.
—You have always known what you wanted, she said, just the way she had in the hospital: Why didn't you help me to know what I wanted. I wish you could stay to help me find out what I want.

While the relief I felt flood me was overwhelming. Even as the moment shook the sky with its pain. Because it had happened so quickly. And come, the briefest cloud over the sun, and gone.

And I knew that she could no longer hold me. For all the sorrow in watching her, for all my need to replay that story over and over, there was so much relief in knowing that it would never again be more than a story. It could not catch me, no matter how much it could move me. And I knew I could no more mother our children than I could her, or the artchildren inside her, I had once loved so much. It was over.

And knowing that, it was easy to smile and say of course, and pat her hand and turn just slightly away from her, toward the sky, as I went back to my fantasy, of another Laura, another Lilac, walking her jungle pathways her subway tunnels, her cosmic discontinuities. While my breath would stop, as I would silence those other words, that seemed to have fallen unbidden from the sky.
—But it is you, my Queen, you. If I have known what I wanted, it was always you. All I have ever wanted is to serve you. Was what the sky had called on me to say.

Only I could laugh at such an impulse now. And shrug my shoulders, and feel for the briefest moment, free. Free of it all. Of her and of Sandro and of my past. So that I would want to laugh at that strange moment, and would not even try to guess what it could mean. Why she could not even suggest we might mother together. Or how badly the moment's meaning could imprison me. Place me behind bars of silence and of pain. Even as I saw so clearly the brief demanding pain in her eyes.

While lying there in the tub
I will find myself falling deeper and deeper into that silence. Into that same, imprisoning rather than liberating, stillness that had stopped my speech. As all that I have regarded in my life as love, as celebration, as freedom, as choice, will suddenly be made sad and sordid and coerced, twisted by the horror of her defeat into the terrible chains of the prisoner. The ones that we never saw, and that always bound us. And I will think, leaning there my hand stretched out above the edge of the water, languid and exhausted at last like the Maya prisoner Jeanpierre and I had seen painted on the walls of Bonampak, in a variation on that terrible old saw about rape that I grew up with, that if defeat is inevitable then you must take the best terms that you can get. And I will wonder at that. Feeling again that I did flee the field. And that all I had done with my life was negotiate and renegotiate the terms of my surrender.

Which is, perhaps, what Our Toad meant. Or could have meant, if he'd been smart enough. About why she had to die. It was not to be the perfect victim. But because she was not meant to surrender. She had chosen long before to fight to the end. So that when she did give up, when her final defeat came, she could not even begin to dictate the terms. But was devastated. Utterly. Losing even the small property of her flesh.

And thinking that. I will cease to think. Dream yes, and occupy my time with the small repetitive tasks and tales of prisoners. Long after the water has drained slowly away. And I have watched intently the grey bits of skin I have rubbed off run down into the drain. When I will briskly towel myself dry and try to whistle a tune that will only turn out a croak as I put on my bathrobe and walk into the room I occupied as a child, that has been converted into a library and a guest room, where Mother has left a last cognac on the bedside table.

And I won't know where she has gotten them, or why it would occur to her, Laura won't be Lilac for a time yet, but there standing just inside the light of the lamp, like the bowl of mush in *Goodnight Moon*, adding a beautiful scent to the stuffy old bookish air of the room, will be a vase full of lilac.

I will settle between the cool sheets and sip slowly while I take the whole night to read a cheap science fiction that I will either find on the shelves or that I will have bought in a train station on the way down. About a society of free love and morals where each child has three parents and three sets of chromosomes and the eggs are implanted into the genetically manipulated wombs of plants, that glow pink when they are receptive and blue as they gestate and purple when they are about to burst open, and there is one that grows in the centre of each city.

Then when citizens pass the square they call out: Good is the morning that carries the child, while sometimes they will go up to the wombs and touch them and speak to them, to start their fruit's education. And parents are called by number from a list when a womb is about to open and they go down to the city centre, where in a large ceremony, in which the whole city hums, the group of them will collect their child. But no one will ever know whose genetic material has contributed to each child, it is just regularly and ceremoniously collected right after the child is given to its nurturers, who will all love the children given into their care.

Then when an exploration crew goes out to rescue some people from a more primitive society, whose sun is about to go supernova or some such, the one thing they can't explain, the natives just won't understand, is where all their extra intelligence comes from, that it is the extra set of chromosomes added when the germ cells are combined in the laboratory, that somehow activate more of the cerebral mass than would otherwise be used, thus giving them telepathy and second sight.

While the space travellers will also go to the orgies of the primitives, staged in a menstrual blood stained temple where a mother goddess is worshipped in all sorts of strange ceremonies of the flesh, that the travellers have forgotten in their civilized state. In which they can hardly remember what the vestigial flesh between their legs has ever been for. And they will watch with great interest as the drums beat, because on their planet they only make the gentlest of love, more a form of tenderness as they stroke the flesh of their partners to the softest music, the way they do the embryos on the womb trees.

They certainly will have seen nothing like this wild beating while everyone does it with everyone else, and all the men, at least once in the night after touching and feeling and entering and leaving the bodies of the masked females, ejaculate into some kind of communal vessel that the same females then dance around, dipping in their hands to massage the mixed ejaculate onto and into all their open throbbing bodies that had so recently held the penises, so that no matter who anyone did it with after that, and whether the men came or not, because the orgy would go on and on, no one would ever know who had fathered any of the children of that night. And then when the women who had become pregnant gave birth the midwives would exchange the children on penalty of death for disobedience, or for in any way marking a child so that its mother might distinguish it, and those children would become the children of the village. And the temple. And they would be the seers of the temple who, until the age of five, were allowed to suck from the breasts of any nursing mother.

And yet it is still true that these orgies will be available only to the temple priestesses and the women who aren't wives, the widows and the divorced and the sterile, as well as the young single women who will not be married until they have proven their fertility by bearing their first child to the temple. Although all the men will be allowed to go, and usually do. Leaving their wives tied at home so that they will not respond to the beating of the drums, although the kindlier men would perhaps leave a hand free, and a little something with which to masturbate as these women imagine earlier years. While every once in a while, a husband would return in the middle of the night, at least for a while, untying his wife, or perhaps not, knowing he would get wilder sex than at any other time during the year. While she would lick him all over, just for the sense of all that flesh of the community that she misses so badly.

Only maybe I will only dream that part. Attaching the faces of the commune members to it. Or imagine it, the way erotic dreams often come, between sleeping and waking, still steeped as I will be, shamefully if I think about it, in the residual horniness of my physically sated self. So that maybe the whole part about the sexual proclivities of the primitive planet will be dream, or yet another reverie. Maybe it will be like my version of *Gatsby*, maybe it won't be in the book at all. While even the artificial wombs might be more mechanical, more laboratory-like, and not plants at all like Tchelichew's tree. And it is only the shock of the advanced civilization's rescue workers at the sexuality that is real. And maybe that is based on shock that the primitives do it at all, not that they do it in large assemblies.

But I will remember that many of the space travellers are attracted by it, and that even with their extra set of chromosomes and their telepathy, they will regress into it, especially the men, and that it will only be through luck and the incredible restraint of the captain and some members of her crew, who blocked their ears from the sound of the orgiastic drums, that the rescue from whatever disaster is about to ensue, which is maybe an epidemic like AIDS, and not an explosion at all, will ever be accomplished. And that everything will come out all right in the end.

Or at least the way it is supposed to.

I won't remember dreaming, though.

Just a vague heaviness in the centre of my body, inside not out, as if my growing silence were a pregnancy that brings pressure down onto the cervix from where it is passed to the vagina and the clitoris, combined with a kind of disgusted horniness that I hadn't experienced since I'd left New York with Jeanpierre. While Laura's and Sandro's faces will float at opposite corners of my mind, at the very edge of my peripheral vision, while the bedbug smell of the old Brooklyn apartment will dominate the room instead of the fresh lilacs.

So that I won't be able to get away from bedbugs and cigarettes and grass and sex, even when I lift the vase of lilacs or the snifter full of

cognac to my nose. I will just drift that way, on the edge of sleep, until I get up with the alarm and go to drink a morning cup of coffee with my mother who will be sleepy and bleary-eyed and morning silent and who will kiss me goodbye as she repeats again:
—I'm sorry.

There will be real feeling and tears in her voice then. Almost as if she could wish I had been Alice B. Toklas after all, the way I will too, one final time. That I could have had that loyalty, or that strength, that nerve to endure. That there had been a steel in me, a temper, as they used to say, that could have done more than mourn the fallen Queen lying in her own blood on that field of battle. That I could have played it out to the end, fought him for her in that game of ours. And even if I had fallen at her side, or in her stead, been at last the true shieldbearer.

Because my questions won't matter any more then. Nor whether I have the best version of the story. Nor even whether I am guilty or innocent. Made the best or even the only choice. Because by then I will have no voice at all with which to speak it. I will be just another of those oppressed who refuse their despair by refusing their story. In the only solution available if you believe there is no other possible ending. Because once you realize that the end you have seen, again and again, is inevitable, there is no point in polishing or beautifying it. Except if, like Laura, you are determined to get out yourself. If you want your version of the universal story of oppression to be your passport to the other side.

Because if that is not what you want then there is no way out but unconsciousness. Like for an abused child who sees no end to the abuse, the refusal of knowledge, even of awareness. A decision to go blind and storyless, without guideposts, into the future. To survive, with your identity as the price. Because a tale cannot even be exemplary if it's the only one. There can be no heroines if there is no choice. If all the thrashing and kicking and singing and inventing and screwing and talking will lead to only the one place in the end.

And if, rather, the tale is cautionary, and the caution in this tale of female submission, like in all the romances, all the tales of the arrival of Prince Charming, is just that you must determine the terms of your surrender early on if you are to get the best deal, as I had thought in the bath the night before, then who would wish to tell it? Snuff film or fairy tale or gilded Victorian pornography, it will still be just another bludgeoning into submission, another form of torture. Because there will be no escape, not even into escapist fiction.

The way I will watch again and again the Queen's shieldbearer deserting the field to go on liberty to her village, to drink and laugh and carouse and talk and find a stablehand with whom to bear her children. Who she will never bring back to serve her Queen because the Queen will have fallen bloody, not on the field in mortal combat against a worthy opponent, against her Achilles, but in her tent, a victim of treason. And of her own illwrought reconnaissance, her own arrogant belief in her own individual power. While her temple priest, her Dionysus, her sworn consort, the bringer of summer and sensuality and joy, will turn into Zeus, into the King, into Jehovah. And call for his vengeance.

His father god on his throne vengeance. And the matriarchy will fall again in her flesh. And there will be no depths or tides of female experience, in the female not simply as experienced but as articulated, enough yet to enclose and drown him. But only enough to cover her body, to raise her up on the tide, and to wash her away. To let her wander among alien space ships and redheaded boys and bingo games and jungles. And fish.

Forever swimming.

Silent I will enter

ny plane, and silent I will get off, and I will not even tell myself: I do believe in Amazons, I do believe in Amazons, I do believe in Amazons. Because I will know that I must once more convince myself to believe in nothing but my children, the firm indissoluble nature of their flesh, the truth of my husband's kiss. So that I will look only at a magazine, and the summer cumulonimbus riding to our right while the pilot speaks of light turbulence and finding a smoother altitude as the plane banks around the edge of the cloud. With all of it equally unreal: sky and clouds and earth far below between them, photos of perfume bottles and skinny models and tropical landscapes, ads for the trip of a lifetime and the trip I had just taken. Even Jeanpierre stern on the other side of the barrier, trying to restrain himself from rushing forward, while he assumes his new corporate personality to approach middle age. Formal in public now with all his promotions, as he will say, taking my one free hand:
—Hello, how did it go? While he will look at me with that never transcended awkward gaze that peeks out of the stalwart body, the only thing in the world that has ever regarded me, like all the earth he maps, as a miracle.

I will answer:
—Okay, I suppose. And then add: As well as could be expected.

And suddenly we will hug each other, very very tight, and there will be tears in both our eyes by the time I get around to hugging the clamouring children, and asking after the baby, safe and sick at home, as Jeanpierre will say, his hand brushing my hair:
—It must have been hard.

And clumsy as he still is in affection, though no longer in bed, he will take my hand and lead me away.

And still it will not seem real.

Even he
will notice it. Even as he drives us home. While I lean back against the seat and close my eyes. So that he will speak to me of it often enough over the next few days, that stretch into weeks. And into months.
—I know she was your best friend, Alma, but don't you think you're taking it too hard? he will say in a casual moment of cooperative cooking.

Or he will look at me over drinks after the children have gone to bed, and suddenly come over to where I sit and he will kneel in front of me.
—Whatever happened in New York, love, you must understand it's not your fault.

And he will as often as not be perceptive enough to add: You're not the one who deserted her. Sometimes when you court disaster, you find it.

And even when I will try to explain, at least a tiny bit about the commune, and about what Sandro did to her, if not to me, it will mean little to him.
—I always knew there was something wrong with that creep, he will say, or call him a bastard in French. And Sandro will be just one of so many men who forfeited their chance at responsibility, at dignity: at manhood. While afterwards he will smile at me and take me in his arms, and repeat it again.
—It's not your fault, he will say. Or even: He's not your fault. She chose him.

And then, faced again with my tears and my silence, he will take to urging me to get out more, to do more things, to try to focus my life, to try to stop blaming myself. He will even start conversations on articles he will bring home, on the nature of schizophrenia.

And still I will only manage to stare back at him. Or wring my hands. Or repeat what I have already said. Or look him in the eyes, to initiate the ritual of our calm and steady lovemaking. That will accompany a wonderful vacation that summer.

And just to humour him, when we return home I will go to the yoga class. And slowly, slowly, Thorne, as you will watch, my mind will awaken from its trauma, just like my body will as it sits in its lotus position.

And then there will come the group,
and its many activities, and our nights out just the two of us, and our laughter and my watching you develop your work, sitting cold on the hardwood floor of the community centre, without genius or histrionics or mad tirades: without even expecting to always be the centre of attention. Or that everyone should work for you.

While over beer there will come laughter, and the brief touching of hands, and what at first will be jokes about how we could, or should, or even must, do New York together. Until one day we will somehow make the opportunity arise, giggling all the way down on the overnight plane. As we watch the sunrise over the prairies on our way to Toronto. And early morning light cover the suburbs of New York.

And there will be SoHo then and the Village and Pier 16 and the Promenade and Union Street and Coney Island and soft shelled crabs and the night that Lilac will come over and look directly at you, so wiry and strong the way you are. So quick. So fox-like with your rich auburn hair. And so many things will happen because she does.

Because her gaze will hold yours until suddenly in her looking at you her eyes will hold no astronomy texts with which to capture the spaceships to take her away, to flee the doctors the nurses the strange creatures who pursue her, or even Sandro. Who my mother will tell me still keeps phoning to ask her when she is planning to come back. Telling her how he misses her, how he will take care of her, how he owes it to her, how he is the only one who has really ever understood her, how he will protect her, as he still tries to cajole her back to the earth of a body she had allowed him once to help make her prison.

And it will only be after she's looked at you many times, openly or surreptitiously looking up, that I will open my arms and hug her for one moment just to be with her, as she will be with me. That the part of my mind that holds me back, still and stiff against all further trauma, will let me go long enough to show off to you before it tugs me back.

But in that moment there is something very important that I will learn, that I will find out about the two of you, far more than my mother will, who will spend the evening measuring with her eyes to see if the two of you will get along. Because there will be a stillness that will last for the longest time, at least for me, a living tension between the three of us that will have its own words, its own scent, that will be lilacs and creosote. And us.

As if we three were all part of that postcard, the way I always see that scene in memory, the room in the colours of the postcard and then the postcard with the two of us added in, where you are covered with red and I with blue and she with yellow, the three pigment primaries, while the cyan blue line shelters us all, a strange trinity. Even as she walks off, a little ahead of us, once more into her jungle.

Then when she leaves. When I take her to the elevator and wait with her for it to come, she will reach out for me once again, just once again with the eyes glowing out of the thin face, the hands coming from inside the pockets. And she will touch me just the way it was before that summer. When we had exchanged notes on Amazons and on goddesses and on school gossip and on boys, and we had crawled through the park and down through the windows along the spiral staircase surrounding the elevator. And swung standing up in the playground across the way and tried to determine, from our relative positions, already in different textbooks even if we didn't know it, our individual frames of reference.

And there will be her hand on my cheek again and her eyes so warm,

so very warm, as she will emerge from deep inside what we are, all of us, where there are no maps, or dynamite, from that inviolate place where she is still magma.
—I like your friend, she will say. Really, I like your friend. She's special.

My breath will catch because it will be the first time she's said that about anyone I ever liked. Man or woman, boy or girl. She will even say you have beautiful hair.
—Beautiful hair, she will say with her high childish giggle as she reaches up to touch mine, severe now in its twist.

It is then that I will go back in and give you the skirt and ask you to dance in it. And when my mother leaves us by ourselves on the naugahyde sofabed I will have you braid my hair. And I will feel your cool cool hands, and I will take them in mine, and I will finally let you do what you have wanted us to do those many nights. When we snuggled and we giggled.

Because this time I will not move your hands away as they brush my breasts. I will let your tongue meet mine as you turn to whisper close while I brush my fingers through your hair, and your tongue will squirrel around in my mouth, harder and more secret than hers.

And after that I will let you do it all, what we had never done, Laura and I, in all our wanting of each other. The same way you will make me want you so badly, so very badly. Far more than Sandro had. With a clear fine desire, missing the edge of difficulty and of pain.
—Beautiful beautiful woman, you will say with your mouth and your hard soft hands until I will know that it is true as I come to want to please you so badly as I laugh and lick you back and let you teach me all the things I have wanted so terribly to know. About myself and about you.

While I will imagine you dancing in that skirt, dancing and dancing with bells on your ankles and bare bare feet, those bony feet like your hands. That when I think of them I always remember the separation between the big toe and all the rest.

Because I will lick in there myself and rest your foot on my shoulder as I throw the covers back and lean back onto my knees in what will always seem a position of worship. For you for me for her for all of us, as I reach down to discover that centre that had always been waiting for me, open and beautiful.

I will even giggle a moment, because I will see what Lilac described in that interview. The beautiful soft and ciliated mussel inscribed in the hard sheltering muscle of your legs. Only when you look at me, asking with your tawny orange brown eyes still reflected in the light from the window, about the origins of my laughter, I will be unable to explain. As I will be overcome with the beauty of you, of all of you, who have just touched all the depths of my body. Whose beauty is mine. And yours alone.
—I am so happy. Happy.

Is all I will be able to say. Because it will be the biggest softest truth and there won't be time for anything else, the interview will flee too swiftly from my mind, transfixed the way I will be with the loving loveliness of you.

As the covers will fall to the floor behind me and I will still remain transfixed, gazing on what I had never seen before except in the mirrors of my birthing rooms. So limpid and warm. And different now, in the labour of love instead of birth. With the bright pink of the clitoris the dark of the vaginal opening the swelling of the labia, the line of the soft red hair. Open. Open to me. As if to the washing ocean. The tide rising in me. As I will drink you down the way you have drunk me and touched me, your hand now in my hair, without minding that I have giggled. Not at all.

Because we will both be laughing, rocking with the strange rhythmic laughter of the sea and being together, as our bodies will catch the light of the full moon shining in the window, almost but not quite caught on the edge of my mother's window shade.

Then with my head bent as if in prayer, I will taste of the waters of the earth. And of the sky. And of the oceans. And of the seasons.

And of us. The world washing through us like stars. Like falling galaxies.

While we will moan and we will groan little tiny cut short moans, accompanied by the tiniest of whines, worried that my mother will come in, that she will catch us. But we will worry only as little girls might worry that the light could flash on at the sleep-over, and there they would be all in each other's beds while the covers would be on the floor as they still talked and giggled. And said the things that must be said.

And that is how it will come to be that we will say those things over and over with our hands and our eyes and our mouths and the little moans deep and shallow in the throat until sleep will be ready for us and dreams will come of you and of lilacs and of forsythia. The changing of seasons and the passing of time as we all of us will watch the spring arrive and then the summer and go to the beach with our old-fashioned straw picnic baskets, you and me and Lilac and Jeanpierre and the commune and Sandro and the children and Our Toad and the women's group.

 When after a while of our walking it won't be the Hamptons of cold clear white to yellow sand where we place our bare feet anymore but an old and dilapidated dock with its dark splintering wood and its smell of creosote from which we will look out over the pastel blue of the river only to find ourselves, just the five of us now, you and me and Jeanpierre and Sandro and Lilac on a boat waving at the rest on shore as the river picks us up in sudden flood. Getting higher and higher as we will manouevre our way through the currents, fighting to hold ourselves steady as the water will push us in waves into canals that might have once been streets all of them banked by buildings constructed like the Statue of Liberty all rusted green molded bronze surrounded by fences, of brownstone and slate and sandstone and brick and chain link and chicken wire and reinforced concrete and wrought iron metal pickets painted in all colours again and again. Blue and green and violet and Rustoleum red, and day-glo yellow and orange, layer after layer peeling from the iron and the concrete and the brick walls with their graffiti, a million names repeated over and over: but mostly hers.

In huge balloon letters again and again, Lilac in purple and Laura in yellow and Lilac Summer in purple with yellow dots and Laura Yer.a.sick in yellow with purple stripes, and Laura Mack in all the colours of the rainbow.

Floating before our eyes until we will come to an island where you three will get out.

To go up a hill of crabgrass and redolent young ailanthus and forsythia still harsh in early leafless bloom, you and Jeanpierre and Sandro, with your picnic baskets and swinging arms. Until you come to a house and go inside. To be surrounded by wallpaper and maps, with no walls behind or none to speak of, just the slight wood slats that serve to bolster plaster in old houses. All torn like the paper where the sky will look in as Jeanpierre examines his graphs all carefully pinned onto the walls to chart the explosions of lilacs and roses.

He will touch the heads of the bright coloured pins as if reading Braille while Sandro unspeaking will look out the window down to where we will stand, the boat no longer a boat but what must have once been a tiny boat-shaped garden. Limited by a picket fence that will curve in just that little bit necessary to suggest a boat sunk into the earth to its high water line, the smoke stack and portholes above wrought in iron too, the decks pounded down earth where once climbing roses or jungle passion vines had grown, the old branches with their thorns the climbing stalks with their tendrils still entwined in the iron, while the water, all polluted now like the Gowanus Canal which ran between the Botanic garden with its lilacs and our apartment with its bedbugs, will rise with its floating turds and condoms. And its shit will creep up to our ankles while the boat will remain wrought iron and refuse to float, and we will climb to the highest deck and we will turn to each other, Lilac and I.

To look into each other's eyes the way we always had by wrought iron and under forsythia and we will hug and we will bring our lips together and her lips will be the softest thing in the world. Softer than they ever were in her tent or among the flowers even as she laughs that laugh, that come here laugh. That deep throated laugh that made me want to go deeper into her, always deeper into her, back down off the deck now and deeper into the water. The two of us slowly drifting alone in each other's eyes until you will hear it and you will come running toward us.

Because whirring and buzzing in the sky the ship will be coming down and you will look up into its light and you will dance in it. On the other side of the garden boat you will dance by us in the light of the ship in the light of the moon while Jeanpierre will read his maps and move his pins, his face one moment close one moment distant while Sandro will lick his terribly chapped lips, his face chapped from nose to chin, and he will rub his bottle shaped prick up and down, up and down, and the ship will approach as he looks and keeps looking and the water rises higher.

Her tongue in my mouth now and the water rising higher.

And that whirring and that whirling and that watching, your watching, Jeanpierre's watching, Sandro's watching, will be so beautiful that I will think I will explode. From the taste of her in my mouth again, another explosion of colour like the light from the ship that will expose us standing there, while I will suck on her and suck on her as if she were a multicoloured all day sucker the spiral kind you used to buy in old-fashioned ice cream parlours, and there will be spiral pinwheels exploding before my eyes, that will change the flavour with the light, the way the flavour of those giant lollipops changed with the colour.

While all of you will add your own tastes with your watching eyes and your dancing feet and your measuring hands, your own pleasures, sweat and ejaculate and glue, adding to the brilliance of the moment, of her moment. Naked between my arms except for the soft green tendrils of the jungle vines she has let grow on her in her journeys. As she will lick the insides of my teeth feel the roughness of my hard palate, and I will moan, ready to travel all the seas all the jungles all the subways all of continuous and discontinuous space with her.

Only then I will feel them.

Not the aliens in the ship. But small alien lumps in my mouth. Like sometimes happens, like it will happen to you that night, the way you will pause. A hair or something gets in your mouth and it's awkward because you have to stop your lovemaking to get it out, licking your tongue again and again on your hand and rubbing your hand along the sheet to make sure whatever it is doesn't make you feel like choking: like a wire cleaving your universe.

That's what will make me lick like that over onto my own shoulder. While I try to get rid of the lumps, all the time looking into her eyes as my tongue will fly once more to her lips, little nips with the teeth and falling into softness and colour and beauty, stopping only to lick my shoulders each time there are too many of them, when it gets too awkward. While all the time her silent eyes will watch and hold my gaze, orchestrating my little moans. My tiniest whispered moans.

Then one time I will let my gaze break away and I will see them. And they will be lumps with the texture of raw liver or gelatin or blood clots. Only so much pinker. So school child's eraser pink that I will almost scream.

Because I will know what they are.

I will suddenly understand exactly what has happened. As she has kissed me and kissed me and I have nipped back at her and savoured her the truth is I have felt less and less of her tongue in my mouth. And I will know even as she pulls me back to her and silences my scream with her softness, that the result of her terrible long exile is that there is nothing left. Or hardly anything.

Hardly anything left in her mouth as I kiss her and kiss her and Sandro rubs his prick and Jeanpierre looks then touches those maps, feeling them and caressing them and moving the small hard pins from place to place until finally he can feel the tremor of the ship approaching with his hands. And he will laugh to feel once more an explosion beneath them, as those tremors will rip through the maps rip through the walls to leave him naked staring at the light of the ship that will be so like the moon in the window the moon on a string the moon of *Goodnight Moon* as you danced me down under the covers and will dance now down toward us. Closer and closer as we stand there in our wrought iron boat that will never float while the water rises about us and I lean to one side to spit out the last remaining pieces of her tongue. And swallow others as the water reaches our waists and the ship sends down a ladder and she lets go of me. To move away. To start to climb.

And she will turn only once to give me one last long look like that look in the apartment that brought me off the couch and onto my knees to hug her, the same look that always hugged me, that would always make me hug her in return. And she will bend down, swinging off the ship's ladder now to touch my shoulder to brush away the rapidly drying desiccated pieces of her tongue. And one she will take and place into my mouth, like a communion wafer, while I will reach up to try to fall into hers, now only a tongueless gaping hole.

But my hand will refuse to reach as speechless she bares her teeth in that toothy smile tucked into the cheeks that will once again be fat and squirrel round the way they were in high school as her eyes crinkle up and fill with tears while the pieces of her tongue continue to fall off my sweater into the polluted water and the spaceship whirls away with her still hanging onto the ladder and her tears pour down over us the way she always said she wanted to be the rain and make love to all the earth.

And Jeanpierre and Sandro will finally reach orgasm, Jeanpierre with his hands still on the shreds of his maps, and their come will follow the ship to become the milky way just as the ship will be the full moon as you dance and you dance and whirl in your skirt and hold it up like a cancan dancer so that it is part of the sky, your sturdy legs the buildings on the horizon as the skirt's colours become the lines of the dawn in the east all pink and yellow and green fading to purple. While I will stand holding onto the wrought iron fence as the water rises, and I too will cry and cry and my tears will mingle with hers that rain down on me.

And where the pieces of her tongue have fallen there will grow forsythia and lilacs under the force of the rain of our tears. So that the empty old garden behind the wrought iron will finally bloom again, its plants grow tall, as it will float up higher and higher to become an island. And wherever the polluted water and her tears have touched trees will grow in red and blue and yellow to bear embryonic fruit from which children will fall to come and gather the lilac and the forsythia and the passion vines and the jungle plants that were once her tongue to weave them into wreaths and into chains, as I will sit among them, those children so tall and straight as befit the children of Amazon warriors, of an Amazon Queen, and we will tell each other stories of our Queen, who is all our Queens, crying at her defeats and laughing at her victories, as we speak too, of the greatness of her spirit, and how she will return, how perhaps she has already returned, fully incarnate in her beautiful woman's body. While we weave and unweave our tales, just as we do our garlands.

While you will continue to dance back and back to the sound of our voices moving over the water as you still hold up your skirt as the house without walls dissolves like a Maya ruin into the jungle, into green and greener green with broad dappled pathways like streets into which the moon and the spaceship will sink on the distant horizon.

As the polluted water is absorbed and the wrought iron boat is now only a temple on a hillside, like the castle in Central Park on its rock, as you float above the green of the park and the reservoir and the buildings and you are the dawn glowing in the eastern sky that will penetrate to every corner of my mother's living room, its colours slowly glowing brighter and whiter until I wake up. And I will move my tongue around inside my mouth and I will look into your face and I will be happy.

Happy.
Happy looking at your calm sleeping face as your hand that has grasped the sheet will slip slowly down onto the skirt where it has been left on the floor by the bed, its ribbons and its faded cotton lying in the sunshine that has crept through the

window onto the floor. And I will touch your face and your eyes will open. And tender and sleepy you will speak.
–Good morning, you will say.
–Sweet dreams? you will ask.

And I will just smile and smile. And kiss you on the lips. And I will feel my tongue that is her tongue and your tongue full inside my mouth and I will know. Even as I lean on your freckled shoulder to get out of bed to go make coffee I will know.

That it is you who have given me the gift to lift my silence. The gift that will finally let me acknowledge her. And give her her place. Because you are the other woman. Dancing out of the centre of your strength your hands stretched out to your companions, the one who makes it possible for there to be another story and another ending. The one who says the story I must tell can be, if never exemplary, then meaningful, at last.

And in looking at you, I will know it is worth the telling. Just as the love between us was worth the making. Even if it could never be all that we wanted. Any more than my story can be. Which is why I must tell it, and tell it. Again and again. In all of its versions. Until I know what it means. And I can leave it, finally, for another.

Which is the answer to your question I guess. Even if it took me a long time to get this far. To what you asked on the phone when I told you I was moving. That you repeated in that note you sent me, that invited me to the performance. When you spoke of touching that skirt and thinking of me. Burying your hands in it, as I bury my hand in the tawny one today, and look out the window at the tawny leaves. And twist that tawny copper ring I still wear on my finger next to my wedding band. The one you bought me for a dollar from that sidewalk vendor in SoHo.

Of course I want you to keep it. To hold onto, while you dance and you dance. That business about an exchange later was just for my mother so she wouldn't understand. My love for you.

Because now, no matter where we go I will always know that you have that skirt, and I will be able to see you dancing, in dreams or in my mind or on stage. So that I can watch those beautiful bony feet of yours move round and round as you leap and you whirl and you stretch, your pink tongue stuck, just a little, out of the corner of your mouth in concentration, your body blue and yellow and pink into purple: forsythia lilacs faded cotton, and time and time and time. And time and time. Forever. As long as I am able to remember.

   To tell and to dance and to dance and to tell and to tell and to dance, and to dance and to dance. The way we did. That time we did New York.

SARAH MURPHY is the author of four critically acclaimed works, *The Measure of Miranda*, *Comic Book Heroine*, *The Deconstruction of Wesley Smithson*, and *Connie Many Stories*. Born and raised in New York City, Sarah Murphy lives in Calgary, Alberta.